retribution

n. punishment that
is considered to be
morally right and
fully deserved.

—The Oxford American Dictionary

continued . . .

RETRIBUTION

JILLIANE HOFFMAN

BERKLEY BOOKS, NEW YORK

THE BERKLEY PUBLISHING GROUP
Published by the Penguin Group
Penguin Group (USA) Inc.
375 Hudson Street, New York, New York 10014, USA
Penguin Group (Canada), 10 Alcorn Avenue, Toronto, Ontario M4V 3B2, Canada
(a division of Pearson Penguin Canada Inc.)
Penguin Books Ltd., 80 Strand, London WC2R 0RL, England
Penguin Group Ireland, 25 St. Stephen's Green, Dublin 2, Ireland (a division of Penguin Books Ltd.)
Penguin Group (Australia), 250 Camberwell Road, Camberwell, Victoria 3124, Australia
(a division of Pearson Australia Group Pty. Ltd.)
Penguin Books India Pvt. Ltd., 11 Community Centre, Panchsheel Park, New Delhi—110 017, India
Penguin Group (NZ), Cnr. Airborne and Rosedale Roads, Albany, Auckland 1310, New Zealand
(a division of Pearson New Zealand Ltd.)
Penguin Books (South Africa) (Pty.) Ltd., 24 Sturdee Avenue, Rosebank, Johannesburg 2196,
South Africa

Penguin Books Ltd., Registered Offices: 80 Strand, London WC2R 0RL, England

This is a work of fiction. Names, characters, places, and incidents either are the product of the author's imagination or are used fictitiously, and any resemblance to actual persons, living or dead, business establishments, events, or locales is entirely coincidental.

RETRIBUTION

A Berkley Book / published by arrangement with the author

PRINTING HISTORY
G. P. Putnam's Sons hardcover edition / January 2004
Berkley mass-market edition / November 2004

ISBN: 0-425-20061-2

BERKLEY®
Berkley Books are published by The Berkley Publishing Group,
a division of Penguin Group (USA) Inc.,
375 Hudson Street, New York, New York 10014.
BERKLEY is a registered trademark of Penguin Group (USA) Inc.
The "B" design is a trademark belonging to Penguin Group (USA) Inc.

PRINTED IN THE UNITED STATES OF AMERICA

10   9   8   7   6   5   4   3   2   1

1

1

CHLOE LARSON WAS, as usual, in a mad and blinding rush. She had all of ten minutes to change into something suitable to wear to *The Phantom of the Opera*—currently sold out a year in advance and the hottest show on Broadway—put on a face, and catch the 6:52 P.M. train out of Bayside into the city, which was, in itself, a three-minute car ride from her apartment to the station. That left her with really only seven minutes. She whipped through her overstuffed closet that she had meant to clean out last winter, and quickly settled on a black crepe skirt and matching jacket with a pink camisole. Clutching one shoe in her hand, she muttered Michael's name under her breath, while she frantically tossed aside shoe after shoe from the pile on the closet floor, at last finally finding the black patent-leather pump's mate.

She hurried down the hall to the bathroom, pulling on her heels as she walked. *It was not supposed to happen like this,* she thought as she flipped her long blond hair upside down, quickly combing it with one hand, while simultaneously brushing her teeth with the other. She was supposed to be relaxed and carefree, giddy with anticipation, her mind free of distractions when the question to end all questions was finally asked of her. Not rushing to and fro, on almost no sleep, from intense classes and study groups with other really anxious people, the New York State Bar

Exam oppressively intruding upon her every thought. She spit out the mouthwash, spritzed on Chanel No. 5, and practically ran to the front door. Four minutes. She had four minutes, or else she would have to catch the 7:22 and then she would probably miss the curtain. An image of a dapper and annoyed Michael, waiting outside the Majestic Theater, rose in hand, box in pocket, checking his watch, flashed into her mind.

It was not supposed to happen like this. She was supposed to be more prepared.

She hurried through the courtyard to her car, her fingers rushing to put on the earrings she had grabbed off the nightstand in her room. From the second story above, she felt the eyes of her strange and reclusive neighbor upon her, moving over her from behind his living room window, as they did every day. Just watching as she made her way through the courtyard into the busy world and on with her life. She shook off the cold, uncomfortable feeling as quickly as it had come and climbed into her car. This was no time to think about Marvin. This was no time to think of the bar exam or bar review classes or study groups. It was time to think only of her answer to the question to end all questions that Michael was surely going to ask her tonight.

Three minutes. She had only three minutes, she thought, as she cheated the corner stop sign, barely making the light up on Northern Boulevard.

The deafening sound of the train whistle was upon her now as she ran up the platform stairs two at a time. The doors closed on her just as she waved a thank you to the conductor for waiting and made her way into the car. She sat back against the ripped red vinyl seat and caught her breath from that last run through the parking lot and up the stairs. The train pulled out of the station, headed for Manhattan. She had barely made it.

Just relax and calm down now, Chloe, she told herself, looking at Queens as it passed her by in the fading light of day. Because tonight, after all, was going to be a very special night. Of that she was certain.

2

THE WIND HAD picked up and the thick evergreen bushes that hid his motionless body from sight began to rustle and sway. Just to the west, lightning lit the sky, and jagged streaks of white and purple flashed behind the brilliant Manhattan skyline. There was little doubt that it was going to pour—and soon. Buried deep in the dark underbrush, his jaw clenched tight and his neck stiffened at the rumble of thunder. *Wouldn't that just put the icing on the cake, though? A thunderstorm while he sat out here waiting for that bitch to finally get home.*

Crouched low under the thick mange of bushes that surrounded the apartment building there was no breeze, and the heat had become so stifling under the heavy clown mask that he could almost feel the flesh melting off his face. The smell of rotting leaves and moist dirt overwhelmed the evergreen, and he tried hard not to breathe in through his nose. Something small scurried by his ear, and he forced his mind to stop imagining the different kinds of vermin that might, right now, be crawling on his person, up his sleeves, in his work boots. He fingered the sharp, jagged blade anxiously with gloved fingertips.

There were no signs of life in the deserted courtyard. All was quiet, but for the sound of the wind blowing through the branches of the lumbering oak trees, and the constant hum and rattle of a dozen or more air conditioners, precariously suspended up above him from their windowsills. Thick, full hedges practically grew over the entire side of the building, and he knew that, even from the apartments above, he could still not be seen. The carpet of weeds and decaying leaves crunched softly under his weight as he pulled himself up and moved slowly through the bushes toward her window.

She had left her blinds open. The glow from the streetlamp filtered through the hedges, slicing dim ribbons of light across the bedroom. Inside, all was dark and still. Her bed was unmade and her closet door was open. Shoes— high heels, sandals, sneakers—lined the closet floor. Next to her television, a stuffed-bear collection was displayed on the crowded dresser. Dozens of black marble eyes glinted back at him in the amber slivers of light from the window. The red glow on her alarm clock read 12:33 A.M.

His eyes knew exactly where to look. They quickly scanned down the dresser, and he licked his dry lips. Colored bras and matching lacy panties lay tossed about in the open drawer.

His hand went to his jeans and he felt his hard-on rise back to life. His eyes moved fast to the rocking chair where she had hung her white lace nightie. He closed his eyes and stroked himself faster, recalling in his mind exactly how she had looked last night. Her firm, full tits bouncing up and down while she fucked her boyfriend in that see-through white nightie. Her head thrown back in ecstasy, and her curved, full mouth open wide with pleasure. She was a bad girl, leaving her blinds open. Very bad. His hand moved faster still. Now he envisioned how she would look with those long legs wrapped in nylon thigh-highs and strapped into a pair of the high heels from her closet. And his own hands, locked around their black spikes, hoisting her legs up, up, up in the air and then spreading them wide apart while she screamed. First in fear, and then in pleasure. Her blond mane fanned out under her head on the bed, her arms strapped tight to the headboard. The lacy crotch of her pretty pink panties and her thick blond bush, exposed right by his mouth. *Yum-yum!* He moaned loudly in his head and his breath hissed as it escaped through the tiny slit in the center of his contorted red smile. He stopped himself before he climaxed and opened his eyes again. Her bedroom door sat ajar, and he could see that the rest of the apartment was dark and empty. He sank back down to his spot under the evergreens. Sweat rolled down his face, and the latex suctioned fast to the skin. Thunder rumbled again, and he felt his cock slowly shrivel back down inside his pants.

She was supposed to have been home hours ago. Every single Wednesday night she's home no later then 10:45 P.M. But tonight, *tonight,* of all nights, she's late. He bit down hard on his lower lip, reopening the cut he had chewed on an hour earlier, tasting the salty blood that flooded his mouth. He fought back the almost overwhelming urge to scream.

Goddamn mother-fucking bitch! He could not help but be disappointed. He had been so excited, *so thrilled,* just counting off the minutes. At 10:45 she would walk right past him, only steps away, in her tight gym clothes. The lights would go on above him, and he would rise slowly to the window. She would purposely leave the blinds open, and he would watch. Watch as she pulled her sweaty T-shirt over her head and slid her tight shorts over her naked thighs. Watch as she would get herself ready for bed. *Ready for him!*

Like a giddy schoolboy on his first date, he had giggled to himself merrily in the bushes. *How far will we go tonight, my dear? First base? Second? All the way?* But those initial, exciting minutes had ticked by and here he still was, two hours later—squatting like a vagrant with unspeakable vermin crawling all over him, probably breeding in his ears. The anticipation that had fueled him, that had fed the fantasy, was now gone. His disappointment had slowly turned into anger, an anger that had grown more intense with each passing minute. He clenched his teeth hard and his breath hissed. No, siree, he was not excited anymore. He was not thrilled. He was beyond annoyed.

He sat chewing his lip in the dark for what seemed like another hour, but really was only a matter of minutes. Lightning lit the sky and the thunder rumbled even louder and he knew then that it was time to go. Grudgingly, he removed his mask, gathered his bag of tricks, and extricated himself from the bushes. He knew that there would be a next time.

Headlights beamed down the dark street just then, and he quickly ducked off the cement pathway back behind the hedges. A sleek silver BMW pulled up fast in front of the complex, double-parking no less than thirty feet from his hiding spot.

Minutes passed like hours, but finally the passenger door opened, and two long and luscious legs, their delicate feet wrapped in high-heeled black patent-leather pumps, swung out. He knew instantly that it was her, and an inexplicable feeling of calm came over him.

It must be fate.

Then the Clown sank back under the evergreens. To wait.

3

TIMES SQUARE AND 42nd Street were still all aglow in neon, bustling with different sorts of life even past midnight on a simple Wednesday. Chloe nervously chewed on a thumbnail and watched out the passenger-side window as the BMW snaked its way through the streets of Manhattan toward 34th Street and the Midtown Tunnel.

She knew that she should not have gone out tonight. The tiny, annoying voice inside her head had told her as much all day long, but she hadn't listened, and with less than four weeks to go before the New York State Bar Exam, she had blown off a night of intense studying for a night of romance and passion. A worthy cause, perhaps, except that the evening hadn't been very romantic in the end, and now she was both miserable and panic stricken, suffering from an overwhelming sense of dread about the exam. Michael continued to rant on about his day from corporate hell, and didn't seem to notice either her misery or her panic, much less her inattention. Or if he did, he didn't seem to care.

Michael Decker was Chloe's boyfriend. Possibly her soon-to-be ex-boyfriend. A high-profile trial attorney, he was on the partner track with the very prestigious Wall Street law firm of White, Hughey & Lombard. They had met there two summers ago when Chloe was hired as Michael's legal intern in the Commercial Litigation Department. She had quickly learned that Michael never took no for an answer when he wanted a yes to his question. The first day on the job he was yelling at her to read her case law more closely, and the next one he was kissing her hot and heavy in the copy room. He was handsome and brilliant and had this romantic mystique about him that Chloe could not explain, and just could not ignore. So she had found a new job, romance had blossomed, and tonight had marked the two-year anniversary of their first real date.

For the past two weeks Chloe had asked, practically begged, Michael if they could celebrate their anniversary date after the bar exam. But instead, he had called her this same afternoon to surprise her with theater tickets for tonight's performance of *Phantom of the Opera*. Michael knew everyone's weakness, and if he didn't know it, he found it. So when Chloe had first said no, he knew to immediately zero in on the guilt factor—that Irish-Catholic homing device buried deep within her conscience. *We hardly see each other anymore, Chloe. You're always studying. We deserve to spend some time together. We need it, babe. I need it.* Etc., etc., and etc. He finally told her that he'd had to practically steal the tickets from some needy client, and she relented, reluctantly agreeing to meet him in the city. She had canceled on her study group at school out in Queens, grabbed a quick change after her bar review class, and had shlepped into Manhattan all the while trying to quiet that disconcerting voice in the back of her head that had suddenly begun to shout.

After all that, she had to say that she wasn't even surprised when, ten minutes after curtain call, the elderly usher with the kind face handed her the note that told her Michael was stuck in an emergency meeting and would be late. She should have left right there, right then, but, well . . . she didn't. She watched now out the window as the BMW slid under the East River and the tunnel lights passed by in a dizzying blur of yellow.

Michael had shown up for the final curtain call with a rose in his hand and had begun the familiar litany of excuses before she could slug him. A zillion apologies later he had somehow managed to then guilt her into dinner, and the next thing she knew, they were heading across the street together to Carmine's and she was left wondering just when and where she had lost her spinal cord. How she hated being Irish-Catholic. The guilt trips were more like pilgrimages.

If the night had only ended there, it would have been on a good note. But over a plate of Veal Marsala and a bottle of Cristal, Michael had delivered the sucker punch of the evening. She had just begun to relax a little and enjoy the champagne and romantic atmosphere when Michael had pulled out a small box that she instantly knew was not small enough.

"Happy Anniversary." He had smiled softly, a perfect smile, his sexy brown eyes warm in the flickering candle-light. The strolling violinists neared, like shark to chum. "I love you, baby."

Obviously not enough to marry me, she had thought as she stared at the silver-wrapped box with the extra-large white bow, afraid to open it. Afraid to see what wasn't inside.

"Go ahead, open it." He had filled their glasses with more champagne, and his grin had grown more smug. Obviously, he thought that alcohol and jewelry of any sort would surely get him out of the doghouse for being late. Little did he know that at that very moment he was so far from home, he was going to need a map and a survival kit to get back. *Or maybe she was wrong. Maybe he had just put it in a big box to fool her.*

But no. Inside, dangling from a delicate gold chain, was a pendant of two intertwined hearts, connected by a bril-liant diamond. It was beautiful. But it wasn't round and it didn't fit on her finger. Mad at herself for thinking this way, she had blinked back hot tears. Before she knew it, he was out of his seat and behind her, moving her long blond hair onto her shoulders and fastening the necklace. He kissed the nape of her neck, obviously mistaking her tears for those of happiness. Or ignoring them. He whispered in her ear, "It looks great on you." Then he had sat back in his seat and ordered tiramisu, which arrived five minutes later with a candle and three singing Italians. The violinists soon got wind of the party downtown and had sauntered over and everyone had sung and strummed "Happy Anniversary" in Italian. She wished she had just stayed home.

The car now moved along the Long Island Expressway toward Queens with Michael still oblivious to her absence from the conversation. It had started to sprinkle outside, and lightning lit the sky. In the side-view mirror Chloe watched the Manhattan skyline shrink smaller and smaller behind Lefrak City and Rego Park, until it almost disappeared from sight. After two years, Michael knew what she wanted, and it *wasn't* a necklace. *Damn him.* She had enough stress in her life with the bar exam that she needed this emotional albatross about as much as she needed a hole in the head.

They approached her exit on the Clearview Expressway and she finally decided that a discussion about their future together—or lack thereof—would just have to wait until after she sat for the bar. The last thing she wanted right now was the heart-wrenching ache over a failed relationship. One stress factor at a time. Still, she hoped her stony silence in the car would send its message.

"It's not just the depo," Michael continued on, seemingly oblivious. "If I have to run to the judge every time I want to ask something as inane as a date of birth and Social Security number, this case is going to get buried in the mountains of sanctions I'm going to ask for."

He pulled off now onto Northern Boulevard and stopped at a light. There were no other cars out on the street at this hour. Finally he paused, recognized the sound of silence, and looked over cautiously at Chloe. "Are you okay? You haven't said much at all since we left Carmine's. You're not still mad about my being late, are you? I said I was sorry." He gripped the leather steering wheel with both hands, bracing himself for the fight that hung heavy in the air. His tone was arrogant and defensive. "You know what that firm is like. I just can't get away, and that's the bottom line. The deal depended on me being there."

The silence in the small car was almost deafening. Before she could even respond, he had changed both his tone and the subject. Reaching across the front seat, he traced the heart pendant that rested in the nape of her neck with his finger. "I had it made special. Do you like it?" His voice was now a sensuous inviting whisper.

No, no, no. She wasn't going to go there. Not tonight. *I refuse to answer, Counselor, on the grounds it may incriminate me.*

"I am just distracted." She touched her neck and said flatly, "It's beautiful." The hell she was going to let him think that she was just being an emotional bitch who was upset because she didn't get the ring she'd told all her friends and extended family she was expecting. He could take what she said and chew on it for a few days. The light changed and they drove on in silence.

"I know what this is about. I know what you're thinking." He sighed an exaggerated sigh and leaned back in the driver's seat, hitting the palm of his hand hard against the steering wheel. "This is all about the bar exam, isn't it? Jesus, Chloe, you have studied for that test almost nonstop for two months, and I have been really understanding. I really have. I only asked for one night out. . . . Just one. I have had this incredibly tough day and all during dinner there has been this, this tension between us. Loosen up, will you? I really, really need you to." He sounded annoyed that he even had to bother having this conversation, and she wanted to slug him again. "Take it from someone who has been there: Stop worrying about the bar exam. You're tops in your class, you've got a terrific job lined up—you'll do fine."

"I'm sorry that my company at dinner did not brighten your tough day, Michael. I really am," she said, the sarcasm chilling her words. "But, let me just say that you must suffer from short-term memory loss. Do you remember that we spent last night together, too? I wouldn't exactly say that I have neglected you. Might I also remind you that I did not even want to celebrate tonight and I told you as much, but you chose to ignore me. Now, as far as having fun goes, I might have been in a better mood if you hadn't been two hours late." Great. In addition to the guilt pangs her stomach was digesting for dessert, her head was beginning to throb. She rubbed her temples.

He pulled the car up in front of her apartment building, looking for a spot.

"You can just let me out here," she said sharply.

He looked stunned and stopped the car, double-parking in front of her complex.

"What? You don't want me to come in tonight?" He sounded hurt, surprised. Good. That made two of them.

"I'm just really tired, Michael, and this conversation is, well, it's degenerating. And quick. Plus I missed my aerobics class tonight, so I think I'll take the early one in the morning before class."

Silence filled the car. He looked off out his window and she gathered her jacket and purse. "Look, I'm really sorry about tonight, Chloe. I really am. I wanted it to be special and it obviously wasn't, and for that, I apologize. And I'm sorry if you're stressed over the bar exam. I shouldn't have snapped like that." His tone was sincere and much softer. The "sensitive guy" tactic took her slightly by surprise.

Leaning over the car seat, he traced a finger up her neck and over her face. He ran his finger over her cheekbones as she looked down in her lap, fidgeting for the keys in her purse, trying hard to ignore his touch. Burying his hand in her honey-blond hair, he pulled her close and brushed his mouth near her ear. Softly he murmured, "You don't need the gym. Let me work you out."

Michael made her weak. Ever since that day in the copy room. And she could rarely say no to him. Chloe could smell the sweetness of his warm breath, and felt his strong hands tracing farther down the small of her back. In her head she knew she should not put up with his crap, but in her heart, well, that was another story. For crazy reasons she loved him. But tonight—well, tonight was just not going to happen. Even the spineless had a limit. She opened the car door fast and stepped out, catching her breath. When she leaned back in, her tone was one of indifference.

"This is not going to happen, Michael. I'm tempted, but it's already almost one. Marie is picking me up at eight forty-five, and I can't be late again." She slammed the door shut.

He turned off the engine and got out of the driver's side. "Fine, fine. I get it. Some great fucking night this turned out to be," he said sullenly and slammed his door in return. She glared at him, turned on her heel, and marched off across the courtyard toward her lobby.

"Shit, shit, shit," he mumbled and ran after her. He caught up with her on the sidewalk and grabbed her hand. "Stop, just stop. Look, I'm frustrated. I'm also an insensitive clod. I admit it." He looked into her eyes for a sign that it was safe to proceed. Apparently, they still read caution, but when she did not move away he took that as a good sign. "There, I've said it. I'm a jerk and tonight was a mess and it's all my fault. Come on, please, forgive me," he whispered. "Don't end tonight like this." He wrapped his hand behind her neck and pulled her mouth to his. Her full lips tasted sweet.

After a moment she stepped back and touched her hand lightly to her mouth. "Fine. Forgiven. But you're still not spending the night." The words were cool.

She needed to be alone tonight. To think. Past her bedroom, where was this whole thing headed anyway? The streetlights cast deep shadows on the walkway. The wind blew harder and the trees and bushes rustled and stirred around them. A dog barked off in the distance, and the sky rumbled.

Michael looked up. "I think it's going to pour tonight," he said absently, grabbing her limp hand in his. They walked to the front door of the building in silence. On the stoop he smiled and said lightly, "Damn. And here I thought I was so smooth. Sensitivity is supposed to work with you women. The man who's not afraid to cry, show his feelings." He laughed, obviously fishing for a smile in return, then he massaged her hand with his and kissed her gently on the cheek, moving his lips lightly over her face toward her lips. Her eyes were closed, her full mouth slightly parted. "You look so good tonight I just might cry if I can't have you." *If at first you don't succeed . . . try, try again.* His hands moved slowly down the small of her back, over her skirt. She didn't move. "You know, it's not too late to change your mind," he murmured, his fingers moving over her. "I can just go move the car."

His touch was electrifying. Finally, she pulled away and opened the door. Damn it, she was going to make a statement tonight and not even her libido was going to stop her.

"Good night, Michael. I'll talk to you tomorrow."

He looked as if he had been punched in the gut. Or somewhere else.

"Happy Anniversary," he said quietly as she slipped into the foyer door. The glass door closed with a creak.

He walked slowly back to the car, keys in hand. Damn it. He had really screwed things up tonight. He really had. At the car, he watched as Chloe stood at the living room window and waved to him that all was okay inside. She still looked pissed. And then the curtain closed and she was gone. He climbed in the BMW and drove off toward the expressway and back toward Manhattan, thinking about how to get back on her good side. Maybe he'd send her flowers tomorrow. That's it. Long red roses with an apology and an "I love you." That should get him out of the doghouse and back into her bed. With the crackle of thunder sounding closer still and the storm fast moving in, he turned onto the Clearview Expressway, leaving Bayside way behind him.

4

THE CLOWN WATCHED with wide eyes through parted branches as her luscious legs stepped out of the BMW. Long and tan, probably from some high-priced tanning salon. She was wearing a short and tight, *oh so tight,* black skirt and a pink silk camisole that showed off her full, perky breasts. Over her arm she carried a matching black suit jacket. Pink was her favorite color—and his too—and he was glad she had chosen to wear it tonight. *Mmmm-hmmm . . . pretty in pink!* A slow smile spread over his face and he began to think that perhaps tonight—well, tonight might not be so bad after all. In fact, things were starting to *shape up* quite nicely. He put his hand over his mouth to suppress an escaping giggle.

Her long blond hair met the small of her back in a cascade of tender curls and he could smell her sweet, sexy perfume, heavy in the humid air. He recognized it immediately as her favorite—Chanel No. 5. The perspiration rushed down from the nape of his neck, soaking his back and armpits.

She seemed to go on forever talking with that preppie little prick of a boyfriend. She didn't look happy. Blah, blah, blah . . . Didn't they know what time it was? It was time to go home. *Time to go to bed.* His fingers drummed impatiently against the black nylon bag. His bag of tricks.

She slammed her door. He, in turn, suddenly got out of

the car and slammed his. Down the street a dog began to bark. The Clown's knees quivered slightly. *What if a nosy neighbor woke up?*

But no neighbors came out to play, and Preppie walked fast to meet her on the sidewalk. He grabbed her hand and they exchanged words that he could not hear. Then he kissed her full on the lips. Hand in hand they walked to the front door of the complex. Her high heels clicked on the cement walk, so close he could practically reach out and touch her ankle. Again, he began to panic. *Was the boyfriend going in, too?* That would just ruin everything. Preppie had had his fun with her last night—tonight was *his* turn.

On the stoop of the foyer they kissed again, but then she slipped in the main door of the complex alone. *Not so lucky tonight, are we, Preppie?* The Clown chuckled softly.

Preppie turned, his head down, and walked slowly back to his car, jingling the keys in his hand. Like a good little boyfriend, he waited until the light went on in the apartment and he saw her wave from the living room window before he drove off into the night.

The Clown smiled. *How quaint! The Preppie Prick walks her to her door and kisses her good night. Don't let those bedbugs bite! And he even stays around to make sure that she is safe and sound and that no bogeyman is lurking inside. What a laugh riot!*

Five minutes later, the lights in her bedroom went on, illuminating the bushes. He pulled himself deeper into the hedge. The air conditioner rattled to life above him and condensation dripped through the evergreen onto his head. He saw her shadow bouncing about in the bushes as she walked around the room, and then she closed the blinds and the light grew dim.

He sat completely motionless for twenty minutes after all the lights went out. Thunder rumbled, louder this time. The rain had started. Soft at first, but he knew that would change. The wind gusts were strong now, and the bushes swayed back and forth, dancing a strange dance in the dim streetlight. The storm was almost upon them. She had made it just in the nick of time.

He grabbed his bag of tricks and snaked his way around the corner of the building until he was directly beneath the window with the broken latch in her living room. Then at precisely 1:32 A.M., the Clown pulled his mask on snug over his face. He stood and brushed off his now *very tight* blue jeans, silently lifted the darkened window and slithered inside out of the rain.

5

CHLOE WATCHED FROM her window as Michael walked slowly
back to the car, rejected, his head down. She waved halfheartedly, purposely closing the curtains on him as he
waved back at her. Another message sent.

She stood alone in her living room and looked around
her. The apartment was silent, lonely, and unbearably hot.
The small feeling of victory melted away as quickly as it
had come. Now she almost wished that she had just let him
stay the night.

The gym had been a flimsy excuse at best. Who was she
kidding? There was no way that she was going to get up at
6:00 A.M. to do aerobics. And if she wasn't going to raise
the "Where is this relationship really headed?" conversation for another two weeks, then what would have been the
harm in letting him stay the night?

*Because you were upset that you didn't get what you
wanted on this Happy Anniversary, and so you certainly
weren't going to give him what* he *wanted.*

Great, even her schizophrenic conscience now thought
she was being a bitch. She knew, though, that if Michael
had stayed the night she would have held a similar conversation with herself at 3:00 A.M., but this one would have
been for being such a lily-livered weak pushover. You're
damned if you do and damned if you don't. It was all too

exhausting and depressing and she hoped a couple of Tylenol would fix the pounding in her head.

The apartment was an oven. The windows had been closed all day, and everything in the place had just baked— even the furniture was still warm to the touch. She grabbed the mail that sat stuffed in the front-door slot and headed into the kitchen.

She flicked on the lights, and the kitchen was instantly illuminated. Chloe sighed at the mess that was her table, littered with breakfast dishes from the morning, dinner dishes from the night before, parakeet seed, and feathers. Pete the Parakeet, temporarily blinded by the fluorescent light, fell from his perch onto the cage floor with a thud.

She piled all the dishes from the table into the already overcrowded sink, squirted some green Palmolive in, and hosed down the mountain of porcelain with the sink nozzle. Pete, meanwhile, had mustered up some dignity and fluttered back to the perch, squawking angrily all the while at Chloe and sending tiny green and white feathers wafting through the air and back onto the table. Chloe gritted her teeth and quickly threw a towel over Pete. Then she took one last look at her kitchen, turned off the lights, and made a mental note to call the Merry Maids Emergency Cleaning Service in the morning. She downed her two Tylenol with a Mylanta chaser before finally heading for the air-conditioned relief of her bedroom.

She tossed the mail on the bed, turned the AC on high, and searched her drawers for her favorite and most comfortable pink pajamas, pushing aside the collection of flimsy Victoria's Secret lingerie that she had gotten as gifts from Michael over the past two years. She found them stuffed in the bottom drawer—cotton, oversized, and not at all sexy. Outside, the hedge branches scraped against her bedroom window, making a desperate, screeching sound, and a spatter of raindrops dotted the glass. The forecast had called for intense thunderstorms tonight. She stood at the window for a moment and watched as the trees bent like straws under the wind, then she closed the blinds and flipped on the television for some company. An old *Brady Bunch* episode came on the screen.

She flopped on the bed with the day's mail and hit the Play button on the answering machine. Bills, bills, advertisements, *People,* and more bills. It never ended.

The female computer-generated voice spoke: *You have no new voice messages in your mailbox.*

She looked over at the answering machine. That was funny. The number 3 flashed red in the machine's message box, indicating three messages. And she had emptied her mailbox messages before leaving for the city. She hit the Replay button on the machine.

You have three stored messages in your mailbox.

First message: Today, seven-nineteen P.M. Her mom's frazzled voice. "Chloe, it's Mom. You must be out studying tonight." Chloe's stomach flip-flopped with guilt again.

"Call me when you get in. I need to talk to you about our visit next month. Your dad and I think maybe we should stay in a hotel, you're just so cramped in that apartment. I need to know some hotels in Manhattan that are nice, but not too expensive and are in a good neighborhood. Call me."

Yeah. Good luck finding *that* short list in New York City.

She went back to the mail. Another bill. When had she found the time to buy all this stuff she was being billed for?

A credit card solicitation. Great, so she could get even more bills.

Finally on the bottom of the never-ending bill pile, an ivory envelope with the familiar chicken scratch of her father's handwriting on it. Chloe smiled. Since she had moved to New York from California for law school her dad wrote her faithfully at least once a week, and his warm, funny letters were a welcome break. Sometimes there were pages and pages, and others only a few short lines, but they all began with the same salutation: "Hey, Beany! How is my big girl in the big city?" Beany had been his nickname for her since she was five, a reference to her sweet tooth for jelly beans. Even at twenty-four, she was still his little girl. She set his letter aside for later and leafed through *People.*

Second message: Today, eight-ten P.M. It was Marie. "Thanks for blowing us all off tonight, Chloe. It was a blast. It really was. You missed our round-robin discussion about the Rule Against Perpetuities. Now *that's* a lot more fun than *Phantom of the Opera.* Hey, don't forget the practice multistate is tomorrow, so I'll be at your door at eight-thirty instead of eight forty-five. Don't be late! Hmmm . . . Maybe I should have told you eight o'clock, then. See ya."

Damn. She had forgotten all about the practice test. Another reason to be mad at Michael.

Third message: Today, eleven thirty-two P.M. A long silence. In the background Chloe could hear a rustle, like the muffled sound of paper tearing. Then, a male voice in a taunting singsong whispered low, *"Chloe. Chloe. Where are you, Chloe?"* More crackling silence. She could hear breathing for just a moment and then the line hung up.

That was bizarre. She stared for a few seconds at the machine.

End of messages.

It must have been one of the guys from her study group. Their study sessions were known to go on until the wee hours anyway. It was probably Rob or Jim just joking around with her. They probably figured that she was home by then and having a good ole time while they studied, and they were just spoofing her for blowing off the study group, hoping to bug her with a message while she was in a compromising position. That was probably it. She hit the button on the machine.

Messages erased.

She got under the covers and propped up the pillows behind her to read her dad's letter. She was an only child and it had hit both of her parents really hard when she left for St. John's. It had hit them even harder when she told them recently that she wasn't moving back. Neither of her parents liked New York, and they certainly didn't trust it. She had been raised in a small town in northern California. Walking a dog on cement and living in a high-rise, fifty stories off the ground, not more than thirty feet across from your neighbor in the next building over, was about as foreign to them as living in an igloo. In fact, given the choice, her parents would probably pick the igloo. Her mother called two to three times a week just to make sure Chloe had not yet been robbed, raped, burgled, or pillaged in the big city, the den of three million thieves, rapists, burglars, and pillagers. And, of course, her father wrote his letters.

Chloe tossed the rest of the mail on the nightstand on top of her Barbri bar review books and grabbed her glasses. She flipped over the envelope and frowned.

The top of the envelope had been neatly sliced open. Her letter was gone.

6

SHE SAT STRAIGHT up in bed, her skin cold. Prickly goose bumps raced up her arm and across the back of her neck, and her thoughts immediately went to Marvin. She stared uneasy at the ceiling above, as if the walls had eyes, and pulled the covers up and around her.

Marvin was her strange neighbor who lived in the apartment directly above hers. An unemployed social recluse, he had lived in the building long before Chloe had moved in a few years ago, and she knew he was definitely odd. Everyone knew he was odd. Each morning he stood watch on the courtyard below from his living room window; his plaid robe open wide, the belt useless and dangling at his side, and his hairy, middle-aged belly exposed, as well as God-knows-what-else under the cover of the windowsill. Thank the Lord for that windowsill. His pudgy, crowded face was always covered with a carpet of gray and brown stubble, and he wore black plastic glasses over eyes that were set too close together. In one hand he always held a black coffee cup. In the other, well, Chloe just didn't want to think about that.

The rumor around the laundry room was that Marvin was unstable emotionally and lived off a government disability check and help from his elderly mother. Behind his back, the residents called him Norman and speculated about what had really happened to his mother, who had not been seen for some time. For years Chloe had thought Marvin weird, but harmless. She would occasionally see him in the hallway or in the lobby, and he never smiled, but sort of grunted as he passed her.

Two months back, though, she had made the unfortunate mistake of waving hello at Marvin in his morning perch as she headed through the courtyard to her car. That night he was waiting for her in the lobby, with her mail in hand. He had smiled a lopsided smile that revealed tiny yellow teeth, and then had mumbled something about how "the mailman must have mixed theirs up" before he shuffled upstairs to spy on his fiefdom again from his living room.

After that, the inept mailman had mixed up their mail at least three times, and Marvin had taken up a new hobby of watering plants in the lobby, conveniently, it seemed, whenever Chloe came home from class. She could feel his stare locked on her from his living room perch when she walked to her car in the morning, and then when she saw him in the lobby at night. His egghead would bob up and down like a cheap car ornament and she would feel his eyes roll over her. Lately, she had been using the laundry room at the back of the building to come and go.

Two weeks ago she had started to get strange phone calls, where the caller hung up as soon as she picked up. When she replaced the receiver, the ceiling would creak above her as Marvin shuffled back and forth. Maybe that had been Marvin tonight on her machine—finally getting up the balls to actually speak.

And just yesterday, she had left some laundry in the dryer while she went back to her apartment for more quarters and had passed Marvin in the lobby on her way back to the laundry room, again pretending to water plants. When she brought her laundry back to the apartment later, two pairs of her underwear had been missing.

Now her mail had actually been opened and taken. The thought of Marvin touching her panties and reading her letters while his fat body got off in his bed over her head made her queasy. After the bar she was going to have to start looking for a new apartment, no easy task in New

York. She could not live beneath this weirdo anymore. Up until tonight she might have even considered moving in with Michael, but now . . .

Too many thoughts filled her aching head. When was she allowed to take more Tylenol anyway? She got up from bed and plodded across the living room to check the front door once again. She peered through the peephole, half expecting to see fat Marvin squatting naked outside her door, a coffee cup in one hand and a plant in the other. No one was there, and the lobby was dark.

She made sure she had double-locked the doors, and then she placed a large piece of duct tape over the mail slot on the inside of the door, so Marvin's chubby fingers wouldn't be able to force an opening wide enough for his peeping eyes to enter her apartment. The next morning she would nail a board over the slot and arrange to pick up her mail at the post office from now on.

She headed back to the coolness of her room and closed the bedroom door. She did a quick check of her ceiling to make sure Marvin hadn't taken up carpentry as a new hobby. Finding no holes in the ceilings and nothing odd, she watched the television for a few more minutes, until the throbbing in her head subsided a bit. A boom of thunder sounded outside, and the lights flickered. The storm sounded like a bad one—she might even lose the electricity tonight. She turned off the television and the lights and settled into bed, listening to the sound of rain as it hit the windows and the back of her air conditioner. It was a soft, soothing patter now, but Chloe knew the heavens would open up soon. Good. Maybe it would cool things off—the recent heat wave had been scorching.

Both physically and mentally exhausted, she finally fell into a deep sleep. She was in the middle of a strange and complicated dream about the bar exam when she heard the raspy, muffled voice directly over her.

"Hi, Beany. How is my big girl in the big city? Wanna have some fun?"

7

HE HAD SLIPPED easily into the apartment through the
unlocked window with the broken latch in the living room.
It had just begun to pour outside, and he was completely
soaked. With the curtains drawn, it was black in the room
and he could see nothing. That was of no concern to him,
though, as he was quite familiar with the layout of her
apartment. The kitchen clock ticked loudly two rooms
away. Carefully, he negotiated his way around the wood-
and-metal end table with its sharp corners in the living
room and the low-lying glass-topped coffee table strewn
with newspapers from three days past.

He had been here many times before. He had stood in
her living room, read her newspapers, her magazines,
touched her law books. He had listened to her phone messages, seen her mail, and looked at her bills and knew, in
fact, that the end table was from Pier 1 Imports and had not
yet been paid for. He knew her slender size four, had
touched her dresses, fingered her silk blouses, and smelled
her laundry, softly scented with Tide and Snuggle fabric
softener. He had secretly nibbled on leftover pizza from
her refrigerator—her favorite: sausage and meatball with
extra cheese. He knew she used Pantene shampoo and Dial
soap and favored Chanel No. 5 perfume. He had stood
before the mirror in her pale green-and-yellow bathroom,
exposed, and rubbed gobs of her luscious freesia body

lotion from Bath & Body Works all over his own body, imagining what it would feel like when it would finally be her hands on his cock. He had allowed the scent to linger on him for days after that: an intoxicating, constant reminder of her. He knew her mother's maiden name was Marlene Townsend and where her daddy worked at his small hometown paper. He knew everything there was to know about Chloe Joanna Larson.

Now he stood silently in the living room, just breathing in the very scent of her. His fingers traced her couch and touched her throw pillows. He picked up the jacket she had worn that night, which had been thrown on the couch, and touched it, smelled it, through the tiny airholes in his mask. Slowly, he made his way toward her bedroom, just down the short hall.

Suddenly, in the kitchen, Pete fluttered his wings about in his cage, sending a hollow, echoing sound resonating from the metal cage bars through the silent apartment. He stopped dead in his tracks and listened for signs of her, beads of sweat forming on his face beneath the mask. His breathing came fast and hard, but controlled. Surprise was essential, and it would not work if she came out now. It would not be according to *the plan*. The second hand on the cheap gray clock suspended in her kitchen ticked off each second loudly, and he remained glued in his position. What seemed like ten minutes passed by, but the apartment remained silent.

At the end of the hallway was the bedroom door. He could hardly contain himself now—the moment had finally arrived. He could hear the air conditioner running inside, the hum dropping low as it changed gears. He clutched the old round glass doorknob in his fingers for several long seconds, feeling the pure electricity of the moment course through his veins.

I think I'll take what's behind door number three, Bob!

Underneath his mask he smiled a slow, sweet smile, and then the Clown simply opened the door with a creak and walked softly into the room.

8

A FEELING OF pure panic pulsed through Chloe's body. She had been dreaming an anxious dream that she had arrived five minutes too late to sit for the bar exam and was arguing with the proctors to let her in. And now, for just a split second, her eyes refused to open while her brain frantically tried to reconcile the words she had just heard with the action that had just played in her dream.

Then, in an instant, she felt the cool smoothness of rubber against her face and tasted the chalky bitterness of the latex glove on her lips. A tremendous weight pressed suddenly on her chest, crushing her lungs and knocking the wind out of her. She tried to cry out but heard no sound. Something smooth and soft was shoved far into her mouth and forced into the back of her throat, making her gag. Her eyes, now open wide in terror, quickly tried to adjust to the virtual blackness of the room. Her hands flew to her face, but in an instant, both of them were seized, forced back above her head and quickly strapped to her metal headboard with a tight-fitting cord. Her legs, too, were grabbed, spread wide apart, and strapped to a metal post at each end of the footboard.

This can't be happening to me. This must be a nightmare. Please, Lord, let me wake up! Let me wake up now!

In less than forty seconds, she had been completely immobilized. Her eyes had now adjusted to the room's blackness and she turned her head frantically side to side, canvasing the room for her attacker.

At the foot of her bed, the figure was crouched, his head down, busy tying off the cord on her left ankle. Chloe's stomach dropped. The face and head were a ghoulish white in the glow of the alarm-clock light. Two tufts of red hair stood out on each side of his head. He looked up then and Chloe saw the bright red smile, the bulbous nose. It was a clown's face, a mask. In his right hand he held a large knife.

Maybe he just wants money. Please, please, take the television, take my stereo! My purse is on the coffee table in the living room! She wanted to shout this at him, but because of the gag, could not speak.

He slowly rubbed the sharp, serrated blade with gloved fingers, as he walked around the base of the bed. His eyes never left her, watching her from their empty, black peepholes in the mask. She could feel his stare, hear his breathing, smell his sweat. Frantically, Chloe flailed her arms and legs, desperate to break the cords on her feet, her wrists, but she could not move. The cord dug into the tender skin around her ankles, and her fingertips began to tingle from the lack of circulation. She tried to spit out the gag to scream, but could not move her tongue. Her body wriggled helplessly about on the bed and he crept closer still, until he stood at the foot post on her right.

His finger touched her toe then and slowly, very slowly, began to trace along her calf, over her knee and up her thigh until it reached the bottom of her pajama top. Chloe writhed under his touch. There was nowhere for her to go. She could hear her own heart pound furiously in her chest.

The air conditioner changed gears and hummed lower. Outside, she could hear the patter of heavy raindrops pounding on the window and on the protruding metal of the AC unit. The storm was here. A crack of thunder rumbled loud outside and lightning lit the sky, some of it sneaking through the sides of the window blinds, further illuminating the figure. She could see the shaggy red fur of his eyebrows, the black outline of his smile. Tufts of white-blond hair escaped onto his bare neck.

He suddenly moved away from her to the night table and set the knife down. He opened the drawer and removed her two coconut-scented votive candles and a pack of matches. She watched as he lit them, their flames casting a soft glow in the room and filling it with the delicate scent. For several minutes he stood staring at her in silence, his breath coming fast through the tiny slit in the rubber. The candlelight cast an exaggerated, distorted shadow on the wall.

"Hi, Chloe." The rubber face with its wide smile stared down at her. His words almost whistled as they escaped the air slit. She thought that she could now see ice blue eyes through the peepholes.

"I've missed you, Chloe. I almost thought you weren't going to show up tonight." He turned and picked up the knife from the night table and then faced her again. "Did you skip out on gym class just to spend a night with your boyfriend? Naughty, naughty, tsk, tsk."

Chloe's skin went cold and clammy. He knew her name. He knew she had missed her aerobics class. *Did he work at the gym?* Her mind desperately tried to place the voice. It was deep and muffled as it escaped through the rubber mouth slit. She thought she detected the hint of a lisp, or maybe an accent he was trying to hide. A British accent?

He bent down and knelt beside her. He moved his rubber face close to her ear, and stroked the hair off her cheek. She could smell the latex of the mask, and the hint of Quorum, a cologne that she had bought Michael once for Christmas. His breath smelled of old coffee.

"You really should have let him stay the night, you know," the Clown whispered right into her ear. Another bolt of lightning crackled outside, illuminating her bedroom with a bright flash, and she saw the knife glisten as he suddenly raised it high, just a few inches above her stomach. Her eyes grew wide.

He laughed and stood up. His finger traced over her body, down her arm, past her shoulder and over her pajamaed breast. The knife moved with him, floating just above his finger. "A pretty girl like my Chloe shouldn't be left all alone." He suddenly lowered the blade and sliced off the bottom button of her pajama top.

"Because you never know what might happen to a big girl in the big city." The knife sliced off the next button. A loud boom of thunder quaked outside to accompany the lightning. A car alarm sounded off in the distance.

"But don't you worry, Beany. I'm gonna take good care of *my* big girl. I'm really gonna make you smile." Another button gone.

Her body shuddered. Jesus Christ, he knew her nickname.

He drew an exaggerated breath in and sniffed at the air through the nose slit. "Mmmm. Chanel No. 5. I love it. I hope you wore it just for me. It's my favorite, too."

He knew her favorite perfume.

"What else are you wearing for me tonight?" The last button came off and slid down her side before dropping to the floor. It made a dull, soft thud as it hit the carpet. The tip of the knife slid between her pajama top, parting it. Slowly and deliberately, it pushed one side away, until it fell limp off her chest and on the bed. Then slowly the knife tip traced back over her exposed stomach and belly button to the remaining part of the pajama top and pushed it, too, aside, revealing both breasts. He stared down at her. His breathing came harder.

He traced the knife slowly over each breast, each erect nipple, and then up toward her neck. Chloe could feel the cold sharp tip gliding over her delicate skin, pressing deep into her flesh, but not yet splitting it open. He stopped at the heart pendant that rested on her throat and hesitated. He slid the knife under the necklace and yanked hard with the blade. The necklace slid down her neck onto the bed. He paused. Chloe could feel his stare penetrating her, up and down her body.

Oh dear Jesus, please don't do this.

The knife angrily sliced down her leg and ripped away what remained of her pink pajamas. Her naked legs squirmed, pulling at the cord on her ankles. He traced the knife now up her bare legs, starting at her toe, and then up her calf, her ankle, and then the inside of her thigh, the knife pressing harder and deeper, but not yet cutting her, as he progressed. He guided the blade under the spaghetti straps on her hip and cut away her panties, exposing her.

"You look so good, I may just have to eat you up," he said in a throaty voice.

Oh God, no, no, no! This must be a nightmare. Let this be a nightmare! She could hear her father's voice. *Be careful out there, Chloe. New York is a big city with lots of different people, not all of whom are nice.*

Chloe struggled to push the gag from her mouth. She could feel her heart exploding in her chest. Her arms twisted frantically under the cord, until she could feel it abrading her wrists.

He watched her wriggle and writhe on the bed. Then he lay the knife down on the dresser and pulled off his black T-shirt. He was tan and his chest was hairless, with well-sculpted muscles and a tight, defined stomach. He unzipped his blue jeans, carefully removing one leg at a time, and folded them neatly over the back of the chair. She saw that his left arm, just above the wrist, held an ugly raised zigzag scar that for some strange reason made Chloe think of a DANGEROUS CURVES AHEAD road sign.

"Lucky for you, Chloe, you didn't come home too late," he said. "We still have lots of time together." He removed his underwear last, revealing his erection.

Details. Get details, Chloe. Remember his voice. Remember his clothes. Look for other scars, marks, tattoos. Anything, everything.

"Oh, and I almost forgot. I brought my bag of tricks with me! I know some fun games we can play." He reached to the floor and opened a black nylon bag. He took out what looked like a twisted hanger, a black glass bottle, and electrical tape. He looked around the room. "But I think I'm going to need an outlet."

In her head, she began to scream and her body jolted about on the bed.

"You be a good girl now, Chloe, and Mr. Clown is gonna give you a real treat," he whispered out loud. Then the Clown climbed on top of her and raped her until the sun came up.

9

HE WHISTLED TO himself as he rinsed the blood off the knife in her clean, white bathroom sink. His and hers toothbrushes sat side by side in a green porcelain cup on the edge of the sink, and her freesia body lotion sat on the opposite edge. The water ran a red river off the blade down into the drain. The Clown watched it, mesmerized, as it twirled around and around in the basin, thinning to a light red and then pink and then finally disappearing.

He felt strong. The night had gone quite well, and they both had had a really good time. Even she had admitted it. Oh, there was that time when he had removed her silk panties from her luscious red, round mouth and instead of thanking him, the bitch had moaned and cried for him to stop. That had irritated him. A lot. But then the knife came out to play again and there was no more of that. In fact, she had actually begged him for more. But after a bit she started to whimper again and he had gotten quite sick of hearing it, so he had put the panties back in.

He dried off the knife blade on her pretty mint-green-and-lace guest towel and placed it carefully back in his nylon bag along with all the other cleaned toys. The mask was off now and he rinsed his gloved hands clean, splashed cold water on his face and neck, and dried himself on the towel. He admired himself in the mirror, his firm, hard body. He gave his teeth a quick brush with her toothbrush and checked to make sure they were clean. Then he pulled the mask back down over his face and headed back into the quiet bedroom.

She lay peaceful on blood-soaked sheets. Her eyes were closed, like an angel. He slipped on his jeans and T-shirt and hummed as he put on his work boots and tied them with a double knot. She still had the panties in her mouth, but she made no sound anymore, not even a whimper. He thought it strange that he actually missed that sound now.

He blew out what remained of the candle stubs. Bending down over her face, he stuck out his lips and kissed her on her cheek through the tiny rubber slit, letting his tongue venture out to taste her soft, salty skin one last time.

"Bye-bye, Beany, my love. My beautiful, beautiful Chloe. It was fun."

On the sheet next to her neck lay the broken heart pendant. He picked it up and put it in his jeans pocket.

"Something to remember our time together by."

He blew a kiss in the air and quietly closed the bedroom door behind him. Then he grabbed the nylon bag from her bathroom and went down her tiny hall and past her kitchen one last time. At the Pier 1 end table, he spotted her small jade statue of the three wise monkeys, their hands covering their eyes, ears, and mouth: Hear No Evil, Speak No Evil, and See No Evil. A present, he knew, from her parents' recent trip to the Orient. He had heard once that folklore said the monkeys were supposed to bring protection and good luck to any home they were welcomed into. *Not tonight,* the Clown thought to himself and smiled. Next to the statue sat a picture of a happy Chloe and her Preppie Prick boyfriend at the Empire State Building. He paused, allowing his fingers to run over the image, before taking his own mental snapshot of this special night.

And then, just as quiet as a church mouse, he slid open the living room window and dropped beneath the dense cover of the evergreen, still wet from the torrential storm that had since passed over. Then the Clown quietly slipped unnoticed into the purple-blue night, just as slivers of orange light began to slice across the sky and day broke over the deserted streets of New York City.

10

MARIE CATHERINE MURPHY stood outside Apartment 1B and simply knew that something was wrong. Especially since it was already ten to nine, Marie was running late, today was the practice multistate exam, and Chloe was not answering her door. And while it was not unusual for Chloe to be late, too, which was partly why they were such great friends, she always eventually answered. Albeit, usually in her pajamas, but always with a great excuse and two enormous mugs of freshly brewed coffee in hand, as well as a box of Stella D'oro Breakfast Treats. They had carpooled to St. John's Law School for the past three years, and Marie could not think of one time that Chloe had stood her up. No matter how late Marie had been in getting there.

An elderly woman had buzzed her in the building, and Marie had practically sat on Chloe's doorbell for the past five minutes. She knew that Chloe and Michael had gone out last night, and she initially thought that maybe he had spent the night and they had both overslept. That thought made her pause for a few moments and hope that Michael would not answer the door in his underwear. Coffee or no coffee, Marie certainly didn't need to see that. But after five minutes there was still no response to the ringing bell, and Marie was getting more than anxious. She tried to peep in Chloe's mail slot, but found that it was covered with something from the inside.

She headed back outside and lit up a cigarette. Upstairs, behind his window, she saw Chloe's strange neighbor staring down into the courtyard at her, black coffee cup in hand. He certainly was creepy, half naked, with those thick glasses and that weird sneer on his face. A chill ran through Marie's body. She saw that Chloe's front curtains were still drawn shut and her bedroom blinds closed. Her car was missing from its usual spot and Michael's BMW was nowhere to be seen.

Don't panic. I'm sure it's nothing.

She padded around to the other side of the brick building to where Chloe's kitchen window was. The window was closed, but the curtains were pulled back. The window towered above Marie's 5'2" frame by another ten inches. She sighed. She had to work that afternoon and was dressed in a skirt and three-inch-high heels. She put down her purse, cursed herself under her breath for not picking out a pantsuit and flats, and crushed out her cigarette. She climbed up onto the brick half wall that ran adjacent to the kitchen window and gated off the steps to the building's basement. Using a garbage can for leverage, she hoisted her husky frame up to the window, holding on to the sill for both dear life and for balance, and peered in. In front of her on the kitchen table was Pete, still covered in his cage. To her left was a pile of dishes in the sink. She could see through the kitchen doorway into the hallway and the living room, and saw the table was covered with newspapers. Marie immediately felt better. If the apartment had been clean, she would have known something was definitely wrong. It looked, instead, as if Chloe had never even come home last night.

She must have stayed at Michael's apartment and forgotten to call me. He probably dropped her off at class this morning with a hot cup of Dunkin' Donuts coffee and a Boston Cream doughnut and she's now learning how to pass the bar and become a lawyer while I stand here with my fat ass flapping in the breeze peering into her dirty kitchen like a moron.

Now she was annoyed. And she was going to be late for the practice test. She had begun her precarious descent down off the garbage can when a thought occurred to her. *If Chloe had not come home last night, who had covered Pete's cage?* She paused for a moment, troubled by something else she thought she had spotted on the hall floor, just outside of the kitchen. Something in the back of her head forced her to turn around again for a closer look, and she pulled herself back up on the garbage can and placed her face up against the window. She cupped her hands around her eyes and squinted hard.

It took several seconds before she recognized that the dark spots she was looking at were actually footprints. It was another several seconds before she realized that they looked like they were made in blood.

That was when Marie Catherine Murphy fell off the garbage can and started to scream.

11

"WE'VE GOT A pulse," a voice yelled out in the darkness. "And a beat."

"Is she breathing?" Another voice.

"Barely. I've got her on O_2. She's in shock."

"Jesus Christ. There's blood everywhere. Where is it all coming from?" Another voice.

"You mean, where is it *not* coming from? She's a mess. I think most of the bleeding is vaginal, though. She may be hemorrhaging. Man, this psycho really did a number on her."

"Cut those cords, Mel."

A fourth voice. A deep, heavy New York accent. "Easy, guys, that rope is evidence—don't hack at it. Touch it with gloves. Crime Scene needs to bag and tag." The room, it seemed, was full of people now.

"Christ, her wrists are completely torn up." The voice sounded disgusted, panicked.

Police radios squawked with static and voices. Piercing sirens, more than one, in the distance and coming closer. The click of a camera, the sound of a flashbulb.

Angry voices now. "Be careful, careful, with her! Hey, Mel, if you can't handle this shit, just step back and get out. Now's not the time to freak."

Silence filled the room for a few seconds, then voice number one. "Start an IV of fluids, and give her some morphine. She's about five five. Looks about one-ten, one-fifteen. Call Trauma at Jamaica Hospital and tell 'em we've got a twenty-four-year-old white female, multiple stab wounds, possible internal bleeding, probable sexual assault, in shock."

"Okay, okay, lift her gentle now. Gentle! On my count. One, two, three."

Pain, intense and biting, rolling in waves over her body.

"Jesus Christ. Poor girl. Does anyone know her name?"

"Her friend outside says that it's Chloe. Chloe Larson. She's a law student at St. John's."

The voices faded away and the blackness folded in on her.

12

CHLOE SLOWLY OPENED her eyes and was immediately blinded by the bright light. For a moment she thought that perhaps she had died and was in heaven, just moments from meeting her maker.

"Follow the light, please." The penlight tracked across her face. She smelled the overpowering smell of disinfectant and bleach and knew that she was in a hospital.

"Chloe? Chloe?" The young doctor in a white lab coat flashed his penlight again in her eyes. "I'm glad to see you're waking up. How are you feeling?" Chloe read his tag: LAWRENCE BRODER, M.D.

It seemed like a really stupid question to Chloe. She tried to answer, but her tongue was thick and dry. She could manage only a whisper. "Not good."

Everything hurt. She looked at her arms, both of which were wrapped in heavy white gauze bandages, and saw tubes connected everywhere. Her abdomen throbbed in the most excruciating pain, which was growing more intense.

Michael sat in a chair in the corner of the room. His body hunched forward, hands folded under his chin, elbows on his lap. He looked worried. Outside the window in the room the sky was tinged pink and orange and light was fading. It looked like sunset.

Another man in green scrubs stood silently by the door. Chloe assumed he was a doctor, too.

"You're in the hospital, Chloe. You have experienced quite a trauma." Dr. Broder paused and looked around the room. The three men exchanged awkward glances. "Do you know why you're here, Chloe? Do you remember what happened to you?"

Chloe's eyes welled up, and tears rolled out. She nodded slowly. The Clown's face flashed into her mind.

"You were assaulted last night. Sexually assaulted. Your friend found you this morning and the paramedics brought you here, to Jamaica Hospital in Queens." He hesitated and shifted his feet, obviously uncomfortable. He spoke fast. "You suffered some severe injuries. Your uterus was badly torn and you were hemorrhaging. You had lost a great deal of blood. Unfortunately Dr. Reubens, here, was forced to do an emergency hysterectomy to stop the bleeding." He motioned to the green scrub doctor, who held his position by the door, his head down, his eyes purposefully avoiding Chloe's. "That was the greatest injury, though, and that's all the really bad news. You do have some cuts and wounds on your body for which we called in a plastic surgeon to do the stitching and minimize any scarring. These other injuries, though, are not life threatening, and the good news is that we expect you will be fine and make a full recovery."

That's all the really bad news. That's it. That's all, folks. She looked around at the three men in the room. All three, including Michael, avoided her stare, their eyes darting among each other and to obscure objects on the floor.

Her voice was barely a whisper. "A hysterectomy?" The words even hurt as they escaped her throat. "Does that mean I can't have a baby?"

Lawrence Broder, M.D., shifted to the other foot and frowned. "I'm afraid that you will be unable to carry a fetus, that is correct." She could tell Dr. Broder wanted this conversation to end. Now.

He quickly continued, twisting his flashlight pen back and forth like a baton in his right-hand fingers. "A hysterectomy is major surgery, though, so you will be in the hospital for at least the next couple of days. The recovery period for something like this is usually six to eight weeks.

We'll start you on some limited physical therapy tomorrow and progress slowly. Are you having pain in your abdomen now?"

Chloe winced and nodded.

Dr. Broder beckoned the sullen Dr. Reubens over. Then he closed the curtain around the bed, blocking Michael out, and lifted the hospital sheets back. Chloe could see white bandages wrapping her stomach, her breasts. Dr. Reubens gently palpated her abdomen, sending fireballs of pain through her body.

He nodded, not at Chloe, but at Dr. Broder. "The swelling is normal. The stitches look good," Dr. Reubens said.

Dr. Broder nodded back and then smiled at Chloe. "I'll have the nurse up the morphine dosage in your IV. That should make it better." He replaced the sheets and again shifted feet. "There are some detectives outside who would like to speak with you. Are you feeling up to it?"

Chloe hesitated, then nodded.

"I'll send them in." He pulled the curtain back. Obviously relieved to end the conversation, Dr. Broder and Dr. Reubens, his eyes still cast downward at the floor, then moved quickly toward the door. Dr. Broder pulled open the door handle and paused. "You have been through a terrible ordeal, Chloe. We are all pulling for you." Then he smiled softly and walked out.

The victim of a sexual assault. A hysterectomy. No kids. The nightmare had been real. The words were coming too fast at her, there was too much information to absorb. Images of the Clown's twisted smile, his naked body, the jagged blade, all flashed in her head. He knew all about her. He knew her nickname. He knew her favorite restaurant. He knew she had missed the gym. He said he was always watching her.

Don't you worry, Chloe. I'll always be close by. Watching. Waiting.

She closed her eyes and remembered the knife, remembered the pain that had engulfed her body when she had first felt him cut her. Michael came up beside her now and held her hand.

couldn't scream . . . he had something in my mouth." She
touched her fingers to her lips, still tasting the dry, soft silk,
heavy on her tongue. She could feel herself gagging, and it
was hard to breathe again.

"He put something in my mouth, then he had my arms
and my feet and I just couldn't move anywhere. I
couldn't move . . ." She looked away from Detective Harrison and reached for Michael's hand, to steady the shaking, but he had turned back toward the window, hands
fisted.

I just wish you had let me stay with you last night.

Detective Harrison glanced in Michael's direction,
reached over and touched Chloe's arm. "A lot of rape victims blame themselves, Chloe. But you need to know that it
is not your fault. Nothing that you did or didn't do could
have prevented this."

"He knew things. He knew where my candles were,
there, in the drawer. He lit my candles, and, I . . . I just
couldn't move!"

"Did he say anything to you, Chloe? Can you remember
what he said?"

"Oh my God. Yes, yes, yes, that was the worst thing. He
kept talking to me like he *knew* me." She could not stop
shaking, and sobbing wracked her shoulders. "He knew
everything, everything. He said he was always watching
me and said he would always be near me. Always. He knew
about my vacation to Mexico last year, he knew Michael'd
been over on Tuesday, he knew my mother's name, my
favorite restaurant, he knew I missed my gym class on
Wednesday. He knew everything!" Pain ripped through her
breasts, and she now remembered why.

"He had a knife, he just cut off my pajamas and then
he . . . he cut me. I could feel him slice my skin open and I
couldn't move. Then he was on top of me and . . .

"Michael, please, I couldn't move! I kept trying, but I
just could not move. I couldn't get him off of me!" She
screamed it until her voice went completely hoarse.

Detective Harrison sighed and slowly stroked Chloe's
arm, repeating herself that Chloe was not to blame. Detec-

tive Sears exhaled a deep breath and shook his head. Then he flipped to the next page in his notebook.

Chloe, sobbing, looked over for Michael, but he was still turned away toward the window, with his fists clenched and his back to her.

13

IT WAS POURING rain on the Tuesday afternoon when Chloe was finally released from Jamaica Hospital. Just five days after she'd been wheeled in unconscious on a stretcher, Dr. Broder came in her flower-filled room and announced with a broad smile that Chloe was now "fine" and was being discharged that afternoon. The news had frightened her—she'd had the shakes all day, and her heart raced as the time of her discharge approached.

Her mother had finally heeded her advice and ignored the real estate section of the *New York Times* and instead had focused on the paper's obituary section. Within two days she had found Chloe a one-bedroom apartment on the eighteenth floor of the North Shore Towers, a high-rise building in Lake Success, just over the Queens-Nassau county line. It had belonged to a ninety-year-old widow and her seventeen-year-old cat, Tibby. Unfortunately for Tibby, the widow had passed on before he did. Chloe, with the help of two new Ben Franklins, was able to have it right away. Her mom said she thought it was nice, for a New York apartment.

Chloe never wanted to return to Apartment 1B, Rocky Hill Road. Never. She never wanted to see Bayside again. Except for Pete the Parakeet, she never wanted to see anything from her apartment again, and especially anything from the bedroom. From her hospital bed, she told her parents to sell it all, burn it all, give it all away. She just did not care, as long as nothing and no one, including Michael or her parents, made the trip directly from her old apartment to her new one.

She knew that Michael thought she was being more than a little paranoid. The idea of her rapist waiting, watching, and following people to find out where Chloe would be moving to seemed, to him, far-fetched. He agreed that she should move out of Bayside, but he could not understand why she did not just move in with him. And he simply refused to give up his Manhattan apartment.

"Chloe, do you know how hard it is to get a rent-controlled apartment in the eighties?" he had asked. "I had to search for eighteen months before I found this one."

Explaining her reasoning to him was almost demeaning. "Michael, he knows *everything*. He knows all about me and he knows all about you. He's probably followed me from your place or he's followed you home. Maybe he was *your* neighbor, and he followed me from *your* apartment. And maybe you are willing to take a chance for a stupid 'rent-controlled apartment in the eighties,' but I'm not. And I am not going there again. Ever. I just can't believe that you can't see any of this!"

The conversation had been heated. Too heated. She had started to cry, he had sighed too loudly. To stop her tears, he promised to "see what he could do," but it would just be impossible for him to move right away. Then he suggested that they instead work on finding her a new apartment out of Bayside. He had stepped outside the room to make a quick phone call and after about ten minutes, returned and announced that he had to go back to his office. A bouquet of flowers had arrived two hours later with a note that simply said, "With love, Michael." That was Friday. He then worked all weekend.

So Chloe's mom had found her the apartment at the North Shore Towers, its windows high above the ground. It offered a single woman in the city the best of amenities: a doorman; double-bolted doors; an alarm system with motion detectors; and, a deluxe intercom system. By Sunday her parents had moved in her television, her kitchen table and chairs, and Pete. Everything else they picked up new at Sears. On Monday the Salvation Army arrived at Rocky Hill Road with their big red van. Two muscled male workers pushed past what remained of the yellow crime scene tape left dangling from the doorjamb of Apartment 1B, and gratefully hauled away the rest of what remained of Chloe's life's belongings. They left a receipt on the empty living room floor. And on a rainy, gray Monday afternoon, as a few curious neighbors looked on, her life in Bayside, Queens, quietly ended. Her father told her that Marvin, her neighbor upstairs, sent his regards.

Her parents, of course, had tried to convince her to move back to California. Anywhere in California would do. Anywhere out west, in fact. Anywhere but New York City. Chloe had raised the subject with Michael, but he had just as quickly dismissed the idea. His career, her firm, his family, their life together—everyone and everything was in New York. So she had lied and told her parents that they were both toying with the idea, but she needed to take the New York Bar first and start at her new firm, where she'd already made a commitment. Then she made an all-important-sounding speech about how she wasn't going to let this maniac ruin her life or run her out of town. Blah, blah, blah. Chloe hoped she actually meant what she said.

In truth, she did not know what she wanted anymore. What had seemed so important only five short days ago now seemed utterly trivial. The bar exam, a new job, an engagement. She jealously watched television from her hospital bed as the world went on as normal, as if nothing at all had happened. People fighting the usual rush-hour traffic in the morning, and then fighting it back home again at night, just struggling to commute. And on TV, the news anchors, busily reporting the world's comings and goings, as if these were major newsworthy events.

If you're headed to the Island, avoid construction on the LIE and delays on the Grand Central Parkway. Tom Cruise is appearing at a star-studded Hollywood premiere in Los Angeles. Another boatload of Cuban refugees is found off the coast of Key West, Florida. Please help the starving children of the world. Unfortunately, folks, the weekend weather calls for continued thunderstorms. Sorry, boaters, better luck next weekend when drier air looks like it'll move on in.

It made her want to scream.

The police guard who had stood by her room for the first two days was now gone and, she assumed, had been reassigned to protect yet another victim. Detective Sears had told Chloe that the guard was taken off her room because she was no longer considered in "imminent danger." And although the police were "actively hunting the perpetrator" and "following up on all possible leads," by Monday, Detective Harrison had stopped her daily visits to Chloe's hospital room, choosing instead to call in once a day to see how she was doing. Chloe suspected that within a few days, the phone calls, too, would trickle off, as her case was shuffled aside to make room for the new arrivals.

Her hospital room overflowed with the many baskets of fragrant flowers that had been sent by well-meaning friends, acquaintances, and associates, but still she couldn't bring herself even to say hello to anyone on the telephone. Other than Marie, Chloe did not want to see friends. She didn't want anyone to see her bandages, and then wonder about all the horrible things that must have happened to her to warrant so many of them. She didn't want to talk about that night, but she also didn't want to make idle chitchat with the curious. After that, she realized, there really was not much to say. She wanted to go back in time, to simply be Chloe again, with all the normal problems and tedious chores that seemed to plague her on any given day, but she knew that that was no longer possible. She hated him for that most of all. He had taken her life, and she did not know how to get it back.

Michael remained at the office, stopping at the hospital on Monday for an hour at lunchtime. She knew that the hospital made him uncomfortable. She knew that seeing her bandages and her IVs, and her medicines and her doctors and her physical therapist only made him feel frustrated and helpless. She knew that the whole *incident,* as he was calling it, made her angry. But somehow she really didn't care anymore how *he* felt about anything. And it made her more than just angry at the thought that his life was going on as normal, as if nothing had happened, when in fact, everything had happened and nothing would ever be the same again for either of them.

Now it was Tuesday and she could finally go home, something she thought she wanted, yet ever since Dr. Broder had told her she was to be discharged, she couldn't stop shaking. Michael was supposed to come for the discharge, but he'd gotten tied up in a complicated deposition all afternoon. So it was her mom and Marie who wheeled her to the front lobby where her dad's rental car stood waiting just outside. She was able to walk, but the wheelchair was hospital policy until she was placed in the car.

The elevator doors opened to the first-floor lobby, and Marie pushed her into the busy hall. People were everywhere. Old folks sat on benches in the corner, and police officers lingered at the reception desk. Distraught parents held crying children, and nurses and hospital personnel crossed the floor to and from the elevator bays.

Chloe's eyes quickly scanned the lobby looking for any sign of him. Some people stared at her in her wheelchair, idly curious. She watched their eyes closely, their body movements. Some were engaged in conversations, others had their heads buried in papers, and still others looked straight ahead at nothing in particular. Her eyes frantically searched them all. Her heart pumped fast, and she felt the surge of adrenaline. The unfortunate and desperate truth was, though, that his could be any one of the many pairs of eyes that she was looking at. She would not know him without his mask.

Just the simple step from the wheelchair to the car brought searing pain to her abdomen. With her mom and Marie's help, she carefully climbed into the backseat, her shopping bag of prescription drugs in hand. She looked out the rain-streaked car window into the vast parking lot. Next stop was busy Northern Boulevard, and then they would hit the Long Island Expressway, which was always crowded with cars. So many faces, so many strangers. He could be anywhere. He could be anyone.

"Are you all set back there, honey?" A pause. "Beany?" her dad asked gently, obviously waiting for an answer.

"Yeah, Dad, I'm ready to go." She hesitated and then added quietly, "Daddy, please don't call me that anymore."

He seemed sad. Then he nodded soberly and watched as his daughter turned her tired face back toward the window. He pulled the Ford Taurus away from the lobby overhang, and the car made its way through the crowded parking lot and onto Atlantic Avenue. Chloe stared out the window as they traveled to her new apartment in Lake Success, passing alongside any number of cars, any number of strangers, with Jamaica Hospital fading farther and farther behind them in the driving rain.

14

CHLOE TOLD HERSELF each morning in the mirror: *Just make it through today and tomorrow will surely be better.* But the tomorrows only seemed to be getting worse. The fear inside her kept growing like an uncontrollable cancer even as her wounds healed and the jagged scars began to fade. Insomnia plagued her nights; debilitating fatigue, her days.

The managing partner at Fitz & Martinelli, the firm where she was supposed to kick-start a brilliant legal career as a medical malpractice attorney after the bar, anxiously called to see how she was and if she would be starting as scheduled in September or needed more time to recuperate. *I'm fine,* she had told him. *Everything is healing, and I'm taking the bar as scheduled in three weeks. Thank you for your concern.*

And she believed what she said. To everyone, every day. But then, without warning, an inexplicable feeling of terror would grip her with its spindly claws, freezing her dead in her tracks—so real she could smell it. Breathing would become labored and difficult; the room would spin. On a subway ride, she would suddenly taste the cloth, feel the cold knife tip. In an elevator, she would hear his voice, smell the sweet, sickening coconut candles. In the car, she would look in her rearview and see his hideous smile. She would instantly be transported time and again back to that night. She tried to maintain some sort of schedule and just resume what was once a normal life. But as the days passed into weeks, she felt the tiny, microscopic cracks take form in her solid façade and then slowly spread and feather, until she was sure that one day she would just shatter into a million pieces.

After two weeks of New York, her parents had finally packed up and left for Sacramento. The bravado that she had spewed at them behind a smiling poker face had worked its magic charm and they hugged and kissed her good-bye as they waited for the elevator, and begged her again to move to California.

I'm fine. Everything is healing, and I'm taking the bar as scheduled in two weeks.

She had waved a smiling good-bye as the elevator doors closed on her mom's tear-streaked face. Then Chloe had turned and actually run inside her apartment, bolted the door, and just sat on the floor and cried uncontrollably for three hours.

She continued to study for the bar exam from home. It was best not to venture out to the live lecture courses because of the many stares she knew she would receive from complete strangers, and the questions she would be asked by well-intentioned friends. Barbri, her bar review course, provided her with videotapes instead. Most days she found herself on her living room floor, surrounded by law books, notepad in hand, staring blankly at the television and watching the professors' mouths move, but hearing them speak words that somehow made no sense anymore. She simply could not concentrate, and she knew she would not pass.

Michael stayed over on the night before the bar exam, and then drove her at 7:00 A.M. into the Jacob Javits Center in Manhattan where the test was being administered. She signed in with the other three thousand test takers, took her assigned seat, and received her thick multistate exam at 8:00 A.M. A hushed, concentrated silence fell over the convention center. At 8:05, Chloe looked behind her, next to her, in front of her, at the sea of unfamiliar faces, some crouched over their papers, some looking around the room in nervous desperation. They all made her feel anxious, terrified. Her head throbbed, her body quivered and broke into a cold sweat. She felt nauseated. She raised her hand and was escorted to the ladies' room by a proctor. She stumbled into a stall and threw up. Then she splashed cold water on her face and neck, opened the bathroom door, and walked straight out the convention center doors. At 8:26 A.M. she took a Yellow cab home and never went back.

Detective Harrison didn't call anymore, so Chloe instead now called her every day to check the status of the case. The answer was always the same, though.

"Be assured, we are actively pursuing the investigation, Chloe. We hope to have a subject in custody soon. We appreciate your continued cooperation."

She swore the detective read the daily response off a cue card titled "Law Enforcement Responses to Pacify Annoying Victims of Unsolved Cases." As days became weeks, Chloe knew that her case was moving its way on a steady course into the cold-case files. Without an ID and no fingerprints or other physical evidence, her case would most likely never be solved short of a confession and a lot of luck. Still, she called Detective Harrison every day, if just to haunt her and let her know that she was not going away anytime soon.

After the bar exam fiasco, her relationship with Michael had all but disintegrated. She knew that he was angry with her for just walking out on the test, for not even trying. There had been no sex since *the incident,* as he still preferred to call it, but now even when they held hands, it felt strained and uncomfortable. Instead of coming by every night, he now came by only on the weekends. And he was getting more and more frustrated that she no longer wanted to leave her apartment, even if it was only to go out to dinner. There was an unspoken cold distance between them that grew every day, but neither knew how to take back the lost ground. Chloe didn't know if she even wanted to go back to the way things were. She knew that Michael, in some way, secretly blamed her for what had happened. She saw it in his eyes when he looked at her and then when he couldn't look at her. And for that she could just not forgive him.

I just wish you had let me stay with you last night.

Chloe supposed that they both knew it was over, yet neither of them wanted to be the one to administer last rites. She suspected that Michael was too afraid of the avalanche of guilt that was sure to fall on his head if he ever conjured up the nerve to break it off. Then she wondered what emotion she would feel herself when and if he finally told her that, although he would always love her, he didn't want her as his wife and could they please just be friends? Would it be relief, guilt, anger, sadness? So as their relationship drifted through the rest of summer and blurred into fall, the two of them saw less and less of each other and neither complained.

Fitz & Martinelli urged her to retake the bar in February and offered her a position as a law clerk in the interim. She declined. It would be just another place where she would be known around the watercooler as "the rape victim." Only now it would be worse because she had also earned herself the dubious distinction of being "the rape victim who walked out on the bar exam."

At her three-month postop checkup, her gynecologist suggested counseling. "Rape victims have scars the rest of us can't see," he had said. "Psychological counseling is recommended to help you cope with things."

I'm fine. Everything is healing, I just didn't take the bar as scheduled. Thank you for your concern. Then she left his office and vowed not to return.

In October she applied for a position as a nighttime reservationist with the Marriott Hotel at La Guardia Airport—a large, constantly busy hotel with hundreds of workers, none of whom even knew her name. She worked in a back room with a headset, away from the public and its probing eyes. It didn't put her on the partner track, and it would not make her parents proud if they knew. Michael was disgusted by what he called her "lack of ambition." But it was a place that allowed her the safety of numbers during the terrifying nighttime hours, and still afforded her the anonymity she needed to avoid intrusive conversation. And it was money. She worked the 11:00 P.M. to 7:00 A.M. shift.

It was only her fourth week on the job, when she received the phone call. It was almost six o'clock, the last hour of her shift.

"Marriott La Guardia. This is Reservations. Can I help you?"

"Yes. I've unfortunately missed my flight, and now American can't get me out until tomorrow morning. I think I'll need a room. Do you have anything available?" She recognized Bach's "Sheep May Safely Graze" softly playing in the background.

"Let me check, sir. Are you a Marriott Rewards member?"

"No, I am not."

"Single or double, sir?"

"Single."

"Smoking or non?"

"Non, please."

"How many in your party, sir?"

"Just me. Unless you care to join me, Chloe."

Her heart stopped. She ripped the headset off and threw it on the floor and stared at it as if it were a cockroach. Adele, the manager came up, followed by several other front-office clerks. From the floor, a tiny voice repeated, "Miss? Miss? Hello? Is there anyone there?"

"Are you okay?" Adele asked. Chloe pulled away from her touch.

Had she really heard that?

The cracks were spreading, branching out all over. The façade would surely fall. She stared at the headset that Adele picked up off the floor.

"Hello, sir? I'm sorry. This is Adele Spates in Reservations. Can I help you?"

Chloe backed away toward the door, grabbing her purse from the table as Adele finished the reservation. The room spun. Voices filled her head.

A pretty girl like my Chloe shouldn't be left all alone.
You look so good, I may just have to eat you up.

I just wish you had let me stay with you last night.
Be assured, we are actively pursuing the investigation.

She ran as if the devil himself was behind her through the Marriott parking lot to her car. She had forgotten her coat, and the cold autumn wind ripped right through her. At seventy miles an hour she sped home on the Grand Central Parkway, frantically checking behind her, expecting to see his clown face in the car behind her, maybe flashing his headlights at her with a wink.

She parked the car and ran to the elevator, rushing past the security guard still sleeping in the lobby. In her apartment, she turned on all the lights, reset the alarm, and dead-bolted the front door.

A fear that Chloe had never known before gripped her, and her body trembled uncontrollably. She frantically raced through each room, flinging open the closets, checking underneath the bed, behind the shower curtain. From the nightstand in her bedroom, she grabbed the small .22 caliber pistol that her father had bought for her before he returned to California. She carefully checked and double-checked to make sure that it was, in fact, fully loaded.

In the living room, the light from the motion sensor continued to blink red, the alarm green.

She held the gun on her lap on the living room couch, her sweaty hand a death grip on the black handle, her index finger toying nervously with the trigger. Tibby the cat nudged his way gently under her arm, purring against her chest. The sun had started to come up, and yellow light began to creep in through the cracks in the drawn curtains. The weatherman had said it was going to be a beautiful day. Chloe stared at the white front door and waited.

The façade had finally come down. And it was in a million pieces.

15

ALL THE ONCE-PRETTY faces gazed back at him with dead, empty stares. Eyes of sea green and smoky violet, their long lashes still thick with mascara, gazed out at nothing—vacant and lifeless. Painted, full mouths now only gaping, twisted holes of black. Eyes whose last witness was one of unthinkable horror. Mouths forever silenced into eternal screams.

Florida Department of Law Enforcement Special Agent Dominick Falconetti sat alone in the gray former conference room. He stared at the montage of photographs that adorned The Wall, his head in his hands, his index fingers gently rubbing away at the pressure that was steadily mounting behind his temples. Police reports, green investigative report folders, newspaper clippings, and interview sheets littered the length of the rectangular cherry conference table. A cigarette burned somewhere nearby behind an old Starbucks coffee container and an empty brown bag from Burger King. Off in a corner of the crowded room, a television monitor crackled with snow from the gruesome videotape that had just played out. Above him, the ceiling's bright fluorescent light cast a glare on the five new grisly photographs that were spread out neatly in front of him on the table. A new girl for The Wall.

The families of the missing eleven young women had been asked to provide a recent photograph of each girl for identification purposes. Prom pictures, high-school and college graduation pictures, yearbook photos, and professional head shots smiled down at Dominick now from their respective positions on the brown corkboard that task force members somberly called The Wall. The task force had actually received from the families three, five, and in some cases up to ten photos of each girl. From his seventeen years as a homicide investigator, Dominick knew that it was impossible to expect a mother to choose just one picture to capture an entire lifetime of memories of her child, or a sibling just one photo to reflect how a sister should be forever remembered. It was almost disrespectful to ask. So the most detailed photograph of each girl had been chosen for The Wall, and the others had been silently filed away. The eleven pretty faces had then been arranged in a row on the corkboard in chronological order—starting with the date of the first disappearance, not with the date that their bodies were ultimately discovered.

Directly underneath, and in startling contrast to the happy snapshots, the naked and broken bodies of nine of the missing women had been photographed one final time. Neon-colored thumbtacks held the five-picture collage of each woman's crime scene and autopsy photos onto a brown corkboard that now stretched almost the entire length of the room. A chilling, ghastly photo album of before-and-after still pictures. Sandwiched between the life and death photos were neatly printed five-by-seven-inch white index cards that listed each woman's name, age, and her brief physical description, and then the date and location of her disappearance. The last line provided the date and location where her body had been discovered, and finally, the coroner's estimated date and time of death. The cause of death was not necessary. From the color glossy photos on The Wall, it was all too obvious.

Dominick took a sip of the coffee, now ice-cold, and stared, as he had done hundreds of times before, at each girl's haunting face, into her once-trusting, terrified eyes. *What had they seen in the last few moments of their short lives before everything mercifully went to black?*

They were all so young. Most of the girls were only in

their early twenties, three were not lucky enough to have made it even that far. The oldest of the eleven was just twenty-five, the youngest, barely eighteen. Photographed in life, the vibrant smiles were inviting, the playful pouts coy. Blond hair fell in golden ringlets off one, spilling onto her shoulders; another wore platinum locks cut short behind the ear in a jagged bob; and another's honey-colored streaks fell pin-straight down her back. All had been blond, and, in life, so beautiful. So beautiful, in fact, that six had their professional head shots on The Wall.

In the past eighteen months, eleven women had vanished into the tropical Miami night, disappearing under the palm trees of Ocean Drive and Washington Avenue from packed, trendy South Beach nightclubs and hot spots where the rich and famous and beautiful liked to frolic. Weeks, and sometimes even months, after their disappearances, the mutilated, nude bodies of nine of the women had been discovered in remote locations across Miami-Dade County. The locations of the crime scenes were scattered and unpredictable: an old sugar refinery plant in the Everglades, a foreclosed crack house in the middle of Liberty City, an abandoned supermarket in Kendall. Their killer had not tried to hide the bodies or cover up his crimes, though; rather, he had obviously welcomed their ultimate discovery. And it was immediately apparent that each woman's cruel death had been as meticulously planned as her disappearance, the brutality of which had sickened even the most seasoned of investigators.

The violated bodies each bore the frightening signature of a serial killer: one who stalks his human prey seemingly at random, for reasons known only in his own twisted mind. A serial killer so brazen that he purposely chose his victims in front of hundreds of witnesses; so savage as to earn him the macabre nickname of Cupid.

Each woman had actually been sliced open, torn apart vertically from her throat to her stomach, and then horizontally under the breasts. The sternum had been cracked wide by an unknown object, the ribs left broken and jagged. The heart of each woman had been cut out of her chest and removed. All were still missing. The butchered chest was left open and exposed, with only a gaping, bloody black hole where the heart had been. Each of the young women had been found nude, posed in a final obscene sexual position, and each had been sexually assaulted before her death, both vaginally and anally, with an unknown object or objects. Some even after.

There were now twelve officers and detectives from five different police agencies assigned full-time to the Cupid task force: the Miami Beach Police Department, the City of Miami Police Department, the Miami-Dade Police Department, and the North Miami Police Department. At the request of Governor Bush, the Florida Department of Law Enforcement (FDLE), the state criminal investigative agency, had originally donated to the cause the use of a conference room at their Miami Regional Operations Center to serve as task force headquarters. And they had also thrown in the services of a criminal analyst, a copy machine, a fax, and a part-time secretary. It was in this very conference room that the corkboard had first been erected. In the beginning it was a standard-sized board, maybe three by two. Then, after eight months, six missing women, three dead bodies, and no leads, the FDLE had also donated the services of Special Agent Dominick Falconetti. The first thing Dominick did was get a bigger corkboard.

Two cheap wooden bookcases and a file cabinet had been pushed into the far corners of the room to make space for the copy machine, three computers, and the many cardboard boxes that were stacked up high against the walls. The commemorative law-enforcement plaques, trophies, awards, and pictures that once decorated the room had been taken down to make room for The Wall, and were now piled facedown in a heap on top of the bookcases. Inside the cardboard boxes were stacks of green investigative report folders, stuffed with police reports, FYI cards, leads, and interviews. Reports and interviews that would expose every detail of the last months, days, and minutes of each young woman's life. A separate stack of boxes contained the financial records of each victim, their diaries, date books, letters, photo albums, and e-mails: the most personal and private of belongings, the most intimate of thoughts, facts, and details—now forever public record in the state of Florida.

Dominick found the thumbtack box on top of the file cabinet in the corner, next to another abandoned, old cup of coffee, this one from 7-Eleven. One at a time, he pushed the hot-pink tacks through the five photos and onto the corkboard, underneath the index card marked MARILYN SIBAN, 19.

Without the index cards, it was virtually impossible to match the crime-scene photos with the right victim's head shot. The once-perfect faces were now swollen and bloated; their creamy silk complexions turned an ashen, pasty gray or, worse yet—a festering, oozing dark black. Brilliant white smiles had been replaced with maggots and swollen, black tongues. The golden curls and platinum locks now stained dark with dried blood. In Florida's hot and humid weather, decomposition came quickly, and, in many instances, bodies were identifiable only through their dental records.

Dominick's eyes moved across The Wall, searching for something that couldn't be seen. Nicolette Torrence, twenty-three; Andrea Gallagher, twenty-five; Hannah Cordova, twenty-two; Krystal Pierce, eighteen; Cyndi Sorenson, twenty-four; Janet Gleeder, twenty; Trisha McAllister, eighteen; Lydia Bronton, twenty-one; Marilyn Siban, nineteen. Two more head shots smiled at him from the far end of The Wall, their index cards incomplete. Morgan Weber, twenty-one, was last seen at the Clevelander Bar on Miami Beach on May 20, 2000, and Anna Prado, twenty-four, was last seen at the South Beach nightclub Level on September 1, 2000. Two more women missing. Two more presumed dead.

Dominick took the last drag left in the burning cigarette and stubbed it out. He had quit a few years back, but ever since Cyndi Sorenson and Lydia Bronton had been found within a week of each other last month, he had been sneaking a couple here and there. He looked out the room's sole, small window. The chain-link fence that surrounded the evidence warehouse next door cast strange, zigzag shad-

ows from the streetlight on the empty FDLE parking lot
outside. Everyone else in the building had gone home long
ago, and it was now completely dark out. On the conference table sat a brown accordion file folder, its contents
spilling out onto scattered police reports and notepads. It
was brand-new. Across the front of the folder was
scrawled: MARILYN SIBAN DOB: 4/16/81 MISSING: 7/28/00
DOD: 9/16/00.

DOD stood for Date of Discovery. Due to the severe
decomposition of Marilyn's body, the medical examiner
had been unable to place a definite date of death. He
approximated it to be within the past two to four weeks.
That meant that, at the very least, Cupid had kept her alive
for three weeks before finally allowing her to die. In the far
right-hand corner of the file folder was handwritten the
number 44 in a circle, indicating the total number of
autopsy and crime-scene photos taken. Dominick had
already placed five on The Wall.

Before dawn yesterday, officers conducting SWAT
training with the Miami-Dade County Police Department
found the body of the nineteen-year-old just west of
Florida City near the Everglades in an abandoned missile
silo and warehouse belonging to the U.S. Navy. The
unmistakable stench of decay had overcome them when
they kicked open the metal silo doors on their practice
search warrant raid. In a far-off corner of the deserted
structure, a five-by-five-foot area had been strung off with
taut nylon rope, from which hung old, dirty blankets and
sheets, forming a makeshift three-sided tent. Initially, the
officers thought it was the camp of a homeless person, or
maybe some kids who had found the old building and built
a fort. They thought the smell was perhaps a dead animal.
Then they pulled back the sheets and discovered what
remained of the once-beautiful model.

Marilyn's nude body sat on the dirty cement floor, her
back propped up against an old rusty oil barrel. Her long,
ash-blond hair had been pulled into a tight ponytail and
then duct-taped to the top of the barrel, forcing her head
back slightly and her neck upright. The mouth and eyes
were open. Most of the skin on the body had festered and

bubbled in the heat, and then sloughed off, exposing black, rotting tissue and muscle. Her legs had been disjointed from their sockets in the pelvis and then spread wide apart, forming a grotesque split, her arms deliberately positioned downward, the skeletal fingers placed inside her pubic area. And as with all his other victims, Cupid had left behind what was now recognized to be his signature. Her chest had been carved open, a concave hole left where her sternum had been split apart. Gauging from the large cover of bloodstains found in the cement under the body, and the blood-spatter patterns on the hanging sheets, she had probably been killed where she was found. The cause of death was found to be massive hemorrhaging and blood loss due to the severing of the aorta and the removal of the heart muscle. The ME had been unable to determine if Marilyn had been conscious, but based on the blood-spatter evidence at the scene, he'd speculated that she was alive when her heart was cut out of her chest.

She had disappeared from Club Liquid on South Beach on a Friday night some two months before. The four friends that had been with her in the packed nightclub said she went to one of the main bars for a drink and had never come back. Because they thought that she had maybe met someone and left with him, Marilyn wasn't reported missing to the Miami Beach Police Department for two days, when she didn't show up at her day job as a waitress. The photograph that her parents gave to the police was from her last photo shoot for a used-car dealer in the Keys, taken just two days before her disappearance.

Crime Scene would now spend the next five days processing every inch of the silo and warehouse and the perimeter surrounding it, but Dominick didn't expect much. If it was anything like the last eight scenes, there would be no prints, no semen, no hairs, no foreign DNA, nothing. The FDLE forensic team out of Key West, along with the MDPD Crime Scene Unit, had spent the last two days scouring the immediate area for tire tracks, footprints, cigarette butts, clothing, or weapons of any kind, and had come up empty. The former military complex was set far away from any main road and any witnesses, smack up against the remote Everglades. The nearest gas station was over five miles away. It was protected only by chain-link fence, multiple NO TRESPASSING signs, and a simple metal arm gate with a lock a two-year-old could pick.

It was so damn frustrating. After eight months on the task force, he was still no closer to finding the killer. Or killers. And the disappearances and murders were happening faster. The violence to each body was escalating, getting more graphic, yet still very organized and controlled. Each crime scene indicated that the killer was becoming even more brazen, more sure of himself. Taunting the police to find him. Some of the victims had been killed where they were found, but others had been tortured and killed elsewhere, their bodies then brought to the locations where they were then flagrantly staged. *Why some and not others?* All the crime scenes were carefully constructed and had been deliberately chosen. *Why? What was the message he was trying to send?* The bodies of two of the earlier victims, Nicolette Torrence and Hannah Cordova, were discovered in what the ME estimated was only days since their murders. Each had been reported missing within the week before they were found. Cupid now appeared to be taking more time with each victim, experimenting more. Months were passing between their disappearances and their discoveries.

The press coverage of the murders had been constant and unrelenting. The media at each scene was becoming a veritable circus of news vans, boom mikes, and strobe lighting. News organizations from across the country and around the world were setting up camp in Miami to report on the "slew of brutal murders that has the police baffled." Perky, eager reporters battled with each other in front of the body bags to be the first on the story, all struggling to contain their excitement on national air at the discovery of yet another Cupid victim. *Now back to you, Matt and Katie.*

Dominick ran his hands through his thick, black hair and slugged down the last of his coffee. He had slept less than four hours in the last two days. He cupped his chin in the palm of his hand, pulling down lightly on the close-cut salt-and-pepper goatee he had been trying to grow. Lately, he had been seeing more salt than pepper in it. Although he thought he looked pretty good on the outside, on the inside, he was beginning to feel all of his thirty-nine years.

It was the job. It was these cases. They drained the very life out of you, no matter how much you tried to distance yourself from them. In every young, beautiful, fresh face, he saw a daughter, a girlfriend, a sister. Staring into those dead eyes, he saw his own niece, just yesterday swinging on a tire swing back in Long Island, now today turning voluptuous and eighteen and leaving for Cornell. He had worked homicides for seventeen years, the first four with the NYPD in the Bronx, and the last thirteen as a Special Agent with FDLE's Violent Crimes Squad. Each year he had vowed would be his last. Each year he swore he would request a transfer to the Fraud Squad, where it was always so quiet and everyone left the office at 5:00 P.M. But the years came and the years went, and here he was, still stuck with the dead bodies and 3:00 A.M. search warrants. For some reason he felt compelled to do what he did. For him, there was no escape until each killer was caught, each victim vindicated—and, unfortunately, that sometimes just never happened.

He knew that every killer messed up. Every single one. And even serial killers left a calling card. He had worked four serials in his career, including Danny Rolling in Gainesville and the Tamiami Strangler in Miami. Historically, if you go back to the original crime scenes of infamous serial killers who had been caught, you could see their screwups. You just had to know where to look. Son of Sam, the Boston Strangler, John Wayne Gacy, Ted Bundy, Jeffrey Dahmer.

You just had to know where to look.

He studied The Wall trying to find the missing piece that no one could see. Aerial photos of South Beach and Miami-Dade County, adorned with red and blue pushpins, took up the opposite side of the room. The red dots littered the art deco area known as SoBe, marking the locations where each of the women had disappeared. The blue were scattered everywhere around Miami.

It was now 9:00 at night. Under the glare of the fluorescent light, Dominick reached for his glasses and again read the interview of Shelly Hodges, one of the last people to have seen her friend Marilyn Siban alive. "It was too crowded to get a drink from a waitress. They were all taking too long. Marilyn said she thought she saw some people she knew at the main bar, and so she went to get a martini. That's the last time I saw her."

Some people she knew. Plural. Could there really be more than one killer? Usually serials worked alone, but there were some notable exceptions, such as the Hillside Stranglers, California's murdering cousins. Assuming for a moment that there was more than one, Marilyn must have known her killers, or trusted them enough to willingly leave the bar with them. It had long been hypothesized that all the victims knew their killer. Why else would they all have voluntarily left their waiting friends in crowded bars?

If that was the case, there should have been a common link of acquaintances between at least a few of the victims. But as far as anyone could tell, none of the victims knew each other and none shared the same circle of friends. None of the girls had modeled at the same job, or worked for the same agency. There was no connection to be found. His thoughts went around and around again, and his eyes returned to the corkboard.

You just had to know where to look.

It was time to go home. There was nothing left to do here tonight and no one left to do it anyway. He gathered the reports off the table and stuffed them into their new accordion file, ejected the videotape of Marilyn Siban's crime scene from the VCR, and unhooked his laptop. His cell phone rang.

"Falconetti."

"Agent Falconetti, it's Sergeant Lou Ribero with Miami Beach P.D. Listen, I think I've got some good news for you and your task force buddies. Looks like we found you your Cupid. And he's brought along his latest victim."

16

DOMINICK RACED EAST down the Dolphin Expressway toward Miami Beach with his blue lights on, weaving in and out of the traffic that snarled the highway even at 9:00 at night. South Florida drivers had to be the worst. The absolute worst. They beat New Yorkers hands down. They either drove twenty miles over the speed limit, or twenty miles below. There was no in between. That was until, of course, the hares caught up with the turtles and jammed on their brakes, thus causing a procession of red brake lights and accidents that would go on for miles.

Just past the 395 ramp to the MacArthur Causeway all traffic stopped dead. Up ahead in the westbound lanes he could see the mass of flashing blue and red lights. The causeway split into a divided long bridge over the waters of the Intracoastal and, but for swimming, there was no way to cross over from the eastbound lanes. He cursed the idiot cop who had chosen the MacArthur Causeway of all places to pull someone over. He pulled to the far right-hand service side of the eastbound lanes and drove on the half mile past the stalled lanes of gawkers and rubberneckers; the turtles and the hares now united in one cause, their heads and necks craned out their windows for a better look at whatever grisly traffic accident they believed lay ahead. Dominick could now see that to his left, a glut of fifteen to twenty police cars had converged on the westbound lanes

of the causeway and a City of Miami police helicopter was
lifting off from the westbound lanes. Florida Highway
Patrol troopers had stopped traffic in both directions, and
in the front rows of cars both east and westbound, the mor-
bidly curious sat on the roofs and hoods of their cars
watching the scene unfold. The frustrated just honked.

Once past the barricade of Florida Highway Patrol
cars, he raced again to the end of the causeway. He exited
eastbound, only to reenter westbound, which was virtually impossible because all traffic had stopped and backed
up on the ramp. He had to radio for an FHP trooper to
help clear the ramp just so that he could get back on the
causeway.

Finally on the westbound side of the causeway, he flew
in the emergency lane past another batch of rubberneckers
and yet another FHP roadblock, parking his undercover
Grand Prix behind a row of what must have been at least
ten marked police cruisers from almost every law-
enforcement agency in Miami-Dade County. The two right
westbound lanes had been cordoned off with flares, and a
freckle-faced FHP trooper who was probably all of nineteen was now motioning for the rubberneckers to move it
along in the reopened left lane.

An ambulance and a fire truck were parked ahead of
the lines of police cars, white and red lights flashing
intermittently with the blue of the police cars. A white
van with the words MIAMI-DADE COUNTY MEDICAL EXAM-
INER written in black across the side sat by itself just up
ahead. It had no flashing lights. If Dominick did not
know what it was he was about to witness, he would have
sworn it was a horrible multicar crash with multiple fatal-
ities.

He walked past the line of empty cop cars, their blue
lights flashing. Sitting in the emergency lane, he spotted
the lone black Jaguar XJ8 next to the concrete guardrail,
surrounded by still more empty police cars. *Shit. The whole
world was out here. Another circus for the media moguls.*

In the immediate background sat the *Miami Herald*
building, butting up against the waters of the Intracoastal,

its tenth-floor windows reaching out and practically touching the causeway. *Great. Some reporter won't even need to leave the comfort of his office to get this picture on the front page.* He looked up at the building, its windows now spotted with lights and dark figures. An intern with a telephoto lens was probably catching the hair up his nose on film at this very moment.

The Jaguar sat empty, its trunk wide open. Inside the trunk, Dominick could see the white sheet gently stirring in the light tropical breeze coming off the Intracoastal. Fifteen feet back from the Jag, a small cache of law-enforcement officers in various uniforms stood talking, their bodies unconsciously forming a protective circle in front of the trunk. Two-way police radios crackled and squawked, each dispatcher communicating something different in garbled, incoherent police jargon.

At one end of the causeway, just to the west, was the beautifully lit skyline of Miami, aglow in neon colors of hot pinks, iridescent blues, and citrus yellows from the People Mover that wrapped around the city. At the other end of the causeway, the twinkling white lights from the high-rises that lined Miami Beach greeted the east.

Directly behind the shiny new Jag sat a marked Miami Beach Police cruiser. In its backseat, behind the protective metal grid that separated driver from passenger, Dominick could see the dark outline of a sole figure.

He approached the cluster of cops and flashed his badge. "Anyone know where I can find Sergeant Ribero with the Beach?"

Another nineteen-year-old in a Miami Beach P.D. uniform nodded and pointed toward a small circle of cops that stood behind an MDPD Crime Scene van. Dominick looked over and saw three uniforms talking with two Blues Brothers stand-ins, *sans* the sunglasses, in dark suits. The dark suits were listening intently and taking notes. He recognized one from the Bureau and automatically felt his jaw clench.

The circle in front of the Jag parted and he passed through, making his way to the trunk. The trunk light illuminated the sheet, and he could see red stains beginning to seep through the heavy material. He pulled his rubber gloves out of the pocket of his khakis, just as a large hand fell heavy on his shoulder.

"Hope you haven't eaten dinner yet, pal. It's pretty bad."

Manny Alvarez, a City of Miami detective assigned to the task force for the past year, stood behind him puffing on a cigarette, the sleeves of his tired white dress shirt rolled up over black hairy arms and too many gold bracelets, the armpits circled with sweat. The collar on his size-eighteen-inch neck was half buttoned and looped with an orange-and-blue Miami Dolphins tie, from which a black-and-white imprint of Dan Marino's face grinned at Dominick. "Where the fuck have you been, anyway?"

"Stuck on that stupid causeway, that's where I've been." Dominick shook his head and looked around him. "Obviously this whole thing has not been kept under wraps, Manny. What a fucking circus."

At an intimidating six five and 250 pounds, Manny the Bear towered over Dominick Falconetti, who stood more realistically at five eleven and 190. Mops of thick black hair covered Bear's beefy frame, and wiry black curls ran down his arms onto the backs of his hands and fingers. He wore a thick black mustache and a five-o'clock shadow so thick that it would have been someone else's full beard. Tufts of hair even sprouted from underneath his collar. In fact, hair was everywhere on Manny. All except for his head, which he kept shaved as bald and smooth as an eight ball. He looked like a mean Cuban Mr. Clean.

"What can I say? When you get invited to a party, you better show up before the cake is gone. Besides, have you waved to our new friends at the *Herald* yet?" Manny gestured to the building behind them and raised his arm in an exaggerated wave. It would probably make tomorrow's front page.

"Alright, alright. I'm over it. What have we got?"

Manny Alvarez puffed on his Marlboro and leaned against the concrete guardrail, with the waters of the Intra-coastal lapping gently forty feet below him. "About eight-fifteen tonight, Chavez, a rookie with the Beach, spots a black Jag speeding down Washington Avenue toward the MacArthur. Doing maybe forty in a thirty. He follows him onto 395 and sees he's also got a broken taillight. So he pulls him over. Only one guy in the car. So he asks for his license, registration, the whole drill.

"Chavez says the guy is Mr. Smooth, cool as a cucumber, no sweat, no tics, nothing. Guy gives him a Florida DL with the name Bantling. William Bantling. Lives on LaGorce Avenue on the beach. Chavez heads back to his car to write the mope a ticket when he smells this funky odor that he thinks is coming from the trunk. So he asks Bantling for consent to search the trunk. The guy says no.

"There's something wrong here, Chavez thinks. You know, why doesn't the guy want me looking in his trunk? So he calls for backup and a K-9 unit. He takes him out of the car and holds him till the cavalry arrives. K-9 shows up twenty minutes later and alerts right away on the trunk— you know, scratching, barking, the whole nine yards. They're thinking coke, right? Papa's packing some nose candy in that trunk. They pop it open and . . . surprise, surprise! Our friend has a dead girl in there. And she's been cracked wide open and is missing a heart.

"Well, everyone freaks. And the radios start rolling. Before you know it, we've got every jurisdiction down here, and everyone's sergeant. It's a circus. They even flew in my chief on the copter to take a peak. You just missed him. He was at some fancy-shmancy fund-raiser for the governor or something. Soon as he heard about it, he claimed he just had to be here, so rather than *drive* the twenty minutes from the Biltmore Hotel, he had the boys fly him and the governor in. We had to clear both sides of the causeway just so the chopper could land and he could waddle his fat ass over for a sneak preview and then brownnose about it on the flight back to his steak and potatoes. Can you believe that shit?" Manny shook his head in disgust and flicked his cigarette into the slow trickle of rubbernecking traffic in the left-hand lane. He hoped it would enter an open window of one of those bloodthirsty gawkers. Right on his lap and maybe burn his balls off.

Dominick nodded in the direction of the Crime Scene van. "Who are the suits?"

Manny smiled slyly. "Need I say? Why they're our good, dependable friends from the FBI, here to take all the credit for solving a case they never even worked on." He rolled his eyes. "It's Stevens and Carmedy. They're making nicey-nice with the Beach Boys so all their facts are straight in the news conference they will undoubtedly be giving tomorrow morning."

"How did they get word on this before me?" Dominick looked around and shook his head. "Damn it, Manny, the whole fucking world is here."

"The Miami SAC from the FBI was at the same dinner. But as far as I know, the feds, always humble, drove themselves here. The rest of the boys, well, as you can see, they just want to be part of this special moment in history."

Dominick shook his head. The Bureau's Miami Special Agent in Charge was Mark Gracker. He and Dominick had had go-arounds long before the Cupid case, on an organized-crime murder that Gracker and his federal pals took over—conveniently after Dominick had solved it and identified the suspect. One minute Dominick had whispered the suspect's name at a closed-door FDLE and FBI powwow and the next he was watching the news dumbfounded as Gracker slapped cuffs on the guy while simultaneously giving an interview to Julia Yarborough of Channel 6. Ten days later, the FBI named Gracker the Miami SAC.

The Bureau was always trying to wiggle their way into something so they could look like the heroes at the end. Good press had been hard to come by since Waco and Ruby Ridge. But now that Marilyn Siban's body had been found on federal land, thereby throwing the case into federal jurisdiction, he didn't think he could actually tell Gracker to fuck off anymore. He looked down at the trunk. "Do we have an ID on the girl?"

"It's Anna Prado, the little hottie who disappeared from Level. She's only been missing a couple of weeks. The body's in pretty good shape, though. Can't be dead for more than a day or so. It's a shame, man. What a beauty."

Dominick slipped on his rubber gloves and lifted the white sheet. Another pair of empty, dead eyes stared helplessly back at him. Hers were baby blue.

"No one's moved her? Touched her?"

"Nope. What you see is what you get. Suits took a peek, but that's it. I played baby-sitter. 'No touchy, boys, and be sure to play nice with the other cops!' Crime Scene did photograph the scene, though. They finished up about ten minutes ago."

Anna Prado's nude body was lying faceup, the knees bent and her legs folded up underneath her body. Her arms were tied together with nylon cord above her head. Long platinum blond hair collected in a pile underneath them. Her chest was cut open in two incisions, forming a cross, the sternum neatly cracked. The heart was missing. Blood had pooled underneath the body, but not in a significant amount—making it clear she had been killed elsewhere.

"He was probably getting ready to move her to some deserted place and fuck with her some more. Then we get to find her skeleton a couple of months from now fucking a sink nozzle or something . . . just in time for the holidays. Let me tell you something, Dom, just in case you didn't know, there are some sick fuckin' people in this world." He moved away from the guardrail and lit another cigarette. He raised his middle finger and smiled at a slow passing car. "Like these sick maggots, stopping to try and get a really good look."

"She looks fresh, Manny." Dominick touched her arm, and the flesh and muscles moved. The skin was cold. Rigor mortis had come and gone, but not too long ago. He figured she had been dead probably less than a day. Dominick stepped back from the trunk, and underneath his shoe he heard a light crunching sound. He bent down and picked up what looked like a piece of red taillight. He slid it into his pocket. "What did they use to pop the trunk?"

"I think a metal jack. Only Lindeman with the Beach actually touched the trunk after they popped it. Crime Scene is going to dig in as soon as the ME takes her away. I wanted you to see the scene, though, before they do."

"Who's this Bantling guy? Does he have a history?"

Dominick looked behind him at the Miami Beach cruiser, where the figure in the backseat sat upright and still, but he could not make out the face in the dark.

"Nope. We ran him. He's got nothing. I called Jannie, the analyst over at the task force, and, as we speak, she is dissecting his scummy little life from the time he first shit in his drawers until the last time it was he took a leak. We'll know more by breakfast."

"What's he do? Where's he from? I never heard of him before. He hasn't surfaced on any of our lists, has he?"

"Nope. He's forty-one and a buyer for Tommy Tan Furniture Designs, some ritzy designer on the Beach. He travels a lot to South America and India. Claimed he was headed to the airport when Chavez pulled him over. The little that we do know is that he keeps to himself. We've got an army out at his house right now, interviewing the neighbors and just waiting for a warrant. So far we're getting the usual from the neighbors: 'He seemed like such a nice guy, but *I* knew there was something odd about him' sort of crap. Tomorrow they'll be on Jerry Springer claiming they were clairvoyant and we were idiots.

"I already called the State Attorney, and Masterson and Bowman from the task force are working on the warrants. They'll walk them through with C. J. Townsend from the State Attorney's and then they can all head to the judge's house for cookies, milk, and a signature."

"Has this Bantling said anything?"

"Nope. He's not talking. Hasn't said a word since he denied the consent to search to Chavez. We've got him in the back of Lou Ribero's squad car with the mikes on and we've been listening, but he's not even breathing heavy back there. I told everyone to leave him alone, that we'll handle it. Our federal friends haven't talked to him either. Not yet anyways, although I'm sure it's on their to-do list."

"Alright. Crime Scene can have it. Release the body to the MEs. Make sure to bag her hands before she's moved." Dominick nodded in the direction of the investigators and techs, sitting on the side of the road, all trying to remain inconspicuous in their blue jackets with the words POLICE and MEDICAL EXAMINER printed in large fluorescent yellow lettering on the back. They descended upon the back of the trunk like termites to wood.

Dominick nodded at the circle of cops that still surrounded the car as he passed through again. In the sky he heard the distinct whirring of a helicopter hovering overhead, and bright lights blinded him from above.

"Hey, Manny, please tell me that is your fat-ass boss coming in for a landing and tour number two," he said.

Manny looked up and squinted hard. Then he shook his head again in disgust. "I'm afraid not. That, my friend, is the Channel Seven Trauma News at Ten O'Clock. Looks like we've made the big time. We're gonna be on at eleven. Be sure to smile."

"Shit. The hordes are descending. Alright, let's get this guy back to the office and talk to him before he realizes that this is a death-penalty state and starts whining for a lawyer and the ACLU. I'll talk to the boys from the Bureau when we get back there, but let's just make it clear that he's *our* suspect."

Dominick opened the back of the Miami Beach cruiser and leaned in. The man inside stared straight ahead. In the overhead car light, Dominick saw that his right eye was puffy and swollen, and blood ran down the side of his face from a deep cut over his cheekbone. Raised red marks covered his neck. He must have tripped on his way into the squad car. It always amazed Dominick how clumsy suspects can be. Particularly on Miami Beach. His hands were cuffed behind him.

"Mr. Bantling, I am Special Agent Dominick Falconetti with the Florida Department of Law Enforcement. I'm gonna need you to come with me. I need to ask you some questions."

William Bantling continued to stare straight ahead, expressionless. His eyes blinked only once.

"I know who you are, Agent Falconetti. And I can assure you that there is nothing for us to discuss at your office, or anywhere else for that matter. I am invoking my right to remain silent. I want to speak with my lawyer."

17

MARISOL ALFONSO WAITED impatiently for her boss at the sec-
ond-floor elevator bay in the Miami-Dade State Attorney's
Office. Her short, doughy frame paced the hallway, a pink
message pad in hand. It was only 9:02 A.M. and she had
officially been on the clock for one hour and two minutes,
even though she hadn't actually arrived at the office until
8:15. She was more than mad—she just wasn't gonna take
this shit anymore. They did not pay her enough.

The doors opened, and Marisol scanned its departing
occupants. In the back of the crowd of police uniforms and
business suits, wearing dark sunglasses and a crisp gray
suit, she found who she was looking for.

"Where you been?" she barked angrily. "Did you know
that I have taken thirty messages since I been here?" She
dramatically flicked through the pink pad and followed her
prey through the security access doors down the hall to the
small office in the Major Crimes Unit, where a plaque on
the door read C. J. TOWNSEND, ESQ., ASSISTANT CHIEF. Now
she waved the pad high above her head. "All these, they are
for you!"

The last person C. J. Townsend wanted to be greeted by
on any morning was her mean secretary, Marisol. It automatically ruined any hope she might have held out for having a good day. Today, in particular, was no exception. She
opened her briefcase on top of her desk, removed her sun-

glasses, and stared back at the glaring, lumpy figure who stood before her, iridescent clawed hands on hips, in a hot-pink Lycra T-shirt and flowered skirt that was two sizes too small and five inches too short.

"The last I checked, Marisol, answering the phone and taking messages were included in your job description."

"Not this many. I haven't been able to do nothing else. Why didn't you call and tell me what to say to these press people?"

Not as if she did much anyway. C.J. smiled through her gritted teeth. "Tell them that there is no comment and just keep taking those messages. I'll get back to whoever needs getting back to, but right now I have a ten o'clock hearing that I need to prepare for. Please make sure that I'm not disturbed." With that said, she began unpacking the files from her briefcase.

Marisol tsked loudly, dropped the message pad on C.J.'s desk, turned on her pink high heels, and stormed out of the office, mumbling angrily in Spanish under her breath.

C.J. watched as Marisol teetered off down the hall to the secretarial pool, where she figured she would now spend the next two hours making her rounds among the secretaries, gossiping about the morning's events and what a bitch her boss was. C.J. closed the door and let out a slow breath. If it was the last thing she accomplished at this office it would be to get that woman moved to another division, on another floor, preferably to the Child Support building across town. Not an easy task. After ten years, Marisol was a lifer. They would probably have to drag her out in a large, pink body bag before the State Attorney conjured up the balls and actually canned her.

She leafed through the message pad. NBC Channel 6, WSVN Channel 7, CBS Channel 2, *Today*, *Good Morning America*, *Telemundo*, *Miami Herald*, *New York Times*, *Chicago Tribune*, even the *Daily Mail* in London. The list went on and on.

The news of an arrest of a suspect in the Cupid murders early that morning had spread like wildfire through the media, and the feeding frenzy had begun. From her office window, C.J. had already spotted the media refugee camps that had staked their claims on the steps of the criminal courthouse across the street, complete with direct satellite feeds to their New York and Los Angeles affiliates.

She had been assigned for the past year by the State Attorney himself to assist the Cupid task force with their investigation. She had been to the scenes, attended some of the autopsies, reviewed miscellaneous warrants, debriefed the medical examiner, scoured police and lab reports, and taken witness statements. She had also shared in the rash of criticism that was seemingly doled out on a daily basis by the press on the lack of progress in the case. But now her devotion to the boys in blue had won her the grand-daddy of all prizes: prosecuting the most notorious serial killer in the history of Miami. That assignment alone apparently now made her the *celebrity du jour* in the eyes of the media, something she absolutely dreaded.

In her ten years with the State Attorney's Office, she had prosecuted everything from fishermen catching spiny lobster out of season to triple homicides committed by seventeen-year-old gang members. She had asked judges for fines, community service, probation, prison, and death. Five years earlier she had been commended on a near-perfect conviction record and promoted to Major Crimes, a small, specialized unit composed of the office's ten top prosecutors. There, she and her colleagues were assigned much smaller caseloads than the rest of the 240 attorneys in the busy office, but their cases were considered the worst type of crimes and the most complex to prove. Most were first-degree murders, all were heinous, and all were judged by the office to be newsworthy. All her defendants faced the death penalty, by electric chair or lethal injection. Most of them got it. Organized-crime hits, child killings, gang-land executions, domestic murders where whole families were summarily annihilated by a despondent man angry because he'd just lost his job—every case, by its very nature, a potential media explosion, although some received front-page press, while others only a two-sentence blurb on the back page of the local section. Others never made it to the big time at all, overshadowed by another case still more atrocious, or an upcoming hurricane, or the Dolphins big loss to the Jets.

In C.J.'s five years with the unit, she had seen her share of her name in the papers. The attention always made her more than a little uncomfortable, and she still loathed giving interviews. She did her job, not for the publicity or limelight, but for the victims, the ones who could no longer speak from their graves six feet under and the innocent friends and family that were inevitably left behind wondering why when the gun smoke cleared and the cameras were turned off. She felt as though she gave the survivors a sense of vindication, a feeling of power in an otherwise powerless situation. In this case, however, the glare of the spotlight would be even more oppressive, since for the first time she'd be dealing with the national and international media, rather than just the local press. She knew when Manny Alvarez called her at home last night to tell her they had a Cupid suspect that this was going to be big. Probably the biggest case her career would ever see.

She had spent half the night reviewing the warrants for William Rupert Bantling's house on Miami Beach and his two cars. Then she spent the other half preparing for the First Appearance Hearing Bantling would be having today, which was set for 10:00. In between the two, she visited the scene on the MacArthur and stopped by the ME's office to get a look at the body. Then she fielded three anxious phone calls from the State Attorney, Jerry Tigler, who was quite upset that although he had been at the same fundraiser for the governor as the City of Miami Police Chief and the FBI SAC, he apparently had not been invited with all the other bigwigs to the after-hours party down on the causeway. He wanted C.J. to find out why he had been slighted. With all that, she had forgotten to sleep.

Within twenty-four hours of his arrest, Bantling was entitled to a determination by a judge in a pro-forma hearing that there was probable cause to arrest him for the first-degree murder of Anna Prado. Was it more likely than not that he had committed the crime of which he was accused? Off the cuff, a mutilated body in the trunk probably met that criterion. And, normally speaking, a First Appearance was a nothing, two-minute hearing that was handled on closed-circuit television with the defendant on one side of a monitor across the street at the county jail and a temperamental, overworked judge with a First Appearance docket of two hundred misdemeanors and fifty felony cases in a tiny courtroom on the other.

The ornery judge would read the arrest form, read the charges aloud, declare probable cause, set the bond or deny one, and move on to the next defendant in the long line that snaked through the jailhouse. And that would be it. It was over so quickly, the defendant usually hadn't even realized his name had been called. He would stand at the jailhouse podium, blankly looking all around until they pushed him off to the line of prisoners headed back to their cells. The prosecutor and public defender sat in the courtroom with the judge, but they were really just decorations. There were no witnesses, no testimony, just the judge reading off the arrest form. And he always found probable cause. Always. It was nothing fancy—just good ol', swift southern justice.

But this one—this one was going to be different. Today the defendant was going to be brought over from the jailhouse across the street and paraded into the county courthouse by the Department of Corrections at a special time for a special hearing in a special courtroom just for him. It would be witnessed by his defense attorney, the prosecutor, the now not-so-ornery judge, and the entire press corps that had camped out overnight on the courthouse steps and were lucky enough to find a seat in the courtroom. A nice, intimate affair that would be viewed by millions in simultaneous live broadcasts across the country and parts of the world. Then replayed again for the five-, six-, and eleven-o'clock news broadcasts.

C.J. suspected that it would take longer than two minutes.

The First Appearance judge was the Honorable Irving J. Katz, a press hound dog. Cranky and old, he had been a judge in Miami long before they had even built a courthouse to put him in. Much to Judge Katz's dismay, the chief judge no longer let him handle trial work, but instead had made him King of the First Appearance, normally an uneventful, tedious job. A case like this one, though, was enough to make Judge Katz salivate. C.J. could expect him to use the first five minutes of the hearing up just in the silent, furious stare of contempt that he would land on Bantling. And the cameras. Then he would ask his bailiff to present him with the arrest form, and he would proceed to slowly read the charges, making sure to enunciate clearly in a voice dripping with disdain. He would pretend to read the arrest form that laid out the facts of Bantling's arrest the night before, which, of course, he had already done in chambers at least ten times, and a feigned look of shock and disgust would creep across his wrinkly, ancient brow. He would demand to know how Bantling pleaded to the charges, even though that really wasn't necessary until the arraignment three weeks later. Then he would wrap up the performance with a stern, dramatic speech that C.J. suspected would sound something like "I pray that these heinous charges, these barbaric, vile acts were not committed by the likes of you, William Rupert Bantling. May God have mercy on your soul if they were, as you will surely burn in hell!" Or something close to that. A real headline grabber for the morning edition of the *Miami Herald:*

JUDGE TELLS CUPID TO BURN IN HELL!

Of course he would find probable cause. Chances were that C.J. would not need to speak at all. But still, she had made sure she was prepared on the facts in case she was faced with an argument from Bantling's attorney.

Judge Rodriguez was the search warrant judge on duty last night, and in his bathrobe at 5:00 A.M. he had signed off on the warrants to search Bantling's house and cars. At this very moment, at least four police agencies were ripping apart every square inch of Bantling's life, literally. But, as of her last report at 8:30, so far they had found no "smoking gun"; no stash of stolen human hearts in a hidden room with an "I did this to them and they each deserved it!" note taped to a mirror adorned with photographs of the dead victims.

This was definitely troubling. Troubling because Bantling had invoked both his right to remain silent and his right to counsel last night and then had completely clammed up. C.J. was going to need more evidence than just Anna Prado's dead body to link him with the other nine dead girls.

Troubling because it was entirely possible that this William Bantling was nothing but a copycat killer and the real Cupid was home reading the paper this morning, laughing his head off at all of them over a cup of hot coffee and a croissant.

18

C.J. LEAFED THROUGH the police reports and the pink arrest form one final time and checked her watch. It was past 9:30. She jotted down a few last-minute notes, grabbed her West's Florida Criminal Procedure paperback, packed up her briefcase again, and headed over to the courthouse. She took the back stairs and the side entrance to avoid the media circus that she knew would be waiting for her, both outside her office building and across the street on the courthouse steps. Then she sneaked in through the underground courthouse garage, waving halfheartedly at the bored security guard as she entered the elevator.

The elevator doors opened onto the fourth floor, and C.J. could tell this whole affair was going to be even bigger than she had originally thought. As she suspected, a mob of cameramen and their chipper reporters waited anxiously in the hallway outside of Courtroom 4-1. Lighting was being set, microphones checked, and lipstick freshened up in hasty anticipation.

C.J. walked straight ahead, focused on the huge mahogany doors ahead of her, her head cast slightly down, the swag of her blunt dark blond bob covering her face. Oblivious to the rush of madness around her.

Frantic whispers erupted from the inexperienced reporters who had not yet done their homework: "Is that her?" "Is that the prosecutor?" "Is that Townsend?" Those more prepared confidently nudged their way past, before the others had a chance to even flip their microphones on.

"Ms. Townsend, what evidence has been found at William Bantling's home?"

"No comment."

"Was Mr. Bantling on the list of suspects that your office had looked at before?"

"No comment."

"Will you be filing charges in the other nine murders?"

"No comment."

"Will your office be seeking the death penalty?"

For that one, she shot the perky doe-eyed reporter a look. *Stupid question.* The doors closed with a heavy thud behind her.

She walked to the front of the walnut-paneled courtroom and took her seat to the right at the prosecution table. Judge Katz had, of course, picked the most majestic courtroom in the courthouse for his hearing. The ceilings soared twenty feet high, with His Honor's mahogany wooden throne towering at least a lofty five feet above the gallery, and three feet above the witness box. Metal domed chandeliers that screamed the year 1972 hung suspended in a diagonal pattern all over the room.

The courtroom was already packed with spectators, most of whom were reporters, and cameras were set up at every conceivable angle on tripods. All around the courtroom were uniformed Miami-Dade officers, and four green-and-white-clad corrections officers guarded the entrance. Another four guarded a back entrance to the small hallway where prisoners were to be escorted in from the bridge over from the jailhouse. Yet another four held positions by the entrance to the other hallway that led to the judge's chambers. In the front row of spectators, C.J. spotted several prosecutors from the office. She nodded in their direction.

She opened her briefcase and glanced over to her left. Ten feet across from her at the defense table sat prominent defense attorney Lourdes Rubio. Seated next to her, wearing a black tailored suit, gray silk tie, and silver handcuffs sat her client, William Rupert Bantling.

The suit looked like Armani and the tie Versace. Bantling wore his salty blond hair slicked back, and on his tan face sat expensive-looking Italian eyeglasses, behind which, C.J. noted, he sported a nice shiner. Probably compliments of the Miami Beach P.D. Although C.J. could only make out his profile from where she sat, she could tell that he was a handsome man. High cheekbones, good chin. *Great. A well-dressed, good-looking serial killer. The love notes from the lonely and demented should start to arrive at the Dade County Jail by tomorrow afternoon.*

C.J. noticed that his handcuffs rested on a Rolex watch and in his left ear he had a large diamond stud. That explained why he sat next to Lourdes Rubio. She was good, and she didn't come cheap. The handcuffs were affixed to a metal chain that connected to ankle shackles. Obviously, the boys over at the jail had really decked him out in the finest in restraint wear just for the cameras—she was surprised they hadn't fitted him with a mask similar to the one Hannibal Lecter wore in *The Silence of the Lambs*. Bantling turned his face then and leaned toward Lourdes, smiling. C.J. noticed perfect teeth. Without the black eye, he was definitely handsome. He certainly didn't look like a serial killer, but then again, neither did Ted Bundy. And pedophiles were almost always nice grandpas who served as presidents of their local Kiwanis Clubs, and the worst wife beaters sometimes were CEOs of Fortune 500 companies. Things were never what they seemed. That was probably how Bantling conned those girls out of those nightclubs. They were expecting a greasy, creepy, three-eyed monster with a knife and bad body odor who they could immediately tell was Cupid. A bad guy all the way. Not Suave Bola, dressed in Armani, full of charm, with perfect teeth, a Rolex, and a new Jag.

"All rise!" The bailiff opened the back courtroom door, and in walked a determined-looking Judge Katz. The first thing he did was scowl in the general direction of William Bantling.

He climbed up the stairs to the bench and sat down. Then he pulled out his glasses and put them on his head to where they just rested on the tip of his nose. The scowl continued.

"Court is now in session!" barked the bailiff. "The Honorable Irving J. Katz presiding! Be seated and be quiet!"

Judge Katz silently surveyed his kingdom with a look of contempt. For several minutes, nervous silence filled the air, and only the occasional rustle of papers or a muffled cough could be heard. This went on for a while. Finally, Judge Katz cleared his throat and said, "We are here on the matter of *The State of Florida* v. *William Rupert Bantling,* case number F2000-17429. Counselors, please identify yourselves for the record." Very formal. C.J. and Lourdes both stood.

"C. J. Townsend for the state."

"Lourdes Rubio for the defendant."

The judge continued. "The charge is murder in the first degree. You have been brought here, Mr. Bantling, for your First Appearance Hearing, as is required by Florida law, to determine if there is probable cause contained in the arrest form to support the charge against you. If probable cause is found, you will be remanded without bond to the Dade County Jail to stand trial. That all having been said, Madame Clerk, please pass me the arrest form in this cause so that I may read it."

He was crisp, he was clear, and he enunciated throughout the whole speech. Judge Katz would look great on the news. Normally, he would have handled at least ten defendants in the same amount of time on any other day. The courtroom buzzed in hushed whispers as the judge pretended to read through the arrest form. Cameras whirred and sketch artists sketched.

"Quiet all!" snapped the bailiff, and the room fell silent.

After almost five minutes of intense frowning, Judge Katz looked up from the three-page arrest form. In a voice dripping with disdain, he declared loudly, "I have read the arrest form. And I find that probable cause does indeed exist in this case to hold the defendant, William Rupert Bantling, for trial on the charge of first-degree murder in the death of Ms. Anna Prado. There will be no bond in this matter. The defendant is to be remanded to the custody of the Department of Corrections." He paused for effect and leaned forward toward Bantling's general direction. "Mr. Bantling, this court can only hope—"

Lourdes Rubio stood up. "Your Honor, if I might address the court. I hate to interrupt, but I am afraid the court is about to conclude this matter on its own before the defendant has had a chance to be heard.

"Judge, my client is a prominent member of the community. He has no prior criminal history. He has lived in Miami for six years and has laid long-term roots here, including a job and a home. He is willing to surrender his passport to the court until this matter is resolved, and to submit to an ankle bracelet with electronic monitoring and house arrest, so that he may assist counsel in the preparation of his defense. We therefore respectfully request that the court take these factors into consideration and that bond be set in this matter."

C.J. rose to respond, but quickly saw there was no need. Judge Katz's bald head turned red, and he glared at Lourdes Rubio. She had thrown off his otherwise-perfect performance. "Your client is a suspect in a string of violent, horrific murders. He was driving his car around Miami with the dead, mutilated body of a woman in his trunk. He's not a tourist who has enjoyed too much of the South Beach nightlife, Ms. Rubio. I am not worried about him *fleeing;* I am worried about him *killing.* He clearly is a danger to society. There will be no bond; he can assist you from his jail cell."

Judge Katz's eyes ran up and down Lourdes Rubio, as if he had just realized that she was a woman. In a low voice he added, "You might very well thank me for *that* one day, Counselor." Then he leaned forward and again set up his closer. "Now, Mr. Bantling, I can only hope for your sake that you are not guilty of the horrible crime with which you have been charged. Because if you are—"

Bantling suddenly stood, pulling away from the table, causing his chair to fall back with a loud thud against the wood railing. He yelled angrily at Judge Katz, "This is ridiculous! Your Honor, I have done nothing! Nothing! I never even saw that woman! This is bullshit!"

C.J. looked over at Bantling, and her head began to spin. He was turned toward Lourdes Rubio, pulling on her elbow with his handcuffed hands and yelling, "Do something! Do something! I am not guilty of this! I'm not going to jail!" Her mouth went dry. She watched, unable to move, as three corrections officers rushed to the table to sit Bantling back down. She saw the judge pound the bench with his gavel, and watched as the reporters stood up, cameras rolling, watching the scene play out on live television. But she heard nothing, just Bantling's voice yelling over and over, "Do something! You have to do something about this!"

C.J. looked down to where his hand grasped Lourdes's jacket and saw the jagged S scar on his left arm, just above his Rolex and his wrist. She knew that voice. She knew in one horrible instant in that courtroom who William Rupert Bantling really was. Her body began to tremble all over as she watched him being dragged from the defense table toward the bridge door, still screaming at Lourdes Rubio to do something. She stared at the image, long after it was gone, not hearing Judge Katz at all as he bellowed her name from the bench.

Strong hands were on her shoulders now from the front row of spectators. It was FDLE Agent Dominick Falconetti, and he was gently shaking her. She looked at him blankly and watched as he mouthed her name. She still could not hear, the courtroom sounded like a vacuum, and she felt as if she would pass out. Then sound began to fill her head again.

"C.J.? C.J.? Are you okay? The judge is calling you."

Rushing, pounding like waves on the shore. "Yeah, yeah, I'm fine. Fine," she mumbled. "Just a bit shocked."

"You don't look fine," Dominick said.

The judge was bright red now. His whole show was ruined. Ruined. "Ms. Townsend, are you ready to play lawyer again? Because this court has just about had it today!"

"Yes, yes, Judge. Sorry." She turned to face the bench.

"Thank you. I asked if there was anything else to add from the state, or can we adjourn today?"

"No, nothing further, Your Honor," she said absently,

looking at the empty chair next to Lourdes at the defense table. Lourdes was looking at her quizzically. As were the court clerk and the bailiff.

"Fine. Then this hearing is adjourned." Judge Katz cast one final glare at everyone and stormed off the bench, letting the door to the hallway slam shut behind him.

A clatter of press people ran to the gallery asking for comment, thrusting microphones in her face. C.J. gathered her briefcase and pushed past them all, not hearing their questions, needing to leave the courtroom, the building, needing to be anywhere but here. Needing to escape.

She rushed down the hall to the escalator, not wanting to wait for the elevator, and pushed past the chattering crowds of defendants, victims, and attorneys that packed the moving staircase. She took the steps two at a time. Behind her she heard Dominick Falconetti yelling for her to wait up, but she pushed down into the main lobby and then out the front glass courthouse doors into the hot Miami sun.

There would be no escape. The nightmare had begun all over again.

19

C.J. DARTED ACROSS the street back to her office in the Graham Building, a parade of reporters behind her, scrambling to keep up. She held her hand up as a continuous sign of no comment and left them all mewling at the security checkpoint in the lobby while she ran up the back stairs two at a time to the second floor. She rushed into the bathroom and quickly checked under the line of stalls to make sure that no one was there, no one was listening. Then she threw her briefcase on the floor and said good-bye to her breakfast.

Leaning her forehead up against the cool tiled wall, colored a nauseating Pepto-Bismol pink, she closed her eyes to stop the room from spinning before venturing out of the stall. She pushed her glasses up on her head and, with both hands, splashed cold water on her face and neck, practically submerging her head in the basin. Her head felt as if it weighed a thousand pounds, and it seemed to take all her strength just to lift it up off her shoulders. In the room-length long mirror that hung over the row of empty sinks against the queasy pink backdrop, she stared at her reflection in the glass.

A pale, terrified woman looked back. She had aged more than what was fair in twelve years. Her blond hair was now cut dramatically short and plain in a blunt shoulder-length bob, and parted to one side. She used a chestnut rinse to drab the honey color down to a mousy blond shade. Unless pulled into a clip or ponytail, the bangs would fall and drape across her face, and she was constantly fidgeting with her hair, tucking it back in place behind her ears. It was just one of the many nervous little habits that she had picked up over the years. Smoking like a fiend was another.

C.J. tucked her hair back behind her ears, and leaned forward on the basin, looking hard at the image before her. She could see the worry lines etched deep across her forehead and the ever-growing crow's-feet that seemed to spread like cracks in a dish out from her green eyes. Dark circles lightened with concealer served as proof of the nightmares she still had and the insomnia that would follow. Normally they were also hidden behind simple gold wire-rimmed eyeglasses. Her lips were full, but drawn in and serious, and she noticed the slight lines that were starting to appear at their edges and feather out. It was almost funny how they called them laugh lines. Her face was devoid of makeup, with just the slightest hint of mascara tracing her lashes. She wore no earrings, no necklace, no rings or bracelets: no jewelry whatsoever. Her gray pantsuit was stylish, but conservative, and she almost never wore a skirt unless she was in trial. Nothing about her person would attract attention. She was a plain Jane, a nobody. Everything about her now was nondescript, even her name.

She knew that voice. She had recognized it instantly. After twelve long years it still spoke to her each night in her nightmares, whispering patiently in her head in that same husky, throaty baritone, with a slight hint of a British accent.

She also knew that she had not imagined it, falsely placed it with William Bantling. The sound of it was like a serrated knife tearing through her brain, an internal alarm ringing so loud in her head that she had just wanted to scream out in the courtroom. Point at him and scream out, "That's him! He's the one! Somebody help me! Somebody get him!" But she had not even moved. Could not move. It was as if she were paralyzed, watching the scene in the courtroom play out on someone else's television screen. At home on the comfy couch you yell at the actors to *do something, don't just stand there!* But they can't hear you and the scene finishes with yet another unsuspecting, doe-eyed victim getting whacked by a fiend with a butcher knife in a hockey mask.

At the sound of that voice, every hair on her body had stood up, goose bumps had rippled in a wave across her skin, and just like that, she was instantly sure it was him. It had been twelve years, but one part of her had always suspected she would hear his voice again, and she was always waiting. The jagged, raised S scar on his left arm had only confirmed it.

He did not seem to recognize her, though. In fact, after all that he had done to her, all that he had taken from her, it was almost funny how now he had barely afforded a glance in her direction, or even acknowledged her presence in the courtroom. Of course, she looked nothing like she did once—once upon a lifetime ago. A dimly lit shadow of her former self. The reflection in the mirror blinked back hot tears. She didn't recognize herself sometimes.

It had been years since that horrible night, but in this instance, time had not healed all wounds, and it certainly had not blurred all memory. She could still recall every minute, every second, every detail, every word. Although she had managed, on the surface at least, to move on with her life, there were things that she could not move past, no matter how hard she tried, and some days were still just an emotional struggle to get through. That night her old life had seemed to end, stripped in an instant of all that was safe, all that was secure. And although most of the physical scars had faded, it was the constant fear that C.J. hated living with. She couldn't force herself just to move on with life, put it in the past and leave it there. It was, instead, almost as if she were stuck in neutral, afraid to go back, but afraid to go forward. She knew it hurt her in relationships, but here she still was, carrying the same baggage she should have checked with her overpriced therapist in New York years ago.

After a nervous breakdown and two years of intense therapy, she'd been forced to realize a fact that she had dreaded knowing all along: Power is all an illusion. In that one night, she had lost all control in her life, of her life, and then had spent years discovering that she had never really had any to begin with. Life was a just a twist of fate, really, which explained why some people got hit by a bus on the way home from a funeral and others won Lotto twice. The key to missing the bus was to avoid walking in a dark street.

She remembered how Michael had referred to that night as *the incident*. Michael, the lousy boyfriend who wound up getting engaged to his skinny redheaded secretary. When the breakdown came, he had agreed to give her the time and space she needed to heal. He promised to wait forever, if that was what it took, for her to "get through this." Well, apparently forever was a long time to wait, and one week after they parted, he was out on the town with the redhead at New York's Tavern on the Green. Within six months they were married. C.J. had not heard from him since. She read about their divorce a few years later in a blurb in the *Wall Street Journal* when the skinny redhead-turned-bodacious-blonde had sued him for all he was worth, which by then was a lot.

But the worst part of the last twelve years was the not knowing. Not knowing who her attacker was, where he was. That fear was always with her, and it never eased up. Was he there in the subway with her? In the diner? At the bank? Was that him on the treadmill or in line at the grocery store? Was he her doctor, her accountant, her friend?

Don't you worry, Chloe. I'll always be close by. Watching. Waiting.

She couldn't escape those thoughts in New York, and after two years, she had decided not to try anymore. So she changed her name, took the Florida Bar, and moved to Miami. The anonymity helped her sleep better at night, when she slept at all. Maybe, she thought, a career as a prosecutor would give her some control in a world out of control, full of senselessness and chaos, full of crazies. A little vindication for the powerless, the ones just tuning in to the illusion.

Images of that night now flooded her brain, flashing slowly, in sequence, like an electric strobe light. This time, though, she knew what the face behind the mask looked like. And with that face she now had a name. Now she just had to remain calm, figure out what to do. Should she tell Jerry Tigler, the State Attorney? Should she call the old detectives, Sears and Harrison, assuming they were still there, in New York? Should she tell the task force? No one in Miami, with the exception of her therapist, knew about her past, about *the incident.*

Break it down as you would any other case.

She exhaled slowly at the mirror. First thing was to get a complete criminal history on this Bantling, and call New York to find out their extradition policy. Pull the New York file on her case to review. Bantling would be held in maximum security without bond until an Arthur Hearing was set, which would take at least two weeks. For that hearing, the judge would then have to take testimony to determine if "proof was evident and presumption great" that Bantling had committed the crime of murder. If the answer was yes, then the judge would deny bond until trial, whenever that was finally set. So Bantling wasn't going anywhere before that, no matter what.

She needed to be thorough and logical. Needed to take her time. She didn't want this to get screwed up yet again. If she was ever accused of not being straightforward with the court, the investigation, she could simply say she wasn't sure at first that it was him . . .

The bathroom door suddenly swung open, and C.J. quickly put her glasses back on. Unfortunately, it was Marisol and she was accompanied by another secretary. She carried a pink glitter cosmetic bag in one hand and a can of hair spray in the other.

"Hello, Marisol." C.J. straightened her jacket and picked up her briefcase. "I'm back from court, obviously, but I still have a ton of stuff I need to get done. Please make sure to hold any calls I get for today. Especially from the media." She noticed that her voice was a little shaky. She tucked her hair back behind her ear and opened the door. Then she turned and added, "Oh, and please call the defense attorney and try and reset those depositions on the Jamie Tucker case. I'm going to need at least two more weeks to prepare now that I've got the Bantling case. I think the depos are set for next Wednesday."

Marisol's face fell in exaggerated exasperation.

"Is there a problem?"

"No, fine. Whatever." She sauntered to the end of the line of sinks, the back of her hand up in the air and shot her friend a look that read, *"Who the hell does she think she is?"*

C.J. walked out of the bathroom and down the hall to the refuge of her office. It was barely 11:00 and she was already drained. She would first call Juan in the State Attorney's Investigations Unit and get a complete criminal on Bantling, including a New York history. Maybe she could get an AutoTrack of Bantling's life as it existed on public records from Dominick Falconetti by this afternoon. That would give her a workup of wherever Bantling had lived, worked, or registered a car for the past ten years. Dominick probably had one run already, and she could just drop by the task force office at FDLE and pick it up. Then she'd head home early, get her thoughts in order, and make the requisite phone calls to New York from home. All she needed was her purse and the rest of the Cupid files that she had left stacked in her office.

The distinct smell of McDonald's and cigarette smoke hung heavy in the hallway outside her office. Her door was closed, and when she opened it, she knew immediately that her quick exit plan was about to be thwarted.

Dominick Falconetti and Manny Alvarez sat facing her empty desk with their backs to her, a new box of files at their feet.

20

MANNY WAS LEANING over the edge of her desk simultaneously eating a breakfast burrito, drinking a *café con leche,* and reading the *Herald,* which was spread all over her desktop. Dominick was on his cell phone. They both turned to face her when the door opened.

Manny looked up from his breakfast and smiled. "Hey, Counselor! How you doing? You had us worried there for a minute."

Dominick looked at C.J. and said into the phone, "I've got to go. The prosecutor just came back from court." He hung up the phone and stared at her. He actually looked worried. "We thought that maybe you had run off on us or something," he said.

Manny extended a small disposable cup of hot Cuban coffee. Just the rich smell of pure caffeine in liquid form made hair grow on her chest. "Want a *café con leche?* I brought an extra one for you. I also got you a *pastelito* with guava jam." He placed a Cuban Danish oozing with pink goo on her desk in front of her chair. "Oh yeah," he said between bites of his burrito, "I also have some of the autopsy photos back on Prado, but you may want to wait on that *pastelito* before you look at 'em."

C.J. dropped her briefcase with a deliberate thud on top of the file cabinet. "How'd you guys get in?"

"Your secretary, Marisol, let us in a while back," Manny

said as he wiped egg yolk and bacon drippings off his mustache. "Hey, Counselor, she's a spicy little number. Maybe you could introduce us?"

C.J.'s opinion of Manny Alvarez, whom she once held in high regard as a homicide detective, immediately plummeted. If he were the Dow Jones, they would have closed the markets for the day. She stared blankly at him and ignored the question.

"So what happened to you back there in the courtroom?" Dominick prodded. He was trying hard to hide his concern. "He freaked you out, didn't he?"

"He's one fucked-up son of a bitch, let me tell you," Manny interrupted. "He actually thought he was going to get a bond—that the judge wouldn't send his sorry ass straight to jail for driving around town with a dead girl in his trunk. Do not pass go, *amigo;* do not collect two hundred dollars. I can still hear him yelling like a girl over at the jail right now." Manny changed his voice to a high-pitched whine. " 'No! Not jail! Not me—I can't go to jail! This must be a mistake! I didn't mean to cut her heart out, Judge. The knife just slipped right out of my slimy little hand into her chest!' " He finished his burrito and then his thoughts. "Just wait till he meets his new best friend, Bubba, over there at DCJ. Now *that* will give him something to whine about."

Dominick was still eyeing her, and she could see that Manny's tangent had not diverted him.

"He is definitely a wacko. I didn't expect him to flip out, though." Dominick was right next to her now, trying hard to get her to look at him. "Then again, you've seen a lot of wackos in your life, C.J., and I didn't expect you to flip out either."

C.J. avoided looking directly at Dominick and instead focused her eyes on the mess on her desk. She hoped her voice sounded stable enough. "He threw me off there for a moment. I just didn't expect him to start screaming like that." She changed the subject and walked past him around her desk. "What happened at the ME's this morning?"

She looked down at the newspaper that lay atop her desk calendar. On the front page, the *Miami Herald* had small color head shots of all ten victims taken before their deaths, lined up dramatically in a row. Beneath them was a large five-by-seven fuzzy picture of Bantling's black Jaguar surrounded by cop cars on the MacArthur Causeway. A smiling photo of a clean-cut and handsome Bill Bantling, shirtless and tan, with a beer in his hand, sat on the opposite side of the Jaguar picture. Obviously not the booking photo. The whole collage of color photos was printed directly under a black headline that blared,

CUPID SUSPECT ARRESTED! TENTH VICTIM'S MUTILATED BODY FOUND IN TRUNK!

Manny had eaten breakfast all over it.

"Neilson says Prado's been dead fourteen, maybe fifteen hours, tops. More likely closer to ten. Says he thinks the body was in the trunk only a few hours before we found it. Cause of death: a severed aorta. Given the amount of air in the lungs, Doc says the heart was cut out while she was alive, Counselor."

Joe Neilson was the Miami-Dade County Medical Examiner. He was well respected at the State Attorney's Office. C.J. exhaled slowly, looking down at the row of beautiful, dead women. "Is it the same guy, or are we looking at a copycat?"

Dominick sat down now in front of her desk. He pulled off the top on the file box on the floor and pulled out ten Polaroids from a brown accordion file. "Identical cuts. A vertical slice down the sternum first, with a sharp instrument, most likely a scalpel. Then the horizontal slice underneath the breastbone. Same cuts on the aorta. Not a hack job."

"Can he match the cuts as coming from the same knife?" Anna Prado's ashen face stared up at her from the Polaroid. Platinum blond hair combed back flat behind her head on the metal gurney. Close-up shots of the chest cavity showed the two deep incisions, the cracked chest, and then the gaping hole where her heart should have been. The cuts were smooth, like the others. For a moment, C.J.

thought of her own jagged scars, but quickly pushed the image out of her head.

"Probably," said Manny. "He's not done yet with the autopsy, but he found something else that's interesting, Counselor. Looks like Prado maybe had a drug in her blood. Same as Nicolette Torrence, the DB we found real quick back in October of last year in that crack-house attic over on Seventy-ninth Street. She had only been laid out a few days."

DB stood for dead body.

"Neilson said her lungs were heavy, indicating a narcotic of some kind. We won't know for sure until toxicology takes a look, though," Dominick continued.

"How about evidence of sexual assault?" C.J. asked.

"Yeah, she was raped with a blunt instrument, both anally and vaginally," Dominick said slowly. She could tell that it was these details that bothered him the most. "Suffered severe trauma to the cervix and uterus. Neilson thinks he used more than one instrument, too, given the different types of distinct scratches and abrasions left on the uterine wall. There was no evidence of any semen. He's taking swabs of everything, though. And he's photographing every inch of her, in case we miss something now and need to go back."

"How about under her fingernails?" Many a victim had been known to scratch their assailant while fighting off an attack, and in so doing, the attacker unintentionally often left a tiny piece of himself behind—microscopic slivers of skin under a victim's fingernails. In those instances, along with the skin, they left behind their DNA calling card, a genetic map that led investigators right to their door, once they had a subject to compare the sample to.

"Nothing. There's nothing on this one either, as far as he can tell." In this case, they had the reverse: a subject, but no sample.

"I'll work on a search warrant to get Bantling's hair and saliva samples. You never know. Maybe he messed up this time. Maybe we missed something on the others." She shrugged and pulled her hair back behind her ears again. "The drug information is good. That might give us the link we need to at least one other victim. I'll call Neilson this afternoon and see what else he has for me on the autopsy.

"Dominick, have you run a complete criminal on him yet? Does he have anything on NCIC?" NCIC was the National Crime Information Center. It provided a federal criminal history that would also tell her if Bantling had a criminal history in any other state. She heard her voice rise just slightly when she asked the last question.

"Nope. As far as we can tell, he's totally clean."

"I want to know everything there is to know about this guy. I'm going to need an AutoTrack on him, by this afternoon, if possible. I also want to take a look at his passport, find out where he's been."

"I'll get Jannie to run what she can on him. I think Manny already has her checking with Interpol to see if he's got anything outside this country, seeing as he's supposedly some big hotshot buyer at Tommy Tan's. We already ran an AutoTrack. The man has lived a lot of places. I'll get you a copy of that today."

C.J. suddenly stood up, abruptly ending the conversation. "I have some things I need to tie up today, so I am going to take off in a little bit. I'll call you later, Dominick, to see what else turns up at that house."

She looked over at Manny, who was already pulling out a Marlboro from the pack. One for the road, so he would be ready to light up the instant he got outside. "And stop smoking in my office, Manny. They keep blaming *me*."

The Bear looked surprised, like a child who has been caught with his hand in the cookie jar and yet still wants to deny he did it. "We didn't know when you'd be coming back, Counselor," he stammered. Then, a thought, and a quick recovery. "Plus, you know, that cute secretary of yours made my heart pound and I got so nervous I had to calm myself . . ." He grinned a big grin.

She had heard enough. "Let's not go there. Anywhere but there, please."

She walked them both to the door and opened it. Marisol stood at the end of the hallway in the secretarial pool. She smiled when she saw Manny. Then she licked her glossy lips coquettishly as if she were in a Revlon commercial. It was all C.J. could do not to slam the door. Manny took off down the hall.

Dominick stayed inside the office and closed the door. He leaned his back against the door and looked at C.J., his chestnut brown eyes heavy and serious. He had taken a shower before court and smelled clean, like Lever soap. His hair was tousled on his head, as if he hadn't had time to brush it before he ran out.

"What is going on with you? Is everything okay?"

"I'm fine, Dom, fine." Her head was tilted down. She wouldn't look at him. She sounded tired, anxious.

"You didn't look fine today in that courtroom, and that's not like you, C.J." He reached out and gently touched the back of her hand where it still rested on the doorknob. His hand was rough, calloused; but his touch was soft and sincere. "You don't look fine now."

She looked up into his serious eyes then. It took all her strength to lie to him. A few critical seconds passed, and then she said softly, "I'm fine, really. Everything is just fine. I'm just tired, you know. I didn't get much sleep last night, what with the warrants and the judge and preparing for the hearing." She exhaled a slow breath. "He just threw me for a moment in the courtroom. I wasn't expecting that reaction." She wanted to cry, but bit the inside of her cheek instead and held back the tears.

His eyes searched hers for signs of the truth, and his rough hand now reached to touch her face. Her body tensed. She knew he had felt it, and his hand quickly dropped back to his side. "I think there's more than what you're telling me" was all he said. Then he turned and opened the door. "I'll get you that AutoTrack when I'm done at Bantling's house," he said, his back to her as he walked down the hallway.

She knew he was worried. Hell, so was she.

21

THE TWO-STORY WHITE house with the neat hunter green awnings and the glass-block front window sat just slightly back from the road. Redbrick pavers led to the chestnut-stained oak double front doors. A six-foot concrete white wall with ornate wrought-iron gates hid the heavily foliaged backyard from view. A cypress tree towered tall, and Traveler's Palms, almost twenty feet high, fanned out dramatically over the wall. It was a pretty house located in a quiet, residential "midbeach" section, which meant it sat between reserved North Miami Beach and trendy SoBe. Until the media hordes descended upon it at 8:00 that morning, the upper-middle-class residents of LaGorce Avenue probably never thought twice about their handsome, well-dressed neighbor. Now he'd been named as the prime suspect in the most intense manhunt Miami had seen since Andrew Cunnanen gunned down fashion designer Gianni Versace on Ocean Drive in SoBe.

Uniformed police crawled over the house like ants. Two white Miami-Dade Crime Scene vans sat in the driveway. Dominick walked up the neat brick path, past flowering planters of bright fuchsia-colored bougainvillea, Manny in tow. A young Miami Beach cop, who looked all of twenty-two, stood guard nervously at the front door, obviously aware that his every move was being recorded and then analyzed on live TV by the two dozen or more media crews who stood watch intently across the street behind yellow crime-scene tape. CNN carried a live feed, as did MSNBC and Fox News. Dominick flashed his badge at the Beach cop, just imagining the feeder band of instant news that, at this very moment, probably ran across the bottom of a million television screens: *Task Force Cops Approach Death House in Grim Search for Body Parts and Evidence.*

Inside, Crime Scene technicians were everywhere—their latex-gloved fingers carefully probing every square inch of living space, collecting and preserving forensic samples of the most ordinary of things, from shampoo to carpet swatches, in a case that was far from ordinary. Everything and anything was now considered evidence, and a piece of every inch of the house, in whatever form, would be packaged up, sealed, and sent off to the crime lab for examination.

Flashbulbs clicked as expert Crime Scene photographers took pictures of each room in the house from every conceivable angle. Fine black powder covered every surface where a fingerprint could possibly be found, and even some where they could not. In the living room, large swatches had already been cut from the expensive-looking Berber carpet, and a two-by-two piece of wallboard had been sliced from its place in the mustard-colored faux-painted wall. The Oriental rug from the front foyer and the Turkish hall runner had been rolled up and bagged as evidence this morning when agents first entered. The contents of every wastepaper basket in the house, the used vacuum cleaner paper bags, the broom and mop heads, the feather duster, the lint tray from the dryer—all had been carefully bagged in white plastic evidence bags and set out in the front foyer to be taken to the Crime Scene van.

In the kitchen, technicians worked to remove the drain trap from the sink, as they would in every drain in the house, and Miami Beach detectives placed dark frozen meat from the Sub-Zero freezer into clear plastic evidence bags. The entire set of razor-sharp Sabatier kitchen and steak knives had been individually bagged and sealed. At the lab, the drain traps would be forensically examined to determine if they contained blood or tissue matter that someone might have tried to wash off. The meat would be defrosted and tested to make sure that it was, in fact, not human. The knives would be tested to detect matches in the cutting patterns of the blades to the wounds made in the flesh of Anna Prado's chest.

Upstairs, every bed had already been stripped and bagged, and in the hall, all linens and towels had been removed from the closets and stacked neatly into larger black plastic evidence bags that lined the hallway. The strong nauseating smell of luminol escaped from behind the closed doors of the guest bedroom, where forensic technicians had just sprayed the powerful chemical all over the rich knock-down walls and hardwood floors, in search of microscopic traces of blood. Once sprayed, otherwise-invisible blood in the dark would now glow a bright yellow—bloodstains that even soap and water could not wash away, but vividly told their story when the lights went out.

In another guest bedroom, technicians carefully vacuumed the carpet with a specially sanitized steel cylindrical container, collecting each tiny fiber, each piece of lint, each strand of hair. The drapes had been removed from the windows and bagged as evidence.

Dominick found MDPD Detective Eddie Bowman and Special Agent Chris Masterson sitting on the floor in Bantling's master bedroom, going through stacks and stacks of videotapes that sat piled in a large decorative wicker trunk. Both detectives had been on the task force since its inception. In the massive oak armoire behind them, a big-screen television played loudly.

"Hey, Eddie. How's it going with the search? You guys find anything yet?"

Eddie Bowman looked up from his stack of tapes. "Hey, Dom. Fulton has been trying to reach you. He's downstairs in the shed."

"Yeah, I just talked to him. I'll head down there in a minute."

On the TV screen, a well-endowed redhead dressed in a plaid Catholic school uniform and garters was bent over the lap of a naked man whose head had been chopped off by the video recorder. Dominick noticed that the uniform

was missing an awful lot of fabric in all the wrong places.
Especially for Catholic school. The redhead's bare ass was
pushed up high in the air and the headless man was swat-
ting it with a metal paddle as she screamed. It was hard to
discern if it was in pain or in pleasure or in both that she
cried out.

"How'd it go in court?" Eddie asked, apparently
unmoved by the screams.

"Good. The judge found pc and denied bond," said
Dominick, distracted, staring at the crying redhead on the
screen. He looked down into the wicker trunk. There were
what looked like at least a hundred black tapes. He could
see the white label on one that read BLOND LOLITA 4/99.

Manny followed Dominick into the room just then, still
breathing hard from the flight of stairs and the short walk
down the hall. "Ah—you never tell the whole story, Dom.
What fun are you, anyway?" He turned in Eddie Bowman's
direction, leaning on the side of the armoire while he tried
to catch his breath. "Bantling totally freaked out. Started
crying like a woman to the judge that he can't go to jail. Oh
no, not him." He chuckled. "Boo-fuckin'-hoo."

A few seconds passed before Manny noticed the disturbing image on the screen that everyone else was staring
at. "What the fuck are you watching, Bowman?" He
sounded disgusted.

"Is that why you're breathing heavy, Bear?" Bowman
returned.

"Fuck you. I need a cigarette, that's all, but Dommy
Boy here won't let me smoke on his crime scene." He
turned his attention back to the TV screen and crinkled his
nose at Eddie Bowman. "Now, what is this sick shit I'm
looking at? That's not your wife, is it, Bowman?"

Eddie ignored the remark and gestured toward the television. "This is what our Mr. Bantling liked to watch on his
boob tube. Not exactly PBS. He's got stacks and stacks of
what looks like homemade video. I'm no prude, but some
of what Chris and I have seen today is just wild. Looks like
it's consensual, but it's hard to say."

A king-sized dark oak bed with a tremendous
chocolate-colored leather headboard took up most of

Bantling's masculine-looking bedroom. The bed had already been stripped down. Besides the bed, the trunk and armoire were the only pieces of furniture in the room.

A high-pitched scream came out of the TV. The redhead seemed to be crying uncontrollably now, telling the man something in Spanish.

"Hey Manny, what's she saying to him?" asked Dominick.

" 'Stop, please. I'll be good, please stop. It hurts so much.' This is some sick shit, Bowman."

"I didn't make it, Bear. I just found it."

The headless man paid no heed. The paddle made a loud thwack as it hit her skin which was, by now, red and raw-looking.

Dominick watched the disturbing image play out on the screen. "How many have you looked at, Eddie?"

"Only three so far. There's gotta be over a hundred videos here, though."

"Any of them have the girls from The Wall?"

"Nope, no such luck. Not yet anyways. Some have labels with dates, others just a girl's name, others, there's no label at all. He's got a collection of regular movies, too, that Chris found in the bottom cabinet of the armoire. Probably fifty or more of those."

"Take them. He might have taped over *Kiss the Girls* with his own version for all we know. We'll have to watch them all. Maybe we can track down some of the stars on that homemade crap." The sound of thwacks continued, as did the crying. Dominick's stare was again drawn back to the TV. "Is that Bantling with the paddle?"

"Don't know. He doesn't say much, and I haven't recognized any of the rooms from this house in the shots. I would think so, but, then again, I haven't seen Bantling naked."

"What happened in the other three tapes?" asked Dominick.

"Same sort of shit. Very sadistic, but it may be consensual. It's hard to tell. Likes 'em young, but I think the girls are of age. Another tough call. Might be the same man in each video, but his face is always cut off, so it's hard to tell.

We're hoping, of course, to hit pay dirt and come up with him screwing one of the dead girls."

"You're twisted, Bowman." Manny had moved to the walk-in closet now. "Hey, you guys didn't search the closet yet?"

"No. Crime Scene already photographed, videoed, vacuumed, and dusted. Chris was gonna bag the closet and the shoes after we inventoried the tapes. They're gonna luminol in here and the master bathroom tonight."

"Mister Psycho has some nice taste in clothes, I'll tell ya," Manny called out from the closet. "Look at this: Armani, Hugo Boss suits, Versace shirts. Why the fuck did I ever become a cop? I could have been a fruity furniture designer and made a mint."

"A *salesman* for a fruity furniture designer," corrected Eddie Bowman. "He was just a salesman. You should see the fruity furniture designer's closet."

"Great. Now I feel a whole lot fuckin' better about my life, Bowman. I should have been a salesman. Do they really make that much money, or was psycho getting some help on the side?"

Dominick entered the master bath, which was right off the master bedroom. Italian marble was everywhere—the floors, the dual vanities, the shower. Fine black dust covered every surface, making the coffee cream marble look very dirty. He called back into the bedroom, "According to his boss, Tommy Tan, his commissions last year alone put him at a hundred seventy-five thou. No kids, no wife—that's all play money."

"No kids, no *ex-wives,* you mean. It's those exes that suck the dollars from your paycheck." Spoken from experience: Manny had three ex-wives. "Jesus! He's gotta have ten suits in here that each cost what I make in a month! And it's all so neat." He stuck his head out of the closet again. "Bowman, check this out—he's got his shirts all lined up in a row according to color, and a color-coordinated tie matched to each shirt. Fuckin' weirdo neat-freak."

"Yeah, go figure, Manny. A guy with a matching tie that doesn't have a cartoon character or a football player on it.

Now that's suspicious, alright." Bowman kept his spot by the TV.

"Hey, what can I say? I'm a loyalist. Besides, Bowman, you're the one who wanted to borrow my Bugs Bunny tie, and everyone in this room heard you ask."

"That was for Halloween, you moron. It was a joke. I was going dressed as Oscar from *The Odd Couple*."

Dominick pulled out the latex gloves from his pants pocket and opened the wood vanity doors under one of the sinks. Neat rows of shampoo and conditioner, racks of Dial soap, toilet-paper rolls, a hair dryer. In the next, a basket of combs and hairbrushes, more rolls of toilet paper, a box of condoms. "Hey, Eddie, Chris," he called out. "What has Crime Scene done in the master bath so far? They haven't bagged anything yet, have they?"

Chris Masterson called back, "Just prints. After the tapes I was going to do the closet and the bath. Fulton said he was coming up after the shed to help out, but I haven't heard from him in a while."

Manny stuck his head out of the closet again. "You two lazy shits. We've been working long and hard all day to put this fucking nut job behind bars, and you're sitting around watching pornos. Let me ask ya: Did you *both* need to inventory the tapes, or could that have been handled by Larry, while Moe did something else besides wait for Curly?"

"Give me a break, Bear," Bowman yelled back. "We took a commercial break from the porno and watched the hearing live on TV, so we know it was all of twenty minutes. You were probably at the Pickle Barrel for the last hour and a half having a *café con leche* and getting the phone number of Señora Alvarez number four."

"Alright, kids, let's not fight now," Dominick yelled from the bathroom. He opened the medicine chest. Bottles of Advil, Tylenol, and Motrin stood in neat rows alongside a jar of Vicks VapoRub, a tube of K-Y jelly, and a bottle of Mylanta. Tweezers, toothpaste, mouthwash, dental floss, shaving cream, and razor blades lined the next two shelves. All the labels were turned facing out, perfectly straight and aligned, like a pharmacy display shelf. Two slim brown prescription containers faced out. Nothing too interesting, though. One was written in February of 1999 for the antibiotic Amoxicillin by a doctor in Coral Gables. The other was from the same doctor in June of 2000 for the nasal decongestant Claritin.

Dominick pulled out the vanity drawer. A small brown basket filled with cotton balls sat next to lined-up tubes of facial cleanser and moisturizer. Neatly folded washcloths placed in stacks of cream and black lined the back of the drawer. He reached his hand in back behind the washcloths and pulled them out. There, underneath the two neat stacks was yet another clear brown prescription bottle. This one was more than half filled.

"Pay dirt," Dominick whispered aloud, cradling the brown bottle containing William Rupert Bantling's prescription of Haldol in his gloved palm.

22

SHE SLIPPED QUIETLY out of the elevator and across the dull
pink-and-gray lobby of the Graham Building, the home of
240 prosecutors and now crowded with people at the start
of lunch hour. Other Assistant State Attorneys milled
about, chatting and waiting for friends and associates to
return from court so they could go to lunch. It was all C.J.
could do to nod in their direction as she passed them on the
way to the parking lot.

She hoped that she looked normal, that some of the
color that had washed away from her face that morning in
court had returned. She also hoped that if she did look out-
wardly different—anxious, nervous, or God-knows-what-
else—that people would blame it on lack of sleep and the
stress of the Cupid case, and not speculate, as lawyers
loved to do. Gossip and rumor ran rampant down every hall
in the five-story building, and news of divorces and preg-
nancies often made the office rounds before the intended
divorcée was served with papers or the lines on the EPT
test turned purple. She hoped that it was only Dominick's
probing eyes that had seen her fear that morning; that it
was not otherwise apparent to all around her that something had just gone suddenly, terribly wrong in her life.
She flipped on her sunglasses as she rushed out, heading
into the bright sunshine. No one seemed to notice a thing.

Several prosecutors waved to her as she left, then, just as quickly, resumed their conversations.

She climbed in the Jeep Cherokee, threw the file boxes and her purse on the passenger seat, and desperately searched her glove compartment for the emergency pack of stale Marlboros that she kept hidden behind useless stacks of road maps and packs of Kleenex tissues. A cigarette had never before been as welcome. Or as necessary. Today, of all days, was not the day to have run out. She had then been foolish enough to think, when she stubbed out her last one at 5:00 A.M., that maybe she should just try quitting again.

The flame on the match head danced and jumped in her fingers, which had yet to stop shaking. Finally, the fragrant snippets of brown tobacco kissed the match and the tip burned a smoldering orange, and the familiar and comforting smell filled the car. C.J. leaned back in the driver's seat, still in the Graham Building parking lot, closed her eyes, and inhaled the smoke deep into her chest, exhaling slowly. The nicotine found her lungs and raced quickly through her bloodstream, finally reaching her brain and her central nervous system, and, like magic, immediately relaxing all those frayed, tense nerves it had met along the way. It was a sensation that nonsmokers would never—could never—understand, but, she imagined, other addicts could. The alcoholic who tasted his first scotch of the day, the junkie who finally got his fix. And even though her hands still shook, for the first time that morning, a sense of calm came over her. She blew a smoke ring through the steering wheel and realized, once again, that she would never be able to quit smoking. Never. She pulled out of the parking lot and turned the Jeep onto the 836 West ramp toward I-95 and Fort Lauderdale.

Dominick. She saw his face at her door, the crease lines from the worried frown he wore etched deep across his brow. She remembered his hand, hesitant on hers, then the surprised look of hurt that had briefly flickered in his eyes when she tensed at his touch, and his intuitive final words to her. *I think there's more than what you're telling me.*

She had turned him away. Unintentionally, but it was still a fact. And she didn't know how to feel about that. Since the moment she had first recognized Bantling in court, an emotional shock wave had washed over her and left all of her feelings numb. Welcoming Dominick's touch in her office seemed wrong at that moment, out of place. Time had stopped again. It was almost like it had been twelve years ago: a dull and exciting and wonderfully normal life with a dull and exciting and wonderfully normal future ahead and then bam!—an instantaneous repositioning of life's priorities. Bantling had robbed her yet again. In one tiny slice of time in that bedroom, in that courtroom, her world was no longer the same.

Twelve hours earlier she would not have moved away from Dominick's touch. Perhaps she would have even moved closer, or met his touch with her own. For the past few months, when they worked together on task force matters, there had existed between them this unspoken flirt, this potential for something more. A sweet, delicious tension that seemed to grow, and no one knew when or where or how or even if it would manifest itself. She noticed that he had called her a few times more than was necessary on legal matters and she had, in turn, called him a few more times than was necessary on police matters. Some pro forma question would be asked, and then the conversation would turn light and airy and a little more personal each time. She had felt the attraction, the strong chemistry that existed between them, and had wondered "what if" more than a few times. And if she had been unsure before of his feelings for her, she certainly knew now. The look of alarm on his face in the courtroom, and then concern in his voice when she had returned from court, the probing questions, and the touch at the door.

But she had pulled away and he had left and that was it. In his eyes she had first seen the hurt, and then the mix of surprise and confusion on his face at having misread the situation, having misunderstood their relationship and where it might have been headed. So the moment had passed. Maybe forever. She supposed she shouldn't even be thinking about Dominick now, but here she was anyway.

She lit another cigarette and tried hard to force those thoughts right out of her head. Now was not the time for the angst of a relationship. Particularly one with someone as complicated as Dominick Falconetti. And especially with anyone who was even remotely involved in the arrest and prosecution of William Rupert Bantling.

At the palm-tree-lined entrance to her condo complex she gave a half wave in the direction of the security guard who sat reading a book in his air-conditioned cubby. He half-waved back, barely looking up from his book, and opened the gate. For the most part, security guards in gated communities in Florida were like cheap car alarms on a Camry in a crowded Home Depot parking lot: useless. She could have been dressed in a ski mask with a sack of burglar's tools on the hood, and a shotgun in the backseat next to a map marked "Victim's Home: The Loot Is Here" and he still would have waved her in.

She pulled into her reserved spot at the Port Royale Towers and took the elevator up to her apartment on the twelfth floor. Tibby II met her at the door with a series of hungry and indignant meows, his big white furry belly sagging beneath him on the tile, tinged brown from the dust balls it collected sweeping up the floor.

"Okay, Tibs. Give me a minute. Let me get in the door and I'll get you a little snack." "Snack" was a comfort word to Tibby, and his woeful meows were momentarily silenced. He watched with the bored curiosity that only a cat can master as she locked the door behind her and reset the alarm, then he followed her into the kitchen, rubbing little white and black cat hairs on her freshly dry-cleaned pantsuit legs. She dropped the files and her briefcase onto her kitchen table and poured out a cup of Purina Cat Chow into Tibby's red bowl. The smell immediately awoke Lucy, her ten-year-old deaf basset hound who meandered from her pillow bed in the bedroom and scuffled across the tile floor into the kitchen, all the while sniffing in the air. A short, happy howl later, Lucy crunched on her own bowl of half-mushy kibble next to Tibby, and all was right with the world. At least for them. The next big decision facing each would be where to continue their afternoon naps, the bedroom or the living room?

She put on a fresh pot of coffee to go with the new pack of Marlboros she had picked up on the way home. Then she headed into the guest bedroom.

In the top of the closet, forced in the back behind the rolls of wrapping paper, gift bags, bows, and boxes was the plain cardboard box with the lift-off lid. She threw the wrapping paper and boxes on the daybed and pulled out the half-empty box. The contents inside shifted. She sat on the floor next to it and, with a deep breath, pulled off the lid.

It had been ten years since she had even looked inside. A musty smell greeted the air. She grabbed the three manila file folders and the fat yellow envelope and headed back to the kitchen. She poured herself a fresh cup of coffee, gathered the folders and envelope and her Marlboros, and went outside on her small screened-in balcony that overlooked the blue sparkling waters of the Intracoastal Waterway below.

She stared at the manila folder with the words POLICE REPORTS scribbled across it in her handwriting. Stapled to the outside corner was the business card of Detective Amy Harrison of the NYPD. She nibbled on the tip of her pencil and thought for a moment about what she would say, how she would say it. God, she wished she had a script. She lit a fresh Marlboro and dialed the number.

"Detective Bureau, Queens County." There was intense background noise. Rushed, hurried voices in different pitches, telephones ringing, sirens wailing in the far distance.

"Detective Amy Harrison, please."

"Who?"

"Detective Amy Harrison, Sex Crimes." It was hard to get those words out—*Sex Crimes*—strangely enough, even though she must have called the Sexual Battery Unit of every South Florida police department at least a few hundred times over the course of her career.

"Hold on."

Thirty seconds later a gruff voice with a thick New York accent. "Special Victims, Detective Sullivan."

"Detective Amy Harrison, please."

"Who?"

"Amy Harrison, she works Sex Crimes out of Bayside, the One-Eleven?"

"There's no Harrison here. How long ago was that?"

A deep breath. A slow exhale. "About twelve years ago."

The gruff New York voice let out a long whistle under his breath. "Twelve years, Jesus Christ. No one here now by that name. Hold on a sec." She could hear him hold his hand over the phone and yell out, "Anyone here heard of a Detective Harrison, Amy Harrison? Used to work Special Victims twelve years ago?"

A voice in the back. "Yeah—I knew Harrison. She retired. Left the department maybe three, four years ago. Went to the Michigan State Police, I think. Who's looking for her?"

The gruff voice began to repeat the information, but C.J. cut him off. "I heard. Okay, how about Detective Benny Sears? He was her partner."

"Sears. Benny Sears," the gruff voice yelled. "She wants to know about a Benny Sears."

"Jesus," said the voice in the background. "Benny's been dead maybe seven years now. Dropped of a heart attack on the Fifty-ninth Street Bridge in rush hour. Who wants to know all this shit?"

"Did ya get that? Detective Sears died a few years ago. Is there something I can help you with?"

Retired. Dead. For some reason she had not anticipated that. Her silence was met with a sigh of impatience on the other end. "Hello? Can I maybe help you with something?"

"Who would handle their old cases then? I need some assistance on a, a . . . case that they handled together back in eighty-eight."

"Do you have a case number? Was there an arrest?"

She opened the folder and began to shuffle quickly through the yellowed papers for a case number. "Yeah, somewhere here, I have a number. Hold on, just give me a sec . . . No, there was no arrest, though, as far as I know. Oh, here's what looks like the numb—"

"No arrest? Then you need the Cold Case Squad. Let me transfer you. Hold on." The line went silent.

"Detective Bureau. Detective Marty."

"Hello, Detective. I need some help on an unsolved sexual assault case from 1988. I was transferred to the Cold Case Squad by Special Victims."

"John McMillan works cold sex crimes. He's off today, though. Can I have him call you, or you want to call back tomorrow?"

"I'll call him back tomorrow." She hung up. That had been totally unproductive.

She picked the phone back up again and dialed.

"Queens County District Attorney's Office."

"Extraditions, please."

The line went silent, and classical music filled the phone.

"Investigations Bureau, Michelle speaking. Can I help you?"

"Hello. Extraditions, please."

"Extraditions are handled out of this bureau. How can I help you?"

"I need to speak with the attorney who would handle felony extraditions back to the State of New York."

"That would be Bob Schurr. He handles all extraditions for our office. But, I'm afraid he's not in at the moment."

Doesn't anybody actually *work* in the city that never sleeps? "Okay. When do you expect him?"

"He went to lunch, and then I think he has a meeting after that. He'll probably be back in the late afternoon."

She left the name Townsend and her home phone number. She hung up the phone and stared out at the water. The sunlight danced off the lapping waves, creating reflections that sparkled like diamonds. A beautiful light breeze blew through her balcony from the east, making her wind chimes tinkle. More than a few boats were out today, in the middle of a Wednesday afternoon, their bikini-clad passengers tanning themselves on small towels spread across the bows, while the proud captains in their bathing briefs, with beer in hand, steered their course. Even better were the bathing beauties slathered in tanning oil lying in lazy lounge chairs off a stern that could easily fit ten lazy lounge chairs. Those, however, were no longer called boats, but rather, yachts. On the yachts, both the bikinis and the briefs tanned together on the stern, martinis in hand, while the crew handled the steerage. And the cooking. And the cleaning. The waves left in their wake splashed the beach-towel bow bikinis and caused the otherwise-proud captains to spill their beers. C.J. watched the rich natives with their healthy, relaxed tans and cool martinis, and the flashy tourists with their Speedos and piña coladas and burned skin, float by without a care in the world. A familiar tinge of envy at the easiness of their lives rose like a lump in her throat, and she fought it back down where it belonged. If life as a prosecutor had taught her any lessons at thirty-six, it was that things were not always what they seemed. And as her dad used to say: *Just be sure to walk a mile in someone else's shoes before buying 'em, Chloe. Chances are you wouldn't make the purchase.*

Her thoughts ran then to both her parents, still living in quiet northern California, still afraid for their Chloe, all alone in yet another metropolitan, unforgiving city, full of strangers, full of madmen. Worse yet, now she works with them, among them, every day of her life, the absolute scum of the earth—murderers, rapists, pedophiles—trying her hardest to win in a system where no one really can. Because by the time the horrible cases reached her, everyone had already lost. C.J. had not heeded their advice, their warnings, and it was painful and tiring for them to keep worrying about her, placing herself like a suicidal fool directly in harm's way. As far as C.J. was concerned, it was really better, this emotional distance that had grown between them since *the incident.* She had enough memories of her own to drag around; she certainly didn't need to share anyone else's. The same was true for all her old relationships from once-upon-a-lifetime ago, no matter how solid they had been at one time. She had not spoken to Marie in years.

She sipped the last of the coffee and opened the thick manila file marked POLICE REPORTS. The corners of the thin white triplicate paper were yellowing, the typewriter ink slightly faded. The date on the first report read Thursday, June 30, 1988, the time 9:02 A.M. Time rushed back, as if yesterday, and the hot tears spilled from her eyes. C.J. wiped them away with the back of her hand as they fell, as she began to read all about the night she was raped, twelve years ago.

23

"FALCONETTI, YOU THERE? Dom?"

Dominick's two-way radio sounded at his side. The screen on the Nextel read "Special Agent James Fulton."

"Yeah, I'm here, Jimbo. Go ahead." His eyes searched the bathroom for an evidence bag, and he walked out into the master bedroom. "Hey, Chris, where are the evidence bags?"

Chris handed him a stack of clear plastic bags, red evidence tape, and white inventory receipts, and he headed back into the bathroom.

"We've got somethin' real interesting happenin' here in the shed out back side of the house. Where you at?" Jimmy Fulton's southern accent made understanding words normally found in the English dictionary interesting. He was an older guy, a seasoned investigator who had been with FDLE for twenty-six years and was currently the Special Agent Supervisor of the Narcotics Squad. His prior experience in violent crime and search warrants made him a valuable asset.

"I'm upstairs in the master bath. I just found something real interesting myself. Bantling has a whole bottle of haloperidol in his drawer, otherwise known as Haldol."

"Haldol? Ain't that for nutty folk?" Dominick could just picture him right now pulling down on his full gray beard, dark sunglasses covering his eyes from sight even inside a dark shed.

"Yee-haw, Jimbo. That it is. And our friend has a prescription for it from a doc in New York." Dominick dropped the prescription bottle into the clear bag and sealed it with the red evidence tape.

"Goddamn! But I think I'm about to top you."

"Oh, yeah? How's that?" He marked his initials, DF, on the outside across the seal of tape in black pen.

"Well, first things first. It looks like our friends from the Bureau have stopped by to pay us a friendly sort of visit. They're out front right now shaking hands and kissing babies and of course giving free interviews to the press about the status of *their* investigation."

Dominick felt his jaw clench tight. "You're kidding me. Please, Jimbo, tell me you are."

"'Fraid not, my friend. 'Fraid not."

"Who is it?"

"Well let me see. The Beach Boy standing guard at the door damn asked them Fibbies for a business card, if you can believe it. He wouldn't let them in at first, so they're out making a ruckus now on the lawn. Remind me to call Chief Jordan over at the Beach and get that boy a raise."

Dominick moved back to the master bedroom and looked out the side of the window. Sure enough, the same two dark suits from the causeway were standing around in their dark sunglasses looking important next to the bougainvillea on the manicured front lawn. Talking on cell phones and writing notes. Why, it looked like Mulder— and Scully in drag. Another feeder band of instant news across MSNBC and CNN viewers' television screens: *FBI Investigators Take Over Investigation from State Authorities.* Or even better: *State Agents Get Fucked Again by the Feds.* It looked like they had even commandeered the best parking spots in front of the house, blocking in the Crime Scene vans in the driveway.

"Well, Dom, I'm looking at the cards here, and I've got an Agent Carl Stevens and an Agent Floyd Carmedy. You know these boys?"

"Yeah, I know 'em, Jimbo. They were all over my scene

last night on the causeway. I'll go down and talk to them. Last I checked, the feds weren't named in our search warrant invitation. If they're not on the guest list, then they're not coming in. Tell Chief Jordan I second that raise and to have him make sure his boys keep the riffraff out."

"Okay, Dom. You're the boss. And I'm mighty glad you are. 'Cause there's one more person from the Bureau that wants to come over and play, and I don't want to be the one to tell him he's not welcome. I got a business card here from Special Agent in Charge Mark Gracker. If you're looking out your window yet, he's the one making the speech on the lawn."

Fuck. Fuck. Fuck. *Gracker.* He pulled his hand through his hair and closed his eyes tight.

"Alright, Jimbo, I'll take care of the feds. I'm coming down now. I just gotta give RD Black a heads up that a tornado might be headed his way this afternoon." RD Black was the Regional Director of the FDLE Miami Regional Operations Center. His boss. Just wait till he had to tell Black that he was about to get in a pissing contest with the FBI SAC. The good thing about Black was he disliked the feds just as much as Dominick did; he just couldn't say it from his position. He would condemn interagency squabbling publicly, but when the cameras went home, he'd shut the door to his office and tell Dominick to make sure he fucked 'em back, just as the feds had done to FDLE in the past. In fact, Black had been the RD on the organized-crime case stolen out from under him by Gracker.

"Well, before you do that, Dom, I have some more news for you, or did you forget what I said about outdoing you before?"

"You mean there's more? I hope you're prefacing the good news with the bad news, because the feds are definitely bad news. This better be good. Go ahead, Jimbo, make my day."

"Oh, you'll like it, alright. Looks like we found ourselves some blood down here in the shed. And maybe a murder weapon, too. Yee-haw."

24

DOMINICK TOLD CHRIS and Bowman to finish up with the tapes and the bathroom, and left Manny to deal with the Armanis in the closet. Then he dashed down the stairs and out the front door. The young Beach cop was still standing guard at the door. He looked pissed off.

Outside on the front lawn in their black suits, black ties, and black sunglasses stood Stevens and Carmedy, notepads in hand. Stevens also had a cell phone to his ear, but Dominick suspected that he was just doing that to look important to the media crowd across the street. He had worked with Stevens once before when he was on the Joint Organized Crime Task Force, and he was, as Manny liked to call him in Spanish, *un maricón*. A faggot. It was probably his mother on the other end asking what he wanted for dinner that night.

Across the street, next to the fleet of black FBI Tauruses blocking the brick driveway, stood FBI SAC Mark Gracker. And right next to him was Channel 10's own Lyle McGregor. Gracker looked serious, somber. Lyle looked excited.

Dominick figured it would be impolite to interrupt Gracker on a live broadcast and tell him to go get a federal search warrant if he wanted to play in the sandbox with the other kids. So he let Stevens finish up with his mommy and approached Mulder first on the lawn. Like a lion, pick off the weak ones first.

"Hey, Floyd. Floyd Carmedy, right? With the Bureau? I'm FDLE Special Agent Dominick Falconetti." *Let's just get this straight right off the bat whose crime scene this really is. Around these here parts you're not FBI Agent Carmedy. You're just Floyd.* Dominick extended his hand.

Floyd Carmedy took his and shook it. "Agent Falconetti. Good to meet you. You're running this warrant?"

"That I am, Floyd, that I am. What can I do for you?"

Gracker, no longer blinded by the television lights that had quickly turned their attention to the Crime Scene tech carting a large black plastic bag out of the front door of the house, must have noticed Dominick on the lawn. He slid his dark sunglasses back on and walked quickly across the lawn, his short legs working extra hard as the heels of his black dress shoes sank into the grass.

Floyd began to speak, but then saw Gracker out of the corner of his eye and quickly shut up, deferentially stepping back a foot to let Gracker take his rightful place in the conversation.

Mark Gracker strutted up, his chest puffed out in his black suit, his black tie dangling off the edge of his pot-belly, and stepped in front of Floyd Carmedy.

"Agent Falconetti. I've been trying to reach out to you all day. We need access to this crime scene." His voice was low and serious. *Just the facts, ma'am.* He was a full four inches shorter than Dominick, and Dominick could see the top of his head, where the hair was beginning to thin and his pasty white scalp peeked through.

Dominick glanced in the direction of Lyle McGregor and his camera crew. *Was Gracker trying to reach him all day by a plea to the media, hoping Dominick might catch him on the news at noon?*

"Hello, Mark. Long time, no see."

Mark Gracker's chalky white face turned red and he pursed his thin lips together. Dominick knew Gracker hated being addressed by his first name. Ever. He sus-

pected that he made even his wife call him Special Agent
in Charge Gracker while they were screwing.

"Yeah, it has been a while, *Dominick*. You know I'm the
FBI SAC in Miami now, right?"

"Yeah, I heard that somewhere. Congratulations.
Things must be real busy over there."

"They are. They're real busy here, too. The Bureau
needs to get into that crime scene, and that baby-faced
prick with Miami Beach won't let us in the door." Gracker
shifted on his feet, looking for higher ground, obviously
uncomfortable at the height difference between the two of
them.

"Hmmm. That is a problem. Well, you see we have a
state warrant that allows only certain state and local agencies access to that crime scene. I'm afraid the Federal
Bureau of Investigation wasn't named. We won't be needing your assistance on this one."

A thin line of sweat droplets had appeared on Gracker's
pudgy upper lip. "You know we have jurisdiction in the
Siban murder. It happened on federal land. The Bureau will
be taking over that investigation."

"That's great. Bully for you. Except Bantling has been
arrested on the *Prado* murder." He made sure he enunciated the name Prado, as he would for a preschooler learning his alphabet sounds. "And we are here on a warrant to
search his house based on facts gathered in *that* homicide.
If we should find something that links him to the *Siban*
murder, I'll be sure to call you."

Gracker's face was beet red now. *Where was Lyle and
his camera when you really needed him?* "You're gonna
make me get a federal warrant, then?"

"I'm afraid that will be necessary, yes. And the Bureau
can look at the house all they want—when we're done."

"I think I'm going to need to contact Director Black on
this."

"Director Black is already aware of the situation down
here, and he sends his apologies in advance for any incon-
venience this may cause the Bureau. Now, if you'll excuse
me, I have to get back inside."

Dominick turned and started across the lawn, leaving an

exasperated and furious Mark Gracker on the front lawn. Scully and Mulder looked around sheepishly, trying desperately again to look important for the cameras that were back to focusing on them. Dominick walked up the stoop to the young Beach cop and said quietly, "Good job."

"What an asshole," the Beach Boy mumbled back.

Then he turned and called across the lawn, "Good to see you again, Mark. Congratulations on that promotion."

And he walked back into the house.

25

HE WALKED THROUGH the house to the French doors leading onto the pool patio. Past the tropical pool, in the corner of the backyard under the fanning palms of a Traveler's, sat the quaint white aluminum-sided shed with the small picture window. It didn't look like a shed, but rather a cute little house, complete with a black shingled roof. The picture window even had a black curtain, which was closed and drawn. He found Jimmy Fulton out by the door.

"How did SAC Gracker take the news that he wasn't needed?"

"Not well. Not well at all. I left him sulking on the lawn." An image of a red-faced Mark Gracker spewing expletives at Stevens and Carmedy as they drove away from LaGorce in their air-conditioned fed mobiles crossed his mind, and he smiled to himself. In the three minutes that it had taken for Dominick to walk through the house to the pool, Gracker had probably already been on the cell phone with RD Black, demanding Dominick's badge on a silver platter. Right next to an invitation to the search warrant, which of course he needed to get into the house. Neither of which he was going to get, but he was still gonna scream like hell.

"This is going to be bad, Jimbo." He sighed. "But then again, as Clemenza once said to Al Pacino in the movie *Godfather,* 'These things have to happen once every five years or so. Gets rid of all the bad blood.' Black is behind us, though. He said, 'Just don't call Gracker a prick to his face.' "

"I'm sure Black would like that honor himself."

"This has been some day." Dominick ran his hand through the top of his hair. "What's in the shed?"

"They're photographing again inside, so let's give 'em a minute. Let me tell you what we got. This Bantling fellow must have liked to cut and stuff animals, ya know? He's got these stuffed owls and birds inside this shed, hanging from the ceiling. Claws still on and all. When I first walked in, well, shit, I thought they was real for a moment. Then I got my senses back and picked up my glasses and realized they was stuffed. But he's also got this long steel gurney, like one y'all might see in a hospital, inside. It's clean, no prints, totally wiped down. So we're thinking there ain't gonna be nuthin' left here to find, right?"

The Crime Scene photographers came out. "It's all yours, Agent Fulton," one yelled. "We took a roll."

"Great. Thanks." Jimbo nodded in their direction. He turned to the forensic tech from the MDPD who was waiting by the door with his black bag. "Hold up for a sec, on taking up that blood, Bobby. I want to show it to Agent Falconetti here first."

They walked inside the shed. Overhead, two stuffed owls, their glass eyes open wide, hung suspended in flight from the ceiling beams on invisible fishing line. A single light with a black round metal shade hung from the middle of the vaulted ceiling between the two owls. The space was deceptively large for a shed, approximately fifteen by ten feet, with a cement floor and drywalled walls. It was impeccably clean, especially for an outdoor shed. Not a speck of dirt on the gray cement floor. A metal gurney sat flush up against the fifteen-foot wall. Directly above it, a row of white Formica cabinets ran across the length of the wall. Next to the gurney in the corner was a beautiful stuffed white egret, its wings slightly spread, as if about to take flight, its long willowy neck and yellow beak turned upward, its black glass eyes staring in the direction of the gurney.

"Take a look at this." Jimbo knelt down next to the gurney. White chalk blocked off a small square-foot area behind the gurney, next to the wall and underneath the cabinets. Three very small pools of reddish brown stained the floor. Jimbo shone his flashlight on them and they glistened slightly.

"Still wet?"

"No. But definitely fresh. Given the spatter pattern and the height of the gurney, Bobby says it looks like the body was on the gurney and the blood maybe dripped from there." He shone the light on the wall, about one foot up from the floor.

Tiny pinpricks of reddish brown dotted the white wall. "Now this—this here looks like where the blood spattered back up from the floor against the wall. Again, it's consistent with the theory that the blood dripped from the height of the gurney. We're pretty sure it's blood."

"Yeah, Jimbo, but is it human?" Dominick said, remembering the glass eyes of the majestic egret.

"We'll know soon enough. Lab can tell that as soon as they get it. But look at this here now," he said, still kneeling on the concrete. He pointed to another chalked-in area, this one a lot larger, and directly off the end of the gurney. It was maybe two feet wide.

Dominick looked with the flashlight and saw the faint swirls of brown, the dark streaks. "Looks like someone tried to clean up a mess."

"Yep. Sure does. The Luminol Boys will take a peak when Forensics leaves. May tell us just how big the mess was before someone tried to clean it up."

"Make sure to take the wheels on that gurney off carefully." Dominick leaned to look under it and shined his light on the black rubber wheels and the underside. "Looks like he may have rolled through something."

"Yeah, we're gonna take the wheels off in a sec."

"What about the weapon?"

"Oh, yeah, I forgot the best part. Take a look at this." Jimmy Fulton opened the middle Formica cabinet. On the bottom shelf was a large rectangular metal tray. Laid out neatly on it were several different scalpels and scissors of varying size. "This idiot should have saved us the time and just given us a confession. Trying him is gonna be fun. Real fun."

Dominick's radio crackled to life again.

"Dommy Boy, oh Dommy Boy, the pipe's are softly calling . . ." It was Manny trying his best to sing in an Irish brogue through his Cuban accent. For amusement, Dominick let him sing for a little while before answering. Jimbo and Bobby grimaced. Manny must have realized that others might be listening in as well and after a few more bars, he stopped singing and barked, "Hey Dom, you there?"

"Yeah, Bear. I'm with Jimmy Fulton out back. What's going on up there? You wrapping up the closet?"

"That I am. And let me just say for the record that in my next fuckin' life I want to be a furniture designer."

"A *salesman,* Bear," Eddie Bowman's voice interrupted in the background. "You want to be a furniture *salesman* when you grow up."

"Fuck you, Bowman. Keep watching for your momma on that TV screen." He turned his attention back to the radio. "This pervert has got the nicest fuckin' clothes. Hey, if he gets the death penalty, do you think I can have them?"

"Yeah, maybe if you drop seventy-five pounds and shrink five inches, Bear. No more *pastelitos.*" Dominick kneeled down and watched as Bobby, swabbed the brown substance off the floor and placed the three samples in separate long, sterile cylindrical tubes.

"I can still wear the ties. Seems a shame to waste these clothes. How'd it go with the Blues Brothers out front? I bet that fucking *maricón,* Stevens, threw a tantrum."

"Not good, Bear. Let's just leave it at that. Not good."

"Well, I've got everything pretty much wrapped in this closet—which is the size of my bedroom, by the way. This fuckin' nut job is so neat, too. Too neat, if you ask me. You know he organized everything? And I mean everything. He's got this black suit bag marked, 'Tuxedos,' as in *plural,* on the outside. Then he's got a box marked winter sweaters, and another that says winter shoes. Maybe he's not our guy, 'cause he sure as hell sounds gay to me. Or could be he's a frustrated homo who hates women because they remind him of his mother. Now there's a motive. At least it explains Bowman's problems with the world today. And listen to this—I found his Halloween costumes in a separate box, all folded neat and shit. Must like to·play dress up, too, 'cause he's got a ton of shit in there: a sick alien mask, a Batman mask, this Frankenstein head, and a _cowboy hat and pants with those gay-looking leather no-ass patches—ya' know, those flaps—to go with it that they wear over their jeans."

"They're called chaps, not flaps."

"Yeah, whatever—chaps. And then get this—just imagine this prick at your kid's birthday party—he's even got a clown mask in there, too."

Dominick stared at the smear patterns on the floor. Two feet away in the corner stood the yellow webbed feet of the stuffed egret. The luminol that the techs would spray soon would glow wherever blood had been. In the course of his years as a homicide investigator, Dominick had seen whole rooms, including spatters on the ceiling, glow a ghastly yellow in the dark. *What would this quaint-looking little shed look like when the lights were turned off? What gruesome picture would it paint for them in the dark?*

"Well, just take it all, Bear. We don't know yet what's going to be important in this case and what isn't."

26

ALTHOUGH THERE ACTUALLY wasn't that much to read, it still
took her some two hours to get through all the police
reports and then the hospital records and lab reports.
Halfway through, she had to stop and walk around the
apartment, put on a fresh pot of coffee, fold the laundry,
wipe the counters—anything to get away from the enormous weight of the memories that rushed her brain. It was
amazing how she couldn't remember what she ate for
lunch most days, but she could still recall every second,
every sound, every smell of a slice in time that happened
more than a decade ago. Partway through reading the statement of her ex-neighbor Marvin Wigford, she went into the
bathroom and vomited for the second time that day. In it he
had stated how Chloe would dress "provocatively" for the
men in the building and "parade around the courtyard"
wearing outfits that "a woman from a Catholic university
shouldn't have been wearing." Then he concluded that "it
was no wonder that something like this happened to her,
because she made men hard on purpose." Pangs of guilt
and blame that she had fought back for so many years tore
at her soul once again, and even though she knew intellec-
tually that his statements were simply the ramblings of a
demented and perverted person, she still felt dirty and
ashamed. There was a part of her, deep down, that had
always felt responsible for what had happened, as if she

had done something to bring this upon herself. For years, her mind had entertained a zillion things that she could have done, should have done, differently and then the zillion other paths her life would have followed. She had found that that was indeed the hardest part of the therapy—learning not to blame yourself.

After the side trip to the bathroom, she had returned to the balcony and watched the boats go back and forth for a while longer, sipping what must have been her tenth cup of coffee for the day. It was almost rush hour and across the Intracoastal in Pompano Beach, the streets were beginning to crowd with cars. Her beeper had gone off a few times, bringing her back from the past to the welcome reality of the present, and she had made sure to call everyone back. The phone calls temporarily took her mind away from the police reports and witness statements, away from the cold, familiar fear and the panic and the blame that was again building inside her head. Particularly the phone calls she fielded from Marisol the Annoyed. She took Lucy out for a walk along the water before darkness made such a thing impossible.

When she got back, it took her another hour to finally finish reading the rest of the reports, including her own statement, where she recollected, in excruciatingly vivid detail, every conscious moment of June 30, 1988. It began with the fight with Michael in his car that had spilled into the courtyard, and rambled to when she awoke to the taste of latex on her lips and the crushing weight on her chest, the pain of him as he climbed on top of her, his penis entering her while she struggled uselessly underneath. Finally, blessedly, it ended with her last conscious memory, when the cold knife angrily sliced across the delicate skin on her breasts, and she watched as her white sheets slowly turned to red. Now, back on her balcony, back in the present, a hand moved protectively to her breast, the other to her throat to free the invisible weight of fear that crushed her larynx and made it almost impossible for her to breathe.

The phone rang just then. The caller ID on the phone said the Queens DA. She wiped the tears from her face and answered in the most sane voice she could muster.

"Hello?"

"Is there a Miss . . ." The voice on the other end struggled as he obviously read from an illegible piece of paper. ". . . Tooso there?"

"This is Ms. Townsend."

"I'm sorry. My secretary left me a butchered name that looked like Tooso. My apologies. This is Assistant District Attorney Bob Schurr of the Queens County District Attorney's Office returning your call. Is there something I can help you with?"

She tried hard to gather her thoughts together. "Yes, Mr. Schurr, thank you for calling me back. Umm, I need to know the necessary protocol to extradite a felon back to the State of New York." She was all business now. The prosecutor in her had taken over, and this whole matter had somehow happened to somebody else.

A long pause. "Okay. Are you an attorney?"

"Yes. I'm sorry. I'm with the State Attorney's Office in Miami."

"Oh. Alright, then. Who's the subject, and what's the warrant out of New York for?"

"Well, there's no warrant as yet. It's an unsolved felony crime that we think we may have located a suspect in."

"Unsolved? You mean there's no indictment? No warrant?"

"No. Not yet. The authorities down here have only just recently identified a possible suspect through interrogation and investigation." She knew she was being vague.

"Oh. Have you spoken with the investigating New York detectives? Are they procuring a warrant?"

"Um, not yet. I believe the case has gone to the Cold Case Squad. We are reaching out to the detectives with that unit, as we speak, to secure a warrant and whatever else is necessary under New York law to arrest the subject here in Florida."

"Well, an indictment would be a necessary first. Then they can get a warrant for his arrest off the indictment, and your detectives down there can execute the warrant and pick him up and hold him down in Miami while we start the extradition paperwork up here. But, we may be getting way ahead of ourselves. How old is this case?"

She swallowed. An uneasy feeling came over her and she remembered something that, as a prosecutor, she should not have forgotten. "Um. I believe the crime occurred more than ten years ago, but I'd have to check with the detectives who are working it down here."

Bob Schurr whistled low under his breath. "Ten years? Uh-oh. Tell me that you want to extradite this guy for murder, and I'll say okay."

"No, it's not a murder." Now her palms were sweaty. She didn't want to know the answer to her next question. "Why the 'uh-oh'?"

"What's the crime you've got this guy on? Assuming, of course, it is a guy. You haven't said."

She cleared her throat and hoped she sounded normal. "It's a sexual assault. A forcible rape. And an attempted murder."

"That's what the 'uh-oh' is, then. You're out of luck, I'm afraid. The statute of limitations on all felony crimes in New York is five years. Except, of course, murder. There's no time limit on that. If there was no indictment handed down within the first five years after the crime happened, you can't touch this guy because the time's up." His pause was met with silence, so he continued. "I'm sorry. This sort of crap happens all the time, especially in sex cases. You finally find the guy through a DNA match, and there's nothing you can do about it. They're just now starting to indict the DNA strands themselves in the cases where they don't have a suspect name and the time is running out. Maybe they did that in your case—did you check with the cold case detective?"

"No. I will. Maybe that's what they did. I hope," she said, although she already knew that there was never any physical evidence found from which to extract DNA to indict in her case. Her voice was drifting in and out, and she knew it. "Thanks for all your help—I'll call you back if I have any more info."

"What did you say your name was again?"

C.J. hung up the phone. This couldn't be happening. The statute of limitations. The arbitrary block of time that some stupid lawmakers had set in stone to define what a fair length of time was to bring someone to trial. What was a fair amount of time for someone to wander through life worrying about when their past crimes would catch up with them? What was fair for the defendant? Fuck the victim. Make sure the *defendant's* rights were protected.

The enormity of the conversation began to sink in. Bantling could never be tried for what he had done to her. Never. Never. Never. He could go to the top of the Empire State Building and shout his guilt to the whole world in all its colorful, vivid, gory, disgusting detail and he could still never be tried. He could take the elevator back down and walk away scot-free, and there was nothing that anyone could ever do about it. She should have remembered the statute of limitations, but in Florida certain sex crimes had none, and, frankly, it had never even entered her mind. She had been so focused on *how* to get Bantling arrested the right way and sent to New York—and how to face her own demons without going crazy again—that she hadn't thought of answering the question *"Can* he be arrested?" Her victim blinders were on, and the whole thing had just been a foregone conclusion in her mind.

She felt as if everything was again coming apart and she needed desperately to pull it together. To think through the fog and the fear that kept pressing against her chest.

She paced the apartment. The sun had slipped down beneath the sky and the warmth of dusk was ending fast. She poured out the cold coffee in the cup and reached for the chilled bottle of Chardonnay in her fridge instead. She poured herself a glass, took a long sip, and picked up the phone again. It took about four rings before the line was picked up and Dr. Chambers answered.

"Hello?" The sound of his voice was instantly comforting.

"I thought I'd still find you there. Even at this hour. How are you, Dr. Chambers? It's C. J. Townsend." She nibbled on a thumbnail as she paced the length of the living room in her stocking feet with her wineglass in hand. She still had not changed out of her suit.

"Hello, C.J." He sounded surprised to hear her voice. "I

was finishing up some paperwork here. You just caught me. What can I do for you?"

She watched as a dinner cruise floated by. The faint sound of laughter and music drifted up on the air.

"Well, something has happened and I think I may need to see you."

27

GREGORY CHAMBERS SAT up straight in his leather chair. He could sense the urgency and desperation in C. J. Townsend's voice, and he was immediately alert. "Not a problem, C.J. Not a problem. How about tomorrow?"

"Tomorrow would be good . . . great." She heard the sound of papers flipping, like an appointment book.

"Can you come in at ten o'clock? I'll just do some creative shuffling to my schedule."

She breathed a broad sigh of relief into the phone. "Thank you so much. Yes. Tomorrow would be fine."

Dr. Chambers leaned back in his chair, his brow furrowed. Her voice was definitely cause for concern. She sounded distraught, a mess. "Do you need to talk now, C.J.? I've got the time."

"No, no. I need to gather my thoughts. Think them through. But definitely tomorrow. Thank you so much for fitting me in."

"Anytime. Call me anytime. I will see you tomorrow, then." He paused. "Remember, you can call me if you need me before then."

She hit the button on the cordless and looked aimlessly around the empty living room. The dinner cruise had floated out of sight and the air was quiet again, but for the sound of the wind blowing through the palm trees and the water lapping gently below against the seawall. Tibby II rubbed against her leg and meowed loudly. The day had gone by, and it was time for him to eat yet again.

The phone rang in her hand and she jumped in her skin, dropping it to the floor. She was too jittery now.

The phone rang again. The caller ID said Falconetti. She hesitantly picked it up in her hand.

"Hello?"

"Hey. It's me. I've got your AutoTrack."

She had forgotten all about that. The day's events had blurred together. "Oh. Okay," she stammered, trying to collect her thoughts, trying to sound cognizant, lucid. "I'll, ah, I'll swing by FDLE in the morning and pick it up. Um, what time are you in?" She reached again for her wineglass and began the pace again, back and forth across the living room.

"No. You don't understand. I have your AutoTrack for you *right now,* and I'm at your condo doors downstairs. Buzz me in."

No. Not tonight. She just couldn't face him. Couldn't talk to anyone right now.

"Um, Dominick, now is not a good time for me. It's really not. I'll just swing by tomorrow and pick it up." She slugged down a long sip of wine. "Or you can just leave it in my mailbox. Stuff it in twelve twenty-two. I'll get it later." She knew that must have sounded ridiculous, but there it was. Take it any way you want to. Just go away.

There was a long pause. She reached for her pack of Marlboros, now almost empty, on the table outside. Then his voice broke the silence.

"Nope. No way. I'm coming up, so let me in."

28

IT TOOK ABOUT three minutes before she heard the ring of the bell followed by the rap of knuckles against the front door. She looked out the peephole and saw Dominick leaning against the door frame, looking down around his feet. He was still dressed in his dress shirt and slacks, with his sleeves rolled up and his tie half off and his collar open. His gold FDLE badge hung on a chain around his neck and his gun was holstered to his side. She unset the alarm and unlocked the door, opening it just a little more than halfway.

He smiled at her, and she could tell he was exhausted. In his hand he held a thin stack of white paper stapled together at a corner. He waved it through the door.

"Hey, thanks for bringing this by, Dom." She took the paper from his hand. "You didn't have to do that. I would have picked it up." She didn't invite him in.

"You said you wanted it today, and so I got it for you today. Last I checked, I did it with three hours to spare, too. It's only nine."

"I appreciate it. How did you even know where I live, though?" The thought that she could be found made her uneasy. She protected her address and gave it to no one. It was also exempt from disclosure on all public records because she was a prosecutor.

"I'm a cop, remember? We're paid to know these things.

Actually I called your office and Marisol gave me your home address and I just MapQuested it on the Internet."

She made a mental note to make Marisol's life a living hell in the morning.

An awkward moment passed between them. Finally, he said, "Do you think that maybe I can come in? I want to tell you about the search warrant. Unless you're too busy." His eyes looked past her, casually perusing the apartment.

She answered quickly, probably too quickly. "There's no one here." She caught herself and finished slowly with "I'm just, well, tired and I've got a headache and . . ." She looked into his face and saw his eyes reading hers, drawing conclusions. She again tried her best at a smile and to look normal. "Oh sure, yeah, I'm sorry, just come on in." She opened the door, and he stepped in out of the hall. They stood facing each other for a moment or two, then she turned away and walked into the kitchen.

"Do you want a glass of wine, or are you still on duty?"

He followed her in. "I thought you said you had a headache."

"I do," she said from inside the refrigerator. "Wine is great for headaches. You don't even remember you have one."

He laughed. "Well, in that case I'll definitely take one, thanks." He looked around the apartment. It was tasteful, colorful. The kitchen was a bright sunshine yellow, with an exotic fruit border in primary colors that ran at chair level across the room. The living room was painted a deep red, and bold artwork dotted the walls. It surprised him. C.J. was always so serious. He had somehow expected her apartment to be white and gray with maybe a hint of cream for color—and bare walls.

"I like your apartment, too. It's very bright, cheery."

"Thanks. I like to use a lot of color. It gives me peace."

"This place is great. What a view." Off of the living room, huge sliding glass doors were open onto a small balcony. He could hear the gently lapping waters of the Intracoastal below and see the lights of Pompano Beach across the way.

"Yes, I love it. I've been here about five years now. It's

small, though. Only a two bedroom. But then again, there's only me and Lucy and Tibby, so I don't need much more, I suppose."

"Lucy? Tibby?"

"That's Tibby rubbing white hairs all over your nice black slacks." As if on cue, Tibby let off a long, woeful meow at his feet. Dominick rubbed the fat cat's head and Tibby purred pitifully, as if he had never known love before.

". . . and that's Lucy. My baby." Lucy, having smelled the contents of the open refrigerator, had just scuffled into the kitchen, sniffing at the air. She found C.J.'s outstretched hand and snuggled over for a pat and a scratch behind her long ears. "She doesn't hear too well anymore, but that's okay. Right, girl?" C.J. put her face down close to Lucy's and Lucy gave her a happy little howl. Her tail wagged back and forth.

"It's quiet up here, too. Different pace than Miami."

"I like it quiet. Like any big city, Miami's got too many nut jobs. I see it every day, I work with them all day long. I don't need to live with them, too. Not that Fort Lauderdale is the epicenter of normality, but it's definitely more reserved. Plus I don't work in this town. And you know what they say you shouldn't do where you eat . . ."

"You like your anonymity?"

"Definitely. It's worth the thirty-five-minute drive to work."

"I've been in Miami too long. It's in my blood, I guess. I can't be more than twenty minutes from a good Cuban midnight sandwich."

"The Broward-Dade county line is only fifteen minutes away. They have black beans and rice in Hollywood and Weston, too. They're just more expensive."

"That's true. Maybe a transfer to the FDLE field office in Broward. Next thing you know, I'll be driving a minivan undercover, chasing truant kids who didn't show up for home ec class."

"Now I know you're exaggerating. This isn't exactly Boringville, Iowa, up here in these yonder parts. I wish it were. Lots of bad things happen over that county line. More and more each year."

"I'm only kidding. Broward County has its own share of problems, and those are definitely growing. Even the nut jobs breed and need a place to live outside the jurisdiction of their court-mandated stay-away orders, but still within a fifty-mile radius of their probation officers." He paused for thought and ran his hand over his goatee. "I just like Miami, I guess. I'm used to it. I like getting used to things. I'm actually a very comfortable type of guy."

"Good. That's good to know," she said softly.

They both said nothing for a moment and just sipped at their wine. She looked tired, drained. Her hair was pulled back with a clip into a soft bun, and strands had fallen out, framing her slightly tan face. Her glasses were off, something he had rarely seen. Even without makeup, she was pretty. Very pretty. She had a natural beauty about her that a lot of women didn't. Funny how she always seemed to try to hide it. But the criminal justice system could be a man's world sometimes, particularly south of that Mason-Dixon line, and even in a city as metropolitan as Miami. It was still filled with chauvinistic male judges, cops, and defense attorneys. In his thirteen years with FDLE in this city, he had seen many women struggle to be respected in court, to be taken seriously by their peers, by the bench. And C.J. was always taken seriously. Always. She was probably the most respected attorney in that office. Even more so than that dippy boss of hers, Tigler. He saw her gray jacket draped over the kitchen chair and noticed that she hadn't changed out of her suit yet.

"I thought you left work early today."

"I did. Why?"

"'Cause you're still in your suit."

"Yeah, I did some work out of here. I just haven't had a chance to change yet." She changed the subject. "How did the warrant go? Did you find anything?" She glanced down and saw that he was simultaneously petting both Tibby and Lucy under the table.

"Yeah. We found a lot. I'm surprised Manny didn't call you to let you know."

"He beeped me before and I called him back and left a

message on his cell. He hasn't called me back again, and that was about two hours ago."

"Well, they just wrapped up over there about forty-five minutes ago. I came straight here. We found blood this afternoon in a shed out back behind the house. Not much, three drops, but enough. Preliminary tests came back about an hour ago. It's human. We'll run the DNA and match it with Prado's to see if it's hers. That will probably take a few weeks.

"We also might have a murder weapon. Bantling apparently liked to stuff animals in the shed—you know, what do they call that?"

"Taxidermy."

"Yeah. He had a few birds hanging from the rafters in this shed. But he also had about six different scalpels. One also has what may be blood on it. Neilson is going to call in an expert on knife patterns to see if we can match the scalpel with the chest incisions of the girls—those that weren't too decomped—and we can get a microscopic skin tear match."

C.J. shuddered. This was hitting too close to home now, and she didn't know how much longer she could hold this conversation together tonight.

"So we boxed and shipped everything to the lab and the ME, and we are just waiting for test results. They luminolled the house. Nothing. No blood anywhere inside."

"What about the shed that you mentioned?"

"Lit up like a firefly. He must've tried to clean it up but he missed a few spatters on the lower part of the wall. But there was blood everywhere. Even the ceiling glowed, with a splash pattern that looks like Prado might have been killed while lying on this metal gurney he kept in there. The aorta would have spurted blood up like Ol' Faithful when cut. We're getting Leslie Bickins, the blood spatter expert from FDLE in Tallahassee, to come down tomorrow and take a look. Of course, the problem is that he also liked to cut up dead animals and stuff them in that shed, so whose blood is whose is the question of the day."

"Anything else?"

"Yeah. I found a prescription for haloperidol that Bantling had from a doctor in New York. You might know it as Haldol—it's an antipsychotic drug. They administer it to manage delirium. So apparently Bantling has a history of mental problems, too. That would fit the pattern, and would make sense in light of the viciousness of the murders.

"He also had a trunkful of homemade sadomasochistic porn videotapes. Different women, some looked real young, our victims' age. We haven't looked at 'em all, because there's got to be over a hundred altogether. From the titles, a lot of them seem to be blondes, too."

C.J. had turned white.

"Are you okay? Jesus, you look like you did in court this morning!" He reached across the table and touched her arm. Her hand clenched the wineglass stem with tight white knuckles. The same look of worry from that afternoon was in his eyes. "What's wrong, C.J.? What is it? Maybe I can help."

"I'm fine. I just think maybe I'm coming down with something. That's all." The words were stammered, distracted. It was time to end the conversation. End it right here before she completely fell apart tonight. She stood up, pulling her hand out from underneath his, moving away from him yet again. Her eyes were cast down, toward the table and away from him. "Thanks for bringing this tonight. I'll definitely look through it." Her voice sounded far away. She fingered the AutoTrack on the table and looked back at Dominick. "And thanks, too, for making the trip all the way up here. You didn't have to."

He stood and followed her back to the front door. He noticed that there were about four different locks on it. And an elaborate alarm system on the wall. *What was she looking out, up here in her tower in nice, quiet Fort Lauderdale suburbia, with the yachts and the party boats?*

She went to open the door, and Lucy rushed to get out. "No, Lucy. No. I've already let you out for the night."

C.J. looked back up at Dominick. He saw the fear in her emerald eyes then as plain as day. "Well, thanks again, Dom," she said quietly. "I'll see you tomorrow, I guess.

Call me after you speak with Neilson. Maybe I'll meet you over there. And I'm sorry that I've been . . . distant, I just—"

His hand found hers on the doorknob, and he grasped it and held it tight. His face was close now, and she could feel his warm breath on her cheek. His breath smelled sweet and cool, like peppermint and Chardonnay. His eyes were serious, but they were also soft. He looked down into hers.

"Don't talk," he whispered. "Don't say anything else or this might not happen."

His lips touched her cheek then, and gently, softly, brushed against her skin, until they reached her mouth. The gruff stubble of his goatee tickled against her face and chin. To her surprise, she found her own lips were already parted slightly, waiting for his mouth to meet hers. She wanted to feel his kiss, to taste his sweet, peppermint tongue on hers.

His lips met hers finally, and she shivered slightly. His mouth moved gently, his tongue probing, exploring hers. Their bodies touched, pressed up against the back of the door, and even through the clothes they both wore, the heat was intense. She could feel him, hard against her thigh. His hand still held hers behind her back on the doorknob. He let go now and ran his fingers up the length of her arm, caressing her shoulder lightly through her silk blouse, then down her side, gently moving over her ribs and the curve in her waist. His hand then slid behind her, where his warm palm fit across the small of her back. His other hand held her face, his thumb surprisingly smooth and gentle on her cheek. Their mouths were still one, and the kiss grew more intense, more passionate. His tongue pushed deeper into her mouth, his strong chest pressed heavily against hers, so close she could almost feel his heartbeat.

She did not move away from him this time. Instead, her fingers hesitantly wrapped around his neck, feeling the short thick hairs on the back of his head curl under her fingers, and she pulled him even closer. The tips of her fingers ran across the top of his back, feeling the definition of muscle through his dress shirt. A surge of emotions surfaced that she had long since buried and left for dead, and the moment completely overwhelmed her.

He felt the hot tears as they ran silently down her cheek, meeting his. The kiss abruptly ended and he pulled back, away from her. She kept her head down, ashamed of herself for letting him see her this way. She should never have let this happen tonight. But then his warm, calloused hands came and held her face, cupping her chin and tilting it upward again, toward his own. She saw again the worry in his eyes and, almost as if he had read her mind, he simply whispered, "I'm not going to hurt you, C.J. I'm not." Then his lips softly kissed away the two rivers of tears on her cheeks. "And we're both going to take this slow. Real slow."

He kissed her once more softly, gently on the lips. And for the first time in a long while, she felt safe, right here in this man's arms.

29

SHE WAS AT her desk, coffee in hand, by 7:00 in the morning, leafing through the piles of papers that had managed to accumulate in just one afternoon out. Despite the sweet good-night kiss, sleep had not come last night without dreams—horrible blood-soaked dreams. The clown's mask was gone—replaced with the handsome, chiseled smile of William Rupert Bantling. It was his face that laughed now at her, his Rolexed hand that slashed her skin to ribbons. She was not even sure if they were dreams she had experienced or maybe it was that she had never even gone to sleep at all, and these tortured images in her head were simply memories come back to play a midnight encore. One thing she'd known for certain was that when she finally opened her eyes, she would not make the same mistake twice and close them again that night. At 4:00 a.m. she wandered out onto her balcony and sat, her body wrapped in the thin sheet from her bed, and watched as the sun came up over Fort Lauderdale and Pompano Beach.

After Dominick had left last night, she'd tried to think. To think about what she could do, should do with the Cupid case. Should she tell Tigler that she had a conflict, or perhaps silently hand the case off to another prosecutor without explanation? One final solution played again and again in her mind that she knew would probably be impossible: Should she go forward and say nothing?

If she told the State Attorney, then the whole State Attorney's Office would have to conflict out of the prosecution and give it to the State Attorney's Office of another circuit, who would, in turn, assign a new prosecutor. That could be very bad—especially in a case so complex and one that was centered all on Miami. Other circuits were not as seasoned as the Eleventh, and so neither were their attorneys. Some circuits had only three or four prosecutors altogether, and had never had a serial homicide even occur in their jurisdiction. And in those old Florida circuits, Miami was considered the armpit, the black sheep of the circuits that no one wanted to visit, much less work a case there.

On the other hand, C.J. was familiar with the facts of each murder. She had been to practically every crime scene, had seen every body, had interviewed every girl's parent, friend, loved one, had spoken to the medical examiner on each case, and had written all the warrants. She had lived, breathed, and worked this case for a year. No one knew the facts as well as she. She doubted anyone could.

If she handed it off silently to another Major Crimes prosecutor in her office, she still had the problem of the new prosecutor not being up to speed with the facts of all the murders. Then she had the added problem of explaining her motivation for doing so. Why would she suddenly give up the most career-defining case of her life? A case any other lawyer only dreamed of getting? The act would raise more questions than she cared to answer. Ever.

As for the last solution, she could go forward for the time being and say nothing. Nothing until she verified beyond a shadow of all doubt that it had been Bantling in New York. Until she made completely sure that it was him. She still had to speak with McMillan from the Cold Case Squad in New York. Maybe by some weird chance some-one had looked at her case in the past ten years since she had stopped calling the detectives every day. Maybe they had retested her sheets, her pink pajamas, her panties, her rape kit from that night and found bodily fluids where none had been found before. Maybe they had by some fluke then indicted Bantling by his DNA strand. Maybe. Maybe. Maybe.

She wanted to do this right, but she wasn't sure what that meant. She wanted to bring Bantling to justice. She sighed and looked out the window of her office down onto Thirteenth Avenue, where street vendors were already setting up their umbrella carts of Sabrett sausages and sodas when it was barely 9:00 A.M. On another, fresh mangos, papayas, bananas, and pineapples dangled from the underside of a red-and-white umbrella, its owner moving to the beat of the Latin music that played on his boom box as he set up his cart.

So last night she had sat on her balcony and thought all these thoughts over in her head a million times. And, of course, she had thought about Dominick. Of all times in her life, this was not the moment for romance or passion. But here it was, and she had not turned it away. She raised her fingers absently to her lips, and remembered what his mouth had felt like on hers. She could still smell the sweet peppermint of his breath, and see the deep concern in his eyes. He had simply held her by the front door, his hand caressing her back, his breath warm by her ear, and the feeling of being safe, of being protected, if only even for five minutes, was an amazing feeling.

She had not been with a man in a long time. The last one had been in a drunken stupor with a stockbroker named Dave whom she had dated casually for a couple of months. She thought he was funny and sweet until he stopped calling. Which happened, coincidentally, right after they had finally slept together. When she asked him why the relationship had ended so suddenly, he only said she had "too many hang-ups." That had been a few years ago, and she hadn't looked back. Intimacy with a man frightened her, and it presented too many issues, opened too many wounds. So in the time since, there had been a few dates, but nothing serious and definitely nothing intimate. Dinner out and a kiss here and there.

But then there was last night, and there was Dominick.

It had only been a kiss, nothing more, and he had left when she asked him to. But she couldn't stop thinking about what he had said, and how he had said it. He sounded so sincere, and she wanted so much to feel safe again, even for just another five minutes. But he was too involved in this case to be told the truth, and how far could a relationship go without the truth? How many thin stories and lies would she have to tell to keep him from it? And even if the truth were a possibility, could she ever even bring herself to tell a man about that night? About the reason her body looked the way it did when the bedroom lights were turned on?

The stack of pink phone messages on her desk was enormous. She was going to have to have the Public Information Officer for the State Attorney's Office return the calls from almost every newspaper and television station in the country. On the top one Marisol had scribbled in large uppercase letters: "THIS IS THE 3 MESSAGE!! WHY HAVE YOU NO CALLED HIM?!!"

The wooden in-box on top of her desk was full of new mail. In addition to the Cupid case, C.J. also had ten other murders she was handling, two of which were set for trial within the next two months. She had a crucial Motion to Dismiss set next week, depositions scheduled through the next two weeks, and next-of-kin meetings. None of these could be neglected just because of Cupid. She would just have to juggle them all and hope she didn't drop anything.

She stared at the back of Bantling's three-page pink arrest form. The names of about twenty-five people, all of them cops, were listed. First initial, last name, department, and badge number. Witnesses. The cop who pulled Bantling over, the first cops on the scene, the K-9 units, the cops who did the search of the trunk and found Anna Prado's body, the investigating detectives, Special Agent D. Falconetti, FDLE #0277.

She had twenty-one days from the date of his arrest to get Bantling indicted for first-degree murder by the grand jury. That meant she had to interview all the witnesses and get their statements and prepare a grand jury memo for Tigler's Chief Assistant, Martin Yars. Yars was the only prosecutor in the entire office who presented cases before the grand jury. And it would be Yars who would then seek the indictment on Bantling, probably with Dominick Falconetti's testimony, as the lead investigator on the case. And the grand jury only met on Wednesdays. Today was already Thursday. That gave her only two Wednesdays to work with. If she couldn't get before the grand jury by then, she would have to at least file a felony Information— a sworn document of charges—for second-degree murder within twenty-one days. Then she'd indict him on first degree when Yars could take it to the grand jury. And to do that, she still needed to take the sworn testimony of all the necessary witnesses in the case, those who could supply the facts to support the charge of murder. In either event, twenty-one days was the magic number and it wasn't much time at all.

Tick-tock, tick-tock goes the clock.

She slugged down the rest of her Dunkin' Donuts coffee, and rubbed her temples with her fingers. Her head was pounding again. She needed to make a decision on how she was going to proceed. On *if* she was going to proceed. Time was a major factor here, and she wouldn't be able to just "mull it all over" for a few days. All the cops had to be brought in, their testimony taken, and that would, at the least, take a few days to arrange and complete.

She looked down at her watch. It was already 9:30. She picked up her purse and sunglasses and hurried out the door, past the secretarial pool and a sulking Marisol, today clothed head-to-toe in purple Lycra.

She vowed to make a decision, one way or the other.

After she got back.

30

THE TWO-STORY SMALL house on Almeria Road in Coral Gables, an affluent Miami suburb, was pretty. An old Spanish style, probably built sixty or seventy years ago, it was perfectly square, the stucco painted a deep, spicy-brown mustard yellow with an orange S-barrel tiled roof. Beautiful flowers, bursting in colors of white, red, and yellow, filled terra-cotta flower boxes that hung suspended from every windowsill, and full flower beds lined the brick walkway to the rounded brown oak door with the wrought-iron handles. It certainly didn't look like a psychiatrist's office. A small sign hung next to the door, just above the terra-cotta mailbox. It read GREGORY CHAMBERS, M.D.

C.J. opened the door and stepped inside. The waiting room was done in Mexican tile, the décor a light yellow and pale blue. Peaceful, calming colors. Large palms fanned out in each of the four corners of the room, and rich, leather chairs lined the two walls. Magazines of every sort were spread out on the beautiful, oversized mahogany table, and Sarah Brightman sang Franz Schubert's "Ave Maria" softly overhead. Peaceful, calming music. Let's not get the rich loonies too excited, too anxious, on their visit to the nice doctor.

The secretary, Estelle Rivero, was seated behind the pale yellow wall that separated the sane from the "needs help" section. Through the small glass window, she could see the top tufts of Estelle's autumn-sunrise-colored red hair that was teased at least three inches off the top of her head.

There was no one else in the waiting room. C.J. tapped gently on the metal bell that sat outside the window. A light ding rang out, and Estelle slid open the glass and smiled through fireball red lips.

"Hello, Ms. Townsend! How are you today?"

I thought the office staff wasn't supposed to ask that question without a doctor in the room.

"Fine, Estelle. How are you?"

Estelle stood up. Her hair cleared the window but her chin didn't. She stood about five foot one.

"You look good, Ms. Townsend. I saw you on the news last night. That is a sick man, no? What he did to those poor women?" She shook her head.

More than you know, Estelle. More than you know.

"Yes, he's definitely disturbed." C.J. shifted, her heels clicked on the Mexican tile. Estelle brought both her wrinkly hands, complete with two-inch bright nails, up to her cheeks and shook her head. On every finger was a gold bauble. "It's terrible. Such beautiful girls. Beautiful girls. He looks so normal, too. Like such a nice-looking, decent man. You can never tell about someone." She leaned forward and lowered her voice to a whisper. "I hope you put him away, Ms. Townsend. Where he can't hurt any more women."

Where he's going, Estelle, except for maybe Lizzie Borden, women won't have to worry anymore.

"I'll do my best, Estelle. Is Dr. Chambers in?"

She looked flustered. "Oh—yes, yes. He's expecting you. Please go right on in." The door buzzed and the "needs help" crossed over into the world of the sane. At the end of the hall, Gregory Chambers's office door sat open. C.J. could see his figure hunched over the huge mahogany desk. He looked up with a smile as she approached, her heels clicking softly on the tile.

"C.J.! Good to see you. Come in, come in."

The office was painted a robin's-egg light blue. A blue-and-yellow floral-print valance decorated the top of the two floor-to-ceiling round windows. Wooden blinds let soft slivers of sunlight into the room, spilling in neat stripes across the Berber carpet and comfortable blue leather wing-backed chairs.

"Hello, Dr. Chambers. I like what you've done with the office. It looks nice." She stood just inside the doorway.

"Thanks. We had it redone about three months ago, I guess. It's been a while since you've been here, C.J."

"Yes. Yes. I've been busy."

There was a brief pause, and then he stood up and came out from behind the great desk. "Well, please. Come in," he said, closing the door behind her. "Have a seat."

He motioned for her to sit in one of the wing-backed chairs and he sat across from her in the other, leaning slightly forward with his elbows on his knees, his hands clasped in front of him. It was all very casual, so informal; C.J. was not sure if he was like that with all his patients, or if she was special, given their long-term relationship. Greg Chambers always made her feel as if her problems with the world were nothing that could not be handled.

"I see they arrested a suspect in the Cupid murders. I caught a bit of the hearing on the eleven-o'clock news last night. Good job, C.J."

"Thanks. Thanks. We've still got a long way to go, though."

"Is this guy the real McCoy?"

She shifted in the chair and crossed her legs. "It looks like it. If Anna Prado's body in the trunk wasn't enough, from what they found at his house last night, there's no doubt."

"Really? Well, best of luck on that." His blue eyes searched hers. "I know it's a real stress case, with all the media attention and all." His voice raised slightly when he said "all" as if it were a question, and she knew he was giving her an opening.

She nodded, and focused on her lap. It had been several months since she had sat in this chair. After so many years it was time to see if all the counseling had actually worked, if the chick could fly, if she could handle it alone in the world—make it past the memories that kept trying to pull her back to where she had just been. In this endeavor, with excuses of too much work and too little time, she had slowed her scheduled biweekly appointments to an occasional visit, finally stopping altogether in the spring. Now here she was back again knocking on his door for help.

"Are you trying it with anyone else from your office?" He sounded like her father, concerned that she wasn't eating right or getting enough sleep.

"No. Just me so far, unless Jerry Tigler appoints someone else."

"Who's the lead, Dom Falconetti?"

"Yes. And Manny Alvarez with the City."

"I know Manny. Great detective. I worked with him on a quadruple homicide in Liberty City a couple of years back. I believe I met Agent Falconetti at the Forensics conference in Orlando last year."

Greg Chambers's black hair was sprinkled with gray, but it was a vibrant, shiny gray, and it accentuated his kind blue eyes, and added some character to his otherwise plain-looking face. The unavoidable march of time had feathered deep wrinkles across his brow and out from his eyes, but they also helped to distinguish him, and C.J. guessed that he was probably a better-looking man in his late forties than he had been in his teens or his twenties. Then she thought of her own tired lines reflected back in the mirror yesterday. Men aged so much better than women. It wasn't fair.

"You've got me more than a little worried, C.J. I could tell from your voice last night that something was wrong. What's up?"

C.J. shifted her legs again and recrossed them. Her mouth was dry. "Well, it's actually about the Cupid case."

"Oh. Do you need some professional advice?"

Therein lay the problem. In addition to being her off-again, on-again psychiatrist for the past ten years, Gregory Chambers was also a professional colleague. As a criminal forensic psychiatrist he regularly assisted the State Attorney's Office and the police departments on violent-crime cases. On dozens of occasions he had testified for her office as an expert in complicated murder and domestic-violence cases, where the core issue that needed to be explained to the jury was simply, why? Why do men do the evil that they do? The same characteristics that made him easy to talk to as a psychiatrist also made him easy to listen to as an expert. With his soft face, easygoing smile, and extensive, impressive credentials, Gregory Chambers would explain the unfathomable in layman's terms: Grown men prey sexually on innocent children because they are pedophiles; boyfriends hunt their girlfriends down with AK-47s because they are psychopaths; mothers kill their children because they are bipolar; teenagers gun down their classmates in cold blood because of a borderline personality disorder.

His diagnoses were always right on target. The police trusted him, respected him, as did the private community. Which, of course, explained his thriving private practice in posh Coral Gables at $300 an hour; when you're rich, you can afford to be crazy. C.J. fortunately got the law-enforcement discount. He had never testified in one of C.J.'s trials. She was always careful to draw a line, so there would never be a conflict in court. She had given tutorials by his side at law-enforcement conferences and seminars, and had sought his professional opinion off the record in some of her own cases. In those roles, he was both her colleague and her friend, and she recalled how she had addressed him in those instances as simply Greg.

Today, however, he was Dr. Chambers.

"No. I'm not seeking your expert opinion. I wouldn't have called you at nine o'clock at night if I needed that." She smiled weakly.

"I appreciate that, but others have not been as courteous, C.J. Jack Lester has called me at one A.M. before." He smiled a knowing smile. "And I don't mind a bit."

Jack Lester was also a Major Crimes prosecutor. C.J. despised him.

"Jack Lester is a pompous, arrogant jerk. And you should have hung up on him. I would have."

He laughed. "I'll keep that in mind for the next time, and I'm sure there'll be a next time." His face grew serious again. "If it's not my professional expert opinion, then . . ." His voice trailed off in a question mark.

Again, she shifted in her seat. The seconds ticked off in her head.

When she spoke, her voice was barely a whisper. "You know why I started coming here. You know why I see you . . . as a patient."

He nodded. "Is it the nightmares? Are they back again?"

"No, I'm afraid it's worse than the nightmares." She looked desperately around the room, and then ran both hands through her hair. God, she needed a cigarette.

He frowned. "What is it, then?"

"He's back this time," she whispered, her voice shattering. "But this time it's for real. He's real. William Bantling is the one. Cupid! He's the one!"

Dr. Chambers shook his head, as if he didn't understand what she was saying.

She shook her head, and the tears that she had held back for as long as she could began to stream down now from her eyes. "Do you understand what I'm telling you? Cupid is the one! He's the man that raped me! He's the Clown!"

31

DR. CHAMBERS STIFFENED, then slowly exhaled the breath he had been holding and said simply, in a calm voice, "What makes you think that, C.J.?" He was a psychiatrist, and his job was to take things in stride.

"His voice in court. I knew his voice the second he started yelling at Judge Katz." She was sobbing, but trying to stop. He reached across his desk for a tissue, and grabbed the whole box.

"Here, here. Take a tissue." He sat back now in his wing-backed chair, his hand covering his mouth, pulling down on his chin. "Are you sure, C.J.?"

"Yes. I'm positive. You can't hear a voice in your head for twelve years and not recognize it when it's spoken again. Besides, I saw the scar."

"The one on his arm?"

"Yes. Right above the wrist, while he was pulling on Lourdes Rubio in the courtroom." She finally looked at him. Her eyes were filled with tears and desperation. "It's him. I know it. What I don't know is what I should do."

Dr. Chambers sat and thought for a long moment; C.J. used the pause to compose herself. Finally, he spoke. "Well, if it is him, then that is, in a sense, good news. You now know who he is, where he is. You can finally have some closure to all of this, after all these years. I'm sure a trial in New York will be tough, but—"

She cut him off right there. "There's not going to be a trial in New York."

"Now, C.J. After all you've been through for twelve years, you're not willing to testify against this man? There is no reason to be ashamed. No reason to want to hide any longer. You've coached enough reluctant witnesses in your career to know—"

She shook her head. "Oh, I would testify. I would. In a heartbeat. But there won't be any trial because the statute of limitations has run—seven years ago. So, now do you understand? He *can't* be tried for raping me, for trying to kill me, for, for . . . butchering me." Her arms were folded, her hands cupped around her elbows. She hunched her body lower, curling them now protectively over her lower abdomen. "He can't be tried. No matter what."

Dr. Chambers sat very still for a few moments, and blew out his breath very slowly through his hand, which still covered his mouth.

"C.J., are you sure? Have you talked to the New York authorities?"

"The original detectives on my case are retired and dead. It's in Cold Case now. There was never any suspect, any arrest."

"Then how do you know you can't go forward?"

"I spoke with the Queens DA's office, the Extraditions Unit, and a prosecutor told me. I should have thought about the statute of limitations before, but I . . . I just didn't. It didn't even cross my mind that when I finally found him, there would be nothing I could do. Nothing." The tears started falling again.

There was another long silence in the room. For once, in the ten years she'd known him, Dr. Chambers was actually speechless. Finally, he said in a low voice, "We'll get you through this, C.J. It will be alright. What do you want to do now?"

"*That's* my problem. I don't know. What do I want to do? I want to fry his ass. I want to send him to the death chamber. Not just for me, but for the eleven women he's killed, and the countless other victims I'm sure he's left out there in his wake. And I want to be the one to put him in that chair. Is that wrong?"

"No," said Dr. Chambers quietly. "It's not wrong. It's a feeling. A justified feeling."

"If I could, I *would* send him to New York. I would tell the world up there that he's the fucking son of a bitch and then I would have put him away up there. I would have looked him in the eye and told him, 'Fuck you, you bastard! You didn't beat me! Say hello to your new roommates, for the next twenty years, because that's the only piece of ass you'll be seeing!'" She looked up at Dr. Chambers. Her eyes were pleading for an answer. "But I can't do that now. What I've been waiting to do for twelve goddamn years. He even took that from me. He even took that from me . . ."

"Well, there is always this case, C.J. He's facing death in the murders of those women, isn't he? It's not looking like he's going to walk away from this a free man."

"Yes, but that's what I'm struggling with. I know that I can't prosecute him, but if I tell Tigler, the whole office conflicts out, and then we get some neophyte from Ocala out of law school three years trucking down to try his first homicide. And I get to watch on the sidelines while somebody once again fucks this up for some reason and he walks!"

Be assured, we are actively pursuing the investigation, Chloe. We hope to have a subject in custody soon. We appreciate your continued cooperation.

"There has to be some solution. Maybe Tigler can get the Seventeenth or the Fifteenth to take it?" The 17th Judicial Circuit was Broward County. The 15th was Palm Beach.

"Tigler has no say. It's potluck, and I am not willing to take that chance. I just can't. You know how complicated serials are. Especially with ten dead bodies and no confession or incriminating statement. And, we've really only got him so far on one. He hasn't even been charged with the other nine murders. It's easy to make a mistake. Too easy."

"I understand that, but I'm concerned about you. Very concerned. I know that you are strong, probably one of the strongest women I've ever met, but no one, no matter how strong her character or steady her conviction, should have to prosecute the person who has brutally attacked her. I think the issue is that you don't want to let go."

"Maybe I don't, until I am offered a viable solution. One that I can trust."

"How about passing it to another prosecutor in your office? What about Rose Harris? She's good, and is very good at DNA and expert testimony."

"How do I pass this to another prosecutor without everyone flipping out? Especially at this late stage of the game? You tell me! Everyone knows how much I wanted this case—shit, I worked at it for a year! I've seen every single bloated, decomped body, met every family member, seen every autopsy photo ever taken, read every lab report, practically written every warrant—I *know* this case. How do I suddenly tell the office and the media that I *don't* want it? Short of being diagnosed with a terminal disease, everyone who knows me knows I wouldn't give it up. And even then I probably wouldn't.

"So bring on the 'whys' and the 'how comes' and the 'what happeneds,' because they will be next. And the media will dig and dig and dig until they find something, anything. And someone will find out about the rape, and hence the conflict that was never revealed but should have been, and I will see that same schmuck from Ocala come down to try *my* rapist, *my* serial homicide, and I'll get to watch him fuck it all up and watch Bantling walk. Only I'll get to watch it on the TV at home since I won't be a lawyer anymore because I'll have been disbarred. So you tell me, Dr. Chambers, how I *can* do it and I'll do it, but only if I can have a guarantee that he's going to get convicted, that he's going to pay for what he's done. Nobody, nobody can give me that. So if this case is going to get screwed up—*I'll* be the one taking the blame, thank you. No one else."

"What are you saying, C.J.?" She could see he was being careful with her as he chose the next question. "I'll ask you again, what do you want to do?"

She sat silent for a few minutes. *Tick-tock, tick-tock goes the clock.*

Her words sounded deliberate, determined, as if she had just thought of an idea and was testing it out, but liked the way it was sounding. "I have to indict within twenty-one days, or else file a felony Information within twenty-one. Either way, the witnesses all have to come in and give a statement, the reports have to be gathered, the evidence reviewed . . ." She paused, and then her voice was even more determined. "I think it's too late to change pitchers now. I have to finish out the inning. So I think that I should at least take it through to indictment. Then maybe I'll bring someone else on board, maybe Rose Harris, to try it with me. If all goes well, I'll quietly hand the reins over to her and bow out with a mysterious sickness when I feel she's up to speed and can handle it all. When I trust her. When I know that she can and will do the right thing."

"What about the office's conflict of interest on this one?"

"Bantling was so busy trying to save his own ass in court that he did not even recognize me. It's almost ironic, considering everything he's done, he barely even managed a glance in my direction," she said quietly, then continued. "He has probably fucked with so many women that he's lost count. They don't even have a face anymore. And God knows I don't look anything like I did back then." She smiled a wry and bitter smile and pulled her hair back behind her ears. "Only *I* know what he did. And if it comes out later, I can just say I wasn't sure that it was him. That I didn't know. He can't be tried in New York anyway, so it's not as if I am sacrificing my own case by saying I can't ID. I don't have a case to make in New York anymore anyway." Her voice had conviction now.

"C.J., this is not a game. Besides the obvious ethical problems that it poses, do you really think you can emotionally handle prosecuting this man? Hearing what he did to those women? Knowing what he did to you? Reliving it every day, every time you hear another gruesome fact, see another picture?" Dr. Chambers shook his head.

"I *know* what he's done to those women. I've seen it. And yes, it will be tough, and I don't know how I'll get through it, but at least I'll know it's being done right. I'll know where he is every minute of the day."

"What about your law license? Keeping this conflict from the courts?"

"Only *I* know there's a conflict. No one can prove I knew there even was a conflict. I would have to admit that I knew it was him all along. I can live with myself if I deny that." She paused for a moment and thought of yet another thing that she should have thought of before. Quietly she said, "Does this put you in an awkward position, Dr. Chambers? Do you need to report it or something?"

As a doctor, he had a duty to disclose to the police a patient's intent to commit a future crime. Everything else said in session was considered confidential. C.J.'s failure to disclose a conflict was perhaps an ethical violation of the Canon of Ethics that a lawyer has a duty to uphold, but it was not criminal.

"No, C.J. What you're considering doing is not criminal. And what is said in this room between us is, of course, confidential. It need not be disclosed. But I personally don't know if it is a good idea for you, either therapeutically as a patient or professionally as an attorney."

She absorbed what he said for a moment. "I need to get some feeling of control back in my life, Dr. Chambers. Haven't you always said that to me?"

"Yes. Yes, I have."

"Well now it's time. I have the control now. Not some tired detective from New York. Not some idiot from Ocala. Not the Clown. Not Cupid."

She paused one final time and rose with her purse to leave. The tears were gone, and anger had replaced the desperation in her voice. "*Me.* I have the control. I have the power. And I'm not going to let that son of a bitch take that from me this time."

Then she turned and left the sanity of the pretty blue-and-yellow-flowered office behind her, waving a silent good-bye to Estelle over her shoulder on her way out.

32

"MEDICAL EXAMINER'S OFFICE."

"Agent Dominick Falconetti and Detective Manny Alvarez to see Dr. Joe Neilson. We have a one-thirty appointment."

"Yes. Dr. Neilson is waiting for you in the lobby."

The mechanical gate arm swung up, and Dominick pulled off of busy Fourteenth Street and maneuvered the Grand Prix into a parking spot marked POLICE VEHICLES ONLY directly across from the glass front doors of the two-story redbrick building. And right next to a late-model black hearse.

Manny slowly opened the passenger-side door and stepped out into the parking lot. He had been unusually quiet on the ride over to the ME's from the task force at the FDLE Miami office. When Dominick didn't get out right away, he leaned back in. "You coming, Dom?" His voice had a nervous-sounding edge to it.

"Yeah. Give me a few minutes, Bear, and I'll meet you inside. I just have to make a quick call first." Dominick had pulled out his cell and held it in his hand. He obviously was waiting for Manny to get lost before he dialed.

Manny Alvarez looked at the redbrick building and gri-maced. He hated the medical examiner's office. It was the only part of being a homicide detective that still made him queasy, even after sixteen years and hundreds of dead bod-

ies. It wasn't the dead bodies in cold storage in the basement that got to him, because he could look at a dead body
all day long at a crime scene and never be bothered. Even
the rotten ones, or the "floaters" that were found missing
an eye or a body part and seemingly surfaced on a daily
basis in any one of the four thousand canals, lakes, and
ponds that existed in and around the city of Miami. Not to
mention the ones that bobbed up next to the fishermen in
the Miami River or freaked out the surfers in the Atlantic.
Those never got to him, unless of course it was a kid,
because he didn't like child victims—those were always
hard. No, it wasn't the bodies that did him in, but the
autopsies, the whole purpose of the medical examiner's
office.

Autopsies were part of his job, and, as a lead detective
on a homicide investigation, he had to attend them on a
regular basis. To find out which of the thirteen bullets that
tore through the victim's back actually took his life? What
stab wound was the fatal blow? Was it murder or was it suicide? So Manny had seen his share of autopsies, and he
wasn't going to quit over them. But the act of the autopsy,
the coldness of the whole procedure—that was what he
hated. He always had, and time had not made it any better.
The human-sized refrigerators, the freezing-cold white-
tiled room, the steel gurney, the bright lights, the organ
scales, the buzz saw and rib crackers, the black thread they
used to sew everything back up when they were finished.
In an autopsy, the dead weren't victims anymore; they
were now cadavers—specimens—to be studied by a bunch
of freaks who actually *liked* cutting up dead people—who
had chosen this as their profession and looked forward to
coming to work every day to do it. In the freezing-cold
white room, the dead bodies lay naked and exposed on the
steel gurney for everyone to ogle, from the interns to the
cops to the janitors, while some doctor with a power tool
cut off the tops of their skulls just to see what was inside
and how much it weighed. It was all too clinical for him,
and he just hated it. Plain and simple. And he thought that
medical examiners on the whole were weird. Why would
anyone pick a career of cutting open dead people and play-

ing with their intestines? Of course, the same could be said
for anyone wanting to become a homicide detective.
Maybe it was because he pictured himself on that steel gurney one day, naked and cold and completely undignified,
the whirr of the buzz saw by his ear while some medical
examiner and his intern snickered over how big his dick
was and how much fat he had in his gut.

Today, he and Dominick were here only to meet with
Dr. Neilson and ask some questions about yesterday's
autopsy on Anna Prado's body. Still, just going in the
building, knowing what was going on in the basement
below them while they chatted over coffee and a Krispy
Kreme, brought on heart palpitations. And he certainly
didn't want Joe Neilson to be the one working on him
when he dropped of a heart attack on that cold, white-tiled
floor.

Manny looked back into the open car door and shot
Dominick a look that read, *Don't fucking do this to me,
amigo.*

"Neilson gives me the creeps. Big time." The Bear
looked nervous, puffing away on the last of his Marlboro.

"Every ME gives you the creeps, Manny."

"Yeah, well . . ." He looked back at Dominick, who was
still holding the phone in his hand and waiting patiently for
Manny to disappear behind a palm tree. "Alright, alright.
I'll tell you what, you make your phone call and I'll wait
for you by the front door. *Outside,* that is."

"For a big, bad detective, you sure are a chicken-shit,
Bear. Okay. I'll meet you by the door. Just give me a sec."

Manny walked off and out of immediate sight. When he
was gone Dominick tried C.J.'s office again, hoping to hear
her voice pick up the phone, but instead, only getting her
voice mail. He left a brief message. "Hey, it's Dominick.
I'm with Manny at the ME's. I've beeped you, but you
must not be wearing your pager. I thought you wanted to
meet with Neilson. Give me a call on my Nextel when you
get this. 305-776-3882."

He held the phone in his hand for a moment and stared
out the window at the disheveled-looking old man in the
driver's seat across from him who was eating a sandwich

and drinking either a Coke or a beer out of a brown paper
bag in the front seat of the hearse. Given the choice of profession, Dominick assumed it was a beer he was downing
with his tuna salad.

He knew he probably shouldn't, but he was getting
more than a little anxious about C.J. He had left a message
with Marisol that morning about the 1:30 appointment
with Neilson, and he knew C.J. had gone into the office.
But when she hadn't called him back to confirm she was
coming, he had beeped her a couple of times and he still
hadn't heard anything, which was not like her. At least he
wouldn't have considered it like her before yesterday.
Something definitely was up with her since the Bantling
hearing, even though she was denying it. He had seen the
fear in her eyes, watched her body language in that courtroom when she had gone white as a ghost and blanked out
in front of Judge Katz. And then last night, when they were
talking about Bantling again, she had turned that same
pasty, drawn color and quickly sent him on his merry way
to the front door. Dominick was no rocket scientist, but it
certainly didn't take one to see that C. J. Townsend, the
prosecutor with the reputation for having balls of steel, was
scared to death of something. *But what could she be that
frightened of? And what did it have to do with William
Rupert Bantling?*

He was still trying to sort out his own confusing feelings
about yesterday as well. When he had seen C.J. that way—
in the courtroom, in her kitchen—looking frightened and
worried and vulnerable, he had felt this sudden compulsion
to just protect her. To wrap her up in his arms and just protect her. It was very strange. A very strange feeling. Very
unlike him, he thought. He knew that they had flirted back
and forth for the past few months, and he knew that he
liked her. Even more important, he respected C.J. He liked
her spirit, her independence, her willingness to take on a
system with more holes than solid flooring. She was a victim's dream: a champion for her causes and a fiery zealot
in court, almost as if she had something to prove not just to
the twelve members of the jury, but also to herself. It was
great to watch her give a powerful summation or argue a

complicated motion to suppress against some of the best
and most egotistical, narcissistic male defense attorneys in
Miami and win. He liked that about her.

Over the past few months when they had chatted
together at the task force or at her office or casually on the
phone, he had come to realize that they had more in common than just defendants and judges and defense attorneys.
Before Cupid, he had respected her as an attorney. Since
Cupid, though, he had begun to like her as a person, as a
woman. He couldn't deny that. He had thought about
maybe asking her out to dinner, or a movie, but for the past
ten months, the Cupid case had him working sixteen-hour
days, seven days a week, and he had never seemed to have
the time. Or, he had never made the time for other reasons.
Probably those same psychobabble reasons that the police
psychologist told him he needed to come to terms with five
years ago after Natalie died. But he had put aside those reasons last night, whatever they may have been, consciously
or subconsciously, and had given in to his compulsion at
her front door. Now he regretted that he had. Maybe he
spooked her with that kiss last night.

The guy in the hearse had finished his sandwich and
must have realized that since Dominick was parked in the
POLICE VEHICLES ONLY parking spot he must be the police,
and the brown paper bag was now nowhere in sight.

Dominick climbed out of the car and headed up the
cement steps to the front entrance. A woman he recognized
as one of the young receptionists at the office stood outside
smoking a cigarette under the overhang, chatting with an
ME investigator twice her age, who Dominick knew as a
former Miami-Dade detective who had jumped ship to the
ME's for a better pension and fewer hours. They were having too much fun to be talking about a case, so Dominick
passed them by and didn't bother to say hello. He looked
around. Manny was nowhere to be found. Either he had
totally chickened out and was hiding around the bushes by
the handicap ramp, waiting for Dominick, or he had been
pulled inside alive by the evil Chief Medical Examiner Joe
Neilson. As he approached the glass front doors, he saw it
was the latter.

Joe Neilson had Manny backed up against the 1970s turquoise sofa with maroon pillows in the lobby, and there was nowhere to escape to. Neilson was dressed in his green scrubs, and his hair was covered by a disposable mint green cotton hair cap. Dominick could see he was talking excitedly, waving his hands up and down right at Manny. From the looks of his outfit, it was quite obvious that the good doctor had been in the basement immediately prior to his ascension to the land of the living. Fortunately, though, he had remembered to remove his latex gloves before coming upstairs and shaking hands with Detective Manny Alvarez, who by this time was looking kind of pasty and in need of either a cigarette or a barf bag.

Dominick stepped inside and tried, with an outstretched hand and a smile, his best attempt at a rescue operation. "Hello, Dr. Neilson. I hope I haven't been keeping you. I just needed to make a quick phone call."

Dr. Neilson walked toward Dominick, freeing Manny up and away from the sofa that held him prisoner, and vigorously shook Dominick's outstretched hand. "No, no not at all. I was just asking Detective Alvarez how the investigation was going. I also told him that I was excited to see you both because there's something very interesting I need to show you downstairs!"

Joe Neilson's unbridled enthusiasm for his job was one reason why he made Manny Alvarez uncomfortable. He was a tall, super-thin wiry fellow with sunken eyes who, Dominick thought, must have had ADD as a kid because this was one man who could never sit still. His hands, his mind, his feet, his eyes. Something was always moving on him. If you kept him in any one spot for too long, his weight would shift from foot to foot, his eyes would blink repeatedly, and his nose would twitch. It was almost as if his head were going to explode.

"Great. Is it Prado, or one of the other girls?"

"Well, right now, I've just reexamined Prado. But I've pulled the files on all the others and I think I'm going to have to take a look again at each of them, now that I know what I'm looking for. Shall we get started, Detectives?" Dr. Neilson's eyebrows were starting to rise and fall, rise and fall, and he began to blink fast. They had run out of time. The train needed to leave the station. Right now.

Manny looked awful. Just awful. He was actually green.

"Manny, you okay? You want to sit this one out?" Dominick asked.

"Of course he doesn't want to sit this one out!" Neilson interjected excitedly. "Come on, Detective. I've got a fresh pot of coffee on downstairs in the lab. That will wake you up!" Dr. Neilson headed for the elevator.

"Yeah, I'm coming. I'm coming. Right fucking behind you," Manny said, sounding resigned.

The elevator doors opened, and all three stepped inside the steel box that was long enough to hold a gurney.

"Dr. Neilson, the prosecutor from the State Attorney's Office wanted to meet us down here as well. I just left a message for—" Dominick began, but the doctor cut him off.

"C. J. Townsend? Yes, yes. She called about a half hour ago. She can't make it. She said she'll have to come over by herself tomorrow or the next day, for us to go ahead. She's tied up in court or something."

Dr. Neilson hit the "B" button, and the metal doors closed with a thud. The elevator car descended to the basement.

33

ANNA PRADO'S BODY was laid out on a metal gurney, the eyes closed. Her skin, which Dominick remembered from her family picture on The Wall to be a creamy white, was now ashen gray, the light sprinkle of freckles across her nose barely visible because of the skin's sallow pallor. Her long blond hair was fanned out underneath her head, framing her neck and shoulders. Some of the ends had fallen off the edge of the gurney, stuck together in clumps and tinged black with dried blood. She had a crisp white linen sheet pulled up to her neck, covering the mess underneath.

"When you called yesterday and told me about the haloperidol that you had found at the suspect's house, I ran some more tests, the results of which came back this morning." Dr. Neilson stood next to the body, his hand casually touching the protruding slender fingers that hung over the edge of the gurney. Dominick noticed that the fingernails were long and unkempt. The pink polish had chipped off of most of the nails.

"Haloperidol is a very, very powerful antipsychotic drug that is prescribed to manage delirium in psychotic or schizophrenic patients. The brand name it is sold under is the better-known Haldol. It's a strong depressant. It relaxes and calms a patient, and brings auditory hallucinations or delusional episodes under control, makes even violent psychotics manageable. For extreme cases, it can be injected into any muscle mass for immediate submission. If it's given in a high-enough dosage, it can bring about catatonia, unconsciousness, coma, and even death. Are you following where I'm going with all of this, Detectives?" Dr. Neilson's eyes blinked rapidly several times. "Now—here's the kicker on haloperidol—our standard toxicology screens that we run on every autopsy won't pick it up. You have to go *looking* for haloperidol to find it.

"So while it was suspected that Nicolette Torrence and Anna Prado both had some form of depressant in their system because of the weight of their lungs in the autopsies, we didn't know what it was, or even what to look for, past the standard list of depressant narcotics, such as Valium, Darvocet, or Hydrocodone. We even initially tested for rohypnol, ketamine, and gamma hydroxybutryic acid or GHB, better known on the street as Roofies, Special K, and Liquid Ecstasy. Nothing. We couldn't identify the narcotic in their systems.

"But, after you called me yesterday, Agent Falconetti, I began to think that haloperidol would fit, it definitely would. It's a very strong depressant. And I got pretty excited. So I ran some more tox screens and . . . Voilà!" He tapped his hand against a brown clipboard that held a yellow piece of paper from the lab. "There she is! Haloperidol! Then I looked back at the stomach contents on Ms. Prado to see if maybe I missed something. Nope. Nothing. But that doesn't mean too much because haloperidol has a half-life of maybe six hours, so if death came within the six-hour half-life period after taking the drug, we would find levels in her tissue and blood, even if complete digestion had occurred.

"So I began to run through some theories in my head. And just indulge me for a moment, Detectives, and see if this would fit into the fact pattern of your cases. The prescribed amount of the haloperidol in the bottle that you seized was twenty milligrams twice a day. That is an extremely powerful dosage, even for a large man who has developed a tolerance to it. For someone who has not, and who has a low body weight, even one twenty-milligram pill would be enough to completely incapacitate her. If your suspect administered just one pill to your victim in, say, a beverage, or sold it maybe as 'X,' within fifteen minutes of ingestion, she would be demonstrating the same clumsiness, slurred speech, depressed motor skills, and slow reaction time consistent with someone under the influence of alcohol. Her thoughts would not run coherently. She could be easily subdued.

"But as I was telling you before, haloperidol is also injectable. Its effects then are immediate. And they are easier to maintain with injection. In fact, for patients who are not good at taking their meds, haloperidol can be given in time-released injections. One injection can work anywhere from two to four weeks. So I went back and looked at the body for the answer."

Neilson held his now-captive audience at bay with a breathless, dramatic pause. Then he pulled down the white sheet from Anna Prado's body the way a magician would a magic cape at a stage performance. Manny half expected him to yell, "Abracadabra!" There was no white rabbit underneath, though. Instead, Anna Prado's naked, violated body lay flat and still on the cold steel gurney. As if he were a used-car salesman trying to point out the model's features, Dr. Neilson rolled Anna onto her side and showed the detectives her buttocks.

It was obvious that she had been killed while lying flat on her back, because the blood had pooled under the skin of both buttocks, and under the elbows and knee joints as well. After her heart had stopped pumping and she had died, gravity took over and settled the blood that had once coursed through her veins to the lowest points in her body at that moment. It was called lividity.

"Now look at this!" he said to Manny and Dominick, handing them a magnifying glass. A small piece of skin and tissue had been removed from the area. Next to it was a small pinprick-sized impression, otherwise invisible to the naked eye.

"There were two such pinprick markings. I missed the bruising because of the lividity that had set in in the area. Plus, I wasn't initially looking for what I found. I cut out the layers of skin that you see missing to examine the blood vessel damage in the area. Both of those pinpricks, Detectives, are consistent with markings of an injection having been given at that site. I believe an injection of haloperidol."

Manny wasn't quite buying it. Now Dr. Death was Quincy the Super Sleuth ME. "Wait a second, Doc. These women were all tortured before they died with all sorts of strange shit. Couldn't those pricks also be from this nutcase sticking straight needles into them just for kicks? What makes you so sure now they are injection sites?"

Dr. Neilson almost looked hurt by Manny's rejection of his hypothesis, but he quickly recovered. With a slight smirk that read *I know something you don't know,* he continued, basically ignoring Manny's question. "Well, Detective, after I found that, I did a little more hunting and found something even more interesting." He turned Anna Prado back onto her back and rolled out her right arm, away from her body. Her arms were bruised, most severely at the wrists where she had likely been tied up with a cord or strap. Dr. Neilson pointed to a small, purplish mark at the inside of her elbow. "This is another mark, also consistent with an injection. But it is not just an injection site. This is a vein that has had an intravenous line put in it. He must have made a few attempts at it, too, because I also found two other blown veins, one on the other arm, and one on her ankle."

"An IV? What the hell?" Dominick was confused now. "So you think he injected her with the Haldol and then gave her an IV of it? Why do both? That doesn't make much sense." He thought about the Hillside Stranglers, two murdering cousins in California who had injected Windex and other household cleaners and substances into the women they had kidnapped, just to see what would happen when they did.

"No. No, that wouldn't make any sense at all." Dr. Neilson was getting increasingly irritated. There was no time for this. He tapped his foot on the tile, gritted his teeth, and continued. "So I went looking and I ran some more tests and I found something else. Something I never would have thought of looking for before. Something that would definitely explain the use of an IV!"

"What? What the hell is it?" Manny sounded grumpy. He didn't feel that this was either the time or place for the tension or enthusiasm of Alex Trebek and his Final Jeopardy question.

Dr. Neilson focused his attention on Dominick now. "I ran another tox screen and found another drug in her system," he said quickly. "Mivacurium chloride."

"Mivacurium chloride? What's that?" asked Dominick.

"The brand name is Mivacron, and it can only be administered intravenously. It's a skeletal muscle relaxant and that's all. Originally, it was developed as an anesthetic and muscle relaxant for use during surgery. But then it was quickly discovered after a trial run on some patients in Africa that while it indeed was an effective muscle relaxant, it unfortunately had no anesthetic or analgesic effect. This problem, though, was not realized until *after* the surgery and *after* the muscle relaxant effects had worn off and the patients were actually able to speak again. Those who lived through the surgery, anyway. Because that was when the patients told them that they had indeed felt pain during the operation. The entire time."

"But they just couldn't say anything . . ." Dominick's voice trailed off as he began to understand the enormity of the conversation he was having.

"That is correct. Their tongues and facial muscles were paralyzed, and they could not speak." He waited a few moments for them to fully absorb the information he had just given them. From the looks on their faces, they did. Finally, he had stunned both Starsky and Hutch. Then he said rather brightly, "I must say, what an ingenious sadist you have captured!"

"How much did you find in her, can you tell?"

"I can't give you an amount. On the haloperidol, she had some pretty decent levels. I think he was maintaining her on that to keep her subdued for a while before her death. On the mivacurium chloride—enough to have paralyzed her completely, I suppose. But remember, Mivacron has no effect on consciousness, so she would have been awake, but unable to move. It is a very short-acting drug, and doesn't last long, which is why it must be administered intravenously and has a very short half-life after death, so she probably expired while she was still hooked up to the IV line. That explains why the bruise is so fresh. It happened right before death."

"So this psycho—and he really is a psycho, I guess, being on this haloperidol—" Dominick began, anger cutting his words. Anger at the whole incredible sick picture that was starting to form now in his head. As if the death of this young woman wasn't tragic enough. Or violent enough. *Look, folks, there's more to come! Stay tuned!* He stopped his thought in midsentence to ask, "What does that mean, anyway, Dr. Neilson? Was he a schizo, or a manic-depressive, or a psychopath? What does that mean, the fact that he was prescribed this Haldol?"

"I'm not a psychiatrist, Agent Falconetti. I can't give you a diagnosis off the cuff. Haloperidol is prescribed for several different psychiatric conditions."

"Oh shit. Here comes the NGI," said Manny. NGI stood for Not Guilty by Reason of Insanity. A plea of insanity was a virtual shoo-in for a defendant with a proven history of mental illness, particularly if it involved paranoid schizophrenia or manic depression or previously substantiated psychotic breaks. If it could then be shown that a defendant was so demented as to not understand the nature or consequences of his actions or discern right from wrong, then the State Attorney could stipulate to the court that he was NGI or a jury could find him NGI. No one wanted that. Skip the *Go Directly to Jail* card and head for the local feel-good looney bin instead. There was no minimum sentence. He could not be locked up necessarily for life. If he regained his sanity, he could be released. It was as simple as that. With a little luck and enough money to buy a few favorable psych exams, one just might be able to buy oneself a ticket back home to suburbia in ten years or so.

Dominick began to play out in his mind the final minutes of poor Anna Prado's short, pretty life. He remembered how her blue eyes stared out at him from the trunk, the terror that they had witnessed in their final moments forever caught in those eyes. Now it was he, not just Manny, who felt sick to his stomach. He stammered for a moment, trying to collect his thoughts, to comprehend the incomprehensible, slowly vocalizing the scenario that played now like a scene from a horror movie in his head.

"So this psycho gives this girl the Haldol that was originally prescribed for him. It knocks her into a catatonic sort of stupor and he then just ushers her right out the door of Level. Right under the noses of a hundred witnesses, half of whom are probably either coked out or drunk themselves and wouldn't notice if their own date was a serial killer. Once he gets her out of there, he keeps her stashed somewhere in la-la land for a while, hooked on that crap through injections or pills, while he just fucks with her. And after he's had his fun for a few days or maybe even a few weeks, and played his games and probably raped her sixteen different ways from Sunday, he lets her wake up and come around again for the grand finale. Then he hooks her up to an IV and gives her a good dose of a drug that completely paralyzes every muscle in her body, but it unfortunately doesn't render her unconscious and she can still feel the excruciating pain while he slices her chest open with a scalpel blade, cracks her sternum, and cuts out her heart. Goddamn it. This one sounds even worse than Bundy or Rolling."

Dr. Neilson piped up again. Fortunately his voice no longer had the same bubbly enthusiasm it did five minutes earlier, or else even Dominick would have hit him, or at least held him down for Manny. "I also found evidence of an adhesive residue on her eyelids, and many of the eyelashes were stripped from both of her lids."

"What does that mean?"

"I believe he taped her eyelids open as well."

"So he made her watch him while he did it? While he tore her heart out? Jesus-fucking-Christ." Dominick shook his head, trying to force that very last image out of his head. "It's a good thing we nailed this guy, Bear."

Manny looked down at Anna Prado's naked, broken body. She was someone's daughter, someone's sister, someone's girlfriend. A girl who was once pretty enough to have been a professional model. Now, industrial-strength black thread held the skin on her chest back together from her navel to her neck and then under her breasts, forming a zigzag black cross, and covering the hole where her heart had been.

"I hate the fucking ME's office" was all Manny could manage to say.

34

134-05 DAHLIA STREET, Apt. 13, Flushing, Queens County, New York.

There it was in black and white. Right there in front of her on the AutoTrack that Dominick had given her last night. William Rupert Bantling's address as it appeared on his New York State driver's license from April of 1987 to April of 1989. A bus ride away from St. John's, a ten-minute car ride down Northern Boulevard to her apartment on Rocky Hill Road, and exactly one block away from the Bally's on Main Street and 135th where she used to work out.

C.J. leaned back in her chair and exhaled a deep breath. Even though she had known deep down in her gut that it was Bantling from the moment she heard his sick voice in the courtroom, she now felt a strange sense of both relief and validation at having been right. To know she wasn't going crazy again. That the voice was real and she wasn't acting paranoid. The connection she had found was more than just coincidence; it was corroboration in black-and-white print.

He had lived just a few miles from her house, just one block from her gym. She remembered his words to her that night, his snicker of delight as he whispered them in her ear.

I'll always be watching you, Chloe. Always. You can't get away from me, 'cause I'll always find you.

And he had said that because, she realized, he physically could watch her. Probably at the gym. Maybe on the subway. Maybe at the Peking House, her favorite Chinese restaurant in Flushing, or Tony's, her favorite pizza place on Bell Boulevard in Bayside. It could have been anywhere, because he was there, just down the road, the whole time. Her mind raced back in time twelve years to remember the face she now knew—somewhere, anywhere, in her life, but she still drew a blank.

A loud thud and jingle sounded at the door, and before she could say "Come in," the door was flung open and Marisol appeared in the doorway. The jingle was from the seventeen gold bracelets that she wore on her wrist.

"You wanted to see me?" she asked.

"Yes. I want to go over the profiles that need to be scheduled all of next week on the Cupid case." She handed her Bantling's pink arrest form. Next to each of the officer's names, she had noted a date and time for their profiles. She had scheduled Dominick toward the end of the week, even though he was the lead investigator on the case and would normally go first. She had made yet another decision today since her session with Dr. Chambers. The first was to go forward on this case to the best of her ability and prepare it for prosecution, one step at a time. And the other was that this was not the time in her life for a relationship with anyone, especially the lead agent on a high-profile case with a defendant who was much more than just a defendant. She needed to get some distance back between them, retreat to professional ground only. No matter what her feelings were for Dominick, no matter what they could be for him, there were too many secrets that could never be shared. And a relationship based on deception and lies is just like a house of cards in the end. Eventually it all comes tumbling down.

"We're running on a tight time crunch, Marisol, and we've got a lot of witnesses." She figured she would try the team approach. "We've got to take this before the grand jury in two weeks. I've noted the dates and preferred times for each officer. Set me up for forty-five minutes with each officer, and three hours with Alvarez and Falconetti."

Marisol reached for the arrest form. "Okay. I'll set them up. You need anything else? It's almost four-thirty."

That's right. The fleeing hour. C.J. had almost forgotten. Come hell or high water, Marisol did not work past 4:30.

"Yes. I have a ton of research to do for the next couple of days. In fact, I'll probably be here pretty late tonight doing it. I need you to reset tomorrow morning's next-of-kin meeting on the Wilkerson case, and the pretrial conference with Detectives Muñoz and Hogan on the Valdon case in the afternoon. We still have two weeks on Valdon before trial. Reset them to next Friday. Oh, and I would really appreciate it if for the next few days, unless it's the State Attorney himself or the building is on fire, you could just take messages from anyone who calls." She smiled, wondering if she could actually get Marisol to laugh.

Apparently not. "Fine" was all Marisol said before plugging back down the hall to her desk, all the while mumbling Spanish curse words that C.J. could hear even through the door that Marisol had closed behind her with a very loud thud. Of course, C.J. doubted that Marisol would bother to tell her if there really was a fire in the building, such was the price of their rocky relationship, but as far as she knew the smoke alarms worked and it was only a two-floor jump anyway. So much for the team approach.

She sat alone now in her office, in her fake burgundy leather chair, and stared out the window, across the street to the courthouse and the Dade County Jail, or DCJ as it was known, where right now her rapist was being held without bond, a prisoner of the State of Florida, a guest of the Department of Corrections. She sipped on her cold coffee and watched as prosecutors returned from court for the day, some with files in their hands, others dragging boxes behind them, pulled on collapsible dollies. After her session with Dr. Chambers today, the thick, blinding fog that had enveloped her thoughts for the past forty-eight hours had begun to clear, and things were again making sense, coming back into perspective. She felt a purpose now, a direction to follow, even if it later proved to be the wrong way.

Although she knew that it was probably fruitless, she

called the Cold Case Squad again in New York, to see if the impossible had happened. She was not surprised to find out from the squad secretary that DNA indictments were considered experimental and, to date, had only been done so far in five cases in that squad. C.J.'s case number was not one of the five. And so it was final—prosecuting Bantling in New York would not be an option.

What she needed was answers. Answers to the many questions that had gnawed at her on the Cupid case for the past year. Answers to the questions that she had asked herself over and over again for the past twelve years about her own assault. She felt a compulsion, an overwhelming need, to know everything and anything there was to know about this stranger, this monster, Bill Bantling. Who was he? Where was he from? Was he married? Did he have children? Family? Friends? Where had he lived? What did he do for a living? How had he known his victims? Where had he met them? How had he chosen them?

How had he known Chloe Larson? How had he chosen her?

When had he become a rapist? When had he become a killer? Were there more victims? Victims that they perhaps did not know about?

Were there more victims just like her?

And then there were the whys. Why did he hate women? Why did he butcher them, torture them? Why did he take their hearts? Why did he kill? Why had he chosen them?

Why had he chosen her? Why had he left her alive?

More than a dozen years and a thousand miles separated her rape and the Cupid murders, yet she found it difficult now to distinguish the questions that needed to be asked. The lines had suddenly become blurred, the questions inextricably intertwined, the answers they demanded the same.

Where had Bantling been hiding for the past twelve years? Where had he played out his sick, disturbed fantasies? She knew from her own experience as a prosecutor of serial rapists and pedophiles, and from the countless seminars and conferences that she had attended over the years, that violent sex offenders don't just happen. Nor do they just stop. Rather, their crimes usually represent the gradual escalation and ultimate realization of their own distorted sexual fantasies. Sometimes those fantasies will take weeks, months, even years to develop in the mind before they are acted upon, and for all outside appearances, the offender will be a regular Joe Good Guy, the best neighbor, the best coworker, the best husband, the best dad. It is only inside his head, where no one can see in, that the hideous, corrosive thoughts boil and bubble, finally over-flowing in his brain, like lava, consuming all in its path, until the fantasy is realized. A "harmless" Peeping Tom becomes a burglar. A burglar becomes a rapist. A rapist graduates to murder. It is just a matter of taking the next step in the fantasy. And with every crime he commits without detection, the offender becomes more and more brazen, the once-forbidden boundaries disappear, and the next step becomes that much easier to take. And serial rapists do not stop until they are stopped. That means jail, a physical disability that actually prevents them from committing the crime, or death.

Bantling fit the classic profile of a serial rapist. He was also a sadist, a person who derives pleasure by inflicting cruelty and pain on others. She thought back again to that stormy June night twelve years in the past, remembering the minutes that passed like hours. He had planned it all perfectly, from beginning to end, even bringing along his "bag of tricks" to live out the fantasy. Raping her had not been enough. He had needed to torture her, demean her, violate her in every way possible. Her agony had set him on fire, sexually aroused him. And yet, the most powerful weapon that he had used lay not in his bag, or in the jagged knife he wielded, but rather in the very detailed information that he had possessed about her. The intimate, per-sonal facts about her, her family, her relationships, her career—from her nickname to her favorite shampoo—that he wielded like a sword, cutting away her trust in others, shattering her confidence in a future. Chloe Larson had not been selected at random that night. She had been chosen. She had been hunted.

So if Bantling was, in fact, a serial rapist who had since

escalated to serial murder, as she believed was the case, where, then, were his other victims for the past eleven years before the Cupid abductions began in April of 1999?

Her newest neighbor across the street had lived a lot of places: New York, Los Angeles, San Diego, Chicago, Miami. She had scoured the criminal histories from every state that he had ever lived in, but there was nothing, not even as much as a traffic ticket.

On paper, Bantling appeared a model citizen. Could it be that he had lain dormant for more than a decade, bottling his anger and his fantasies deep inside, finally exploding with a merciless and savage fury as Cupid? She doubted it. The careful, meticulous planning of her assault probably meant that she was not his first victim, and his brutality with her demonstrated little self-control. He would have had difficulty controlling his fantasies, his anger, for the few months it probably took for him to stalk his next victim, and there would be no way he could have controlled himself for a decade. C.J. was not even sure if she herself was supposed to have been a murder victim, but instead had survived. *Or had he left her alive on purpose?*

She knew that the task force would be ripping Bantling's life apart, piece by piece, looking for answers as well. They, too, already had a history from every state and local jurisdiction that Bantling had ever lived in. In a matter of days, detectives would be sent all over the country to interview ex-neighbors and ex-bosses and ex-girlfriends, with the hopes of finding that Bantling had been an ax murderer in California before becoming a scalpel-wielding psycho on South Beach. His name and a description of the Cupid murders had already been run through the FBI VICAP database and Interpol, the International Police Agency, to see if any similar unsolved crimes had occurred in any other jurisdiction or country. Perhaps a sudden rash of young women disappearing in the cities that Bantling had visited on business? But there was nothing. Of course, though, the task force would be looking for a murderer.

Using Westlaw, the on-line legal research company subscribed to by the State Attorney's Office, she began her search for answers. She started with a search of old newspapers in the cities where Bantling had lived since 1988, beginning with L.A., where he had spent the majority of his time, living at two different residences in the city from 1990 through 1994. She began with the *Los Angeles Times,* first entering search terms for that period fitting the Cupid murders: *blond, women, disappeared, dismembered, mutilated, murdered, attacked, knife, tortured.* Twenty different words in twenty different combinations. She even asked the Westlaw service representative on the phone for help on how to best word the search, but there still was nothing. A few missing and murdered prostitutes, as well as several unrelated domestic incidents, and a few runaway teenagers, but nothing like Cupid. There were no missing coeds or models that looked to be related, no unsolved ritualistic murders, no severed hearts. She ran the same search in the *Chicago Tribune,* the *San Diego Times,* the *New York Times,* the *Daily News,* and the *New York Post,* but, again, there was nothing. Then she tried a new search, once again in the *Los Angeles Times.* But this one had only five search words: *women, raped, knife, clown, mask.*

Three articles came up.

In January of 1991, a female college student at the University of California at Los Angeles awoke at 3:00 A.M. in her off-campus apartment to a stranger in a rubber clown face standing over her bed. She was brutally raped, tortured, and beaten for several hours. The rapist was not identified and escaped through her first-floor window.

In July of 1993, a female bartender who had just gotten off her shift at 1:00 A.M. was surprised in her Hollywood apartment by an unidentified man in a latex clown mask. She, too, was brutally raped. She also sustained several knife wounds from her attacker, but was expected to recover, according to the article. Her assailant was not caught.

In December of 1993, a college student in Santa Barbara was found in her first-floor apartment, the victim of a heinous rape and assault by an unidentified man who had broken in through a window in the middle of the night. The perpetrator had worn a rubber clown mask. He had not been identified or captured. There were no suspects.

Three articles. Three assailants with a rubber clown mask. The same MO for all: ground-floor apartments, masked strangers, brutal rapes. It was the same rapist. She expanded her search criteria and found another case farther up the coast in San Luis Obispo with the same MO, but this rapist wore a rubber alien face mask.

Four victims. And she had just started to look. They had happened three years and four counties apart in probably three different police jurisdictions, and so no one had made the connection. She continued to search the *Times,* but found nothing that linked the cases together. Only one small two-paragraph blurb appeared as a follow-up on the female bartender from Hollywood. It ran about four days after her rape and reported that the unidentified woman had been discharged from the hospital and was recuperating with relatives. It also said that, although the police were still investigating, there had been no arrests made yet and no suspects had been identified. The public was urged to call the LAPD with any information. The *Times* had not bothered doing follow-up articles on the other three victims.

She ran the same search in the other cities Bantling had lived in before arriving in 1994 in Miami. She found a rape with the same MO by an assailant wearing an alien mask in Chicago in September of 1989, and another with a clown mask in San Diego in early 1990. Now there were six. And those were the ones that had been reported. But was it Bantling, or merely coincidence? She MapQuested Bantling's old addresses in Chicago and San Diego that appeared in his AutoTrack with the addresses of the rape victims in the two articles. He had lived no more than ten miles from each. She held her breath and checked the South Florida papers since 1994: the *Miami Herald,* the *Sun Sentinel,* the *Key West Citizen,* and the *Palm Beach Post,* but there was nothing.

She flipped through Bantling's passport, which had been surrendered to the court. Brazil, Venezuela, Argentina, Mexico, the Philippines, India, Malaysia. Bantling had traveled extensively throughout the world on business with Tommy Tan and before that, Indo Expressions, another upscale furniture design house out in California. Business trips that lasted anywhere from two weeks to a month at a time. The furniture-manufacturing plants and galleries that Bantling had visited, according to the list provided to her office by Tommy Tan, seemed to be located in poor towns on the outskirts of big cities where it was easy to remain anonymous. He had made repeat visits to many of the cities. Could he have victims overseas?

C.J. flipped through her Rolodex and found the number for Investigator Christine Frederick with Interpol Headquarters in Lyons, France. Christine and she had worked together a few years back on a murder suspect who had killed his whole family with a shotgun in a hotel room on South Beach. He had fled to the mountains of Germany where Interpol and the German police found him eating schnitzel in Munich, and Christine had helped with the extradition back to the States. They had struck up a friendship in the months that it took to finally get the guy back to Miami. It had been a long while since they had spoken.

On the first ring she got Christine's voice mail. In French, German, Spanish, Italian, and, fortunately, English. C.J. looked down at her watch. It was already 10:30 at night. She had totally lost track of time. With the time difference between them, it was barely sunrise in Lyons. She left only her name and number and hoped Christine would remember her.

It was dark out, the sun having set behind the Everglades hours ago, and her office was lit only by the banker's desk lamp with the pull-chain cord that her father had given her. The bright office fluorescents made her eyes hurt after a while, and she liked the intimacy and coziness of her desk lamp. The halls outside her closed office door were black and long since deserted. She would have to call security in the lobby downstairs to have them escort her to her car.

She turned once again to her office window and DCJ across the street, where lights burned on every floor in the building. Strange, desperate people milled about just outside the chain-link fence topped with razor wire, waiting for their boyfriend or their girlfriend or their pimp or their business associate or their mother to get booked in, or get released. Cop cars flanked the building, bringing in new criminals to replace the ones who could post bond. And in that dirty gray building of steel doors and iron-mesh windows, behind the razor wire, in the custody of the Department of Corrections, sat William Rupert Bantling. The man she had been running from, hiding from, for the past twelve years was now directly across the street from her, no less than fifty yards away. If he was near a window, he could be watching her at this very moment, just as he had promised her he always would. The thought made her shudder, and her skin went cold.

She turned her attention back to her desk to pack up her briefcase and head home. The light from her computer screen glowed brightly in the otherwise-dim office. On the screen was the last newspaper article that Westlaw had pulled up in her search. The state searched was New York. The paper was the *New York Post*. She stared at the words, but it was not necessary for her to read them. The date read June 30, 1988. And although the twenty-four-year-old rape victim's identity was not being disclosed by the paper, it made no difference. C.J. knew who she was.

She quickly pulled the chain on the banker's lamp and turned off the computer. Then she put her head in her hands, and in the darkness where no one could see in, she started to cry.

35

BY TEN MINUTES of eight on Friday morning, she was back at her desk once more. Sleep had again been fitful and completely unproductive, filled with screaming, familiar nightmares. So at 5:00 A.M., she had finally stopped staring at the red numbers on her clock and had gotten out of bed and gone to the gym, before heading back down I-95 into work.

In addition to the two messages on her office voice mail that Dominick had left for her yesterday, she had another one waiting for her last night on her answering machine at home. He wanted to know why she hadn't shown up at the ME's yesterday, and if everything was alright with her. Apparently, they also had some new developments in the case after speaking with Dr. Neilson, and he had asked her to call him when she got in.

It was so strange. Here it was, after so many years, that she had finally met someone who could be special in her life. Whom she could talk to, relate with, maybe even eventually allow into her cubbyhole life. When she talked to Dominick, the words came easily. There were no strained gaps of silence. No fluffy conversation. It was all real, every word she had shared with him in every conversation they had had, even when the subject matter was inconsequential. And it sounded silly—juvenile, perhaps—but she felt this anxious excitement just listening to him when he talked, wondering what he would say, what he would tell her. Each word, each fact, just another piece of the big zillion-piece puzzle to finding out who this man was, what he was thinking, what he was about.

She had never been physically attracted to cops. For the most part she found that too many of them were controlling, on their own personal power trips, such was the nature of their work. And C.J. was not one to be controlled. So it struck her as almost odd how different Dominick was from other cops. He was strong, but not in an overpowering way, and he was in control of every situation without being controlling. He headed a task force that under someone else's command could be full of egos, but under his they were a unified front—even with all the lights and cameras on them for the past year. She also noticed that Dominick listened before he spoke—another trait that was not too common in cops, or many men for that matter. Over the past ten months she found that they actually had a lot to say to each other outside of defendants and pretrial conferences. And, if they had been given the chance, they could have explored all the things they had discovered that they had in common—biking, traveling, the arts.

She hadn't wanted to know that much before with any man, not even Michael. With Dominick, she realized that she had almost craved that knowledge. And now that he had shown his feelings for her the other night, she thought that maybe he felt the same way about her. That perhaps he wanted to know every drop of her as she did him. And she just might have let him in, too. That's what was so hard. To sacrifice all those intense feelings and emotions before experiencing their full potential, always left to wonder what could have been. Because she just might have let him into her heart, and now that was impossible. He had become another victim in the game.

She toyed for a moment, though, with the idea of calling him back, to hear his voice, to maybe have one more grasp at the incredibly warm feeling she had experienced by the door two nights ago. But she dismissed the idea as quickly as it had come. Her decision to go forward on Cupid came with consequences. She knew that, accepted that.

Nevertheless, she had to talk to him eventually, to

regain the ground of professionalism and to go forward on this case. As she was figuring out just how to accomplish this, the phone rang.

"State Attorney's Office. ASA Townsend."

"*Bonjour,* Madame Prosecutor."

It was Christine Frederick.

"Christine? How are you?" C.J. was not even going to attempt hello in French. Everyone concerned would be better off if she didn't.

It didn't matter. The voice spoke back to her in perfect English, with just a hint of a German accent. "C. J. Townsend! Well, hello there! How are things in your sunny part of the world?"

"Sunny. How about you?"

"I always said if I was going to be a criminal, C.J., I would be a criminal in Florida. It is always so sunny and warm. Things here are good! I cannot complain. It's not too sunny, though. It has been raining a lot in the city."

"You don't want to be a criminal in Florida, Christine. Stay put on the Riviera where the international criminals are at least rich and the food is—what's that word I learned in high-school French class? *Magnifique?*"

Christine laughed. "*Très bien, mon amie!* Very good! I got your message from yesterday. Is this a good time to talk to you?"

"Yes, it is. Thanks for calling me back so quickly. I need your help with something, if I might ask. I don't want to go through Washington just yet, though, on it. I don't want anything official."

"Sure, C.J. What can I help you out with?"

"I need you to run an MO through Interpol and see if anything comes up. We've got a possible serial rapist here in Miami who has extensive travels outside the U.S., mainly to poor South American countries. Also Mexico, and the Philippines. I need to know if you have anything that matches up."

"What have you got?"

"He's a white male in his early forties. Uses a mask. He seems to prefer a clown face or an alien face, but he may use some other Halloween figure–type latex mask. Breaks

into usually ground-floor apartments and targets young
women who live alone. He seems to stalk them for a while
before he acts. His weapon of choice is a knife, and he
forcibly ties down his victims in most instances." She took
a breath and continued in what sounded, at least in her own
head, to be a calm, steady voice. "We also have evidence
that he is a sadist. He likes to torture. We have a few girls
who were cut up pretty badly, physically disfigured on their
breasts and in the vaginal area."

She could hear Christine jotting down notes on the
other side of the phone line. "Is that it?" she asked.

"Yes. Look back over the past decade. In fact, begin
with 1990. He started traveling right around then."

"How about DNA?"

"No. Nothing. No prints, semen, hair. He leaves a
squeaky-clean scene."

"Do you have a subject name for me?"

"I've already run his name through Interpol. I'm trying
something new. Do me a favor and run it through without
his name. Let's just look for similarities."

"Okay. Will do. What South American countries are we
looking at?"

C.J. picked up the photocopy of Bantling's passport and
started reading off countries. "Venezuela, Brazil,
Argentina."

"Okay. Then you said the Philippines and Mexico. Do
you want me to try anywhere else?"

"Yeah. Look at Malaysia and India."

"You got it. I'll call you back when I've got something."

"Thanks, Christine. Let me give you my cell number in
case you find something out this weekend. 954-346-7793."

"You bet. Hey, whatever happened to that guy who
killed his family while on vacation on Miami Beach? The
one we found in Germany?"

"He got the death penalty."

"Oh."

She hung up the phone and thought about Dominick's
message last night. She needed to know what she was in for
with Joe Neilson at the Medical Examiner's. So she picked

up the phone and called Manny on his Nextel, hoping that Dominick wasn't in the room with him.

"Counselor! *Buenos días!* Where were you yesterday? We missed you at the Medical Examiner's."

"Hey, Manny. Are you at the task force yet?"

"Are you kidding? I just got up maybe twenty minutes ago. I'm in my car heading down Eighth in Little Havana, looking for my morning shot."

"You sound like a junkie needing his fix, Manny. If that Café Cubano crap doesn't wake you up, nothing will."

"Tell me about it. It's gotten to the point where I can't even think without it."

"I'm about to call Neilson, but I wanted to speak with you first and find out what happened down there yesterday."

"Have you talked to Dom yet? I think he was looking for you yesterday."

A tinge of guilt ran through her, and she felt her face go hot. *What had Dominick said to him about their relationship? About the other night?* "No. Not yet. I'll try to catch up with him later."

"Oh. Well, Neilson—who is a mother-fucking freak, if you ask me. Pardon my French, Counselor—Neilson says that Prado had been shot up with haloperidol. He found decent amounts of it in her system."

"Haloperidol?"

"Yeah, the brand name is Haldol."

"Isn't that what Dominick said Bantling had a prescription for? That he found in the search of the house?"

"That's right, Counselor. Fucking psycho laid us a neat brick path right back to his door, didn't he?" She could hear loud Latin music in the background and a ton of voices chattering in what sounded like a rushed mixture of both Spanish and English. Manny was obviously on foot now, because C.J. could hear him huffing as he walked.

"Where are you, Manny?"

"I told you. I'm getting a shot." In the background she heard him say, *"Me puede dar dos cafecitos."* Then he spoke back into the phone. "Actually I'm getting *two* shots. It's gonna be a long day. I need to look my best."

The Nextels were clear. Too clear. She actually listened to him gulp down both shots, and then he let out an "Aahh" and began huffing his way back to the car, she assumed. The Latin music faded away.

"So they found Haldol in Prado's blood. Why would he have done that? What effect would that drug have had on her?" she asked. "Did Neilson tell you?"

"It's a depressant. It quiets the crazies. Docs give it to mentally ill people who are having a psychotic episode. It relaxes them, subdues them. In fact, Neilson the Super Sleuth thinks Cupid used it to relax her right out the door of Level."

"And you don't agree?"

"No, I agree. I think he may be on to something, especially if this Haldol would have the same effect as a Roofie or Liquid X. We've seen some crazy shit go down with those date-rape drugs. In front of lots of witnesses, too. Girls snuck out of clubs, practically unconscious. Fucked so many times even their grandchildren won't be virgins, and then they wake up in some roach hotel like Sleeping Beauty not remembering a thing and asking, 'Where am I?' to the pervert that raped 'em.

"It's not that I don't agree with him, Counselor. He just gives me the creeps with all that twitchin' that he does. His fucking eyes keep blinking."

"Yes. I think he may have a medical condition."

"He's still fuckin' weird, if you ask me. I didn't even tell you the good part—Neilson is happy as shit about this, too—he found this other drug in her system. Seems she had to be hooked up to an IV because that's the only way to dose it. Probably was still hooked up with this crap flowing through her veins when she died. It's called Mivacron. That's the brand name, anyway. Have you ever heard of it before?"

"No."

"Me neither. Stuff is a muscle relaxant, but it doesn't knock you out; it only paralyzes you. And here's the kicker: It has no effect on pain. You can still feel everything—but you just can't move. How's that for some sick shit? Neilson says she was hooked up to that crap when

Cupid cracked her chest and cut out her heart. Says he found evidence her eyelids had been taped open so she could watch him while he did it."

C.J. could not say anything. A scene flashed in her head. Bantling had made her open her eyes and watch him as he sliced the knife across her breast. Her hand rushed protectively to her chest, and she remembered the intense pain that had flooded her brain, the scream that she heard over and over again, but only in her head. She felt dizzy, as if she would vomit. The two cups of coffee that she had drank that morning churned in her stomach, and she quickly sat back in her chair.

There was a long silence before Manny piped back up. "Counselor? You there?"

"Yeah, Manny. I'm just thinking," she said, her voice a soft whisper. Her head was hung between her knees as she tried to get the blood flow back into her brain, to rush the images out of her mind that she could no longer bear to witness. She needed to toughen up, to be stronger. She was determined to get through this.

"I thought I might have lost you there for a sec. Neilson thinks Prado wasn't the only one he did it to, either. He's redoing tox screens on the other nine girls, now that he knows what he's looking for. He might even have some of the results back later today. Dom was going to call in if he didn't hear from him by four. You should get with him."

She sat back up in the chair. The feeling of dizziness had passed.

"I'll call Neilson myself. I want to look at Prado's body. We might need to exhume the others, the ones that weren't cremated. I also need you to get me the doctor information on Bantling's Haldol prescription. I want to find out who was treating him and for what."

"Eddie Bowman called the doc yesterday. Name is Fineberg, I think, or Feinstine. Something like that. Doc told Bowman to pound sand without a warrant. Wouldn't even acknowledge if Bantling was his patient. Doctor-freak privilege. 'Oh no, Detective, I can't tell you how many women my client has killed because that wouldn't be right! People should be able to discuss these things with their therapist without the fear that they might actually have to go to jail for cutting out a beautiful girl's heart.'"

"Alright, then. Get me the info and I'll start the warrant."

There was a long pause. C.J. heard Manny puffing away on his cigarette, with the whiz of traffic going by his car window. Finally he spoke again.

"We sure nailed one sick fuck, didn't we?"

"Yeah, we sure did, Manny," she said quietly.

"Well it's up to you now, Counselor. You better do the right thing by us all and fry this motherfucker."

36

SHE GAVE HERSELF a quick pep talk at her desk in her compact mirror and headed over to court to handle a quick matter on a case that was set for motions next Friday. She needed to get a tight grip on her emotions if she was going to continue this prosecution. Dr. Chambers was right—she probably would be seeing and hearing things on a daily basis that would cause torturous flashbacks to June 30, 1988. She already had, and each one had been a sucker punch in the stomach. The worst nightmares had already returned. What else was in store for her if she didn't control herself? Another complete breakdown? Another padded room and more psychotherapy?

It was all about control. She needed to remain in control. Control her feelings, control her emotions, keep everything in check, but be prepared for anything. *Don't let him beat you this time. Don't let him win.*

After court she headed over to the ME's to meet with Neilson and see Anna Prado's body again. She had seen it on the night Anna was found, but needed to look at the injection sites herself, see where he had run the intravenous line in her vein. She was going to be buried on Monday, and the family wanted her wake to be held on Saturday and Sunday, so this would be her last opportunity before they sent the body to the funeral home.

Manny was right. Neilson was way too enthusiastic

about his job. He hopped and twitched about the room, excitedly showing C.J. the injection sites on her buttocks, and the blown veins in her ankle and right arm, then, finally, where the line had took, allowing the Mivacron to run into her system, paralyzing her body before death.

Neilson had used the pictures that he had taken during the autopsies of the other nine victims, to locate suspicious markings that he believed were again consistent with injection sites on at least four of the bodies. The preliminary toxicology tests for haloperidol were in on six of the victims, and all were positive. The mivacurium chloride tests would take a few more days.

The living like to console themselves with the idea that when someone dies and leaves this world, his or her soul is finally "at peace." Maybe it was a coping mechanism, a way for people to avoid the cold reality that death brings, but C.J., for one, didn't believe any of it. Not that she was an atheist—she believed in God and a better place and went to church on most Sundays. But about death, she knew better than to believe people were at peace, particularly those who had died a premature, violent death, who had been robbed of life in a cruel manner, without warning. They were not at peace. They would never be at peace, always wondering why they had to leave when the thief who had stolen their life, in most instances, still got to walk the earth and kiss his mother and see his family. And now, today, it was Anna Prado's turn to see the mortician, make ready for the final party. She lay on that cold metal gurney with dried black blood in her hair, and eyelashes ripped from her lids, her chest sewn back together with black thread, the color of life drained from her face, and all C.J. could think of was how incredibly sad she looked. Sad and terrified. There would be no peace for her.

She skipped lunch, opting instead for a Coffee Coolada from Dunkin' Donuts with extra whipped cream and another pack of Marlboros. Sequestered back in her closed office that afternoon, she opened the file that contained the six different newspaper articles that she had found and printed out late last night. She needed to know for sure what had happened to those cases. It was impossible to tell from a newspaper search alone. So she started in chronological order, picked up the phone, and called the Chicago P.D.

"Records. Chicago P.D. Officer Rhonda Michaels."

"Hello, Officer Michaels. I'm a prosecutor in Miami with the Miami-Dade County State Attorney's Office, and I'm hoping you can help me. I need some information on a rape that happened many years ago in your jurisdiction and was handled by your department. But I'm afraid I only have limited information—"

"What's the case number?" Officer Michaels abruptly cut her off in a gruff, tired voice. She probably pulled hundreds of documents and records a day for people and she obviously wasn't in the mood for engaging in conversation.

"As I was saying, I don't have that. Unfortunately, all the information I have is from an old newspaper article that ran in 1989."

"Do you have a suspect's name?"

"No. From the article it appears that a suspect was never identified. That's my problem. I need to know a little more about this case, as it may relate to one that I am handling down here."

"Hmmm. No suspect name. Do you have a victim's name? I may be able to search by that."

"No. Her name wasn't in the paper."

"I don't think I'm going to be able to help you, then." There was a short pause. "Do you have the date that it happened? An address? A detective's name? What do you have?"

"Yes, I have a date, September sixteenth, nineteen eighty-nine. The address is one-one-six-two Schiller. It doesn't give an apartment number. It says here that detectives with the Chicago Police Department are investigating."

"Alright. That may be enough. Hold on. I have to run something through a system and then do some checking. This may take a while."

Exactly twelve minutes later she came back on the line. She sounded nice again.

"I've got it. The number on the police report is

F8922234X. Three pages. The victim's name was Wilma Barrett, twenty-nine. Raped and assaulted in her first-floor apartment, Apartment 1A, it says. Is that what you are looking for?"

"Yes. That must be it. Can you tell me whatever happened to that case? Was it ever solved?"

"Hold on, let me take a look at the history. No. No, it was never solved. No arrests were made. The detective that was assigned to it was Brena, Dean Brena. He might still be around. Of course, there are thousands of officers with our department and I don't know them all, and that was a long time ago. Do you want me to transfer you to Sex Crimes?"

"Not right now. I first need to look at that police report to see if it is even related to the one I am handling here. Can you fax my office a copy?"

"Sure can. It'll probably take a couple of minutes, though. What's your number?"

C.J. gave her the number and dashed out to the fax machine to wait for it to come through. The secretarial pool, where both the fax machine and Marisol were located, was a maze of about ten desk units separated from each other by Formica half-wall partitions. It was located in the center of the Major Crimes Unit, surrounded on all sides by short hallways that ran to the window offices of the Major Crimes prosecutors, and a long hallway that ran out to the security access doors and the elevator bay.

C.J. felt like the fat kid who shows up uninvited at a summer pool party in jeans and a parka. She knew she did not belong in the maze. The laughter and chat that had gone on unchecked just seconds before her presence was detected immediately ceased when she was spotted waiting at the fax machine. A silent alert rippled through the pool, and the laughter and chat were replaced by an uncomfortable silence.

There existed within the State Attorney's Office, as, she supposed, existed in other corporations and offices as well, an unspoken sort of social order among the workers. Administration socialized with administration, attorneys socialized with attorneys, and the secretaries, victim witness coordinators, and paralegals socialized with the secretaries, victim witness coordinators, and paralegals. Breaking ranks was not unheard of, but it certainly was uncommon and infrequent. And C.J. had three strikes against her. As an assistant chief, she was a member of administration, and, of course, as a prosecutor, she was an attorney. She was also Marisol's boss and although that would drive any normal person perhaps to the bottle, Marisol was still a member of the pool and the wagons closed around her protectively just the same. So when C.J. entered the maze, the enemy was watching, and shoptalk just shut down as quickly as it had set up.

She smiled awkward smiles at the secretaries who glanced over at her, while silently praying for the fax to come through, and most of them smiled awkward smiles right back at her. After a short eternity, the machine finally beeped and the five-page fax came through. Behind a final awkward smile of good-bye, she retreated back into her office and closed the door again.

By seven o'clock that night she had spoken to the records departments of all six different police departments and had gotten a copy of each police report faxed to her.

It was as if she were rereading an account from her own rape six times over. The method of entry was the same in each one: always a first-floor apartment, always in the middle of the night while the victim was sleeping. The modus operandi was the same: the victims tied down and gagged first, then assaulted by a muscular stranger in a latex clown mask with shaggy red polyester hair and eyebrows and a huge red smile or a latex alien mask with black eyes and a glowing mouth. His weapon had been a jagged knife that he had used to subdue them, and also to terrorize. His tools of torture differed with each victim, but each had left their scars. Victims described being raped with beer bottles, twisted metal objects, hairbrushes. Each woman was physically maimed, suffering substantial trauma to her vaginal area and uterus, her breasts disfigured with his jagged knife, but he had left no trace of himself behind. No semen, no hair, no fibers, no prints, no physical evidence whatsoever. Completely clean, completely untraceable scenes.

However, it was not in the physical similarities of each crime scene that she came to know with certainty that it was Bantling, but in the personal, private, simple details that the rapist knew about each woman. The intimate details that were used like a weapon, a form of torture themselves. Favorite restaurants, perfumes, soap brands. Dress sizes and designers, work hours and boyfriends' names. For the college student from UCLA, he knew every grade she had received in college; for the bartender in Hollywood, he knew the exact amount of her Visa bill for the preceding three months. Birthdays, anniversaries, nicknames.

It was Bantling, of that she had no doubt. Not anymore. None of the cases were ever solved, none were ever linked. There had been no arrests, no leads, no suspects. Until now.

But would that even matter anymore? Her thoughts ran to the conversation she had had with Bob Schurr at the Queens County District Attorney's Office just two days ago. She was almost afraid to know the answer that she already suspected. Even if a case could be made—which, she knew as a prosecutor, did not look hopeful given the lack of physical evidence cited in each case—but supposing each victim was still willing to testify, would the very notion of commencing a prosecution be quashed by the statute of limitations? The rape in Chicago had occurred more than a decade ago. She doubted that there would be any time left, and, in fact, wasn't very surprised when she pulled up the Illinois state statutes on Westlaw and learned that ten years was the limit. Like hers, that case was gone, no matter what.

But the last California rape had happened on March 23, 1994, just a little over six years ago. She knew that in recent years, some states had changed their statutes of limitations and had enacted lengthier time limits on certain sex crimes. California was definitely one of the most liberal states. There may be some time left after all on these cases. She pulled up the California Code at the California state legislature Web site and searched the state statutes for the statute of limitations on sexual batteries. She almost wanted to cry when she read the answer.

Six years from the date of the crime. She was five months too late.

37

DOMINICK SPENT THE weekend interviewing present and former bosses, co-workers, neighbors, and girlfriends of William Bantling. Trying to figure out who Bantling was, and how no one was able to notice that he was not like them, that he was in fact an inhuman monster. A wolf living, working, playing among sheep, picking them off one by one, but no one—not even the shepherd—had ever noticed his clawed feet, or big ears, or razor-sharp teeth.

Although most of the original interviews had already been done by other task force members within the first forty-eight hours after Anna Prado's body was found, he felt it necessary after a few days to go back to each witness. The detectives had done a thorough job, but he liked to give people a day or two after their initial statements to absorb what had happened, think about it all. Usually after a few days they came to think of other things they hadn't thought of before that now, in hindsight, probably looked suspicious or out of place.

Now that I come to think of it, Agent Falconetti, my nice neighbor Bill always seemed to like to move his large rolled-up Oriental rugs from his house to his car at three A.M. Do you think that might be something?

After a few more weeks, he would go back over and see them all again in person and repeat the process. He had found that if you scrape the bottom of the river enough times, sometimes you find gold.

Bantling was born in Cambridge, England, on August 6, 1959, to Alice, a homemaker, and Frank, a carpenter. He had moved to New York in 1982 to attend college at FIT, the Fashion Institute of Technology, which he graduated from in 1987 with a degree in interior design. He had held a few assistant jobs with small interior design companies in and around the New York City area for the first couple of years after graduation, bouncing from job to job before moving to Chicago in 1989 to accept a position as a designer with a small furniture design company. In eight months, that company had gone bankrupt, and by December of 1989 he had landed a sales job at Indo Expressions, a furniture design company based out of L.A. He had stayed with them out in California for five years, moving to Miami in June of 1994 and hooking up with Tommy Tan Designs out on SoBe.

Neighbors on LaGorce all said the same basic thing: *He seemed like a nice-enough guy, but I didn't know him.* He was described by coworkers as a diligent, hard salesman. Charming with customers, lethal as a snake in negotiations behind closed doors. He had not made many friends it seemed so far—none in fact—just a series of acquaintances who all said they did not know him very well at all. Dominick found that to be a common problem, though, in homicide investigations. When someone finds out that their best friend is a serial killer, they usually don't want to admit they even knew the guy, much less that they were best buddies. It creates a bit of a social stigma. But if what the neighbors and coworkers and associates were all saying was taken to be true, then Bantling was indeed a loner.

The only exception to the social stigma caveat was Tommy Tan, Bantling's boss in Miami for the past six years. Dominick had spoken with Tan twice himself. Shocked to find out his best employee was a suspect in a string of serial homicides was not quite the word Dominick would use. *Devastated* was more like it. Tan had broken down and cried, fortunately choosing, instead of

Dominick, Hector, one of his assistants, to lean on for comfort during the first interview, and Juan, another assistant, during the second. Other than acknowledging that Bantling was a bit arrogant, a character trait Tan found to be "strong and exciting," he had nothing but praise for Bantling, who had been his top sales agent, finding "magnificent, hidden gems throughout the world." Magnificent gems bought for pennies from the Third World and resold to the trendy, artsy, capitalistic world for thousands. Tan was a rich man. No wonder he had loved Bantling so much.

Although Dominick had asked the question, Tan denied any sexual relationship between him and Bantling and swore that Bantling was straight. In fact, he insisted that Bantling always had a girl on his arm, in his car, out clubbing on SoBe. They were always very pretty and flashy, real head-turners. And he seemed to prefer blondes, too. At that, Tan had again thrown himself in tears onto Juan's pink Versace-clad chest and Dominick had called it quits on the interview.

There had been no Mrs. Bantlings, not even a potential future Mrs. Bantling, and, as far as the task force had found out, there were no little Bantlings running around anywhere either. Bantling had had his share of girlfriends, for sure, most of whom the task force were still trying to track down. But none seemed to last beyond a date or two, and for good reason. From the six or seven who had been interviewed so far, the task force had learned a lot. Bantling was definitely kinky. Whips, chains, bondage, sadomasochistic paraphernalia, video recorders. It spooked most of the girls whom they had spoken with, even though they'd all been around the block more than a few times and, Dominick was sure, were used to seeing some interesting things in the bedroom. But they all had a common opinion about Bill Bantling: His was a true night-and-day personality. Quite the gentleman over expensive dinners. Quite the asshole in bed. Three of the girls whom they had interviewed had shown up starring in a couple of the homemade movies that Eddie Bowman and Chris Masterson had found in Bantling's bedroom. When a few of the girls had balked at what even they perceived to be his over-the-line ideas of sex, he got angry and kicked them out of the house, not even bothering to call them a cab or drive them home. He had even thrown one girl right out on his neatly manicured front lawn stark naked and crying, leaving her to pound on the neighbor's door for some clothes and a phone call.

Come to think of it now, Agent Falconetti, you're right! Maybe there was something a bit strange about my neighbor Bill!

He had no family here in the States, and his parents had both died five years ago in a car crash in London. The media had beaten the task force members to the friends and family left in England, but no one really seemed to even remember the boy they described as quiet and surly. There were no friends from elementary school, no buddies around town. There was no one.

On Saturday night, Dominick and Manny had hit the clubs where all the girls from The Wall were last seen: Crobar, Liquid, Roomy, Bar Room, Level, Amnesia. They reinterviewed all the bartenders and lounge staff, this time equipped with a color lineup. Bantling, they knew already, was known for clubbing. And several of the wait staff definitely recognized him as a frequent customer. Always dressed to the nines and always with a different, young, pretty blonde. No one, unfortunately though, could place him with any of the victims from The Wall, and no one could place him definitively in the right club on the right night when any one of the victims had disappeared.

He fit the description that Agent Elizabeth Ambrose, the FDLE profiler, had prepared when they were looking to develop a Cupid suspect after the first three murders: a white male twenty-five to fifty-five, a loner, probably average-to-good-looking, intelligent, employed in a high-pressure professional position. Of course, that profile also fit a lot of other men he knew, including himself. Still, the pieces were all beginning to fit into place, the case was being made, fact by fact by fact. A neat stack of facts that, when stapled together, would read like a good book. The girlfriends painted Bantling as a sexual deviant, an arrogant, angry narcissist who did not handle rejection well. He exhibited sadistic, violent behavior and had a thing for blond women. He was known to frequent all the clubs where his victims disappeared from. The prescription for Haldol connected him with the narcotic found in the systems of at least six of his victims. He practiced taxidermy as a hobby—the art of gutting and stuffing animals to mount them—and thus worked with straight-edge razors and scalpels. Human blood that Dominick was sure would turn out to be Anna Prado's had been found in the shed of his home, on a probable murder weapon in that shed: her mutilated body found stuffed in his trunk.

What had caused this otherwise good-looking, wealthy, successful man to go so wrong was anyone's guess, but Dominick didn't need to prove that to make his case. The reasons why didn't matter so much, as long as they did not bring with them the plea of insanity. Because the murders were so bizarre and heinous, the jury just might think that there was no way that a human being could actually commit them, unless he was insane; add to that scenario a defendant with a history of mental illness, and the prosecution could have themselves a definite problem. So Dominick's job was not just to provide evidence that Bantling had committed murder, but gather facts that would prove that Bantling knew exactly what he was doing when he did it. That he understood perfectly the consequences of his actions, the difference between right and wrong. That he did not torture and kill ten women because he was mentally insane, but simply because he was evil.

Now, at 10:00 on Sunday night, he sat back once again in the dark task force offices at FDLE, staring at the images collected on The Wall, trying to find all the facts he needed, trying to write the book. Almost 70 interviews had been completed since Tuesday, 3 search warrants executed, 174 boxes of evidence seized from Bantling's house and cars, hundreds of man-hours put into the investigation.

You just had to know where to look.

His eyes went back to the aerial maps, the blue pins that showed the locations where each girl had been discovered. *Why had Bantling chosen those locations? What did they mean to him?*

He massaged his brow with his fingers, and looked over

at his cell phone, wanting to dial her number, but knowing he wouldn't. He had not heard from C.J. since Wednesday night. She had not returned his calls or his beeps, and he was no stalker, so by yesterday he had stopped leaving them. She was obviously going through something that she didn't want to let him in on, and he'd obviously been way off target about the two of them. He was a big boy, he could handle her rejection, but now he was afraid that this rift was going to damage the case, and he was quite sure that neither of them wanted that. He needed to figure out a way that they could just get back to where they were on a friendly, professional level.

But he sensed that there was more to C. J. Townsend— that he had seen more, felt more, that night in her apartment—than she cared for him to see. He had held her in his arms, knowing that something was terribly wrong in her life, wanting to fix it for her. He had seen her vulnerable and scared—completely defenseless, a side of her he was sure she wanted no one ever to see. And having been witness to it, he was sure she was now finding it difficult just to face him again.

What had made her so afraid, in the courtroom, in the apartment? Was it Bantling? Did this case have a different, special meaning to her for some reason? He had seen her try difficult, complex, very violent cases before. She was always in control, always in command. Not now—now she was scared and anxious. *What made this case so different for her?*

And why did he care so much?

38

OFFICER VICTOR CHAVEZ stood in the doorway and rapped loudly on her office door at exactly ten past nine on Monday morning. He was already ten minutes late.

"ASA Townsend? C. J. Townsend?"

C.J. was seated behind her desk, where she had been since 7:00 that morning. She looked up and saw the young rookie in her doorway, holding the prefile subpoena that had been sent to him. Behind him in the hall stood two other Miami Beach cops in uniform. On one shoulder she recognized sergeant stripes.

"We're here for our prefiles," said the striped shoulder as he pushed his way past Chavez, who had stalled in the door frame and had yet to actually enter her office. "Lou Ribero," he said, extending his hand across her desk. He nodded behind him. "This is Sonny Lindeman and Victor Chavez. Sorry we're a little late. Traffic."

"I thought I had scheduled all your prefiles separately, Sergeant Ribero. At least that's what I told my secretary to do." C.J. shook his hand, frowned, and looked down at her day calendar as murderous thoughts flooded her vision. She envisioned Marisol's thick neck in her hands the next time she saw her in the bathroom.

"Yeah, you did, but well, all of us were there on the scene on Tuesday, and we all came together, so we figured we'd do it together, if it's no big deal. We do joint prefiles all the time. Saves everyone some time."

Her hands released Marisol's throat. "Thanks, Sergeant, but I prefer to prefile all my witnesses separately. I think I've got you at ten-thirty and Officer Lindeman at eleven forty-five. Why don't you both head to the Pickle Barrel and I'll beep you when Officer Chavez and I are done? I'll try to finish you all up early, if I can," she said.

The young man in the doorway finally stepped forward into the room. "Hello, ma'am," he said and nodded. "Victor Chavez."

C.J. immediately felt old. She *could,* by a very wild stretch of the imagination, be this guy's mother, he looked that young. And with the lack of sleep she'd had in the past week, she probably looked that old. He couldn't be a day past nineteen.

"Have a seat, Officer Chavez. And, please Sergeant, close the door behind you."

"Alright, then," said Ribero, carefully eyeing the back of Victor Chavez's head. "Have fun, Victor. We'll see you soon."

"Thanks, Sarge." Chavez flopped down and took an easy seat in one of her fake-leather chairs. He was a good-looking guy, no doubt, with olive skin and smooth features. She could tell from the size of his forearms in his short-sleeved uniform that he worked out. A lot. His jet-black hair was cut in the close-cropped style that rookies had to wear in the academy, and she wondered how long he had been out. His gum cracked as he looked around her office. C.J. thought he looked maybe a little too comfortable.

"Raise your right hand, please," she said. "Do you swear to tell the truth, the whole truth, and nothing but the truth so help you God?"

"I do," he said and dropped his hand. In his lap he held a notebook, the arrest form, and a police report. He crossed his ankle casually across his knee, and C.J. spotted his ankle holster, which was, she suspected, exactly what he wanted her to see. Those were not department issued, only his side arm was. *Great. A cowboy.*

She pulled out her legal pad. "Officer Chavez, have you given a prefile before? Are you comfortable?"

"Yes, ma'am. I've actually given a few before."

"Okay, then let's do the preliminaries. And stop calling me ma'am. It ages me." She smiled. "How long have you been a police officer?"

"Since February."

"February of what year?"

"This year."

"Two thousand?"

"Yes."

"Are you off probation yet?"

"No. I have four more months to go."

"Do you work with an FTO?" FTO stood for Field Training Officer.

"Nope. That ended in August. I'm in my own car since then."

"When did you graduate from the police academy? January?"

"Yes, ma'am." *Not just a rookie. A newborn.*

"Look, Officer Chavez, we're going to get along just great if you stop calling me ma'am." She smiled at him again, but this one was not as friendly.

He smiled a full smile of white teeth back at her. "Okay. I got you this time."

"Alright, then, let's get to Tuesday the nineteenth. You were the one who pulled over William Bantling. Can you tell me what happened that evening?"

"Yep. I was in my car and I saw this black Jaguar go speeding past me, doing maybe thirty-five, forty miles per hour. So I pulled him over."

This was going to take some work. "Thank you. That was very informative, but I think I'm going to need a few more details."

She watched him for a moment. He was fidgety, playing with the shoelace on his shiny black uniform shoes, and although he was trying to come off to her as cool, calm, and collected, she could see underneath that he was very tense. This was, without a doubt, the biggest case his short seven-month career had ever seen. He had a right to be nervous, she supposed. But she also unfortunately detected in him more than just a hint of arrogance, a smirk behind the bright smile. She found that rookies right out of the academy usually went in one of two directions the first year. They were either total dependents: never taking the initiative, waiting for instructions, constantly asking questions of their superiors, unsure of themselves and what needed to be done in a situation. Or they were Rambos: totally independent, know-it-alls, don't-have-to-ask-a-thing types. The latter category—the ones already packed for their power trip, with mega-egos—were the ones of whom she had grown most wary. Inexperience bred mistakes, no matter what, and she accepted that, but the Rambos—although inevitably being the ones who made the most mistakes—never cared to own up to them.

"Were you on patrol alone that night?"

"Yes."

"Where?"

"Washington and Sixth."

"In a marked unit?"

"Yep."

"Is that when you first saw the Jaguar?"

"Yep."

"Where?"

"Speeding down Washington toward the MacArthur Causeway."

"Heading south?"

"Yeah."

"Were you using a radar gun?"

"Nope."

"Then how could you tell he was speeding?"

"He was weaving in and out of traffic in an unsafe manner at a speed that I could visually tell from my training and experience was higher than the posted limit of twenty-five miles per hour."

Taken straight out of the *How to Properly Word Trial Testimony If You're a Cop* textbook.

"How fast was he traveling?"

"I approximated it to be about thirty-five, maybe forty miles an hour."

"Okay. What did you do then?"

"I followed the vehicle onto the MacArthur Causeway, heading west toward the city, where I eventually pulled him over."

The MacArthur Causeway, which ran from the beach to downtown, was about two miles long. "Officer Chavez, Bantling was pulled over at almost the very end of the causeway, was he not? Right across from the *Herald* offices?"

"Yes."

"That's a pretty good distance from Washington. Was this a high-speed chase, Officer?"

"No. I wouldn't say high speed."

Of course not. High-speed chases were not permitted in the Miami Beach Police Department unless in pursuit of a fleeing violent felon. And only then with approval from a sergeant. That being said, they happened all the time anyway. "Okay. If not high speed, what speed would you put it at?"

"I'd say maybe fifty-five to sixty mph on the causeway."

"So you're basically telling me that you were *following* this guy on the causeway and doing the speed limit with your lights and sirens on until he finally just pulls over?"

"Yeah. But I don't think I had my sirens on, maybe just my lights."

"Did you call for backup at this time?"

"No."

"Why not? This guy has been going since Washington, heading straight out of the Miami Beach limits and you didn't call anyone?"

"No, no." Officer Chavez now began to look uncomfortable. He uncrossed his legs and shifted in his seat.

"How did you finally get him to pull over?"

"He just did. Right there on the side of the causeway."

This was beginning to sound interesting. Too interesting.

"Would you consider this a chase, Officer?"

"No. Look, he might not even have seen me in his rearview. Maybe that's why he didn't pull over right away. All I know is that he finally did."

"Okay. What happened when he finally pulled over? What did you do?"

"I got out of the car and asked him for his license and registration, which he gave me. I asked him what his hurry was, where he was headed to, and he told me he was going to the airport and that he had a plane to catch. Then I asked him where he was going to and he didn't answer me. I saw one bag in the backseat and I asked him if he had any luggage in his trunk and he still didn't answer me. Then I asked him if I could maybe look in the trunk, and he told me no. So I headed back to my car to write the guy a ticket for speeding. And for this broken taillight that he had."

"Let me understand this. This guy whom you've been chasing for a couple of miles—okay, *following* for a couple of miles—tells you to pound sand when you ask to look in his trunk and you just shrug it off and head back to your car to write the ticket?"

"Yes."

Never happened. No Beach cop that she had ever met took it that nicely when a person he's just pulled over won't let him look in the trunk. Forget whether they even had probable cause to look in the trunk in the first place.

"Okay. Then what?"

"Then I'm heading to my car and I pass the trunk and I smell this smell. This rotten smell, like maybe, maybe a dead body or something.

"So I ask the guy again for consent and he tells me no, that he's got to go. So I tell him he's not going nowhere. And I call for K-9 units to respond. FHP shows up, along with Beauchamp from the Beach and his dog Butch. Butch goes nuts on the trunk, and so we popped it. The rest is history. There's a dead body inside with her chest cut open, and I know we just nailed Cupid. I tell this Bantling to get the hell out of the car, and we all just waited for about six minutes on the causeway while the whole world showed up."

C.J. read the arrest form again. Then she remembered what Manny had told her after she was called out on the warrants on Tuesday night, and she knew she had more than a little problem on her hands.

"Where were you again when you first spotted Bantling's car, Officer Chavez?"

"I was on Washington and Sixth."

"Was your car on Washington or on Sixth?"

"Sixth. I was sitting on Sixth when I saw him go by."

"But on Washington, Sixth is a one-way, Officer Chavez. It only heads east. If you were watching Washington, you must have been facing west."

Chavez shifted again. It was obvious he was uncomfortable, but he never missed a beat. "Yeah, I was on the corner of Sixth facing the wrong way when I saw the car go by. I do it all the time. Great way to catch speeders. They don't expect you to be there."

"And when you saw him heading south toward the causeway, you pulled right out after him?"

"Yeah."

"Never lost him?"

"Nope."

"Okay. Now that we both know you're lying, Officer Chavez, why don't you tell me what really happened?"

39

SIXTH STREET WAS not only a one-way street, it was also not a through street. Even if Chavez was facing west, the wrong way, small cement pilings prevented his turning left, or south, onto Washington. He would have needed to turn north on Washington and make a U-turn a block or two up. There was no way that he could have kept that Jag in his sights, assuming he had ever even seen it speeding in the first place.

Chavez was now visibly shaken. His face was red. She had caught him, and he knew it.

"Look. Alright. I was sitting on Sixth. I saw the Jag and I headed down Sixth to Collins. I made a quick right and went back up Fifth straight to the causeway. I only lost him for a minute, if that's what you're getting at."

"Wait. Wait. You headed back down Sixth?"

"Yes."

"So you were never facing the wrong way at all, were you? You were never even watching Washington?" She could not believe the words she was hearing. She stood up and leaned over the desk, her voice shaking with anger. "So help me, Officer, I am about to have your badge. You are under oath and I want the truth, you got that? Or else I'll be talking to your cheap PBA lawyer while you're kissing your youth good-bye in a crowded cell at South Florida Reception!"

There was a long silence. The arrogance was all but gone now, the air let out of the balloon. Chavez's brow was furrowed, his eyes dark. He finally looked worried.

"Jesus Christ, I never knew this was going to be this, this . . . big case! How the fuck was I supposed to know this guy would turn out to be Cupid?" He pulled his hands through his hair, and C.J. sensed that her case was about to fall apart. "Alright. Look, I was on Sixth, out of my car on the corner, talking with some tourist kids who were having some words or something. I got this radio call. Some anonymous tip had just come in about this guy running dope out of the back of his car. Caller said a late-model black Jag XJ8 was heading south down Washington. The dope was in the trunk."

"An anonymous tip?" C.J. was stunned. This was the first she had heard of such a thing.

"Yeah. Tipster said he had two kilos of cocaine in the trunk and was heading for the airport. So I see this Jag go by me, I say *adiós* to the fighting friends, and hop in my car down Sixth to Collins. I swing up Fifth, but he's gone. I knew he must've headed for the causeway over to the airport, so I hop on the MacArthur and about a mile or so up, past Star Island I see him. Just as calm as a fucking cucumber. I'm thinking, you know, this jerkoff's just gonna hightail it the hell out of Dodge, all cool and shit, not even breaking fifty-five. So before he can get off the Beach limits and I lose jurisdiction on him, I pull him over."

C.J. sat back in her chair. Her mouth was dry, her heart pounding in her chest. This was not good. "So you never saw him speeding? You pulled him over based on this anonymous tip, and that's it?"

Chavez said nothing, just looked down at the paperwork, which was still on his lap.

"What exactly did the tip say?"

"I just told you. A black late-model XJ8 was heading south on Washington with two keys of coke in his trunk."

"Heading for the airport?"

"Heading for the airport."

"Did the tip give a description of the driver? Did he at least give a plate number? Did he say how it was that he knew this information? Did he say anything at all that would lead a reasonable police officer to think this guy is trafficking?" Her voice was rising almost to a shout, and she knew it. Anonymous tips are always looked at skeptically by the courts—anyone can call one in, and there's no way for the caller's credibility to be assessed. And without sufficient detailed facts in the tip, there is no probable cause. A black Jaguar heading south on Washington with two kilos was not going to cut it.

"No. That's it. There wasn't any more time, Ms. Townsend. He was about to leave the jurisdiction, and I didn't want to lose him so I pulled him over."

"No. You had already lost him over on Sixth. In fact, how is it that you know that the black Jaguar you 'caught up to' on the MacArthur was the same one you saw pass south on Washington in the first place? How is it that you know that the car you pulled over was the same one the tip referred to on Washington, assuming, arguendo, that the tip was good in the first place?"

Again there was silence.

"That's right. You don't know that, because that tip was shit and you knew it. That's why you didn't even tell me about it in the first place. Okay, so you've got him pulled over. Tell me exactly what happened next."

"I made him get out of the car and asked him for his license and registration. I asked him where he was going, and he said the airport. That's when I asked him what was in his trunk. You know, luggage? He only had that one bag in the backseat, and the tip said the dope was in the trunk. And he told me to fuck off. So I knew he had something in there. I told him he's gonna miss his flight, and I called K-9."

"What was in the bag in the backseat?"

"Clothes, his passport, and a day planner. Some other papers and shit, too."

"And when did you search the bag?"

"While I was waiting for K-9."

"There was no smell, either, was there? Coming from the trunk, then?"

"Yeah, yeah, there was!" he stammered. "It smelled funky, like a dead body, maybe."

"You are a goddamn liar, Officer. You never smelled jackshit, and you and I both know it. First you tell Manny Alvarez that you thought he had drugs, and now you've changed your tune because there were no drugs to be found. Anywhere. You also wouldn't have smelled Anna Prado's body, because she was only dead a day. So fess up and tell me that you wanted to look in the trunk because you were pissed he wouldn't let you and you knew you didn't have enough pc to open it yourself. Ten minutes on the job and you're a tough guy. No one says no to you. You never even had probable cause to pull him over, do you know that? All because you didn't bother to check the tip. Do you know what kind of case you have just royally fucked up, Officer?"

He stood up and paced the small office. "Christ, I didn't know it would be Cupid! I thought this guy was maybe dealing. Maybe I'd nail a doper, out by myself, just on intuition. My FTO says this shit happens all the time in Miami. If someone doesn't want you looking in their trunk, it's because there's something to hide in it. And he had a fucking dead body in there! He had a dead body! You're gonna tell me that doesn't mean anything?"

"Yeah, that's what I'm gonna tell you, because if the stop is suppressed and the search is suppressed then we don't have a dead body in the trunk, got it? It never comes in—it's not admissible in a court of law. Didn't they teach you the law in the police academy or were you too busy strapping extra weapons on your ankle that you forgot to actually listen?" They sat in silence while the cheap wall clock ticked off the seconds and minutes. Finally, she asked, "How far does this go?"

"My sergeant, Ribero, he responded after we popped the trunk. I told him the whole story. And he freaked, just like you, said the whole case would be tossed. But then he said we couldn't let this guy just walk, no way. So he said there had to be another reason why I pulled him over, that it couldn't be the tip."

"Who broke the taillight?"

Chavez didn't answer; he just stared out the window.

"So it's you and Ribero?"

"Lindeman knew about the call, too. How bad is this, Ms. Townsend? Am I gonna get fired over this?"

"Your welfare is the least of my concerns, Officer Chavez. I need to think of a way to keep a man who has butchered ten woman in jail, and right now, I am drawing a complete blank."

40

SHE SAT QUIETLY behind her desk, trying to think through the white noise of confusion. Chavez was back in his seat, but this time the broad shoulders were meekly bowed, his head slumped over his lap, the hands folded in what looked like—and probably was—prayer.

Summoned back over from the Pickle Barrel, Lou Ribero now sat, his arms folded across his chest, glaring at the rookie next to him. He was obviously thinking of the shit patrols he was gonna put Chavez on for the next ten years.

After a long while she finally spoke. Her voice was low, her words carefully chosen.

"While the facts of the cases may all vary, the law on anonymous tips in Florida is pretty clear. Because there is no way to cross-examine the caller, to verify where and how he received his information, or test his motives, in order to serve as the basis of a vehicle stop, an anonymous tip must be sufficient in detail so that it is quite clear to the officer that the person providing the tip has intimate knowledge of the facts of which he speaks. If those facts are then independently corroborated by the officer, the officer will then, and only then, have sufficient probable cause, or at least a reasonable suspicion, to believe that criminal activity is afoot, and may pull the vehicle over to investigate further. A tip that is devoid of necessary facts, that is not sufficiently detailed to be considered credible, cannot be the basis of such a vehicle stop. Period. And of course we all know that any search that is conducted after an illegal stop will also be considered illegal unless there is independent probable cause to support the search. Any evidence obtained as the result of an illegal search will be suppressed and is inadmissible in a court of law as fruit of the poisonous tree.

"That all being said, a vehicle may also be stopped for any traffic violation that the driver has committed in the officer's presence, such as excessive speed or an illegal turn, or for any mechanical infraction that the officer sees, such as a broken headlight or taillight or blinker.

"Officer Chavez has informed me that on September nineteenth at approximately eight-fifteen P.M. he was in his marked patrol unit on Washington and Sixth in South Beach. That at that time he saw a late-model black Jaguar XJ8, license plate TTR-L57 proceeding southbound on Washington toward the MacArthur Causeway with a blond white male thirty-five to forty-five years of age in the driver's seat. The car passed him at a speed he approximated to be higher than thirty-five miles per hour in a posted twenty-five miles per hour zone. Officer Chavez proceeded down Sixth Street to Collins and then back west up Fifth Street and onto the MacArthur Causeway, heading westbound. He again spotted the black Jaguar XJ8 with the license plate, TTR-L57 and the same white male in the driver's seat. He stayed behind the vehicle for approximately two miles on the causeway, at which time he also noticed that the Jaguar had a broken taillight and he observed the vehicle do an illegal lane change without signaling. At that point, Officer Chavez decided to conduct a traffic stop. He activated his lights and siren and pulled the vehicle over.

"He asked the driver, subsequently identified as William Rupert Bantling, for his license and registration. Mr. Bantling appeared nervous and jittery. His hands shook as he handed the license to Officer Chavez, and he failed to maintain eye contact. On his way back to his patrol car, Officer Chavez stopped to look more closely at the broken taillight. At that time he observed a substance on the bumper of the vehicle that looked like blood. He returned to the vehicle to give Mr. Bantling back his license and registration, at which time Officer Chavez also thought he detected an odor of marijuana in the vehicle. He asked Mr. Bantling for permission to search the vehicle and was denied. Based on the totality of the circumstances, the substance on the bumper, the smell of marijuana, and Mr. Bantling's actions, Officer Chavez suspected that the vehicle contained contraband and so called for a K-9 unit to respond. Beauchamp with the Beach responded and his dog, Butch, alerted on the trunk of the vehicle. The alert gave the officers the necessary probable cause to search the trunk, at which time they discovered the body of Anna Prado."

She looked at the two men for a long moment now. "Is that what happened, Officer Chavez? Did I understand you correctly?"

"Yes, ma'am. You did. That was exactly what happened."

She looked at Ribero. "Is that how the incident was reported to you, Sergeant?"

"Exactly."

"Very well. Why don't you finish up your coffee with Officer Lindeman, Sergeant Ribero, and then I guess I'll see him for his prefile at twelve o'clock."

Ribero stood to leave. "Thanks so much for your help on this, Ms. Townsend. We'll see you, I'm sure, for the depos." He nodded grimly at C.J. and then threw a glare in the direction of Chavez. "Let's go, Chavez."

The door closed behind them and that was it. The deal was done. The secret pact had been made with the devil, and there would be no turning back for any of them.

41

FOR THE FIRST time in her career, C.J. had compromised herself on a case. It was for the greater good, she had told herself. The small sacrifice of her professional integrity for the greater good. To put away a monster, to slay the dragons, even the good guys sometimes had to play dirty.

The stop was bad—there was no way around it. Legally, there was no probable cause to support it, and so the search was bad as well. She just wished that Chavez had been a better liar so that she wouldn't have to know what it was she now knew. So she wouldn't have to play the part that she was now forced to play.

Without the search, there was no body. Without the body, there was no case. If Chavez didn't clean up his story, Bantling would walk. It was as simple and horrible as that. No matter what evidence the police had found at his house that had connected him to the murders, everything would be thrown out, because without the illegal stop and search, the police would never even have known William Rupert Bantling existed. They would not have searched his house. They would not have found the Haldol, the blood, the probable murder weapon, the sadistic porno tapes. Such was the way the law read.

The phone rang at her desk, pulling her out of the fog.

"C. J. Townsend."

"C.J.? It's Christine Frederick with Interpol. Sorry it's

taken me a few days to get back to you. I had to run the information that you gave me through a few systems."

"Did you find anything?"

"Did I find anything? Yes, well I think I found quite a lot for you. I think your suspect may have a home in a few other countries when you're done with him. The MO hit in all three South American countries: rapes in Rio, Caracas, and Buenos Aires, Argentina. White male with a mask. He likes to cut and tickle. The mask changes, though. I have an alien, a monster mask, a clown face, and a couple of latex faces that the women did not recognize. I then found a similar BOLO in the Philippines, where they had four rapes matching that MO, but those ran from 1991 to '94. Nothing there since. The wanted sheets from the eighties are mainly inactive and outdated, so I couldn't find anything that far back, and there was nothing in Malaysia. All in all, it looks like maybe ten victims, four countries. But this is all off of the wanteds. I haven't called any of the consulates or police agencies to confirm. I figured you'd want to do that yourself, if this guy matches the pattern, which it looks like he does. Let me fax you over the wanted sheets and you can see for yourself."

Ten more women. She didn't even need to read the wanteds that Christine faxed over to know Bantling was the one. He was a serial rapist, a serial murderer, a sexual predator of women. He had raped and tortured more than seventeen women. He had killed another ten, probably eleven—maybe even more.

Without Chavez, there was no case. Bantling would walk on the Prado murder. The time had run on the rapes in the U.S., so he would walk on those as well. She knew that the rapes in the foreign countries would never be prosecuted. The scenes were the same—there was no physical evidence, and the criminal justice systems in poor South American countries were not to be trusted, to say the least. He would walk on those, too. William Rupert Bantling would walk away a free man. Free to hunt and stalk women. Free to rape and torture and kill again, which is what he inevitably would do. It was simply a matter of time.

A small sacrifice for the greater good.

There was no getting off this case now, or ever. Only one question remained. One that she could not ignore, but did not think she could ever answer.

Who had called in the tip?

42

"YOU'VE BEEN AVOIDING me."

In the door frame of her office stood Special Agent Dominick Falconetti, a Dunkin' Donuts bag in one hand, a black leather briefcase in the other. He was sopping wet.

She tried her best to look shocked at his accusation and opened her mouth to protest, but then quickly closed it again and leaned back in her chair. *Guilty as charged, Officer.*

"Don't try to deny it. You have. In the past week, you have stood me up at the Medical Examiner's office and dodged at least six of my phone calls. You call Manny back, but not me, and you schedule my profile last."

"You're right. I guess I have been avoiding you."

"Now I want to know why. Why do you like Manny better than me? He's definitely more irritating. And he smokes in your office when you're not here." He came in from the doorway and sat down in front of her.

"Along with Glocks, don't they issue you guys umbrellas?"

"It's a Beretta and no, they don't. They don't care if I get soaked and sick, just as long as I can still fire off a shot if necessary. Don't change the subject."

"Look, Dominick, this, this thing between us . . . it should be professional. And nothing more. You're my lead on this case and it's not a good idea for us to, well, get involved. I guess I just didn't know how to tell you that."

"Sure you did. You obviously have been rehearsing what you were going to say to me in your head for over a week now." With his palms on her desk, he leaned over close to her face. His wet black hair curled against his forehead and small drops of water trickled down his temples in zigzag lines, onto his neck. He smelled like Lever soap again. She watched the droplets run down his neck, disappearing into his blue dress shirt, which clung to his chest from the rain. "Maybe I'm being arrogant, but I don't believe you. I thought we . . ." He hesitated for a moment and she watched his mouth as he searched for the right thing to say. "I thought that we had something going there. That maybe there was something between us. And I was pretty sure from that kiss that you thought so, too."

She felt her face flush and she hoped no one had chosen that moment to walk by her door, which was still open. She looked down quickly, away from his probing brown eyes.

"Dominick, I," she stammered, trying to collect her thoughts. "I . . . *we* need to keep this professional. My boss . . . the media would have a field day if they knew—"

He sat back in the seat in front of her desk. "Oh, the media wouldn't give a shit. Maybe for two minutes. And even if they did, who cares?" He reached into the Dunkin' Donuts bag and pulled out two containers of coffee. He handed her one over the desk. "One sugar and cream, right?"

She smiled weakly and nodded. "Yeah. One sugar and cream. Thank you. You didn't have to." There were a few minutes of strained silence between them while she stirred her coffee. The rain was pounding hard against her window. It had rained nonstop now for three days. Outside, you could not see the other side of the street, and the parking lot looked flooded. Tiny figures tried desperately to run to the courthouse, taking large galloping steps through the puddles. Someone had lost a file, and white papers were everywhere on Thirteenth Avenue, cemented by the driving rain to the pavement.

In a low voice she broke the silence in the room. "Then you understand where I'm coming from?"

He sighed and leaned toward her desk again. "No. No, I don't. Look, C.J., let's just put this out on the table. I like you, I do. I'm attracted to you. And I was pretty sure that the attraction was mutual. I thought that maybe we could take this somewhere, to another level, but I suppose not now.

"I do know this much, though. Something has gotten to you since Bantling was arrested, but I don't know what it is, and I don't think it's the media. Or your boss. So if you want me to accept what you're saying—fine, I accept it. If you want me to *understand* it, then I can't help you." He ran his hand through the top of his wet hair, slicking it back off his face again.

"But, whatever. I'm here for my pre-file. Friday at two P.M. Right on time." His voice was resigned now, and he put his briefcase on the chair next to him and opened it. "Oh, and I forgot one other thing . . ." He reached back into the Dunkin' Donuts bag. "I brought you a Boston Cream. I threw my body over it so it wouldn't get soggy."

Only the first twenty minutes of his prefile seemed awkward, and after that the tension in the room lightened, and for a while, the conversation even felt comfortable again, like putting on old slippers. She knew he was mad at her and that he was hurt. It was ironic that after promising that he wouldn't hurt her, *she* had been the one to hurt him. And that was the last thing she wanted to do. She wanted to tell him how she really felt, how she wished it could be as he said, taken to another level. But she swore him in, took his statement, and said nothing. *Chalk up yet another small sacrifice for the greater good.*

The Chief Assistant, Martin Yars, had the case set to go before the grand jury on the following Wednesday, September 27, just a few days before Bantling's scheduled arraignment date on Monday, October 2. Dominick would be testifying before the grand jury, presenting the entire investigation into Anna Prado's death in the hope that they would return an indictment against Bantling for capital first-degree murder. On the surface, in all the reports, the case was strong. They had a mutilated body, and although DNA wasn't yet back, the blood in Bantling's shed matched Anna's blood type, O negative. It also looked like they had a murder weapon. The scalpel SA Jimmy Fulton had found also had trace amounts of blood on it, and the narcotic drug haloperidol, found in her system, matched the prescription found in Bantling's house. It all made for the perfect case, except for Chavez and his troubling revelation on Monday. Nevertheless, she fully expected an indictment would be issued and that it would be for capital murder. Before the grand jury at this stage of the prosecution, only the state gets an opportunity to present its case, not the defense; there is no presiding judge, and hearsay is totally admissible. So as C.J.'s criminal law professor at St. John's once pointed out, the state can pretty much indict a ham sandwich if it wants to.

C.J. did not tell Dominick about the bad stop. No one else could be brought into that dark coven, even though the question of who had called in the anonymous tip still burned in her mind without an answer. After careful consideration, C.J. had finally decided that it must have been a coincidence. There were a number of black XJ8 Jaguars in SoBe—maybe Chavez had pulled over a Jag other than the one the caller had tipped about. Or maybe Bantling had shot someone the bird out the window and pissed off some idiot who thought it would be neat to call in a false tip. To question it any more than that would be like leaving open a door to a room you wanted no one to enter.

It was still pouring rain outside when they ended their profile some three hours later and Dominick rose to leave. The wind whipped sheets of water against her window, and she reached into her desk and pulled out an umbrella.

"You just now got dry. Save yourself. I'll have security walk me to my car with theirs."

"Security? Ha. It's after five on a rainy Friday. Security went home hours ago, along with the rest of your office, I think. Thanks, but no thanks. I'm a tough guy. Water runs right off me."

"Suit yourself. Don't catch cold, though. You're needed in front of the grand jury on Wednesday—and oh, I almost forgot. I just got notice today of the Arthur Hearing. Go figure, Bantling wants a bond. It's set for one P.M. next Friday, the twenty-ninth. I'll need you for that, too. Can you make it?" An Arthur, as it was known, was much more involved than the preliminary First Appearance, where the judge simply read off the arrest form to find probable cause. Even if an indictment had already been issued by that time, C.J. still would need to prove through witnesses that "proof was evident and presumption great" that Bantling had committed first-degree murder, which meant, at the very least, calling her lead detective to the stand. Hearsay was again admissible, but, unlike grand jury testimony, all witnesses now would be subject to cross-examination. Defense attorneys often used an Arthur Hearing as a discovery tool to see what kind of a case the state had, and how good their witnesses held up under cross, knowing full well that there would be no way the judge would grant them a bond. C.J. suspected that to be Lourdes Rubio's goal in this case.

"Are you handling it?"

"Yes. Yars only handles the grand jury. It's all me from here on out."

"Then how could I say no? Of course we need to keep this strictly professional, so you better send me a subpoena anyway."

She felt her face go hot again. "Very funny. Thanks for, um, understanding, about keeping this—our friendship, that is—professional between us."

"I never said that I understood. I said I accepted it. Big difference."

She walked with him past the deserted maze of the secretarial pool to the security access doors just outside the elevator bay.

At the door he turned to her. "Manny and I are meeting for drinks at the Alibi to go over some things. You're welcome to join us if you'd like. All three of us can remain professional over a couple of beers."

"Thanks, but I'd better not. I've got lots of things to finish up."

"Alright, then. Have a good weekend, Counselor. I guess I'll see you on Wednesday, after the grand jury."

"Stay dry," she called out just as the elevator doors closed, leaving the dark office hallway deserted once again.

43

IT TOOK THE grand jury less than an hour to indict William Rupert Bantling on first-degree murder in the death of Anna Prado. And it only took them that long because they had ordered lunch during deliberations and the bill was on the state only if they ate *before* they finished with the case.

Within a matter of minutes after the indictment was handed down, the media hordes had descended on the news and devoured it, and then instantaneously regurgitated the information on the pristine marble steps of the Dade County courthouse through dazzling white smiles, analyzing "what it really meant" for captive TV audiences around the world.

C.J. had not expected a decision to be that quick. In fact, she was in a hushed meeting with the State Attorney himself, Jerry Tigler, when one of the secretaries ran into the conference room with the news and turned on the TV. C.J. and Tigler, along with the U.S. Attorney for the Southern District, and the FBI's Miami Special Agent in Charge all watched on live television as a flustered and red-faced Martin Yars, Chief Assistant for the Miami-Dade State Attorney's Office, painfully stumbled through even the simplest of words on the courthouse steps, ineptly trying to satisfy the insatiable questions of the dozen or so press corps who had nailed him unexpectedly for interviews on the way to his car. It looked bad. It sounded worse.

The impromptu meeting at the State Attorney's Office had been called at the joint request of both the Federal Bureau of Investigation and the U.S. Attorney's Office. It seemed the feds wanted Cupid, and they didn't want to share. All eyes in the room were silently glued on Yars, who had chosen now, of all times, to develop a bad stutter. After a few more difficult moments, blessedly, even Channel 7 took pity and went to commercial. Tom de la Flors, the U.S. Attorney for the Southern District, broke the uncomfortable silence in the room.

"See, Jerry? That's exactly the sort of thing that I was talking about. Our office has the resources and the experience to handle this media circus." He shook his head and dropped his voice a few octaves to a more personal whisper that could still be heard by all in the room, and he looked straight at Tigler, who was squirming uncomfortably in his fake-leather high-backed chair. "Can we be honest here, Jerry? This case is a political firecracker, and we all know it. One drop, one mess-up, and the whole thing can explode. Right in your face. Right in an election year. And I know how rough it can be to keep the opinion polls friendly and the voters turning out on election day chanting your name. I was a state judge once; I know how it works. And the polls don't lie, Jerry. They haven't been happy with how your office has handled this case from the get-go. Eighteen months before a suspect was arrested, and he's only been indicted on one of the murders. The other victims' families are all screaming bloody blue murder to every reporter who will listen. And they are all listening, Jerry—they are all listening."

As if on cue, the FBI's Miami SAC, Mark Gracker, chimed in. "The FBI is prepared to assume the entire criminal investigation. We will, of course, need all evidence obtained to date by the Cupid task force to be submitted to the FBI crime lab for reexamination."

De la Flors paused for a moment to let what had just been said sink in. Then he leaned back in his chair and in a resigned voice that sounded to C.J. strikingly similar to that of a father who has just had to reprimand his child, continued on. "The U.S. Attorney's Office is prepared to go forward on *all* the murders, Jerry, not just Marilyn

Siban's. I think it would all just be smoother if we could agree beforehand and save each other a lot of unnecessary bickering in court."

C.J. sat in her chair doing a slow but steady boil, listening to the thinly veiled threats escape de la Flors's mouth through his perfect white teeth and slick smile. She wanted Tigler to get up and slug him, but knew that he would have to find his balls first, and that could take years.

Tigler looked around the table and squirmed again in his seat at the helm of the long table. Finally, after a long moment, he cleared his throat and found his voice. "Well, Tom, I appreciate your concern. I do, but I think at this stage of the game we have things under control over here. C. J. Townsend is one of our finest prosecutors, and I'm confident that she can handle this case."

Jerry Tigler looked out of his league. His brown suit was frumpy and outdated, and his hairpiece had shifted across his head during the meeting due to the nervous buildup of sweat underneath. He was no match for the diamond-smiled, Calvin Klein–wearing, former judge and now larger-than-life, appointed-by-the-president, U.S. Attorney Tom de la Flors.

"I'm not so sure you understand, Mr. Tigler," Gracker started in again. C.J. watched as he jabbed his pudgy little finger on the conference table, an attempt to command more attention to his small self. "The Bureau has worked hundreds of serial homicides. We have the resources available to work the murders of all eleven victims."

That was it. C.J. could take it no more. "That would be *ten* victims, Agent Gracker. So far we have only *ten* bodies, so unless the FBI knows the location of Morgan Weber's remains, we have *ten* victims. And perhaps I can explain why we have not prematurely arrested or indicted on the other nine murder victims. To date, there is no physical evidence linking Bantling to the other nine women, and our office thought it prudent to go forward only on the case that we can actually prove at this time."

"This is not a slam against you, Ms. Townsend," Tom de la Flors began, but C.J. cut him off.

"Oh, yes it is. It's a slam against me, my prosecutorial

judgment, and this whole office, Mr. de la Flors. And even, assuming the state did hand over the prosecution of all ten murders to the U.S. Attorney's Office, under what legal theory would you have jurisdiction? Only Marilyn Siban's murder occurred on federal land."

De la Flors looked stunned. He hadn't expected any backtalk from the prosecutor, and only minimal whining from Tigler himself. It took him more than a moment to recover. "I believe each victim was found with the controlled substance haloperidol in her system, Ms. Townsend. Presumably, that substance was administered by their captor, namely, William Bantling. Mr. Bantling has thus engaged in a continuing criminal enterprise under the United States Code."

Tom de la Flors had picked the wrong day and the wrong person to try to bully with his interpretation of the law. "The drug information is correct. However—and correct me if I'm wrong—I believe for a CCE you also need five or more conspirators to form the enterprise. Again, if the Bureau knows of additional suspects in this case, we'd love to listen to what you have, but to my knowledge, Bantling is it. So we're four suspects short of a CCE. And of federal jurisdiction, I'm afraid." Well, there it was. She could now kiss off any future at all within the federal government, particularly one as an esteemed federal prosecutor. De la Flors glared at her from across the table.

"Well, I'll have to look into it more closely, Ms. Townsend, but that was only one legal theory I was throwing out to you. There's also the Hobbs Act." He turned his attention to Tigler now. "We have used it before, successfully, to prosecute tourist robberies, right here in Dade County."

"Yes. But that was only on the robberies," C.J. continued. "That's still not going to give you jurisdiction on the murders."

De la Flors was more than a little annoyed now at the pesky gnat that was C. J. Townsend. He was a politician, not a prosecutor. He probably hadn't even seen a courtroom or a copy of the United States Code in the four years he had served as U.S. Attorney, and was not prepared to argue subtle nuances in the law. He raised his voice up the few octaves that he had given to Tigler earlier. "If it's part of a robbery, it will—or it will at least make for a great argument, I can assure you. But if your office does want to fight us on jurisdiction over this, we can always just go forward on each robbery."

"What robbery are you speaking about, might I ask?" Tigler the Timid spoke up again in a meek voice.

"You might, Jerry. Each victim was found nude and missing a heart, correct? Including Ms. Prado? Then they were each robbed. And on that the case law is quite clear, Ms. Townsend. We do have federal jurisdiction. So we can just tie Mr. Bantling up in federal court for a few years trying him individually on each robbery. It's better than what your office has managed to do till now. And when we're done you can have him sent back from Leavenworth for whatever state cases you have finally managed to indict him on. Assuming, of course, Jerry, that you're still the State Attorney and can still make those kinds of decisions.

"But you think it over and let me know if we can maybe work this from a team approach before I move forward to indict. In the meantime, I have a warrant and a court order from U.S. Magistrate Carol Kingsley authorizing us to have access to Bantling's house and cars and any evidence seized pursuant to a previously issued state warrant." He tossed a thick document onto the conference table.

C.J. never took her steely eyes off de la Flors. "I'll get you a copy of all documents seized, Mr. de la Flors. I will personally walk you through the evidence stored at FDLE and, as for evidence at the lab, I will get you a report on everything tested. Any more than that, and we can both pay a visit to Judge Kingsley, because as much as I would love to cooperate, I have a murder to prosecute, and from the sound of the threats in this room, I'd better hurry before I have to file a habeus motion to get my murder defendant back from the Neverland of federal court where he's to be tried for *robbery*."

She stood up and grabbed the warrant off the table. "Now, if you'll excuse me, gentlemen, I need to get started copying all the documents you requested in your court order."

Jerry Tigler looked envious of all the things C.J. had said, wishing he had been the one to say them. Nonetheless, he sat up an extra two inches taller in his frumpy brown suit and smiled as a frustrated and furious Mark Gracker and Tom de la Flors stormed out of his conference room.

44

C.J. FELT THE maddening flutter of butterflies in her stomach as she made her way through the courthouse to Courtroom 4-8 where the 1:30 Arthur Hearings were being held before Judge Nelson Hilfaro. With each floor she ascended on the wobbly steel escalator, her heart raced a bit faster, and the butterflies fluttered their queasy wings about like bugs trapped in a jar, until she was pretty sure she would be physically sick. And although her hands dripped with nervous perspiration on the handle of her oversized leather briefcase, still, her face remained stone. The raw fear that grasped her belly and reached up around her throat was invisible to all around her; she made sure of that. To the rest of the world, she was the strong, confident prosecutor. Only inside was she afraid that she would fall apart.

She must have handled over two hundred Arthur Hearings in her career. Probably closer to three hundred—maybe more. They were routine in her cases. Every defendant who was charged with a nonbondable offense punishable by life in prison or death was entitled to an Arthur, and while they could be time-consuming, generally speaking, if you had a good case and a competent lead detective they were *only* that. But this was no ordinary case.

It had been almost three weeks since she had laid eyes on William Bantling in Judge Katz's courtroom. Three

weeks since her mind first realized the horrible truth that
had since become her living nightmare. And while the initial shock wave may have passed, and her brain may have
come to accept the facts that she had force-fed it in the time
since, she had not been made to sit in a room with him
across from her, his ice blue eyes upon hers. She could
hardly bear the thought of his breath mixing with hers in
the same air—his scent, his *presence,* everywhere—with
no escape short of running out of the courtroom with a
string of reporters in tow and an angry judge blasting her
from the bench. How would she react, coming face-to-face
with her assailant just steps from her seat? Would she
freeze, the fear in her throat closing in on her, choking for
a gasp of air, as she had at the First Appearance? Would
she break down and cry, as she had every night in the
weeks since? Would she stand and scream at him and
point, as if he were a creature from some late-night horror
movie? Or would she simply grab her steel letter opener
from her briefcase and with a cold smile stab him straight
through the heart before any corrections officer could stop
her? That was what was so frightening, and why the butterflies danced their maddening, sickening dance in her stomach. She did not know what she would do. And she didn't
know if control was even an option.

She flung open the huge mahogany courtroom doors
and, with a deep breath, strode into the packed courtroom.
There were seven cases set down on the Arthur Hearing
calendar and none of the prisoners had yet been brought
over from the bridge. The jury box—or box, as it was
known, where all the defendants scheduled for an Arthur
would be seated, shackled to one another in chains—was
empty. C.J. felt an enormous weight lift off her chest and
was happy to find that she could breathe. At least for the
moment. Up ahead in the gallery next to the state's table
she spotted the bald head of Manny Alvarez. At six five, he
was not hard to miss, towering above the prosecutors and
detectives who had all nervously milled about at the table
to look at the court calendar and avoid the prying lenses of
at least a dozen cameras that were set up around the courtroom. Her eyes took in the rest of the room quickly,

searching for Dominick's familiar shoulders, black hair, and salt-and-pepper goatee, but there was no sign of him. Then, from behind her she felt a heavy hand, warm on her shoulder.

"Looking for me?" It was him. He was dressed in a crisp white shirt and dark blue suit, a midnight-blue-and-silver tie tied around his throat. His hair was brushed back off his head, but one piece had managed to escape, curling delicately on his forehead. He looked very neat, very professional. He looked very good.

"Actually, yes, I was. I see Manny is here," she said. His fingers felt warm on her shoulder as he ushered her protectively through the crowd toward the gallery.

"Yeah. You can't miss him, alright. He even brought a jacket and tie in case you needed him to testify. But, before you get too impressed, I have to warn you that the jacket smells like mothballs and the elbows have brown suede patches. I haven't seen the tie yet. You may want to wait for an emergency to break him open."

"Thanks for the warning. I think I'll start with you, then. You look dapper. They must be paying you well at FDLE. Nice suit."

"Only the best for you. Only the best. What number are we?"

"On the calendar we're number six, but I don't know if Judge Hilfaro will go in order today."

They found Manny leaning against the state's table, chatting with a young prosecutor. Female, of course. When he saw C.J. he smiled broadly and shook her hand, his huge hairy paw swallowing up her fingers. "Counselor! *Hola!* Long time, no see? How you been? Keeping out of trouble?"

"Hey, Manny. Thanks for getting all dressed up. You look good."

"Yeah, Bear," said Dominick. "You look nice, alright. Just don't raise your arm without your jacket on when you swear to tell the truth, buddy."

"Damn. You're kidding me, right?" He raised his arm and looked at the dark sweat stain at the armpit. "I just can't get those pit stains out."

"You need a good cleaners," said Dominick.

"Nah. I need a good wife. You know anyone cute, Counselor?"

"No one cute enough for you, I'm afraid."

"What about that secretary of yours?"

"We're not going there now. I still want to respect you at the end of the day. But don't worry about the jacket, Manny, I'm only going to put Dominick on the stand."

The jury box door opened just then, and in walked three corrections officers in dark green suits. Following them came a stream of handcuffed and leg-shackled defendants, their chains clanking together as they filed into the two rows of the box. Most of the inmates wore street clothes, which they were allowed to wear for court appearances. Nothing fancy, and usually, for most prisoners, it was just the same clothes they had been arrested in, recycled for every court appearance until their defense attorney finally borrowed a donated suit jacket from some charity for their trial. But there, in the second row of seats, separated and seated apart from the rest, sat a handsome blond man in a lone bright red jumpsuit, a corrections outfit assigned to identify those "special" defendants—the ones charged with capital murder. C.J. felt the room begin to spin, and she quickly looked away.

"There's our man, now," Dominick said, turning his attention for a moment to the box.

"Hmmm . . . I don't think jail is agreeing with him, Dom. He looks a bit gaunt. Must be the food. Or maybe the entertainment." Manny laughed.

Dominick looked back carefully at C.J. again, but she had her head buried in her briefcase and he could not see her face. "Speaking of the devil himself," Dominick said, "that grand jury came back pretty quickly on the indictment, didn't it? Even I thought it might take them at least an hour, and I'm an eternal optimist."

"Yes, Yars told me you did a great job on the stand. The consummate witness, which, of course, I had always expected." She inhaled a deep breath and looked up from her briefcase, carefully keeping her back to the jury box, her eyes straight ahead and focused on Dominick. She fought down the creeping, paralyzing fear that worked its way relentlessly out of her belly up into her throat, reaching up into her crazed mind, trying to force her to turn around and look into the eyes of madness. Not yet. Not until she was ready. She knew Dominick was watching her, waiting to see her reaction, so she was careful not to give him one. "But that reminds me, Dom, I need to talk to you about something else that happened around here on Wednesday, just in case you hadn't heard yet."

"Heard what?"

"About the visit Jerry Tigler and I were paid from our friends downtown."

"Oh no. Friends downtown? You mean the feds, don't you?"

"None other."

"Who? The Bureau?"

"Yes. The Miami SAC, a short, pudgy guy with a bad attitude by the name of Gracker, I think. Mark Gracker. And he was accompanied by none other than his majesty, the U.S. Attorney himself."

"Tom de la Flors?"

"That would be the one."

"You're kidding me. What did they want?"

"In a word—Cupid."

"All rise!" barked a loud voice next to the bench, and the courtroom fell silent. The heavy double doors to the judge's chambers swung open and the Honorable Judge Nelson Hilfaro waddled his way in and up to the bench, his black judge's gown trailing after him on the floor.

"I'll have to tell you the whole sordid story later," she whispered.

"Can't wait," he whispered back.

"Be seated," commanded the bailiff, and everyone in the courtroom sat.

"Good afternoon, all," began Judge Hilfaro, clearing his throat. "Given the rather, um, *special* case that we have set here today which, apparently, most of you present are here for"—he nodded in the direction of the press, which packed the ten rows in the courtroom—"I have decided to call the matter of *The State of Florida* v. *William Rupert Bantling* out of turn, and take it as my first case, so that we may clear the courtroom, after which I will call the rest of the calendar and proceed as usual. State, are you ready to proceed?"

C.J. was a bit stunned. She'd thought that she would have had at least the calendar call and a case or two to ready herself emotionally. But, then again, maybe it was better to dive right in without too much thought. She stepped up before the judge to the state's podium.

"Yes, Judge. C. J. Townsend on behalf of the State of Florida. We are ready to proceed."

"Counsel for the defendant?"

Lourdes Rubio, dressed in a conservative black suit, hair pulled back in a tight bun, made her way from the back of the courtroom to the defense podium.

"Lourdes Rubio for the defendant, Bill Bantling. We, too, are ready Your Honor."

"Very well. How many witnesses, State?"

"Just one, Your Honor."

"Good. Let's get started. State, you may begin." Judge Hilfaro was a no-nonsense judge. He did not like the spotlight, and so he did not care much for media cases. That was one of the reasons the Chief Judge had sent him from a trial division to the land of Arthur Hearings. It wasn't that he was not competent, because, in fact, just the opposite was true. It was really that Arthurs did not attract much attention normally. Usually just the First Appearance of a bloodthirsty defendant caught the eyes of the press, and then, if they were still interested, maybe the trial itself. But, then again, it was not every day that a serial killer who had made international headlines landed in Judge Hilfaro's quiet courtroom.

"The state calls Special Agent Dominick Falconetti to the stand."

Dominick strode to the witness box, all eyes in the courtroom upon him, and was sworn in.

After a few preliminary questions establishing his credentials, C.J. brought Dominick to the night of September 19, when he'd been called to the causeway. He was an easy witness—he knew what legal elements she needed to make her case, and he knew what facts would enable her to establish those elements. Other than a "What happened next?" question, he needed no further direction. He took the courtroom through the stop of Bantling's car, the discovery of Anna Prado's body, and the search of Bantling's house, where human blood matching Anna's blood type was found on the walls and flooring of the shed, as well as trace amounts of blood on the probable murder weapon, a scalpel.

No mention was made of any drugs found in Anna Prado's system, or the porn tapes found in Bantling's bedroom. To hold Bantling without a bond until his trial, all that was necessary for the state to prove at this stage of the proceedings was that a murder had been committed and that proof was evident and presumption great that Bantling had committed it. All other aggravating, extraneous facts could be used later at his trial, when motive and opportunity became issues to a twelve-member jury, and when the standard of proof was raised to reasonable doubt and the penalty became death.

The press eagerly gobbled up every word that Dominick spoke, and the sound of dozens of pens could be heard scribbling furiously together, almost in sync. Most of the details that were being testified about today were new to them, and their excitement was almost palpable.

She felt Bantling's cold eyes upon her, moving slowly, deliberately up and down her body, probably undressing her in his mind, right there in court. Inmates did not sit next to their attorneys for Arthur Hearings, and from where he sat in the box, he had a perfect view of the whole courtroom and of her as she questioned Dominick on direct. She could see him from the side of her eye, watching her. She wondered for a moment if he might recognize her, and then, what she would do if he did, but then just as quickly dismissed that thought. She looked nothing like she did once upon a lifetime ago, and she was sure his interest in her at that moment was simply a manifestation of his sick curiosity for any female in the room. For a split second she thought she could actually hear the sound of him breathing, the same labored hissing sound his breath had made when it escaped the clown's rubber mouth, and the air smelled faintly of coconut. She pushed the thoughts out of her head and tried to keep her back to the box, forcing her mind to listen to Dominick. *Don't look too closely, now. Don't go too crazy.*

"Thank you, Agent Falconetti," said Judge Hilfaro when he had finished testifying. "Defense, any questions?"

Lourdes Rubio stood up and faced Dominick. "Just a few, Agent Falconetti. You were not the arresting officer, were you?"

"No."

"In fact, the initial stop of Mr. Bantling's vehicle and the subsequent search of the trunk and discovery of Ms. Prado's body had been conducted by officers with the Miami Beach Police Department before you even were called to the scene, correct?"

"Yes."

"And the stop of Mr. Bantling's vehicle and discovery of Ms. Prado's body actually occurred much by chance, did it not?"

"No. The stop of Mr. Bantling's car was based on excessive speed and faulty equipment as observed by a Miami Beach police officer."

"What I meant was, prior to September nineteenth, your task force of police agencies did not have Mr. Bantling's name on one of its lists of Cupid suspects, did it?"

"No."

"In fact, prior to that day, not one task force member had even heard the name William Bantling before, had they?"

"That is correct."

"So the stop of Mr. Bantling's vehicle on the MacArthur Causeway was pure chance? A random, routine, run-of-the mill vehicle stop by our esteemed, above-reproach boys in blue at the Miami Beach Police Department?" That comment drew a snicker from the crowd. Everyone in the room knew the reputation enjoyed by the MBPD, and it was not always glorious.

"Yes."

"And, of course, they would never just pull someone over for no reason, or search someone's trunk without obtaining the proper consent?"

"Objection, argumentative," C.J. interrupted. She did not like where Lourdes was going with this, and she felt more than uneasy. *Had she spoken with Chavez or Ribero? Did she know about the anonymous tip? Or was she bluffing?*

"Sustained. Move on, Counselor. I got your point. If you want to make a motion to suppress, then write out a motion and set it down before the trial judge, but I'm not going to let you argue it here. Anything further, Ms. Rubio?"

"No, Judge, no further questions. But I would like to offer an argument as to bond."

"That won't be necessary, Ms. Rubio. I have heard all I need to hear. Based on the evidence presented here today, I find that proof is evident and presumption great that the crime of murder was committed by the defendant. The defendant is considered by this court to be a danger to society and a risk of flight, and as such, he is remanded without bail until his trial."

"Your Honor," began Lourdes, her voice raised. "I believe the stop of Mr. Bantling's vehicle was unlawful, as was the search of his trunk. I would like to make an argument on that point."

"Fine. As I said, make it as a motion to suppress before Judge Chaskel. You won't make it here. Not without proper testimony. I've made my ruling."

"May I at least be heard on forms of alternate release?"

"Sure. Go ahead. Tell me some forms of release you would propose to keep society safe from a man accused of ten murders."

"He has not been charged in any other murder, Judge, and that is the point I am trying to make. In the eyes of this court and the court of public opinion, my client is being tried and convicted as a serial killer of ten women, when he has, in fact, only been charged in the death of one woman."

"That's more than enough for me, Ms. Rubio." Judge Hilfaro looked over at Dominick. "Is Mr. Bantling considered a suspect in the other nine Cupid murders, Agent Falconetti?"

"Yes, sir," replied Dominick.

Judge Hilfaro scowled at Lourdes Rubio, but let her

argue pointlessly for ten more minutes for an alternate form of release for her client. When she asked for house arrest, he actually laughed out loud.

At the state's table, with Dominick at her side, C.J. quietly sighed a breath of relief. Bantling would definitely be held behind bars until trial. She had gotten him that far.

The next step was to get him all the way into the death chamber.

45

BILL BANTLING KNEW he wasn't going to get a bond. He knew that his lawyer was not good enough to get him one, but the hell if that was going to stop him from trying. From going all the way. He was going to make that bitch work for her $300 an hour one way or another.

So he had to say that he really was not very surprised when the Honorable Nelson Hilfaro denied him a bond. He was not surprised, but he was pissed. Pissed at the ignoramus judge who looked at him like he was some sort of communal leper; pissed at the tight-assed haughty prosecutor who traipsed around the courtroom like her shit did not stink asking questions from that sneaky FDLE agent on the stand. Who, he might add, was the only one of the lot he had any respect for, as minimal as it might be. He was even pissed off at his own bitch lawyer who would not let him say anything in his own defense, not a single word. That he did not like. Not one bit, being ordered around by some overpriced female. Damn it, if he was going to be fucked by a woman it better be in bed.

Not in a million years would he ever have trusted a woman to even represent him on line at the local grocery store, much less as his attorney in a court of law, particularly with a matter as delicate as his own life or death. But Billy Bantling was no fool. No, siree. He knew what the papers wrote about him. He knew that people thought him a monster—the devil himself incarnate. He had already been tried and convicted in the simple, zoned-out minds of millions of TV viewers everywhere. And knowing all this, he also knew that Lourdes Rubio, a straitlaced and serious-minded schoolmarm in a conservative but slightly short skirt and jacket was the smart choice as his attorney. He had done his homework on her long before her services were ever needed. Okay-looking, but nothing to write home about, she was well respected in both the Latin community and the legal community in Miami and just pretty enough to make a jury stop and think. Think and wonder how this nice, pretty, educated, conservative little Cuban girl from Hialeah could represent such a heinous monster like himself. How she could stand up next to him, whisper in his ear, share the same table, and drink from the same water pitcher and yet still confidently proclaim his innocence to the world knowing full well the crimes he stood accused of committing. Well, if the nice Cuban girl didn't think him guilty of rape and torture and murder, then maybe it's just not so. After all, a woman wouldn't just let a sociopathic serial rapist go free, now would she?

He knew deep inside that his thinking on this point had been correct all along, and that he had been right in his choice of counsel, when and if the time ever came that he needed one. He was just frustrated at the gloomy prospect of remaining locked up in the piss-smelling, vermin-infested hole across the street for even one more day, and it took every fiber of strength in him to stop himself from screaming at the fat judge on the cheap mahogany bench or the tight-assed bitchy prosecutor, or his own okay-looking attorney. But he sat silent, just as his nice attorney had asked, handcuffed hands patiently folded together in a feigned look of prayer, and he chewed away the inside wall of his cheek to prevent the sneer of contempt that threatened to escape his otherwise-pious-looking poker face.

He watched as they all hacked at his freedom before the judge, his own attorney asking for electronic monitoring, house arrest, weekend release, suicide watches. Then the mousy blond Madame Prosecutor, arguing for solitary confinement, a suspension of phone privileges, no more visits from the press. She was definitely a hard-ass. C. J. Townsend. He had read her name in the papers, but now he took a good long look at her. He watched as she chatted back and forth with Agent Falconetti at the prosecution's table. And something bothered him about the scene, something else that he couldn't quite put his finger on.

There was something very familiar about her.

46

"SO WHAT'S THIS about the feds taking Cupid?"

C.J. and Dominick were outside the courtroom now, hiding out in the judge's hallway just waiting for the press to finally go home. Besides the two of them, the hallway was deserted. Judge Hilfaro had managed to kick everyone out of his courtroom after the Bantling hearing to finish up the rest of his Arthurs, and even though the representatives of most of the major news agencies had left, some less reputable members of the press were still sniffing around downstairs for crumbs.

"De la Flors served me with a court order and a warrant from Judge Kingsley, a federal district judge," said C.J. "They want everything. Labs, evidence, documents. Everything we have."

"You have got to be kidding me!" In anger, Dominick slapped the wall with his palm, and the flat sound resonated down the empty hallway. "Well, we're not going to give it to them, are we?" From the look on her face, he knew the answer. "Damn. Can we fight it?"

"Here's the thing. The U.S. Attorney's Office wants to prosecute Cupid on the murders, but other than Siban's, whose body was actually found on federal land, they have no federal jurisdiction. That means yes, we can fight it. And I can assure you, de la Flors was none too happy to hear me tell him that."

"Okay. So if they legally can't get the other nine murders, why do we have to hand everything over to them? All this just for Siban?"

"Well, yes and no. They want what we have to go after Bantling on Siban, but they also want to go after him on the—get this—robberies."

"Robberies? What the hell? What robberies?"

"De la Flors wants glory and fame. He wants his name in the papers is what he wants. And he wants Cupid. So if he can't get him on murder, he's gonna drag him over to federal court to get him for robbing women of their clothing and their hearts. Although I'm not sure in what order that will read in the indictment. He intends to tie him up with the Hobbs Act in federal court for a few years to make Tigler look like a buffoon, which is not that difficult a task. After Tigler loses his reelection bid and de la Flors gets nominated as a federal judge, maybe he'll cut Bantling loose to pay his hometown a visit and we can finish what we started."

"The Hobbs Act? He really thinks he can make that stretch that Cupid is affecting interstate commerce?"

"He's certainly going to give it the old college try."

"And what's Gracker's role in all this? That tubby little shit."

"He's de la Flors's cheerleader, I suppose. He sat in the back of the room singing 'I can investigate better than you can.' But when it comes down to it, he's nothing without de la Flors."

"What did Tigler do?"

"What do you think? After asking the vampires in for coffee and doughnuts and a pint of A negative, nothing."

"So we're gonna give them what they want?"

"Not all of it. Copies of documents, copies of lab reports. I'm going to stuff them so full of paper, they'll need magnifying lenses for glasses when they're done, their eyes will be so bad. I told de la Flors to get ready for a fight if he even thinks I'm giving him actual evidence. That's when he decided to go home."

Dominick smiled and leaned in close to C.J.'s face, his

arm above her, palm resting on the wall. "I like you. Not only are you pretty, but you're pretty tough."

She felt her face flush. "Thank you. I'll take that as a compliment."

"You should. That's how I meant it."

The door to Judge Hilfaro's courtroom opened just then, and in walked Manny. Dominick dropped his arm and quickly looked over at the detective, who looked unhappy. C.J. felt her heart return to a normal beat.

"Where have you been, Bear? Don't tell me giving interviews to Channel Seven," said Dominick.

"Are you shitting me? While both make me laugh, Cartoon Network has a better cast of characters. What are you two doing back here? Lying low?"

For some reason, C.J. felt her face flush again with embarrassment. Dominick answered quickly. "C.J. was telling me all about the visit the feds paid her Wednesday. It seems Gracker found himself a pigeon—Tom de la Flors. The U.S. Attorney's Office wants to lay claim to Cupid. They served C.J. with a warrant."

"As if my day wasn't going crappy enough. Fuck them. Pardon my French, Counselor."

"You don't have to worry about C.J.'s virgin ears. She told de la Flors and his stoolie just that. Now let's hope they go away."

"Something tells me that won't happen, Dom. Especially now."

"Why? What happened?"

"They just found Cupid's latest work of art. Looks like Morgan Weber's body, or what's left of it anyway, was discovered about an hour or so ago. Duty calls, my friend."

"Where was she found?" asked Dominick.

"In a fishing shack in the middle of the Everglades. Some drunk fisherman went to crash there and burn off his hangover and found her strung up from the ceiling. It's pretty bad, I'm told. ME's heading out now. Miami-Dade and the Florida Marine Patrol have the scene secured. The buzzards have gotten wind, though, and the choppers are hovering overhead."

"Alright. We're out of here," said Dominick. Damn; even the slightest hope he had held out for finding Morgan Weber alive had now been snuffed out.

"Let me follow you out there. I'll need to see the scene," said C.J.

"Ride with me. I'll take you back later, or I'll get a uniform to take you back."

"Alright." She nodded.

"Hey, Counselor, nice job in court today," said Manny as all three headed toward the security doors that led to the main hallway and the elevator bay.

"Thanks, but I think Dominick was the star of the show. He didn't even need me."

"Don't be so modest. Trust me, Counselor, you have your share of fans, too."

"What are you talking about?" she asked as the doors swung open. Clustered around the elevators and Courtroom 4-8 was a mass of reporters. They had obviously heard the news about Morgan Weber. When the security doors opened, the crowd ran toward all three of them, their camera lights burning brightly before them. They smelled blood.

"Well, Mr. Psycho sure seems to like you," Manny said under his breath as he composed his face for the cameras. "In fact, he just couldn't keep his eyes off you the whole hearing."

47

IT SEEMED LIKE forever since C.J. had actually slept eight hours through the night. After spending Friday night at the grisly scene in the Everglades where Morgan Weber's remains were found, she had then accompanied Dominick and Manny over to the medical examiner's office to watch Dr. Joe Neilson perform the early-morning Saturday autopsy. After that she had spent the afternoon at her office trying to figure out if the fishing shack stood on federal land in the Everglades, or county property in Miami-Dade. Finally satisfied that the answer was the latter, she spent Saturday night on the phone getting yelled at by that prick de la Flors and his entourage of prick attorneys in the Justice Department. It was only when she broke out the actual land survey and threatened him with both trespassing and obstruction-of-justice charges did he call the FBI hounds off of her murder scene, all the while vowing revenge against her and her office for all eternity. That left the boys in blue on the task force cheering her name, but by Sunday night, she was both so emotionally and physically exhausted that when she actually fell into her bed, even her nightmares could not wake her.

Morgan Weber. Nineteen. Blond. Vibrant. Beautiful. Dead. As C.J. headed to court for Bantling's arraignment on the murder of Anna Prado, on Monday morning, visions of the smart wannabe model from Kentucky filled her head. Having seen the horror in the fishing shack, she could not dismiss its image from her brain. Strung out on fishing line and hanging from the rickety wooden rafters of the small shack's ceiling, Morgan Weber's petite body dangled like a bat's, her arms and legs spread far apart, like an acrobat or contortionist, her neck tied back so it curved upward toward the ceiling, like a swan, held in place with wire and tied back to a beam. She had been dead for so long, her body was all but a skeleton, with just a few black chunks of meat clinging to her tiny bones in a few spots. They had managed a quick, tentative ID because her driver's license had been found underneath the body, splattered with her blood. The identification was later confirmed through dental records.

They knew it was Cupid. From the huge amount of bloodstains on the floor underneath the body and the blood spatter at the scene, it was clear that Morgan had been killed where she hung. The savagery and viciousness of the murder, the precise staging of the remote crime scene were in keeping with his style. But ironically, it was this preciseness, this attention to detail, this staging of his victims that might just prove to be Bantling's downfall on this murder. Because from where Morgan Weber's body hung in the dark shack from invisible fishing line, she looked like a bird in flight. A vision hauntingly familiar to that of the stuffed birds caught on film by Crime Scene technicians in Bantling's own shed.

An indictment for capital murder was never before so warranted. Even the staunchest death penalty opponents would be able to say little in defense of William Rupert Bantling when the time came for him to hold out his arm.

C.J. held her copy of the indictment in her hands and walked into the crowded courtroom, full of Monday-morning motions, arraignments, and trial calendar calls, not to mention, of course, the antsy members of the press, who were all waiting with bated breath for the big official announcement from the state. The crowd let out a low whisper of excitement when she walked to the left-hand side of the gallery where the prosecutors waited for their cases to be called from the calendar.

The defendants in custody had been brought over from the jail already, and from the corner of her eye she could see the bright red jumpsuit and blond hair in the back of the box, again separated from the other inmates, and flanked by corrections officers. She made sure to avoid eye contact with him, and instead looked down at the paper in her sweaty hands.

Judge Leopold Chaskel III looked up from his Monday-morning calendar and spotted the cause of excited commotion. Ignoring the speech then currently being made by a whiny defense attorney begging for drug court for his client, the judge addressed her from the bench.

"Miss Townsend. Good morning. I believe you have something on my calendar this morning."

"Yes, Judge, I do," said C.J., moving toward the state's podium.

"It seems that I have been the lucky judge selected to hear the case of *The State of Florida* v. *William Bantling*, have I not?"

"Yes, Judge, you are the winner—he's all yours from here on out."

"Good. Is the defense present for your case this morning?"

"Yes, Judge. Lourdes Rubio for the defendant, and he is also present, Your Honor," said Lourdes. She rose like a shadow next to her client in the box.

"Good. Let's get this taken care of, then." Judge Chaskel turned to the defense attorney who was still in midwhine and said in a stern voice, "I'll deal with you and your client in a moment, Mr. Madonna. Don't mope, now, please. It is, after all, only Monday and you're on my calendar three more times this week. Hank, bring me the Bantling case."

Judge Leopold Chaskel III was a state's dream-come-true for a trial judge. He was a former state prosecutor who didn't put up with a lot of shit that other mousy judges might, particularly those worried about the defense bar. He gave a fair hearing to both sides, but with minimal whining and no stunts, and he had a very low reversal rate.

"Okay now. Counsel, make your appearances for the record, please."

"C. J. Townsend for the State."

"Lourdes Rubio for the defense," said Lourdes, coming to the defense podium.

"We are here on the matter of *The State of Florida* v. *William Rupert Bantling*. Today is the twenty-first day. State, do you have an announcement?"

"Yes, Judge. The grand jury has handed down an indictment against William Rupert Bantling in case number F2000-17429 for first-degree capital murder in the death of Anna Prado." C.J. handed the clerk the indictment.

"Very well," said Judge Chaskel, taking the indictment from the clerk. "Mr. Bantling, the state has charged you with first-degree murder. How do you plead to these charges?"

"Not guilty, Your Honor," said Lourdes. Bantling remained silent in his seat in the box. "We waive formal reading of the charges, enter a plea of not guilty, and demand trial by jury."

"Discovery within ten days, State."

"No, Judge. I have spoken with my client, and he has decided that he does not want discovery in this matter. Just a quick date," said Lourdes.

Judge Chaskel frowned. "Ms. Rubio, in case you didn't know, this is a first-degree-murder trial, and a lot is at stake. What do you mean your client doesn't want discovery?"

"Just that, Judge. I've explained to him that he has a right to discovery, but he has declined."

Judge Chaskel looked past Lourdes now and stared quizzically at Bantling. "Mr. Bantling, you have just been indicted on first-degree-murder charges. You have a right to know the evidence that the state has against you, the right to speak with the witnesses they intend to call to the stand to prove their case. That is called discovery, and in the State of Florida, you have a right to this, if you so choose."

"I understand," said Bantling, his eyes never leaving the judge's.

"And if you choose not to participate in discovery, you cannot come back later if you are convicted and complain.

Do you understand that? You will be waiving your right to appeal on that issue?"

"I do understand that, Judge."

"And with that in mind, do you still decline to participate in discovery and depose the state's witnesses?"

"That is correct, Judge. I have spoken with my attorney and I am aware of my options and I do not wish to engage in discovery."

The judge shook his head. "Very well. Let's set a trial date. What do we have, Janine?"

Janine, the clerk, looked up. "February twelfth, two thousand one, for trial. Report date, Wednesday, February seventh."

Lourdes cleared her throat. "Judge, Mr. Bantling wishes to expedite this matter as quickly as possible and clear his name. Can we get a quicker date?"

"You do understand that this is a first-degree-murder case, Ms. Rubio?"

"Yes, Judge. That is my client's decision."

The judge shook his head in amazement. "Okay. We aim to please. Janine, give me a closer date. One in December, please."

"December eighteenth, two thousand. Report date, Wednesday, December thirteenth."

"Okay, all. We are set for December. Merry Christmas. Happy Hanukkah. Joyful Kwanza. Now I hope you won't come whining to me in two months that you're not ready, Ms. Rubio. You're the one who wanted a quick date."

"No. I don't expect I will, Judge."

"Very well. I'll see you all then in December. Motions within thirty days, please. And no surprises. I hate surprises."

"Judge," said C.J. "I do have one further announcement for this court."

"I suspected you would, Ms. Townsend."

She cleared her throat and handed a piece of paper to the clerk.

"Pursuant to the Florida Rules of Criminal Procedure, the state is filing a written notice of its intent to seek the death penalty in this case. The death of William Rupert Bantling."

48

HE'D JUST HAD it. Had it with this show that everyone was putting on before him. The flavorless judge stopping his calendar in the middle of that poor schlep's speech, to make an all-important speech of his own. To fix the cameras onto his own bland face. Now here was the bitch again, Miss Madame Tight Ass Prosecutor waltzing into court in her plain black pantsuit and glasses and making a big announcement. As if all eyes were on her. *Bullshit.* It was him they wanted to see; she was just some decoration. Eye candy on the cake. *Ooh, do take my breath away with your announcement, Miss Tight Ass. I'd love to loosen up your tight ass. Just give me five minutes to get it nice and loose.*

How was he supposed to get a fair trial with any of them? Mugging the cameras for attention, when it was he who had handed them their notoriety? They cared not for the fucking truth. They didn't even listen when it was screamed in their faces.

He sat back in his seat and grumbled, watching the show, the farce, play out in front of his eyes. He wanted to turn his head and smile his best right at those fucking cameras. Maybe crack a lens or two. Maybe get one of those cute blond reporters to send him a love note in jail or, better yet, visit him for a live interview. *Step up to the mike, my dear. That's it, put your mouth on the mike and take it all the way in.* That would be sweet. And she could bring her own camera, too. His mind started to wander away from the hearing and his cock rose in his bright red jumpsuit.

Then Miss Tight Ass made her haughty proclamation.

And the state would like to announce . . . blah blah blah . . . its intent to seek the death penalty in this case.

It wasn't that he hadn't expected the *announcement,* as it was being called; it was just that he hadn't expected it today, in this circus. Today was just to be his arraignment. Just sit there and say nothing. Today is the day we enter your plea to the charges; that's it. At least that was what his useless lawyer had said. So they wanted to put him to death? They were going to need some heavy-duty rope then to haul his kicking, screaming ass in, that was for sure. There would be a fight, yes, siree. Count on it.

He heard the cameras click and whir and focus on his face and he watched as Tight Ass teetered her haughty little self back out of the courtroom right past him. So close he could spit on her. So close he could smell her perfume as she passed. Chanel No. 5 it was. He could see her cute little upturned nose and fair skin and full, pouty mouth.

Then the Grinch got an idea. A wonderful, awful idea.

Bill Bantling smiled a sheepish, calculated smile for the cameras. For just then, he'd finally remembered exactly why Miss Madame Prosecutor looked so familiar.

49

"IT TOOK THE lab a couple of weeks, but they've finally ID'd it. The fishing line that he used on Morgan Weber is identical to the line found in the shed," said Dominick.

It was Monday, October 16—exactly two weeks since Bantling had been arraigned. Manny, Eddie Bowman, Chris Masterson, Jimmy Fulton, and three other task force members sat at the cherry conference table in task force headquarters at the FDLE's Miami office. C.J. sat next to Dominick at the head of the table. It was a case strategy meeting. A powwow.

"That's great. Now tell me the bad news. How many spools of that fishing line were manufactured and sold within the past ten years to bait and tackle shops all over Florida?" asked Manny.

"A lot. We're working on getting a number," replied Dominick. "Another bit of good news just in: Jimmy and Chris finished up with Tommy Tan's crazy-ass business records. Even though our love-seat salesman of the year was out of the country six months out of each year, he was nice enough to stay home in cozy South Florida on every day a girl vanished."

"Have we gotten anyone to ID him with a victim?" asked C.J.

"No. A few Jerry Springer wannabes, but no one credible," said Dominick.

"Well, he hasn't filed an alibi notice and he isn't participating in discovery, which worries me a bit. So I don't know what defense he plans to spring on us. Maybe we're in for a big surprise at trial," said C.J.

"Like an evil identical twin brother?" piped up Chris.

"Sit down, Matlock, before you hurt yourself," yelled Manny. Everyone laughed.

"So when are we gonna move on him on the other murders?" asked Eddie Bowman, as the laughter died down. He was scratching the back of his head impatiently. "It would make me sick if this pervert walks for some reason on Prado, and we ain't got nothing to hold him on his way out the door in the middle of the night."

"He's not walking on Prado," said C.J.

"The case is pretty much airtight, isn't it, C.J.?" asked Chris.

"As airtight as a case can be. The DNA's back, and it's a match to Anna's. That was her blood all over his shed. We have the body in his trunk. We have the murder weapon in his shed. The mutilation of her body and dissection of her heart is cruel and heinous, not to mention the drugs he used on her to paralyze her and keep her conscious while he killed her, and we have her abduction from Level, which shows premeditation, all of which are the aggravating factors that we'll need to get death. All I really would like to seal this case is her heart, and, of course, the hearts of the others. But at least on Prado we have enough at this point to go forward."

"Then why not file on the others?" asked Bowman again. He looked annoyed. For all his twelve years spent in law enforcement, sometimes he just didn't understand how the legal system worked once a perfectly good case got passed off to a lawyer. Take a mope with an armful of priors and a two-hour taped confession—and five bucks will get you ten that for some fucked-up legal reason, a jury would never hear about either of them. That's just the way it seemed to be, and it pissed him off more and more each year. One minute he would be looking at a commendation for great police work on a case and his name on a plaque, and the next, he was sitting in a courtroom listening to a not-guilty verdict on the same fucking case. So he was not holding out any hope on Bantling, no matter how "airtight" the prosecutor was calling it.

"Because Bantling is a stickler on the clock. He wants a speedy trial on Anna Prado, and I don't want to act prematurely and later lose something on speedies because all my ducks were not in a row. If I can get a conviction on Prado, I can then Williams Rule not only the conviction itself, but also the facts of her murder into the other cases and try them all together. That way, even without any physical evidence directly linking him to the other murder victims, the jury can still hear about all the murders and Bantling's conviction for at least one of them. Of course, it's still circumstantial and that makes me nervous, especially with Miami jurors. I want some physical evidence—and the fishing line is certainly a start—some evidence that directly connects him to those women. I want the smoking gun, Eddie. Find me the trophies he collected from each of his victims. Find me their hearts."

"Well, we're looking, but he could have burned them or eaten them or buried them for all we know, C.J. I just don't see why finding them is so necessary." Bowman scratched the back of his head again.

"Hey, Bowman, what you got? Fleas?" Bear yelled. "Maybe they're breeding in your ears, 'cause you ain't fucking listening. She's going forward even without them. Give her time." Not everyone shared Bowman's gloomy pessimism.

"I don't think he did any of those things, Eddie," C.J. responded. "I think he has them preserved someplace. Someplace where he can look at them and remember. I spoke with Greg Chambers, the forensic psychiatrist who consulted on the Tamiami Strangler. All serials take trophies from their victims. Snapshots, jewelry, hair snippets, underwear, some personal artifact. He thinks Bantling's trophies were his victims' hearts. It fits the pattern. And he wouldn't destroy something he went to great lengths and ceremony to take. They would need to be preserved someplace where he had access to them at his leisure so he could look at them, touch them, remember. So I think that they're still out there, Eddie. We just need to know where to look.

"In the meantime, I've subpoenaed Bantling's medical records from New York. He still hasn't filed an insanity plea, and I don't think Judge Chaskel is going to let me look at the actual records and charts unless Bantling calls his sanity into question. But the actual *diagnoses* of his medical condition and *what* he was prescribed by his doctor is directly relevant and I'll get that. That will show a strong link between him and all the murder victims that the ME found with haloperidol in their systems."

She pulled her hands through her hair and tucked it behind her ears. Then she began to pack up her briefcase. "But, we might not even have to try that hard. He may make it very easy for us."

"How's that?" asked Dominick.

"I got a call yesterday from Lourdes Rubio. They want to talk. Probably on how he can plea and still avoid the death penalty."

"Oh that's just bullshit!" groused an excited Bowman. "He's not gonna sit in jail forever eating three square meals a day on *my* tax dollars after hacking eleven women to death, is he?"

"Don't be such a fuckin' grump," growled Bear. "Counselor is not gonna let him walk. I've seen the size of her balls in court and I can tell you that they sure as hell are a lot bigger than yours, Bowman."

"Taking the death penalty off the table is not an option," said C.J. "But if he wants to save the state the time and trouble of trying him for eleven murders, I'll certainly let him. He can argue to the sentencing jury in the penalty phase that he has found Jesus and his cooperation in pleading was a valuable asset. Valuable enough to spare his life. That argument didn't work for Danny Rolling in Gainesville and I doubt it will work for Bantling, either."

She had her briefcase in hand and was headed toward the door. "I'll let you know how it turns out. In the meantime, I've sent the feds enough paperwork to ticker tape all of Manhattan for a parade. When they're done reading, I'm going to walk them through whatever evidence they want to look at on Friday. They're getting quite antsy. So I'll need a warm body to open up the evidence room and supervise. Any takers?"

"Yeah. Bowman. He loves to baby-sit. Don't you, Itchy? Maybe you can pass off some of those fleas to the FBI SAC." Bear laughed.

"He don't have much hair left on that shiny head of his for them to hide in, Bear," said Jimmy Fulton from the back of the room.

"Now don't be making fun of guys with no hair. Me and Bowman are pretty sensitive," said Manny sternly.

"Fuck you, Bear. I ain't losing my hair," protested Eddie Bowman.

"No. You're fucking scratching it off your head, Itchy," snorted Manny.

"We'll just call you follicle challenged, Eddie. And I ain't calling Bear nothing. He's a hell of a lot bigger than me," said Chris Masterson.

"I'll walk you out," said Dominick to C.J. "Now behave yourself, kids. No spitballs."

Dominick and C.J. walked out the conference room doors and down the hall. Rain poured down outside the glass main doors that led to the parking lot. A big boom of thunder quaked outside.

C.J. stood at the main doors. "Damn. I forgot my umbrella," she said.

"Let me walk you." Dominick took an umbrella from the hall stand outside Dispatch. He led her outside, and they walked close together under the small umbrella in the driving rain to her car.

"How have you been sleeping?" he asked suddenly.

She gave him a funny look, as if he knew something he shouldn't have known. "What?"

"You said you got almost no sleep last weekend after we went to Morgan Weber's crime scene. I just wanted to know if you had caught up."

"I'm fine, thanks." She climbed into her Jeep. He held the door open with the umbrella still over his head, the rain pouring off the sides and soaking his pants. The palm trees in front of her car bent under the rain and wind—a typical vicious Florida afternoon thunderstorm in the height of hurricane season. Then Dominick suddenly leaned his whole upper body inside the car and into the front seat. His face was now inches from her own. The faint scent of his cologne tickled her nose. His breath smelled of sweet peppermint, and she could see the very faint lines that ran out like cracks from his soft brown eyes. She remembered his kiss from weeks ago and felt her breath suck in. The butterflies flew free.

"When this is all over, will you go to dinner with me then?" he asked.

She stuttered, taken aback by his question, which she had not seen coming. When she finally found her voice a few long seconds later, she was surprised to hear her own answer. "Yes. When this is over I will."

"Good." He smiled and the faint lines spread, cutting deeper into his tan face. He had such a nice smile. "When are you meeting with them? Bantling and his attorney?"

"Day after tomorrow, at DCJ. I'll call you and let you know how it went." She could not help but smile back at him, a warm, intimate smile. The butterflies danced.

He closed the door and watched under his umbrella as she pulled out of the parking lot and drove off toward the expressway in the driving rain.

50

THE MINT GREEN halls of the Dade County Jail smelled of bad body odor and urine and shit, an odor so offensive that it was hard to breathe. C.J. hated coming over to the jail. Whenever possible she had inmates brought over to either the courthouse or her office for depos or statements or plea negotiations, but because of the high security surrounding Bantling, that just wasn't going to be possible. So here she was, behind the same iron bars as the criminals, walking past the peeling green paint under the bright fluorescent lights, trying to tune out the whistles and jeers from the inmates above her on the metal catwalks outside their cells. She silently prayed that nothing dripped on her head from above. *Keep moving—it's hard to hit a moving target.*

On the seventh floor, where the maximum-security cells were located, a corrections officer in a bulletproof plastic booth in the center of the floor directed her down a corridor to a solid steel door with a small, thick, bulletproof window at the end of the hall. When she reached it, a loud buzzer sounded and it slid open. She stepped inside and it instantly slid shut again with a thud, as she faced another short hallway with more peeling green paint, and a steel-bar door at the end. Three video cameras recorded everything from their mounted positions on the wall. From where she stood behind the bars, inside the room she could see a metal table and two bodies seated at it—one of whom she instantly recognized in his familiar red jumpsuit as Bill Bantling. Cupid. Just steps away from her. She sucked in her breath and exhaled slowly. *Time for the show.* She walked to the door and it, too, slid open automatically. She steadied herself and stepped inside. The doors slammed shut behind her with a loud clang: She was locked in.

Bantling looked up at her when the door slid open, but C.J. kept her focus on Lourdes Rubio, who was seated at the table, directly to his right. She felt his eyes follow her as she walked across the room. But for the metal table and three chairs around it, the room was empty. The room was cold, and a strange and uncomfortable shudder ran through her.

"Hello, Lourdes." C.J. took a seat across from the two of them and opened her briefcase and removed a legal pad.

"Hello," Lourdes replied, looking up from a stack of papers in front of her. "Thank you for agreeing to meet with us this morning."

"You wanted to talk about a plea. Well, I'm here and I'm listening." C.J. looked only at Lourdes.

"We have some matters to discuss that will definitely factor in on any plea considerations, that is true." Lourdes sighed and after a brief moment, took a thick packet of paper and laid it in front of C.J.

"What's this?" asked C.J., frowning.

"My motion to suppress the stop."

C.J.'s eyes quickly scanned the motion while Lourdes continued on in a soft, resigned voice. "We have reason to believe your judgment is being clouded in this case, Ms. Townsend. We are making a formal request tomorrow before Judge Chaskel to have you removed. I am also planning on personally calling the State Attorney to discuss the matter."

C.J. swallowed hard. A feeling of panic, one that an animal must feel when the trap springs closed around him, caging him in, rushed over her. She felt as if she had just been sucker-punched from behind and all she could manage to say was, "Excuse me? And just what makes you think that my judgment has been clouded?"

"We have reason to believe . . . Well, we have come upon facts . . ." Lourdes blinked twice and went silent.

Then she looked down at her notepad, and an uncomfortable long moment ticked by. C.J. could feel Bantling's eyes
on her, never leaving her. She could smell his scent, heavy
in the cold air. His long fingers picked the peeling green
paint off the metal desk that he was handcuffed to; flecks
of olive green fluttered to the floor. The corner of his
mouth was turned up in a sneer, as if he was about to laugh.
He looked like a kid who knew something that no one else
in the class knew. C.J. focused her attention on Lourdes,
but underneath the table her knees began to shake.

Lourdes spoke quietly, her eyes still downcast at the
notepad. "I know that you have legally changed your name
from Chloe Larson. I also know that twelve years ago you
were the victim of a brutal rape in your apartment in New
York. I have read the police reports." She hesitated and
looked up at C.J. now. "I would like to say that I am sorry
about what happened to you." She cleared her throat and
repositioned her glasses on the bridge of her nose before
continuing. "My client maintains that he is the one who
raped you. He believes that you have recognized him. Due
to the expiration of the statute of limitations, he can no
longer be prosecuted for that crime in New York, and he
believes that you are aware of that fact and are now on a
vendetta. A vendetta against him. We believe that you are
withholding evidence in this murder because you know
that he is innocent." Lourdes exhaled deeply, obviously
relieved to be done speaking.

It was interesting, Lourdes's choice of pronouns in her
speech. Bantling was actually smiling now, and his head
nodded up and down as Lourdes spoke, as if she were a
preacher delivering a great sermon. His probing eyes
moved purposely up and down C.J.'s body. She knew what
he was thinking, and she instantly felt dirty: naked and
exposed in a roomful of voyeurs. She sat completely
motionless, stunned by the announcement. *What could she
say? What could she say?* Her mind raced for an answer.
Her face grew hot, and an awkward silence filled the room.

Then he spoke. The voice from her nightmares, now no
less than two feet in front of her.

"I can still remember how you taste," said the voice. Smiling still, he leaned forward toward her across the table and opened his mouth, slowly licking his top lip with his long pink tongue. He closed his eyes, as if in a deep fantasy. "Mmmmmm, mmmm good, Chloe. Or should I call you *Beany?*"

Lourdes sat up stiffly and yelled in his face, "Mr. Bantling! This is not helping you. Shut up!"

Chloe's knees shook uncontrollably now and she lifted her feet slightly off the floor so that he could not hear her heels click on the cement. She felt as if she would vomit. A rush of sweat poured over her body, and she had an overwhelming urge to run. Just run. For she had been ambushed again.

But she couldn't move from her seat. She could not leave because now was the moment. The moment she had wanted; the moment she had dreaded.

Speak now or forever hold your peace.

C.J. found his eyes and held his vile stare with her own for a few long seconds. His lip was pulled up in a sneer and his eyes danced with excitement, and she struggled inside to find a voice. When it came, it was low, but forceful and determined; she was amazed to hear how strong she actually sounded.

"I don't know how you found out about the crime of which I was a victim, Mr. Bantling—I really don't. Police reports, I suspect. That was a long time ago. And your allegation is truly sickening, especially if, in your twisted little mind, you thought making it would give you some sort of advantage in this litigation."

Now it was her turn. She felt the anger inside her gain momentum, knocking aside the weak Chloe who wanted to run and hide. She leaned closer, holding his icy blue stare with her own. In those eyes she saw a flicker of shock, a hint of confusion. She lowered her voice to all but a whisper, but she knew he heard her. "But I can assure you that nothing, nothing will give me more pleasure then seeing them strap your scrawny little body onto a metal gurney and pump a needleful of poison into your veins. Your

scared eyes will desperately search the audience of spectators called to lay witness to your death for someone, *anyone,* who can help you get that needle out of your arm, who
can help you stop the poison that's pulsing into your body,
shutting it down forever. And you'll find no allies in that
audience. No, you won't. But what you will find is me. And
rest assured, Mr. Bantling, I will be there to watch. In fact,
I'll be the one who puts you on that gurney. It's just a pity
that they don't usually fry people anymore. It would've
made it that much sweeter to see your whole twisted face
melt off."

She smiled a dry, knowing smile at him and stood up,
turning to address Lourdes now, who sat watching with her
mouth open as the scene unfolded before her. "And as for
you, Ms. Rubio, that was the single most unethical display
of lawyering that I have ever seen. I'll be sure to advise
Judge Chaskel as such when I get back to my office. Perhaps I will even address it with the bar."

Lourdes opened her mouth as if to speak, but C.J. shot
her down, her voice shaking with anger and contempt. "In
the future, don't even think about communicating with me
again unless it is through written motions filed with the
court. There is nothing that you need to say to me that cannot be said in front of a judge. You are as despicable as
your client." She grabbed her briefcase, headed to the iron
bars, and buzzed for Corrections.

Bantling had turned a frightening white, and droplets of
sweat had begun to drip slowly from his forehead down his
cheeks. Suddenly a loud, inhuman screech that sounded to
C.J. like a cat being skinned alive bellowed out in the steel
room.

"Jesus Christ, Bill! Stop it!" Lourdes shouted.

C.J. kept her back to him, waiting for the door to open.
The anger in his voice was all too familiar to her, and she
began to silently pray.

"I didn't do this!" he hissed. "You know I'm innocent!
You can't put an innocent man on death row!"

The heavy bars slid open. C.J. stepped through them
and tried not to run down the hall.

Bantling stood up now, his metal chair slamming on the

cement floor behind him, his handcuffs clanging against the metal leg of the table that held him in place. He screamed behind her. "You fucking dirty bitch! You can't run from *me,* Chloe! Just remember that—you fucking tasty bitch!"

The bars slammed shut, and she hit the buzzer to the outer steel door of the reception area. The guard looked up from his magazine in the bulletproof booth. *Come on, come on. Open.* Her legs were knocking together, and she could barely breathe. Air, she needed air. The door buzzed.

He was screaming now, pulling violently on the table. C.J. wondered if anyone had ever actually pulled a table out of the floor before. Would he get to her before the guard put down his magazine and made it out of his booth?

"Twelve years and you're still running, Chloe! But I found you! I found you again, *Beany*! I told you I'd be back! I'm back for you now—"

The scream cut off as the metal door slammed shut behind her. She reached the elevator bay and with shaking hands hit the Down button. It seemed like hours before the doors opened and she could step inside, alone at last. She knew, though, that video cameras still recorded her every move. Her legs felt like jelly, and she leaned against the steel walls for support. The doors opened and she walked quickly to the reception counter and signed out, her hand trembling violently under the pen. She held it still with her left hand.

"You okay, Ms. Townsend?" The corrections officer was Sal Tisker. He used to work security at the courthouse bringing the inmates over for court.

"Yeah, Sal, I'm fine. Just fine. It's been a bad day, that's all." Even her voice shook. She cleared her throat and took her purse from Sal across the counter. She pulled out her sunglasses and put them on.

"Have a good day, Ms. Townsend." Sal buzzed her through the last security door, and she walked out into the brilliant sunshine.

She quickly headed across the street to her office, passing the same three hookers on the jail's dirty cement stairs that she had seen on her way in. They were obviously wait-

ing for their meal ticket to make bond. Boy, was he going
to be pissed when he found out his best three ladies had
taken the day off from making money on Biscayne just to
fart around at the jailhouse. Everything around her in the
sunshine seemed surreal now. She resisted the urge to bolt
back at full speed to the safety of her office. *Just act normal a little bit longer. You're almost home. Then you can
fall apart.*

From behind her a voice shouted out from the steps of
DCJ. It was Lourdes Rubio. She sounded frantic.

"Ms. Townsend! Jesus, Ms. Townsend! C.J.! Stop,
please!"

51

"I HAVE NOTHING to say to you."

"Please, please, just give me a moment. I'm sorry. I didn't know he would be like that, that he would say those things." Lourdes trotted alongside C.J., trying to get her to look at her. "C.J., please, hear me out."

"Let me guess—you pulled strings and got the police reports from New York. You give a loaded gun to a madman and act surprised when he shoots someone? Give me a break, Lourdes." C.J. kept up her brisk pace.

"He knew facts that were confirmed in those reports, C.J. I only let him read them after the fact."

"I was assaulted over twelve years ago, Lourdes. He had twelve years to read those reports before you were kind enough to order him his own set. Don't be fooled so easily."

"C.J., the fact is, I'm sorry for how it came out, for how it was handled. I know this must be painful for you—"

C.J. stopped walking and faced Lourdes Rubio with a look that would have frozen water. Her voice shook. "You have no idea. You cannot even begin to imagine. Imagine what it's like to wake up in the middle of the night with your hands strapped to a headboard and a madman in a mask slicing your skin to ribbons with a jagged steak knife."

Lourdes closed her eyes and cringed, turning her head away.

"Does hearing it make you uncomfortable, Lourdes?" Her words were a low, contemptuous hiss now, and she spat them like venom at Lourdes. "You know, the word *rape* by itself sounds so neat, so clean. So easy. Okay, you were raped. So is one in every four women on college campuses across the country. Just get over it, already. The fact is, there is so much more to it than that. Like four hours of torture, of being raped over and over and over again with a penis, a bottle, a coat hanger. Of writhing under a man determined on pleasuring himself by cutting your skin open and watching the blood seep out. Of screaming so much in your head that you thought you would explode from the pain and from the pure fear. Maybe you didn't read those reports you ordered for your client. Because if you had, you would have known that the man who raped me didn't just leave a boo-boo. He left me sterile. A freak when the lights are left on. He left me to die on sheets soaked in my own blood. Now did you think that you could just come in and toss out your accusation and that it wouldn't be painful or shocking or completely devastating? Did you really think you could do that? Who gave you that right?"

"He's my client, C.J. And he's looking at death row." Her voice was a choked whisper, the words pleading for understanding. But there was none to be found.

"And your client tells you that he's a monster. That he viciously raped a woman twelve years back, and that woman just so happens to be his prosecutor now while he stands accused of raping and then butchering eleven women to death. How convenient. And without thought as to the consequence, you actually toss out those accusations to a woman you know has been raped *while he is sitting right there*. Now I don't know how your client found out about my assault, I really don't, but I will tell you this much—my conscience is clear. And if by some chance he should walk, if he should get out of jail someday, and rape and torture and kill some other innocent woman, which he will inevitably do if given the chance, I know that I can face that woman's family and truly say, 'I'm sorry for your loss.' I can live with myself, Lourdes. Can you?"

Lourdes was silent. Tears rolled down her cheeks.

"Now you do what you feel you have to do for your client. And I'll do what I know is right. I have an appointment."

With that, C.J. turned and crossed Thirteenth Street, leaving Lourdes Rubio crying on the sidewalk just outside the Dade County Jail.

52

"C.J. TOWNSEND. STATE Attorney's Office." C.J. flashed her credentials at the dispatch officer.

"Who do you need to see, again?"

"Special Agent Chris Masterson."

"Yeah, hold on, he's coming down."

C.J. nervously paced the reception waiting room at FDLE headquarters, her heels tapping softly on the white tile. Commendations and plaques decorated the walls, along with an enormous detailed color photograph of a gold Special Agent's badge. On yet another wall, plastered practically on top of each other inside a glass case, were missing-person flyers. C.J. glanced over the photos on the flyers. Most named teenagers who had either run away or children who had been abducted by a noncustodial parent, but there were a few others who had simply vanished under suspicious circumstances. Those were labeled "endangered." A flyer remained in the case until the person was found or the case was solved. The new additions were thumbtacked alongside the older ones, so that the more dated flyers were caught underneath. C.J. spotted the black-and-white photograph of a smiling Morgan Weber, her flyer half covered by the freckled face of a teenage runaway. They had not yet removed her flyer from the case.

The door opened, and Chris Masterson walked in. "C.J. How are you doing? I'm sorry it took so long. Dominick didn't tell me you needed to get into the evidence room today, so it just took me a minute to set everything up for you."

"I was going to go through it Thursday, Chris, but I have a depo set then and I'm walking the FBI through it all on Friday. So I need to get in there now. Thanks for taking the time to set it all up."

"No problem." They walked down several twisting hall-ways until they reached the locked conference room. Task force headquarters. Chris opened the door. The long conference table was stacked with large cardboard boxes. On the side of each box was scribbled CUPID, with the FDLE case number. "I left you the inventory sheets from the search warrants on the table. Everything's marked in order. Just make sure you sign out when you're done and let Becky know that you're through. She's the evidence custodian across the hall. I have an interview in an hour, or else I'd help you out. In fact, just about everybody's out this afternoon."

"No. There's no need. I just want to take a peek at what we've got. I won't be too long."

"Dom's on the Beach doing interviews, I think. I don't think he's coming back here tonight. Do you need me to raise him on the radio?"

"No. I don't need any help. Thanks, anyway."

"Alright, then. Good luck. I'll leave you to your work." He closed the door behind him, leaving her alone in the dimly lit room. It was already almost five, and the light outside was beginning to fade as the sun set. The dead girls on The Wall stared down at her as she lit a cigarette with shaking hands and carefully read through the sixteen pages of inventory sheets on the table. She didn't know exactly what she was looking for, but she knew that if it existed, this was where she was going to find it.

Lourdes was on a fishing expedition on the pc issue— either that, or her motion to suppress was incomplete. Lourdes had given her a copy of the motion that would be filed tomorrow morning. She'd read it over carefully three times and there was no mention of, or hint at, the anony-mous tip. The motion was based solely on Bantling's protestations that he was not speeding, that his taillight had not been broken, and that the search was without consent or probable cause. And to be sure that neither Chavez, Lindeman, nor Ribero had talked to either Lourdes or one of her investigators, or anyone else for that matter, C.J. had also called the sergeant himself at MBPD, almost giving him a heart attack with news of Bantling's accusation that the search had been devoid of pc. No one had talked to anyone, Ribero had assured her. A boilerplate motion: an arrested defendant's words against that of an esteemed police officer. It was not hard to see in that instance who would win the war of words.

But while she may have breathed a sigh of relief, it was short-lived, for the second half of the motion was devoted to the allegations Lourdes had made in DCJ. That C.J. was raped, that Bantling was her rapist, and that C.J. was now actively involved in a fraud and a cover-up to conceal that fact. And C.J. knew that Bantling may just have something in his possession to prove that true, to elevate this past just a boilerplate war of words.

The inventory sheets listed every piece of evidence seized from Bantling's house and cars, and assigned it an FDLE exhibit number. She purposely passed over boxes containing swatches of carpet, bedding and linens, kitchen utensils, and personal hygiene items and moved to a set of three large boxes marked Exhibit 161A, B, and C. The top of the inventory sheet was marked "Personal Effects," and then listed on a separate line the evidence seized in that category: "photos, misc."; "photo albums numbered 1 through 12"; "black VHS unlabeled videotapes numbered 1 through 98"; "books (44)"; "magazines (15)"; "CDs numbered 1 through 64"; "clothing, misc."; "shoes, misc. (7 pr)"; "costumes, misc."; "jewelry, misc." It was this box that interested her.

She looked at each photo album, every photograph, and, finding nothing, then moved slowly through the box of miscellaneous clothes seized from Bantling's house. There was nothing. The books were mainly contemporary novels, except, appropriately, for a few titles from the Marquis de

Sade and Edgar Allan Poe; the magazines ranged from soft- to hard-core porn—*Playboy, Hustler, Shaved.* The CDs were all popular music, and her office had already been forwarded a copy of all the videotapes, which she had watched in their entirety in one hellish, long weekend. There was nothing there, either.

FDLE Exhibit Number 161C, Item 11: miscellaneous costumes was handwritten on a white evidence receipt and taped directly to the top of a blue plastic storage container in the last evidence box. There was no other detailed description noted anywhere on the inventory sheet. C.J. opened the lid, which had not been taped shut, and drew in a breath.

There, resting on the top, with its bloodred smile and shaggy polyester eyebrows, was a ghoulish clown mask. C.J. instantly recognized it. Her blood ran cold, and she trembled uncontrollably as memories rushed her like ghosts freed from a closed-off attic. That face at the end of her bed, glowing white in the electric flashes of lightning that escaped into her bedroom. The sound of his breath as it hissed through the rubber mouth slit. She felt his gloved hands on her skin, the tickle of the polyester hair on her legs and stomach. She smelled the latex and his old coffee breath and tasted the dry silk of the panties on her tongue, her throat gagging with the memory. After a few dizzying moments, with her own gloved fingers she picked up the mask by its fuzzy red hair, holding it far away from her person, as if it were a dead, putrid animal. She knew what had to be done. Then she stuffed it into a waiting black plastic bag and closed up the lid on the storage container.

The final evidence bag in exhibit 161C was a clear plastic bag stapled with a white inventory receipt marked *FDLE 161C Item 12: jewelry, miscellaneous—upper-left-hand bureau drawer, master BR.* She laid the bag on the conference table and spread out the jewelry inside, looking at it carefully. A TAG Heuer watch. A gold cuff bracelet. A gold rope bracelet. Necklaces. Cuff links. A man's black onyx ring. Several mismatched earrings.

And then she saw it. The gold double-heart diamond

pendant that Michael had given her for their anniversary twelve years before. Tears flowed down her cheeks, but she quickly brushed them away, and delicately sliced under the red evidence tape that sealed the bag, careful not to disturb the initials of C.M., the officer who had bagged the jewelry as evidence. Probably Chris Masterson. She removed the pendant, fingering it flatly in her fingers as she had the last time she had seen it, when it was around her neck. She remembered Michael's words to her that night.

I had it made special. Do you like it?

A one-of-a-kind piece—and the only thing that could incontrovertibly connect her with Bantling. The ghosts rushed her again, tackling her and leaving her breathless and drained. She remembered the knife as it angrily sliced the pendant from her throat. His labored coffee breath as it hissed harder and faster from the mouth slit. *She couldn't go crazy again. She couldn't. It took too long to come back last time.*

The earrings and maybe the bracelets and necklaces were probably taken from Bantling's other victims: maybe the bartender from Hollywood, or the UCLA student from L.A., or the nurse in Chicago. Tokens, trophies taken from each conquest. How many times had Bantling looked at that pendant and thought of her? Remembered Chloe and who she used to be? Got himself off thinking of her dying on those sheets? She slipped the pendant in the black plastic bag next to the mask and she shoved the bag in her purse. Then she carefully resealed the evidence bag and placed it back in the cardboard box. She had found what she had come for. Now the playing field was again level. It would be his word against hers. And she knew who would win that battle.

She had become a thief, a criminal. She had become one of the bad guys.

Yet another small sacrifice for the greater good.

53

SHE HAD PACKED up her briefcase to go when the door opened suddenly. She jumped in her skin and caught her breath. Dominick stood in the door frame looking at her quizzically.

"Hey, what are you doing here?" he said. "I came back to get my laptop and saw the light on from the parking lot. I thought you might be Manny."

"You scared me. I didn't hear the door," she said, holding her hand over her heart.

"Sorry. I didn't mean to scare you. You do look a bit pale."

"Chris let me in. I needed to get familiar with the evidence. I'm walking Gracker and the FBI through it all on Friday. I didn't want to be surprised," she said quickly.

"Well, keep an eye on him. He just might take a few things when you're not looking." Dominick looked around the conference room. "Where's Chris now?"

"He had an interview."

"Where? Upstairs?"

"No. I think in the city."

Dominick looked upset. "He shouldn't have left you with the evidence. He needs to sign it in and out of the evidence room. He should be here."

"He told me to sign out with Becky."

"Becky left at five, along with everyone else. The building is deserted. I'll need to sign this stuff back in and secure it. Let me open up the evidence room."

"Sorry."

"It's not your fault. I'll get with Chris in the morning about it. Did you find everything you needed?"

"Yes. I've seen everything I needed to see." She helped him carry the boxes down the hall to the evidence room and watched anxiously as Dominick logged each exhibit back in. Her palms were in full sweat as she watched him check off the items on the last exhibit, namely the bag of miscellaneous jewelry and the costumes box. She breathed a sigh of relief when he finally stood and double-locked and secured the evidence room, set the alarm, and signed out.

"How did your meeting go today with Bantling and his attorney? It was this afternoon, right?" he said as they headed back down the hall.

C.J. bit the inside of her lip. Other than Chris Masterson and Lou Ribero, Dominick was the only other person she had spoken with since all hell broke loose at DCJ. She didn't know if she could have this conversation right now without falling apart. She felt her eyes well up, and she looked down at her purse on the long cherry table. "Okay. Not much to tell."

"Does he want to cop a plea?"

"No. No plea. He's filing a motion to suppress the stop."

"A motion to suppress? On what grounds?"

"No pc for the stop. That Victor Chavez, the Beach cop who pulled him over, was lying and didn't see Bantling speeding. He just used that as an after-the-fact excuse to justify the stop. He also says that the taillight wasn't broken, and that excuse was bullshit, too. He says, basically, that Chavez is a rogue cop looking to make the big time using Cupid as his pole jump." She purposely left out the second half of the motion, the real reason she was called down to the jail today.

Dominick remembered the broken piece of taillight that he had picked up at the scene and slipped into his pocket the night Bantling was arrested. It certainly wouldn't be the first time that a cop had taken matters into his own hands with an asp or flashlight or his foot. Make the facts fit the crime.

"That's just great," he said shaking his head, trying to shake loose the image he now had of Chavez tossing pieces of taillight off the MacArthur Causeway. Right in front of the *Miami Herald.* "You prefiled that cop. What do you think about his story?"

"He's a rookie—he lacks experience. But I think he'll be okay." C.J. was feeling more than uncomfortable now. She was not good at lying. Avoiding, maybe, but not lying. "If I could have picked someone else to have done the stop, I would have, but that's not possible, so we go with what we have. I'm working with him."

"I don't get it. Rubio asked you down to the jail to file a motion to suppress? That doesn't make much sense. She could have done that in court. She didn't need to drag you into that shit hole. Was Bantling there, too?"

"Yes." She started to shake slightly.

"Anyone else?"

"No."

"Just you, Rubio, and Bantling in a lockdown cell?" He watched her face drain with every question. *Why?*

She knew he was reading her, looking for an answer and at this very moment, she was an easy read. She reached for her purse and held it close to her side. "Dominick, please. It's been a long day. He's a freak. I don't want to get into it."

"C.J., what has he got on you? Why does this case upset you so much? What is it? You can talk to me. Maybe I can do something . . ."

God, how she wished she could talk to him. How she wished he could make this whole nightmare go away, maybe hold her in his arms and make her feel safe the way he had that night in her apartment four weeks ago. Safe and protected and warm. Now, more than ever before, she needed that feeling, because her life seemed to be spinning furiously out of control yet again, and she'd been left desperately grabbing at strings to pull it back in and hold it together. "No, no. As I said, he's a freak, that's all. I've got to go home. It's late, and I'm exhausted."

He watched her as she picked up her briefcase. "Is the motion good?"

"No. It's boilerplate. Shouldn't be a problem."

"Can I get a copy?"

"It's at the office," she lied. She knew that the press would be all over the facts in that motion once it was actually filed with the court and became public record. Her rape would be all over the news, analyzed by some twenty-something reporter trying to make a name for himself on MSNBC. She would relive it again and again and again until the public wasn't interested anymore. And even though it would not be grounds in and of itself for her removal on the case, she knew that Judge Chaskel would not be happy that she had not disclosed it. She also feared that Tigler would remove her and assign another prosecutor: one who didn't carry allegations of impropriety and bias with her as baggage into the courtroom. She knew she should give Dominick a heads-up before the allegations came out, practice denying them without crying every two seconds, but not tonight. Tonight she couldn't.

"Alright. Let me walk you out." He knew not to push her; it would just drive her further away. So he decided to change the subject. "I'm gonna try to raise Manny and see if he wants to get some dinner. I just spent my whole afternoon club-hopping on Miami Beach, and it's really no fun in the middle of the day." He locked the conference room and waved at the duty officer alone in the dispatch room on the way out.

They walked to her Jeep in silence, and she climbed in. It would not be a sweet send-off like the other day. "Thanks, Dominick," was all she said.

"Good night, C.J. Call me if you need me. Anytime."

She nodded and pulled away.

He turned and walked to his own car. In the dark, deserted parking lot, he sat thinking for a few moments about what had just transpired, about C.J.'s quirky reaction yet again to the mention of Bill Bantling's name. He left a message on Manny's cell and then checked the voice messages on his own cell phone. The faint tap on his window more than surprised him.

It was C.J. He rolled down the window.

"Jesus. You shouldn't sneak up on people. Especially those with guns in dark parking lots. Are you okay?" He looked around the parking lot for her car, expecting to see it disabled with the hood up.

"Is that dinner invitation from the other day still open?" she asked with a strained smile. "Because I'm starving."

54

IT WAS NOW 8:00 at night and Lourdes Rubio still sat at her hard oak desk in her empty office, still staring at her law degree from the University of Miami, and still wondering how the day had gone so terribly wrong. Next to the law degree, the cream-colored walls were adorned with the miscellaneous community-service awards and plaques that she had received over the years from various legal and charitable organizations.

She could still remember verbatim the oath she took as a lawyer when she was sworn in by old Chief Judge Fifler, and the horrible magenta suit with the quarterback shoulder pads that she had worn for the occasion. That had been fourteen years ago. Judge Fifler had since died, the purple suit burned, and the years had somehow flown by.

Much to her mother's disappointment, Lourdes had always wanted to be a criminal defense attorney. She actually *wanted* to uphold the Constitution and protect the innocent from having their rights trampled upon by the intrusive eyes and ears of bad big brother. All that shit that she had learned and taken for gospel in law school. Then she had hit the real world as a public defender and watched as her naïveté fell from grace.

There was no place for the homeless, no help for the mentally ill. Lawyers wanted to make money and cut deals. Judges wanted to lighten their caseloads. Prosecutors wanted to build a name for themselves. For many, the justice system was nothing but a cruel revolving door. And still, she wanted to be a criminal defense attorney.

Until today.

She had coped with the shortcomings of the system by leaving the bureaucratic Public Defender's Office and starting her own criminal law practice. As a Cuban female in a solo practice she had struggled for years to build a name for herself in a profession dominated by men, where she was surrounded by men, including her own clients. And after eight hard years she had made that name, playing hardball with the best of them. She was at the top of her game, one of the highest paid and most well-respected criminal defense attorneys in Miami. She had won the brass ring. Now she looked at her law degree with disgust rather than pride. She thought of her client with contempt, instead of compassion.

How could she allow herself to get caught up in the cycle, in the very system that she despised and for years had claimed on a daily basis she wanted to change? How could she actually allow a rapist to confront his victim, allow him to use his crime against her as a legal weapon to gain his freedom? Because in this system, to win sometimes meant playing tough, at whatever cost, and she knew that his allegations would be a quick fix to this case. A fast victory.

She began to put her files in her briefcase, to pack up and go home and fix dinner for her elderly mother and maybe watch a movie on HBO, but then she just as quickly stopped and put her head in her hands.

She had mistaken victory for justice today, and for that she was truly sorry.

55

CHLOE LARSON. THE cute little lawyer-to-be from Queens was now all grown up and playing prosecutor. Boy, had Father Time been rough on her. He had barely recognized her, what with that mousy hair and her grandma suits that covered too much of her once-tight ass and perky tits. But that face. Well, he could never forget a face. Especially one like Chloe's. That's why she had been chosen in the first place. Because she was not just pretty—she was *exceptional*.

And now he had found her again. Twelve years and he had found her, and they were reunited. The look on her *exceptional* face when his useless attorney had sprung the news on her was priceless. Simply priceless. Shock. Then fright. And finally, terror. She had been caught. Caught by her captor. Forced to look back in his face again with those pretty green eyes and admit she couldn't play this game. She had failed at that, too.

He picked his teeth clean with a cardboard notebook cover while he sat on the lumpy cot that smelled like old fish and piss.

Shut up and sit down. That's actually what his useless attorney had yelled at him. *Shut up and sit down.* Who the fuck was she? He had to rethink her part in all this. He had originally thought her to be a good choice as his attorney, but now . . . Then again, she had gotten the police reports for him from New York and that had made for some great bedtime reading. To actually read about what he had done, as recalled through the eyes of others. Particularly the dumb NYPD Blue cops who couldn't find their asses from their elbows. It was pretty cool. And his useless attorney had helped him scare the shit out of Madame Prosecutor with her heretofores and whereases and overall legalese. But now she said she couldn't file the motion yet, that she had to do some more investigating. So now he was left to wonder if she could play ball with the Big Boys in the Big Top.

Let me handle this. You are admitting that you are a brutal knife-wielding rapist. You want to say, "I did it then, but I didn't do it now" and get off by accusing the prosecutor, your victim, of wrongdoing. But understand this, Bill: Everyone will despise you even more, and they will take pity on her. It is a very delicate situation, and we can't just level these charges. She is denying your accusations, and frankly, your word means nothing to the court—not over hers. You need proof.

I'll give you proof, alright. Although I'd hate to part with it.

Outbursts like today's are certainly not going to help your case. You look the part of a serial killer. You need to let me handle this in the way I think it should be handled. And you need to say nothing. Just shut up and sit down.

She sure was scared, though. Now that Lourdes Rubio knew who she was dealing with, sitting next to in the courtroom, whispering with in the cellblock. And he didn't know if she could be as convincing to a jury as before, when she actually believed him innocent. The trusting doe eyes were gone.

Bill Bantling paced like a wild animal in his cage, locked away from the others in solitary confinement because he was a security risk. *Bullshit.* It was simply because, he now realized, *Chloe, Beany, Madame Prosecutor,* had known who he was all along, and she needed him contained for her own protection. For her own sanity. The more bars he was locked behind, the better she told herself she could sleep. But now he knew her game, and it was up. It would actually be fun watching her come apart.

It's just a pity that they don't usually fry people anymore. It would've made it that much sweeter to see your whole twisted face melt off.

Oh, she talked a big act. But he knew that was because he was locked up in handcuffs and shackles and chained to a fucking table, and because of that she *could* actually say those things to him.

He knew, though, that she was scared, scared out of her mind. And she should be.

Because when he got out, he was going to kill her.

56

"I'VE BECOME INVOLVED with Dominick Falconetti."

"When did this happen?"

Greg Chambers was back in the role of therapist now. He sat quietly, his chair pulled conversationally in front of his desk. The late-afternoon sun streamed in through the wooden blinds, basking the room in a warm caramel light.

"I guess it's been happening. I've been trying to stop it, especially since Bantling's arrest, but, it just sort of developed." He watched as she stubbed out one cigarette, only after lighting another. The smoke hung in the air, dancing on the beams of soft light. She exhaled slowly and pulled her hair back again off her face and behind her ears.

"How do you feel about this? Is this something you want?" His voice was soft, devoid of judgment or opinion. Anything but, and she would clam up, hold it all inside, where it would eat at the lining of her stomach.

"How do I feel? I feel scared, nervous, happy, excited, guilty. All in one. All at the same time. I know I shouldn't have let it get this far, but . . . God, he takes my mind away. Away from all of it. And that's a good thing. That's good therapy, Doctor. When I'm with him, I'm with *him*. I'm in a safe place. That's the only way I can describe it. I can let this security fence, this *radar* that I have always going on, well, I can let it down. Turn it off. That psycho's face is finally out of my head, for just a few hours out of my day, anyway, and I'm someplace else, and this invisible weight in my heart . . . it's gone. It's a feeling I haven't had with any other man—one I don't want to let go of."

She rose out of the blue wing-backed leather chair and paced nervously about the room. "But I'm also scared. Actually, I'm petrified. I don't want to let him get too close. There are things he can never know about."

"Are you referring to yourself, perhaps? That you don't want him to see the real you for fear he may not like what it is he sees?"

"No. Yes. Emotionally, maybe sometime in the future I could totally let down my guard. Share myself, as you like to say. But, there are things, factual matters that, well, I can never share with him. Things that he would never accept. And I just don't think that a relationship can be built on half-truths."

"Are you speaking about your assault, the rape? Facts you don't care to share with him about that?" he prodded. "Perhaps sharing those facts can make you grow together."

"No. Besides the rape there are other things, but I don't want to get into them today. Not now." She remembered what was not covered by patient-doctor confidentiality, and that was future crimes. Withholding of evidence, tampering with witnesses, tampering with evidence, suborning perjury. All were criminal acts. She had to be very careful not to take this any further.

"Have you become intimate with him?"

The question made her a little uncomfortable. In the past, perhaps, these details would not have been difficult to share, but now Dr. Chambers had a professional relationship with everyone concerned. Unconsciously, she moved behind the chair. "Yes," she said.

"And?"

"And it was"—she paused for a moment, as if remembering something—"it was *nice*. It didn't happen right away, though. We just went to dinner that night after . . . after, well, what happened at DCJ."

"After Bantling and his attorney confronted you in the jail?"

"Yes. That night." She had shared with him Bantling's

allegations that he was her rapist. She had not told him of Lourdes's accusation that she had willfully withheld evidence. "I couldn't go home that night. I needed him around me. I was scared out of my wits—everything rushed back as if it were yesterday, and I could not go home to an empty apartment. I know that shouldn't be a basis for a relationship—fear—but, we didn't sleep together that night. It was just dinner. It was company. It was something more that had started awhile back. I needed to be close to him that night. I can't explain it."

She moved to the window and looked out on the busy Coral Gables street outside as it settled into rush hour. Busy people hurrying to and fro with their lives.

"Anyway, it just happened between us. Slowly. Last night, actually. I haven't been with anyone since that stockbroker a few years back, and frankly, I didn't think it would ever be *nice*. But it was, and it was warm and it was sweet and it was *nice*. Even in the pitch-black darkness, I was terrified about the scars, what he would say when he touched them, what he would think . . ."

She remembered her bedroom and Dominick's warm hands, softly rubbing the small of her back as he gently kissed her, his tongue touching hers, those hands moving slowly to undo the buttons on her blouse, and to press his own shirtless chest against hers. And she remembered the instant, sobering wave of terrifying anxiety that had come over her, because she knew he would feel them. Maybe even see them once his eyes adjusted to the darkness, the ugly raised lines that haphazardly crisscrossed her chest and abdomen.

They had had a couple of bottles of wine—too much wine—while watching the boats pass on the Intracoastal below. Wine and funny conversation. She had felt relaxed and comfortable and *happy* for the first time since she could remember. And when he had leaned over in his chair on the small balcony with the moonlit palm trees as a backdrop and kissed her, she did not resist. Instead she had moved closer and they had ended up in the blackness of her bedroom, his probing hands electrifying her body and terrifying her mind. But then her blouse, and then her bra, had come off and their skin had touched and he had said nothing. He hadn't even paused. He just kept kissing her in the darkness, his body dancing slowly in time with hers to soundless music, as if nothing else in the world mattered. And that morning when she had awoken, he was still next to her, playing softly with her hair and the back of her neck.

". . . but he didn't care," she continued. "He never said anything. I knew he must have felt them, so I told him I was in a car accident. I just blurted it out."

"And what was his reaction?"

"He asked me if they hurt me now. He asked me if they hurt when he touched them. I told him no, but that it had been a very long time since I had been with someone. And then he made love to me. Very slow, very gentle . . ." Her voice trailed off.

"I shouldn't be telling you this. It's very intimate, and you know everyone involved. But you're the only one who knows the whole story at play here, Greg—Dr. Chambers. I know I am falling for him, that I may already have fallen for him. I need to know if I am a fool to see a future in this."

"Only you can answer that, C.J."

"I can't even bring myself to tell him about the rape. He can never know about Cupid. There are so many secrets now, so many lies . . ."

"What about the motion to suppress? Didn't you say it detailed your rape? Won't he learn about your assault when the motion is heard?"

"Yes, the draft of the motion that Lourdes gave me did detail the rape. But I guess after I talked to her outside the jail she must have had second thoughts. At least for the time being. The rape is not mentioned in the copy of the motion she actually filed a week later with the court. Chaskel is hearing the motion next Tuesday morning. Halloween, of all days. Of course, she may surprise me still and call Bantling to the stand. If that happens, I guess the world will then find out about my rape at the same time Dominick does."

"How do you feel about that possibility? Your inability to control these events?"

"*Everything* is out of my control, it seems. But I can't let go of this case; I won't. And in the event that it does happen and I fall apart in front of the world, I was hoping that . . . well, that you might be there for support. Because if he does take the stand, I just might go crazy again."

"If you would like me there, then I will be there."

C.J. felt relieved; she would have at least one person in her corner should the world collapse in around her. "You'd better come early to get a seat—it's a hot ticket. CBS pitches a tent the night before, I've heard."

He laughed.

She mused aloud. "Maybe Lourdes has a conscience in that pretty head of hers. Maybe she thinks her client is lying about the rape: Maybe she knows better than to raise this as a defense. I guess we'll see on Tuesday."

He folded his hands under his chin and rested his elbows easily on his knees. "I'm glad you've decided to resume therapy, C.J. I really am. I would like to see you back on Wednesday evenings, at least weekly while this case progresses. I believe it will be more stressful than even you can realize."

She smiled. "Do I look as if I'm going crazy? Do my eyes roll? Do I sound coherent to a nonlawyer?"

"Let's not let it get to that point. You are not sharing these events with anyone else, and that is a factor to consider in returning to a weekly therapy schedule. It doesn't mean I think that you are 'going crazy' again, as you call it."

She nodded nervously. *If the metamorphosis did begin again, would she recognize the signs, or would someone have to point them out to her?*

"I'm sorry," she began in a low voice, "about ending therapy the way I did last spring—without . . . without speaking to you first. I wanted to see if I could muddle through life on my own . . ."

"Say no more. I understand. The important thing is that you've recognized that you need help, that you won't go through this alone. Now," he continued, changing the subject and letting the awkward moment pass as quickly as it had come, "how is the case going otherwise?"

"Everything else has fallen into place. The feds have backed off a bit. I think de la Flors is waiting to see how the motion goes. If I lose, he'll hang me high and rush in like a hero with an indictment. If I win, well, he might just do the same. It depends how the political winds are blowing.

"I just got Bantling's medical records from that doctor in New York City," she went on. "The diagnosis, anyway. Chaskel took a look at the records in his chambers and said only the diagnosis was relevant since Bantling has not yet placed his sanity in issue. So I'll get that and his meds into evidence. That will give me another link to Anna Prado, and a link to the other six girls that the ME has found haloperidol in. His doc had him on twenty milligrams of Haldol a day."

"That's an extremely high dosage. Was he still being treated by this doctor?"

"Dr. Fineburg. Occasionally. Enough so that he kept writing him refills every three months."

"And what was the actual diagnosis?"

She stubbed out her last cigarette and sighed wearily before rising to leave. "Borderline personality disorder with extreme and violent antisocial tendencies. In other words, he's a complete sociopath. As if I needed a doctor to tell *me* that."

57

HALLOWEEN MORNING WAS hot as hell. A warm front had come in and sat over Miami for two days, cursing it with 88-degree temperatures, 95 percent humidity, and nasty afternoon thunderstorms. Dominick stood outside the Graham Building, his dress shirt already sticking to his chest under his suit jacket. It was a quarter of ten in the morning; he'd barely made it.

He had cut short his meeting on the Cupid case with RD Black and the FDLE Commissioner because he knew he had to be here. Even though she had not asked him, and would probably never ask him, he knew he had to be here. He had witnessed her anxiety at the mere mention of Bantling's name enough times; and he had seen her strange, tense reaction when she was forced to be in the same room as him. Her eyes full of fear, her body trembling slightly, uncontrollably. In the past few days as she prepared for today's motion to suppress he had watched her become more withdrawn, definitely more stressed. And she did not want to discuss it with him, instead blaming her mounting stress on the pressures of trying a capital murder case where the stakes were high if she failed. Too high. He still did not know what it was, but he did know it was more than the stress of a murder case that drove the fear in her eyes. And he knew that he had to be here now, even if she protested, to escort her into the courtroom through the mob of nosy and pushy and completely obnoxious reporters, the curious onlookers, and those who silently prayed behind a smile for her downfall. To, if nothing else, sit behind her, while she struggled with the unseen, untold demons before her.

The glass doors of the Graham Building opened. She stopped when she saw him, a look of surprise on her face that he could detect even behind her dark sunglasses. She was dressed in a sharp black suit, her dark blond hair pulled into a soft bun. With her heavy briefcase on her shoulder, she towed a pull cart of three file boxes behind her.

"I just figured I'd give you a hand with those files," he said finally.

"I thought you had a meeting with Black," she replied slowly.

"I did. But this seemed more important."

It was still so new, this *relationship* they had fallen into. Even though they had spent the night together last night, it felt awkward between them at that very moment. He wasn't quite sure where they were headed, where he even wanted them to go, but right now what he did know was that she was worried about appearances. Their appearance together. So he kept a comfortable distance as they walked across the street to the courthouse in silence side by side, with him carting the enormous box of files behind him.

58

VICTOR CHAVEZ WAS nervous. Hell, he was sweating bullets what with all those damned reporters buzzing about like vultures inside, waiting for a chunk of meat to fall from the bone so they could take it back to their nests and pick it over. Waiting for someone to fuck up in this case so they could be the very first to report it. He sat on the bench just outside Courtroom 2-8 waiting for his turn on stage to be called. Everyone was here. Everyone was watching. His sarge, his lieutenant, all the boys downtown.

It wasn't as if he'd never testified before. In fact, this was his third felony arrest that he had to come in on, and he thought he was rather smooth on the stand. But of course, nothing was like Cupid. And, of course, he hadn't totally fucked up those other cases. And now he was being called as a witness for the defense in this stupid motion to suppress. Suppress *his* stop. *His* search. Guy drives around Miami with a dead girl in his trunk and it's a bad stop? *What the fuck was that about?*

Sergeant Ribero hadn't let him out of his sight, practically, since it had happened. Shit, he had to report taking a fucking leak when he was on duty now, and it was damn annoying being baby-sat, no doubt. But he knew it would be much worse if he fucked it up now, at a crucial motion to suppress, on the record with the lights and cameras on. Not only would he be out of a job; he would also become the subject of a criminal investigation himself. And of course, that fucking nut job would walk. He had to remember the story down to the last letter.

That was the hard part. Remembering every fucking detail, just as the prosecutor had said, in the order that she had said it. *That's the problem with telling a tale,* his mother had always said. *You often can't remember exactly what tale it was that you told.* Especially since he was always being asked by somebody what had gone down that night, how he had caught Cupid on the causeway. Not just downtown, either. It was everyone, it was everybody, it was everywhere. His neighbors in the building. High-school buddies. Strangers on the street. Girls at the beach. Girls by the pool. Girls in bars. Girls on patrol. He was a regular celebrity now, *The Cop Who Caught Cupid,* and even though his Sarge had told him to shut up unless he was in court, it wasn't Sarge that the girls wanted to blow to hear him tell his story. How he, Victor Chavez, while still on probation, basically single-handedly and on intuition, had caught the most notorious serial killer in America.

But now was the midnight hour, and he had to make sure every detail was right. Every single one. They ran together in his head like a garbled tape.

He sat on the bench in his MBPD uniform, his sweaty hands clasped together, just waiting his turn to walk the plank, when the mahogany doors swung open and in a loud, deliberate voice the bailiff called out his name.

59

BANTLING WAS ALREADY seated in his red jumpsuit at the defense table next to Lourdes when C.J. walked in the courtroom. She felt his eyes move with her as she crossed the gallery before the bench to the prosecution's table and, with Dominick's help, unpacked all the files. Even though she could not see him, she knew he was smiling. She could feel it. *Focus. Focus. Just like any other case.*

Dominick took a seat with Manny and Jimmy Fulton behind her in the front row. Chris Masterson and Eddie Bowman had shown up late and had to badge their way into a seat in the back row next to Greg Chambers. On the other side of the courtroom, still in their black suits, dark sunglasses tucked into their pockets, were the Blues Brothers, Carmedy and Stevens, and the bandleader, Gracker. Although she had not seen him, she was sure de la Flors was here, or had at least sent two Assistant U.S. Attorneys in his place, probably readied with a federal indictment in each hand, in case C.J. lost. As usual, every network was here, their cameras set up all over the courtroom. And then there were the newspaper reporters who were present from every major paper in the country. It was a packed house.

Lourdes had not looked at her when she walked in, instead keeping her head down, purposely focused instead on reading the paperwork before her. C.J. still did not know what to expect from her today, and her heart was definitely caught in her throat. The door to the judge's hallway swung open and Hank the bailiff quickly shouted, "Court is now in session. The Honorable Leopold Chaskel III presiding. Be seated and be quiet. No cell phones. No beepers."

Judge Chaskel took the bench and wasted no time with speeches or announcements to the anxious crowd; he appeared not to notice they even existed. With ten years on the bench and another twenty as a prosecutor, he had seen it all, and seeing his name in the papers was no longer a thrill. It was simply an irritating part of the job. He turned to Lourdes and started in right away.

"Well, Ms. Rubio, we are gathered here today to hear your motion to suppress the stop and subsequent search in the case of *The State* v. *William Bantling*. I've read your motion, so go ahead and entertain us. Call your first witness."

60

SINCE IT WAS the defense's motion to suppress, the defense also bore the burden of proof. They had to prove the stop was bad; the state did not have to prove the stop was good. And the only way to prove that the stop was bad was through, of course, witnesses who had themselves observed the stop. Lourdes's first witness was Miami Beach Police Officer Victor Chavez.

Chavez walked calmly in through the double doors of the courtroom and nodded somberly in the direction of Judge Chaskel before taking a seat in the witness box next to the bench. He straightened the tie on his uniform and cleared his throat, and a hush fell over the courtroom.

Lourdes finished shuffling her paperwork and jotting notes and after a few long seconds stood from her seat next to Bantling and approached the witness box. That was precisely when a cold fear gripped Victor Chavez's belly and his mouth suddenly went dry, and right then and there he knew that he was fucked.

A few weeks back he had been out on SoBe with his brother. In fact, they had gone to the Clevelander, the same bar that Morgan Weber, the last Cupid victim found, had disappeared from. And as always, when word got out that he was there, *The Cop Who Caught Cupid,* women were everywhere, all over him, wanting to know how he had done it. Wanting to know if he was packing now. And where. Wanting to know if they could see the back of his squad car. It was incredible. There were always enough women left over for his brother, too. And that night was no exception.

As soon as he had sat down, this cute redheaded chick with a tight pink shirt and her dark-haired friend had sat next to him, asking if it was true, if he had caught Cupid. He had had a few drinks before hitting the Clevelander and then there were some more and before you knew it, he was feeling pretty good. His brother was totally screwed up, barely able to walk, if he could remember right. And this redhead was getting so hot—falling all over every fucking word he said—he'd known it would be another night of easy pickings.

Now he sat in the hard-backed wooden chair with every eye in the crowded courtroom on him and the cameras rolling, and he knew he had totally fucked up. Sweat rolled off his forehead and down his temples. He could feel it run down his neck, and he rubbed his dry lips together.

The defense attorney who stood before him in a conservative gray suit, her arms crossed in front of her slight frame, was the dark-haired friend from the Clevelander.

And he knew she had heard everything.

61

WHAT HAD HE said? *What had he said?* The same garbled words streaked in front of him. A thousand tales, but which one had he told? Which one had she heard? There was so much liquor that night, he'd barely been able to remember his name when he got home.

"Please state your name for the record," she began.

"Victor Chavez, Miami Beach P.D.," he stumbled. *Easy, easy. Take it easy.*

"How long have you been an officer with the Miami Beach Police Department?"

"Um, since January. January two thousand."

"So we can cut to the chase, Officer, you were working the three-to-eleven shift on September nineteenth, two thousand, the night my client, William Bantling, was arrested. Is that correct?"

"Yes. Yes, I was."

"In fact, you were the officer who initiated the stop of his vehicle, were you not?"

"Yes."

"What events had transpired that led to Mr. Bantling's vehicle being stopped?"

Chavez looked around dumbly, perhaps for an assistant from the shadows to run up and whisper the answer in his ear.

"In other words, what happened that night, Officer Chavez?"

Chavez looked down at his reports, but Lourdes stopped him. "In your own words, from memory, if you would, Officer."

C.J. rose from her seat. "Objection. The witness is allowed to review documents that may refresh his recollection."

Judge Chaskel leaned over and looked skeptically down at Chavez. "Well, he has not yet told this court that he needs his memory refreshed, Ms. Townsend. Besides, Officer, I would imagine that this was the biggest night of your short career in law enforcement and that you would remember practically every minute of the evening. Why don't we try it first without the reports and see how we do?"

C.J. exhaled slowly, trying not to make eye contact with the desperate-looking officer.

"I was on patrol. Down on Washington, when I saw this Jag, um, Jaguar, license number TTR-L57, go speeding past me southbound, toward the causeway. The MacArthur Causeway. So, I took off after him. I followed him on the causeway for a while, just watching him. And then he made an unsafe lane change—he didn't signal—and I saw one of his taillights was out. So I pulled him over. I approached the vehicle, right in front of the *Herald* building, and asked him for his license, which he gave me. He looked kind of nervous, you know, sweaty, jittery. I took the license back to my car and stopped at his bumper to look at the broken taillight. That's when I saw what looked like, um, blood. Right there on the bumper. I gave him back his license and when I did, I thought I smelled marijuana in the vehicle. I, ah, I asked him, Bantling, if I could look in his trunk and he told me to get lost. So I called K-9 and backup. Beauchamp with MBPD showed up with his dog, Butch, and Butch went nuts on the trunk. Excuse me, he alerted on the trunk. So we popped it open and found the girl's body."

"Were you alone on duty, or with someone else?"

"I was riding by myself that night."

"What speed was Mr. Bantling traveling at when you first observed him?"

"Um, approximately forty miles per hour in a posted twenty-five-mile-per-hour zone."

"And you clocked his speed using a radar device?"

"No."

"Oh. So you were following behind him and observed that on your speedometer he was traveling at a speed of forty miles per hour?"

"No." Chavez twisted in his seat uncomfortably.

"Where were you then, Officer Chavez, when you first noticed this excessive speed violation? This fifteen-miles-over-the-speed-limit bandit in a new Jag, zipping down Washington?"

"I was on Sixth Street. Sixth and Washington."

"What direction were you facing?"

"My car was facing east. I was out of the car."

"Out of your patrol car? So that I am straight up to this point, Officer, you are not using radar, you are not following my client in your patrol car, you are not even in your own patrol car, you are standing on a street corner when you see this car go by you, barely breaking the speed limit?"

"Yes."

"And with your naked eye, just nine months out of the police academy, you were able to determine that this black car was traveling approximately fifteen miles over the speed limit?"

"Yes. Yes, I could. He was weaving in and out of congested traffic. He was proceeding in an unsafe manner." *Right out of the manual.*

"And what were you doing out of your patrol car at that time?"

"I was breaking up a fight between these two kids who'd had some words."

"And you left this fight where people presumably were in danger of being hurt, jumped in your patrol car, which was facing the opposite direction of Washington, and did what?"

"I, ah, followed your client onto the causeway."

"How did you get back on Washington to follow my client onto the causeway?"

"I went up Sixth over to Collins and then up Fifth, past Washington onto the causeway."

"So you first went down Sixth, and lost sight of my client in his speeding car, I presume?"

Chavez nodded.

"Please speak into the microphone, Officer Chavez, because the court reporter can't record when you nod your head."

"Yes. That is correct. I lost sight of him. I found him again, though. Right away. The same car with the same tag TTR-L57 five seven, on the causeway." Chavez was not only becoming noticeably uncomfortable under this questioning; he was obviously beginning to despise Lourdes Rubio. His answers were terse, cutting.

"Was he speeding then?"

"Um, yes. Yes, he was. He was doing about sixty to sixty-five in a fifty, if I recall."

"But you did not pull him over right away, did you?"

"No."

"Approximately how many miles passed on the causeway before you decided he posed such a safety risk to the citizens of Miami he needed to be pulled over?"

"About two. I pulled him over by the *Herald,* before I lost jurisdiction on him."

"Hmm. And did he pull right over?"

"Yes."

"He didn't try to flee?"

"No."

"And you say he was jittery, sweaty, nervous when you approached him?"

"Yes."

"Kind of like you are now, Officer Chavez?"

The courtroom tittered.

"Objection." C.J. rose again.

"Touché, Ms. Rubio. Move on," said Judge Chaskel.

"And then you stopped at his bumper to examine this broken taillight that you had suddenly noticed two miles into this pursuit?"

"Yes. I had noticed the broken taillight when I first caught up to him on the causeway."

"That's when you saw the blood on his bumper?"

"Well, it looked like blood. It was a dark substance. It turned out later that it was blood. That girl's blood."

"What time of night was it, Officer?"

"It was approximately eight twenty-five P.M."

"Did you have a flashlight with you?"

"No, not on me. I had one in the car."

"And at eight twenty-five at night with the whiz of busy traffic rushing by all around you, you observed a dark substance on this man's bumper that you automatically assumed must be blood?"

"Yes. There was enough light from the causeway lights and the buildings off the causeway. I could see. It was dark and sticky. It looked like bloodstains."

"And you then approached Mr. Bantling to give him back his license?"

"Yes."

"Did you draw your gun?"

"No."

"You observe bloodstains. You say my client was nervous and jittery. You suspect something's amiss, and yet you did not draw your gun?"

"No. Not at that time. I did when I found the dead girl in his trunk, though."

"You've already reminded this court that there was a dead body in his trunk, Officer. Several times, in fact, and that issue is not in dispute."

Chavez tried a more civil tone. "I again approached Mr. Bantling in his car and that's when I smelled the marijuana smell in the car."

"The car was thoroughly searched that night, was it not, Officer Chavez?"

"Yes."

"And no trace of marijuana was found in the car, was there?"

"He was obviously smoking it, ma'am. For all I know, he ate the roach before I gave him back his license." Chavez was irked. She was making him look like a complete fool.

Lourdes Rubio stared at the rookie for several moments.

Then she turned and looked directly at C.J. while she asked her next question.

"What did you really think you would find in that trunk, Officer Chavez?"

"Drugs, weapons—I wasn't quite sure. Butch sure knew something was up, though. He damn near tore that trunk to shreds with his paws."

"Isn't that what you suspected you would find in there all along, Officer Chavez? Drugs?"

C.J. felt her hands begin to tingle.

"No. I pulled him over for excessive speed. Traffic violations. As it turned out later, there were additional facts that led me to believe he was concealing contraband in that trunk. The dog alert confirmed it."

"Let's be honest here, shall we, Officer? Didn't you think from the moment you saw that Jag on Washington that he was carrying dope?"

"Objection," C.J. said. "The question has been asked and answered."

"Overruled. The witness may answer," said Judge Chaskel.

Chavez remembered what he had told the redheaded chick at the bar, but it was too late to turn back now. He was backed in a corner. His whole career as a cop rested on the right answer. "No. I pulled him over for speeding."

"What would make you stop breaking up this fight, get in a car, and chase down a speeder? What would your gut instincts tell you might be in that trunk? What had someone else told you might be in that trunk?"

She knew about the tip. C.J. sprang to her feet. "Objection! Asked and answered!"

"Overruled. Let's get through this, Ms. Rubio."

"He was speeding. That was it. There was nothing else." Chavez was not going to budge, and it would be war between them. Unless she had proof. "It just so happened that when I did get to look in the trunk, ma'am, your client had a dead body in it."

"Fucking liar," Bantling suddenly said in a loud voice from his seat.

Lourdes Rubio left Chavez and turned toward her client.

"Mr. Bantling, do not interject during testimony. And that language will not be tolerated by this court," said Judge Chaskel sternly. He had heard about Bantling's antics during the First Appearance, and he simply wasn't going to allow it here—not in his courtroom.

Bantling stood in his seat, his leg shackles clinking. "I am sorry, Judge, but he is a liar. They all are. Just look at him."

"That's enough, Mr. Bantling. Sit down."

"I want to speak, Your Honor." Bantling looked over at C.J. and a slick smile bloomed on his face. "There is something this court needs to know."

C.J. felt the room spin again, and she clutched her pen tight in her hand. She looked away from Bantling, straight at the judge. The moment had finally come when it would all come crashing down. *How would it feel to stand accused in front of all these people?* She held her breath waiting for Bantling's next line.

"Anything the court needs to know, your counsel will tell me. Now please sit down or I will have you removed. Ms. Rubio, is there anything further?"

Lourdes Rubio watched as her client was sat back in his chair with the help of two burly corrections officers. All the while he stared at the prosecutor, a look of contempt and pure hatred painted on his otherwise-chiseled and good-looking face. He enjoyed this mind game he was playing with her, this cat-and-mouse, this *I know something you want no one else to know* game. Well, Lourdes wasn't going to let him play it. Not today. Not with her.

"Nothing further, Your Honor," Lourdes said abruptly, and sat down.

62

C.J. SAT AT the prosecution's table for a long while after the hearing ended, letting the courtroom empty out behind her. She had caught Lourdes's eye briefly as she packed up her briefcase at the table next to hers, but there was nothing there to be shared between them. Lourdes had rushed out just as soon as Corrections had carted off her obviously unhappy client back to his maximum-security jail cell.

Chavez was an idiot. A horrible liar. A buffoon. And Lourdes had had him dead to rights. But then she'd backed off suddenly. *Why?* She also knew about the tip. *But how?* And then there was the rape. She had never even mentioned Bantling's allegations to the court, even though Bantling had practically pushed her through that door after opening it up himself. *Was that simply case strategy or was there more to it?*

An enormous, anxious wave of guilt rushed over C.J. Before Bantling, she had actually liked Lourdes. They had worked together over the years on two other murder cases, and she always found Lourdes to be straightforward. Not whiny or unscrupulous like most of the defense bar. And now, she knew that Lourdes was compromising herself. And for that, C.J. felt bad. But since that day in DCJ, C.J. had also grown wary of Lourdes, and now she wondered if perhaps Lourdes was taking this opportunity to throw her off and plan a more effective time to explode with her damning information? Perhaps right after a jury was sworn and double jeopardy had attached? Because once jeopardy had attached, should Lourdes make her allegations in court and the judge declare a mistrial for prosecutorial misconduct, Bantling could not be retried. Ever. And he would walk away a free man. C.J.'s thoughts returned to that day in the jail, when a smiling, gleeful Bill Bantling had sat at the side of his once-scrupulous attorney, while she fired her deadly bullets across the table directly at his victim. Lourdes had known before that day that her client was a madman. He had told her as much himself, showed her the proof in the police reports. And Lourdes had still allowed herself to be used as his pawn, as his conduit. She had arranged for C.J. to look into the eyes of her attacker in a lockdown cell. Just for effect. Just to win a motion. And with that last thought, C.J.'s guilt was gone.

With Bantling out of the room, and the mob of reporters focusing their energies on task force members and FBI agents outside, she felt as if she could breathe, at least for the time being. After a while, she didn't know exactly how long, Dominick sat down next to her in the empty courtroom.

"Good job," he said quietly.

"I didn't do much of anything," she replied.

"You won the motion; that's enough. With no help from that cocky SOB from the Beach. Someone needs to fine-tune him before he gets before a jury."

"He doesn't tune very well. I've tried. So has his sergeant."

"Maybe we'll have Manny work on him. He has a way with words." He paused for a moment, trying to find her eyes, which were still staring at the files on the table. "I know you're worried, but the case is strong, even with Chavez trying his best to screw it up."

"Let's hope so."

"And Bantling doesn't help his case any, either. I think Chaskel is going to wind up letting Cupid attend his own trial from closed-circuit TV across the street if he doesn't shut up."

C.J. said nothing.

"I liked your summary argument."

"Thanks. It's been a day."

"Yeah. The spooks are definitely out today. By the way, Happy Halloween. Can I help you back to your office?"

"Is everyone gone out there?"

"Yeah, pretty much. I think only Manny and the boys are out in the hall, with your secretary."

"Marisol's here?"

"She came to cheer you on, I think."

"I doubt it."

"She stayed the whole hearing. Now she's talking to Manny outside. Interesting outfit she's wearing."

"It always is. Okay, then. I'll take the help."

He lifted the files off the table and placed them on the pull cart, one on top of the other. With one hand he pulled the cart behind him, and in the other he held her heavy briefcase. They headed together to the courtroom doors that led to the main hallway.

"How about dinner tonight?" he asked.

"That would be nice," she said. This time she didn't hesitate. Not at all.

63

LOURDES RUBIO OPENED the bottom drawer of her desk and pulled out the amber bottle of Chivas Regal, the good stuff that she kept on hand for celebrations, favorable verdicts, acquittals. Today, though, it would serve a different purpose. Today she would drink it to get good and drunk and calm the nerves that rattled her whole body.

She poured herself a glass and looked down at her desk, which was covered with grisly crime-scene photos. Anna Prado's butchered, bloody body lay, wide-eyed and terrified, staring out from the trunk of her client's new Jag.

She hated herself. Hated herself for what she had said in court. For what she had almost said. For what she had not said. There was no winning for anyone. No celebration or victory party today.

She knew her client was a rapist. A sick, sadistic, brutal rapist. And she knew that he had raped that prosecutor, and that he was not at all sorry for what he had done to ruin her life. Lourdes also suspected that he had raped other women, although he had not admitted that to her. Not yet. Bill Bantling admitted facts to her only on what he felt was her "need to know" basis. There was no surprise in that; most clients enjoyed that same trait.

Was he a killer?

In the beginning, when he had first retained her, she would have adamantly said no. It must be a cover-up, a frame job, a mistake. There was no way this man was a rapist, a killer. No way that he could possibly be Cupid. He had fooled her completely, and that was a rarity. Especially as a criminal defense attorney, where you know and accept that most clients hold back and lie, even to the person they've hired to save their ass. But Bill Bantling was not most clients. He was a successful businessman, good-looking, charming, sincere. He was her friend long before he was even arrested, jogging with her on SoBe on Saturday mornings and sharing a cappuccino at the bookstore sometimes on the weekends. She had bought his whole story, and now she saw that she had been fooled. Completely blindsided by a smooth-talking psychopath. That was what stung the most.

And then there was C. J. Townsend, a prosecutor whom she had always respected and admired. One who didn't play bullshit political games or offer nasty backstabbing pleas that only served to make her office look good. Lourdes knew C.J. was lying, too, and although her motivations might be more justified, they were certainly not honorable. She had reviewed the inventory sheets left behind when the police searched her client's house and cars. She had looked through the boxes of evidence seized with those warrants. There was nothing there. Nothing that, according to her client, should have been. Another blind side. It was now at the point that Lourdes could not trust her own judgment of people any longer.

She downed the first drink, still staring at the gruesome pictures. *Where was the justice for Anna Prado? Where was the justice for her client, whom she had taken an oath to zealously defend? What the hell did justice even mean anymore?*

She had dropped the ball as his attorney today. She'd had that cop running right into a brick wall with his own words and she stopped. She'd stopped because she knew her client was a rapist, and in that moment in the courtroom when he had stared down his victim, with no remorse or pity, with nothing but hatred and loathing in his eyes, she knew he would do it again if he could. And she could not let herself be the one who made it possible for him to do it to some other woman. She herself was a champion for women's rights in the Cuban community, this community where she lived and worked and played. In fact, she was the chairwoman of La Lucha, helping immigrant Hispanic women who are victims of domestic violence seek shelter and safety from their abusers. How could she call herself an advocate for women and in the next breath use her talents to let a brutal rapist walk free? She had seen firsthand the damage he had done to one victim; she knew what he would do to the next.

Lourdes downed the second scotch, and this one was much smoother. It was easier to swallow. It didn't burn as much. Perhaps the same analogy could be drawn to her own participation in this charade. Perhaps each step would be easier to take as she helped walk her client into the death chamber. Perhaps it wouldn't burn as much when she watched them stick the needle in. An accomplice to her own client's murder.

Because she really did not believe that he was a killer. And she knew that she could get him off, that she could have gotten him off today. She knew all about the strange, anonymous tip that had been phoned in to the Miami Beach Police Department on September 19. That stupid cop, drunk and hoping to get laid, had shot his mouth off last month to her and her intern at the Clevelander, and she knew that was why he had really pulled over the Jag, even though now he chose to sing a different song. He thought he could deny what she had heard in that bar, just deny it and it would all go away. But things don't ever work out that way, do they?

She flipped the cassette tape that she had ordered from the Miami Beach P.D. over in her hand. On the outside was scribbled *9/19/2000 8:12 P.M.* 911 tapes were routinely held for thirty days before they were erased. Fortunately, she had gotten her copy on the twenty-ninth day.

The scotch was working its magic, making her light-headed and dizzy and pain-free. Lourdes stared at the pictures of Anna Prado and poured herself a third.

This one just slid down her numb throat.

64

HE WATCHED THE scene play out before his eyes in the packed courtroom. It was even better than he had ever expected it would be. To see the different players interact off each other, with each other. Emotions running high, the tension so thick one could cut it with a knife. The breathless, nail-biting crowd nibbling on their proverbial popcorn and taking their pictures as a cheap tourist would, while they watched with him, alongside him. He melded into them. He was one of them. This game that he himself had set in motion was spinning quite nicely now into subplots, and the suspense of just how it would turn out was killing him.

But he needed more. It had been months now that he had contained himself, and he could wait no longer. The feeling inside him was akin to that of a desert man in search of water. An insatiable thirst, a quenching for life. For death.

He could not risk ruining the drama that unfolded now, calling into question the innocence of the guilty. He needed to break away from what police liked to call his "modus operandi," his "method of operation." It would cast suspicion if he should choose another blond-haired vixen, no matter where he selected her from. And, of course, unlike the others, she could never be found. For what he would do to her body was simply unmentionable. And what he would do to her mind before that was unthinkable. If only they knew of the horrors in store, they would think William Bantling a timid rabbit.

Yes. A dark-haired beauty. Someone with hair as dark as ebony and skin as white as snow and lips red as the rose. His own little Snow White to play with. He could only hope to win her heart.

And then the killer known to police as Cupid rose with the others in the crowded courtroom and followed them out into the hallway, down the escalators, and into the hot Miami sun, where he left them in search of his next true love.

3

65

C.J. FOUND MANNY and Dominick downstairs in the Pickle Barrel nursing their *cafés con leche*. She grabbed her own cup of coffee from the self-serve urns and pulled up a chair.

"How'd the status conference go?" asked Dominick. Today was December 13, Bantling's report date before Judge Chaskel. At a report date, the attorneys met with the trial judge to discuss the status of the case, plea negotiations, and finally, to firm up their trial schedules for the following week.

"There was no request for a continuance. It looks like I'm picking the jury on Monday morning."

"No shit?" said Manny. "I could've sworn that nut was gonna come up with a hundred and one excuses why we shouldn't move to fry his ass before the holidays. Well, good. Let's get this thing over with."

"I have to say I'm surprised, too," said Dominick, cautiously. "Two months' prep on a capital case, here in Miami, the land of defense continuances and wishy-washy judges? No depos, no discovery? Not even an attempt at a change of venue? That's not going to cause a problem later on down the road, is it C.J.?"

"You mean as a basis for an appeal? No. It's Bantling who wants the quick trial, not Rubio. And it's Bantling, I think, who wants to keep it here in Miami, rather than risk having it tried in some northern county where the median age is sixty-five and whatever a cop says is gold. It's not ineffective assistance of counsel either. Judge Chaskel has had Bantling state on the record all along that he knows he has a right to discovery and that any waiver of that right is done with his full knowledge and consent and can't be used as a basis of an appeal after he's convicted. You know, the 'But, Judge, nobody told me!' defense. And Chaskel has pretty much made me give him everything anyway, because he doesn't want to see this case come back. Lourdes hasn't taken on any new clients since Bantling. She's a well-respected attorney who has six capital cases under her belt, so she's experienced at what needs to be done, and I don't think she's been rushed. She's handled cases before without discovery, and sometimes a defense attorney will try to use it as a tactic: 'You don't show me yours, maybe, but neither do you get to see mine.' Maybe she wants to surprise us. I hope not."

"What's Bantling in such a rush for? Does he really think he'll get off in time to finish up his Christmas shopping?" asked Manny.

"Hey, it's better for us if he wants it quick. I hate when these things linger in purgatory. Witnesses forget, evidence gets lost, all sorts of bad shit happens," said Dominick.

"I agree," C.J. said, "but there is one thing that a continuance would have bought us and that would have been more time." She stopped deliberately for a moment before continuing. "Tigler called me this morning. De la Flors is taking the Siban murder and the robberies before the grand jury next week. If we lose on Prado, he'll whisk Bantling out the door and downtown to Club Fed so fast we won't even get to say boo. Then we'll have to wait our turn in line while he tries Bantling on each federal indictment."

"That should buy him enough time and attention then to get that federal judgeship he wants," said Dominick.

"Exactly," said C.J.

"Well, then, why don't we beat him to the punch and just indict on the other murders, Counselor?" Manny asked. "We've got plenty of time so that speedies won't be an issue now. Not with you going to trial next week."

"Because other than the fishing line found at Morgan Weber's scene, there's still no direct physical evidence linking him to the other victims, and the fishing line is not enough. And I don't have a conviction yet on Prado." She turned to Dominick. "I need those hearts. I need you to find his trophies."

"I thought you said we didn't need to find those to convict?" asked Manny.

"We don't. But you saw how Victor Chavez was on the stand in that motion to suppress. He comes off evasive, cocky, arrogant."

"An asshole," Manny interrupted.

"Right. He's a horrible witness, but I can't proceed without him. I just don't want him to turn the jury off so much that they buy into Bantling's defense that he was framed. Then, if they let Bantling go on Prado, I don't even have a murder conviction to Williams Rule in. The judge might not even let the next jury hear about the facts in Prado. We'll have nothing."

"C.J., we've looked everywhere," said Dominick. "We've talked to three hundred witnesses, analyzed hundreds of pieces of evidence. I don't know where else to look."

"Maybe his shrink in New York would know what he did with them. Have you talked to him, that Dr. Fineburg?" asked Manny.

"No. Bantling is not pleading insanity and that's final, according to Lourdes. I can't look at his records. I can't have him examined by the state shrinks. My hands are tied, and any info that he told his psychiatrist is confidential and privileged. He won't talk to you even if Bantling buried the hearts in his own backyard."

"What if Bowman was right, and this guy pulled a Jeffrey Dahmer and ate them?" said Manny. "We may never know."

"I don't think so, Bear. I think C.J.'s right. I've worked serials before. They always keep a trophy. It fits that it's the hearts. He *wants* us to look for them, I think. Bantling is teasing us, taunting us to find them. He went to such great lengths to horrify us all by taking them, he wants to horrify us again when we find them."

"Go over all the evidence again. Look at his records. Maybe we missed something," said C.J. "Some otherwise insignificant storage receipt, a locker key. I don't know. Let's just try. We have probably three weeks of trial. If I can indict on the others by then, then no judge will let him leave for Club Fed until I've tried him on the murders."

"Three weeks of trial, huh?" Manny sighed. "Well, Ho-Ho-Ho and a Happy Fucking New Year, too. I guess there will be no trip to the North Pole for any of us this Christmas. No matter how good we've all been."

66

MANNY WAITED UNTIL C.J. had left to go back to her office until
he said, "I like the Counselor, but I think she's crazy thinking we can maybe find those hearts this late in the game.
Unless Bantling has them in a freezer someplace, they are
probably decomped."

"Alright. Let's find the freezer, then."

"Ever the optimist. How long have you and the Counselor been an item?" said Manny suddenly, looking coyly
up at Dominick between bites of his *pastelito*.

Dominick blew out a breath. "I wouldn't call it an item,
exactly. Is it obvious?"

"To me, your good buddy. I like to think I can read
women, Dom. And I can read that the Counselor has a
thing for you."

"You can, can you?"

"Yep. And that you have a thing for the Counselor. So
how long?"

"Just a couple of months."

"And?"

"And, that's it. I don't know. I like her, she likes me. She
won't let me get too close. We're kind of at a standstill, I
think."

"Women. They want a relationship, a relationship, a
relationship. You give 'em one and they don't want a relationship. That's why I've been married three times, Dom. I

still can't figure them out completely. But no matter how many times I've sworn off them, I always go back for something hot and spicy. Then, just like *picadillo*, they give me indigestion and I wonder why I tried it again."

"Well she doesn't want this out, so keep it between us, and tone down those sharp instincts of yours. She'll get spooked if she thinks people suspect anything. She's worried about Tigler and the press."

"Mum's the word. No smooching in the squad car, though."

"I do think she's right, though, Manny. I really do," Dominick said slowly, wondering if he should utter his next thoughts or keep them to himself. He looked around to make sure no one was listening in, but the Pickle Barrel had pretty much emptied out and they had the back of the cafeteria to themselves. In a low voice he continued, "I've been thinking, Bear, looking over the crime-scene reports, the photos. Looking for what we've been missing all this time. Why is it that there is nothing physical left behind? Because Cupid doesn't want us to find it? No, that doesn't quite fit because if that was the case, he wouldn't even have left us a body to pick over. I think it's because he's too smart, Bear. He took so many chances with those girls. Walking them right out of those clubs, past security guards and right past their own friends. He took his time killing them, setting the scenes, playing with the bodies, arranging them in death. It's all very controlled, very calculated.

"He wants us to see what he's done, Manny. He wants us to know what he did to them before he killed them, with that drug, Mivacron. He wants us to be horrified, mesmerized, amazed at how smart he is. He can be this ruthless and open, and we still can't catch him. Every crime scene, with the exception of Anna Prado's, was planned out. Planned out for when and how he would kill his victims and planned out for when and how *we* would find them. Down to the positioning of their fingertips."

"Okay. So he's smart. He planned everything, even how he wanted us to find them. Where are you going with all this? What's the link?" asked Manny.

"Think of Marilyn Siban, in that abandoned army base.

I think he knew cops trained there. He knew cops would find her, and that the scene would make the most hardened among us rethink our careers. Nicolette Torrence. Found by those kids in that abandoned crack house. A crack house that coincidentally was the subject of forfeiture proceedings by South Florida IMPACT and the Coral Gables P.D. for drug violations. Hannah Cordova. Found in an abandoned sugarcane factory that had been raided by U.S. Customs on a heroin tip four weeks earlier. Krystal Pierce. Found in that abandoned supermarket where a triple homicide had happened not six months earlier. That one was investigated by Miami-Dade P.D. Almost all the crime scenes have some remote connection back to a police department, law-enforcement agency, a task force."

"So what are you saying, Dom? You think Bantling's a copycat? You buy his 'I've been framed!' bullshit? That police crap could very well be coincidence. Hell, according to the bleeding hearts at the ACLU, almost everyone in Miami has had their house searched by cops at one time or another. And God knows the feds are like cockroaches when they're looking for dope. The bodies were not found in the most savory of locations, Dom, but bodies generally aren't."

"I don't think Bantling's a copycat, Bear. I think he's the original. The cuts on the torso across the sternum were in the same location, the same order as the others. Anna Prado had the same drugs in her system as the others. A copycat wouldn't have known to do that, wouldn't have known about the drugs. I do think there is a police connection, though."

"Like maybe Bantling's a wannabe cop and we missed that, or his cat was killed by a cop? There're a lot of reasons people take on cops, Dommy Boy. We're everyone's scapegoats."

Dominick nodded and slowly sipped at his cup of coffee before continuing his last thought. "Maybe. As for Anna Prado, I think Bantling had other plans for her, though. Plans that we interrupted perhaps by catching him prematurely. If we can figure out what those plans were, we may be able to figure out where his trophies are."

Manny was shaking his head. "I don't know, Dom. A cop connection. If there is one, how would Bantling have known about the raids, the searches, the training, all that shit you just said?"

Dominick was silent.

Manny picked up on his friend's thoughts and blew out a low whistle under his breath. "Oh shit, Dom. You think there's another one, don't you? You think that this guy has a partner out there somewhere who's just laughing his head off right now. *And you think he may be one of us.*"

67

FIVE DAYS. C.J. had just five days before the biggest trial of her career began. She had lived, breathed, slept with this case for over a year, and as a lawyer, she knew she was prepared in almost every way one could prepare. She knew the witnesses, she knew the evidence, she knew the victims. Inside and out. Backwards and forwards. She had rehearsed a closing statement in her head on almost a daily basis ever since she had been assigned to the task force, updating her closing with every new fact that had emerged, each new body that was discovered, and finally, last September, she'd been able to add a name to accuse. To point at from across the crowded courtroom, to hang high in front of an angry, vindictive jury.

But now the accused might just become the accuser. It had been six weeks since she had laid eyes on Bantling in that crowded courtroom, when he had sought to stand up and point at her, to hang *her* high in front of her peers in the court of public opinion. Judge Chaskel, unwittingly, had restrained him, his attorney had soothed him, and the moment had flared, but not erupted. For six weeks since he had remained silent, and almost daily C.J. had wondered to herself when the phone call would come from Judge Chaskel's chambers, when the mailroom would deliver another motion, when the front page would blare the news: *Prosecutor Raped by Cupid! Her Plot for Revenge Foiled!*

How much longer could Bantling be contained? Voir dire? Opening statements? Chavez's testimony? Dominick's testimony? The ME? Closing arguments? Or perhaps, the big bang would come when he decided to take the stand in his own defense. Not to deny the accusations against him, but to accuse his accuser. Every day in that courtroom would take an eternity to tick by, the pressure in her head and chest mounting with his daily staredown, the licking of his chops with that long pink tongue, until, she supposed, her heart finally ruptured from the stress.

And she knew that was exactly what he wanted. With a beautiful white smile, he dangled his secret over an open black pit while she sweated profusely trying to grab it back. He had total control over her in this regard, and he relished it. It was a mind game that he could play even from his jail cell, behind iron bars and steel doors, where she could not hear him or see him.

She had to win this case. If she did not, he would walk. Maybe not right away—maybe the feds would get him for a while to try out their Hobbs Act robberies on him, but there was no more physical evidence linking him to a robbery than there was to a murder. And then he would be free, and she would not know where he was. Until he showed up maybe as her neighbor in her condo building, or on the escalator at the courthouse, or at the restaurant where she ate dinner, the diner where she ate lunch. Just like in New York, when he could be everywhere, anywhere—he would be again. Only this time would be different, because even if she saw him, there would be nothing she could do. She could scream and scream and scream on a busy street as he walked past her, on the bus as he took the seat next to her, at the restaurant as he held the door open for her, and there would be nothing that anyone could do, not until he touched her again. And by then she knew it would be too late.

The gray glow of the computer screen in the dim room forced her to squint at the words as she finished up the first draft of her voir dire, the questions that she expected to ask potential jurors during jury selection. She now kept her blinds closed when in the office alone at night, to protect herself from the watchful, prying eyes of her neighbor across the street. Spread out on the desk were the first three drafts of her opening statement. Each draft was different, depending on if and when the volcano decided to erupt and spew its molten lava. And depending on if Dominick and the task force could locate the additional physical evidence she wanted. The answer was out there somewhere, she knew it, and she would not stop looking for it until . . .

What if Bantling was not the killer?

She really did not believe that, but, *what if?* What if they could not find the hearts or any additional evidence because there was none to be found? What if it was someone else? Someone who, while she struggled to keep the devil across the street behind bars, was sharpening his best knife and waiting for another opportunity to emerge from a darkened alley? What if he had struck again, but they didn't know because they weren't looking anymore? Her mind refused to go there, to play that treacherous game. Every piece of evidence that they had collected pointed irrefutably to Bantling, with only one exception.

C.J. fingered the cassette tape in her hand gingerly, before she popped it in the boom box on top of her file cabinet.

"Nine-one-one. What's your emergency?"

"There's a car. A late-model black Jaguar XJ8. Right now he's headed south on Washington from Lincoln Road. He's got two kilos of cocaine in his trunk, and he's headed to the airport. He's going to take the MacArthur to MIA, just in case you miss him on Washington."

"What's your name, sir? Where are you calling from?"

The hum of a telephone line going dead.

She had listened to the tape at least thirty times since getting a copy from the MBPD. The voice was muffled, as if the caller had placed a cloth over the phone. But it was deep and definitely male. He was calm, not rushed or hurried. In the background the faint sound of soft music, an opera perhaps, could be heard.

Why would someone call in a fake tip that the car was carrying dope? Who would want the Jaguar pulled over, the trunk searched? An angry fellow motorist who sought revenge because he had been cut off? The deep, calm voice on the phone did not sound angry or upset. It did not sound like a car's cell phone. There had never been any evidence ever found to suggest that Bantling even did illegal drugs, much less dealt them.

Who would want that trunk searched?

The only other possible answer left made C.J.'s blood chill.

Someone who knew the gruesome contents the police would find inside.

68

THE SMELL OF roasted lemon pepper chicken and hot buttermilk biscuits rushed her when she opened the front door. Lucy scrambled to find the source, trying desperately to dash through C.J.'s legs into the hall, but C.J. caught her with her feet. Tibby II found the person holding the goods and coquettishly rubbed his body up against Dominick's calf, purring incessantly, as if he had not seen food in a week.

"I see you brought dinner," she said.

"Hey, we can't powwow without food," said Dominick as he made his way into the apartment. "Don't be too impressed, though. It's Publix. Although I did spring for extra biscuits." He whipped out a bottle wrapped in a brown paper bag from behind his back and handed it to C.J. "And, what fine dining would be complete without a bottle of Kendall Jackson Chardonnay?"

Then he bent down and found Lucy's head. "Hey there, Lucy, old girl! That mean momma of yours hasn't fed you yet? Well, have I got a surprise for you!" Tibby mewled loudly. *Et tu, Brute?* "And for you, too, Tibby. Of course." From behind his back he pulled out another plastic Publix bag. In it was a container of cooked chicken livers. Lucy howled with delight. Tibby almost jumped on Dominick's head. "Let's get you both a bowl."

C.J. watched the show from the kitchen table while she

put out the roasted chicken and biscuits and wineglasses. "She's gonna howl now for twenty minutes. She's also going to have to go out again tonight."

"That's okay. I'll walk her later." Dominick walked into the kitchen and, reaching for the wine, came up behind C.J. as she set the table. "I'll get that," he said as she turned to face him. He pressed her up against the table and kissed her softly on the mouth, his hand finding hers and moving over it with his fingers. "Now, who needs food?" he said lightly.

"Okay, Casanova. Show me those muscles and open the wine."

"No sweat." But he didn't move. With his body still pressed to hers, backing her up against the table, he reached his arms around behind her and found the wine bottle and corkscrew. Then his mouth found hers again, his tongue sensuously wandering to touch hers. She ran her hands up over his polo shirt, feeling the hardness of his chest, the strength of his shoulders, the curve of his muscles, until they were wrapped around his neck. Through her thin silk blouse she felt the cold wine bottle on the small of her back, dripping condensation as it hit the heat of her body, and causing the silk to moisten and mold to her skin. The cork popped free of the bottle, but their kiss did not end. Dominick put the bottle on the table and pulled her blouse out of her pants and away from her back, replacing the wet silk with his own hands, made damp and cold by the wine bottle. They ran up her back with a delicious chill, over her bra straps, stopping to caress her shoulders. Then they moved back down and unhooked her bra, and the fingers feathered out over her ribs until they finally found her breasts. He moved her loose bra out of the way and his fingers delicately moved over her, massaging her firm breasts, feeling them heave under his touch as her breathing became heavier.

One hand moved free and progressed down her stomach, ignoring the ugly scar lines, and finding the button on her pants. She could not extricate herself from his kiss, and in less than a second, the button was open, the zipper down, and his hand moved down lower, moving aside her panties, his fingers finding her warm and moist and waiting for him. Her black suit pants fell in a pool onto the kitchen floor. With the strength of his body, he lifted her buttocks onto the table, his fingers never leaving the inside of her, his penis pressed hard against the inside of her thigh through his slacks.

She knew what was about to happen, and she forced herself to break from the kiss. She opened her eyes and saw the bright track lights on the kitchen ceiling above her.

"Dominick, let's go into the bedroom," she said in a whisper. His fingers moved faster inside her and she felt a tingling sensation erupt over her body.

"Let me make love to you here. Let me see you, C.J. You're so beautiful," he whispered back next to her ear, his tongue wrapping around her earlobe. His other hand moved from her breast and his fingers began to unbutton her blouse.

"No. No. The bedroom. Please, Dominick." The tingling sensation from his touch was rushing her whole body now and she began to quiver on the table. Her orgasm was not far off.

"Let me see you. I love your body. I want to see what I do to you." His hand had pushed down her panties, and they slid off onto the floor. Only the thin white silk of her blouse covered her, and he had gotten all the buttons open.

"No." She shook her head. "Please."

He pulled back slightly and looked into her eyes. Without another word, he picked her up gently in his arms and carried her down the hall and into the dark bedroom, leaving the telling lights of the kitchen behind them.

69

THEY LAY TOGETHER in the darkness, front-to-back, like two spoons from the same set. He watched in the dim red light of the alarm clock while she dozed, his fingers playing with her hair on the back of her neck, where the roots grew in blond. After they had made love, as she always did, she had quickly put on a T-shirt in the dark before getting back into bed to cuddle. He ran his hand now under the T-shirt, feeling her warm back against his palm, the slightness of her delicate bones, the definition of muscle covering them, and her soft skin. He watched as she slept, her body gently rising and falling with each breath under his hand.

As they often did, his thoughts ran to Natalie, and in the alarm-clock light he saw the long whispers of her dark hair that rested on her shoulders and spilled onto her back while she slept. Natalie. His fiancée from years past, and the only other woman in his life whom he had felt as much for, whom he needed to be with as much. To just be near and to watch sleep next to him. He remembered how intense the pain had been when she slipped away, when he had finally lost her. His grief had been overwhelming. It had taken over him so completely that he felt as if a part of him had actually died with her, as if someone had punched a hole in his chest and physically torn his heart out. Her death had made him understand what the relatives of the victims on his cases had meant when they spoke to him of the enormous pain they experienced at the loss of a loved one. A pain so deep and so profound that it touched everything they did, every relationship they had—it touched their very soul. And then there was the final, brutal secret that this macabre club membership had let him in on: Time does not necessarily heal all wounds.

He couldn't go through that pain again. He remembered the torture of just waking up and looking around his apartment at each happy memory they had shared together encapsulated in a picture frame, or some end table they had bought together, or a favorite coffee mug. The daily agony had stretched on and on until it finally numbed him, and he had vowed he would never again get that close to a woman. He placed the memories far away, back in deep storage, but then the familiarity of a moment would trigger them, and they would tumble out, seeking to be reexamined. He would see Natalie's bright face and her sweet smile before it turned before him into a cold and empty mortician's stare.

He lay next to C.J., his body touching hers, the scent of her hair driving him crazy. Against his better judgment, he found himself wanting more with her, wanting to know all there was to know about her and who she was, this beautiful, mysterious, troubled woman.

He kissed her neck and felt her stir. She moved closer to him. "What time is it?" she murmured sleepily.

"Twelve. You slept for about an hour."

"I hope I didn't snore."

"Not tonight."

She rolled over and put her head on his chest. "I'm starving," she said and looked at the closed bedroom door. A sliver of light sneaked in through the bottom of the door. All was eerily quiet. "I wonder if the chicken is still out there."

"I never even fed them the chicken livers. I doubt there's anything left of the chicken."

"It's almost like a bad horror movie," she mused lightly, "when the sexy coed makes her boyfriend go get her a beer after they've fooled around. Nothing is left alive in the kitchen after the attack of the hungry pets."

"It's a good thing I closed the door, or that fat cat might be in here with my gun demanding more. He's the leader, you know."

"I think I have some frozen pizza. Maybe some soup. That's about it."

They lay there in the darkness for a moment before Dominick spoke again. "What do the initials C.J. stand for?" he asked suddenly. "I realized that I've never asked you that question."

Her body stiffened. She'd been taken off guard, and so found herself answering him. "Chloe," she said, her voice barely above a whisper. "Chloe Joanna."

"Chloe. I like that. It's pretty. Why don't you use it?"

"Don't call me that, please."

"I won't if you don't want me to, but just tell me why."

"I don't care to get into it. It's personal." She rolled away from him.

He waited a moment and then with a sigh asked, "Why are you so full of secrets? Why won't you let me in?"

"That name is part of my past. Something I don't choose to discuss."

"But the past is a part of you." Then in a low voice he added, "And I want to be a part of you, C.J."

"The past is who I was, not who I am now. That's all I can give you, Dominick." She sat up stiffly in bed.

He sat up also, and pulled on his slacks. "Alright, alright. Whenever you're ready," he said, his voice resigned. "How about I whip us up an omelet? Do you have any eggs?"

She waited a moment before she spoke. "Look. We need to talk, and I don't want you to take this the wrong way." She sat still in the darkness at the edge of the bed, her back to him. "The trial is going to start in just a few days, and, during the trial I don't think that we, well, that we should be together. I think we're both going to be under a lot of scrutiny by the press and by our bosses and, I think my feelings for you are written all over my face when I'm with you. I think we should give ourselves some distance."

Her words hit him like a smack across the face. "C.J.,

what does it matter if people guess our feelings for each other? What does it matter?"

"It matters to me. I can't jeopardize this case, Dominick. I can't. Bantling needs to go away for what he's done."

"I agree with you, C.J., and he's going to go away. I promise you." He sat next to her on the bed. "We're doing all we can. We've got a great case. You're an awesome prosecutor. He's going to go away." He looked into her eyes, pulling her face toward his. "Why has he gotten under your skin like this? What else has he done, C.J.? Talk to me, please."

For a long moment he actually believed she would tell him. Her lip trembled and a line of silent tears rolled down her cheek. But then she composed herself. "No." She wiped the tears away defiantly with the back of her hand. "Dominick, I really do care about you. More than you know, but we need to have distance between us during this trial. I need to have perspective, and I need you to understand that. Please."

Dominick reached for his shirt and pulled it over his head. He finished getting dressed in silence while she sat on the edge of the bed, her back still to him. The door to the bedroom opened, and light rushed into the room. His words were distant and cool. "No. Don't ask me again to understand it, because I don't."

Then he grabbed his gun and his keys off of the coffee table in her living room and walked out her front door.

70

THE DOOR TO the judge's hallway was flung open and Judge Chaskel hurried out, his black robe billowing in a puff of black behind him as he quickly took the bench.

"All rise! Court is now is session! The Honorable Judge Leopold Chaskel the III now presiding," Hank the bailiff announced with a startled shout.

The courtroom hushed to silence and the judge quickly put on his glasses and frowned as he scanned the jury pool sheet that Janine, his clerk, had left for him on the bench. The box was empty, as were all the rows on the entire right side of the courtroom, which had been blocked off with rope. That was where the prospective jury pool would be seated during voir dire. Trial watchers, and, of course, the press, covered the rows on the left. It was 9:10 on Monday morning, December 18.

"Good morning, everyone. I'm sorry I'm late. I had a judges' holiday breakfast that I had to attend. 'Tis the season." He looked down over his bench and over his glasses to where Janine sat at her desk, which was directly in front of the bench. "Speaking of the season, no hats please while court is in session, Janine," referring to the pointy red-and-white Santa hat the clerk wore on her head. She sheepishly pulled it off and stuck it in her desk. He cleared his throat. "Now, we are here today on *The State of Florida* v.—" he began, then stopped himself, looking around the courtroom. "Where is the defendant?" he asked, his brow furrowing.

"On his way over from DCJ. They're walking him right now," Hank said.

"Why isn't he here now? I said nine A.M., Hank. Not nine-fifteen. Only the judge is allowed to be late."

"Yes, Judge, but it seems he gave them a little bit of trouble across the street this morning," said Hank. "He didn't want to cooperate."

Judge Chaskel, obviously irritated, shook his head. "Well, I don't want the defendant being brought in by Corrections in front of the jury pool. That will taint them. Hold off on bringing them in until he gets here. How many potential jurors do we have downstairs waiting, Hank?"

"Two hundred."

"Two hundred? This close to the holidays? That's pretty good. Let's start with the first fifty and see how we do. And I want a word with Mr. Bantling before we try sitting a jury in this case." He looked down at Lourdes over his glasses. "Ms. Rubio, your client is getting a reputation for being a troublemaker both in and out of the courtroom."

Lourdes looked embarrassed, as if the conduct of her client when out of her presence were somehow her fault. Last week's status conference was the first time C.J. had actually seen her since Halloween, and like that day in the judge's chambers, she noted that Lourdes would not look directly at her. "I'm sorry, Judge—" she started, but was interrupted by the thud of the jury box doors being opened. Three beefy corrections officers walked into the room with William Bantling in shackles and handcuffs. He was dressed in an expensive charcoal Italian suit and white shirt with a light gray silk tie, also designer. Despite having lost what C.J. guessed to be about twenty pounds, he looked quite dapper, except for the left side of his face, which was red and bruising. The officers sat him down hard next to Lourdes, who, C.J. noticed, moved her chair ever so slightly away from his.

"Don't take off those cuffs, just yet, Officer. I need to have a word with Mr. Bantling," the judge said sternly. "Why was he late being brought over here?"

"He had a fit, Judge," the corrections officer responded. "He started cussin' and screaming that he wasn't going to the courthouse without all the jewelry he came in with. Called us a bunch of thieves. We had to restrain him to get him out of the cell."

"Why can't he have his jewelry?"

"It's a security risk."

"A watch is a security risk? Let's not cross over into the absurd now, Officer. I'll allow him to wear his jewelry here in court."

Judge Chaskel narrowed his eyes and looked at Bantling. "Now, listen here, Mr. Bantling. I have seen your outbursts in this courtroom and I have heard about your tantrums elsewhere and I am going to warn you right now that I am neither a tolerant nor a patient judge. Three strikes and you're out, and you already have two. If necessary, I will have you bound and gagged and dragged over here for court every day in your red jumpsuit if you do not conduct yourself properly. Do I make myself clear?"

Bantling nodded, his cold eyes never leaving the challenging stare of Judge Chaskel. "Yes, Your Honor."

"Now, does anyone have anything else, or are we ready to pick a jury?" Bantling turned his stare toward C.J. His secret dangled precariously over the open pit.

Judge Chaskel waited a moment and then continued. "Okay. No one else has business. Let's get on with it. Officer, remove those cuffs and shackles on Mr. Bantling, and Hank, go fetch the first lucky fifty. I want to pick a jury before the week is out. Let's not drag it on past the Christmas break."

Even as she felt her lungs constrict and the room spin nervously, C.J. met Bantling's stare defiantly with her own. Ever so subtly, his pink tongue crept out of the corner of his mouth and moved across his upper lip, and then a slow, knowing smile spread across his face. His mouth glistened in the bright courtroom lights.

She knew then that it would not be on this day that he would break his silence to the world. He would make her

72

"IF I WERE to remain seated and say nothing, just sit here and not say one word—you would think him guilty, although the law has told you he is not." Lourdes sat still in her chair, as she made her opening statement. She faced the judge's bench, and spoke to the jury as if she were voicing her own private thoughts aloud.

C.J. had just sat back down in her seat after delivering what she thought was a good, solid, to-the-point opening that left no room for speculation, to the hushed crowd of spectators and camera crews. And now it was Lourdes's turn.

Lourdes allowed moments to pass in silence, and then she turned finally in her seat and faced the jury with a mixed look of disbelief and disappointment. "You all look at my client now as if he were a butcher. You are obviously frightened and sickened at the very vivid, very gory picture that the prosecutor has just painted you for the last hour. Without question, Anna Prado was a beautiful young woman, brutally mutilated by a madman. And you think him guilty, as if the prosecutor's words were enough to lead you to that conclusion. And you want to be frightened and sickened at the very sight of William Bantling as well, although common sense tells you this good-looking, well-educated, successful businessman certainly does not warrant that reaction." She put her hand casually on Bantling's shoulder and rubbed it as a subtle sign of her support. Then she shook her head.

"But what the prosecutor has offered you in her opening statement is not proof, ladies and gentlemen. It is *not* evidence. It is *not* fact. It is assumption. It is conjecture. It is speculation. It is an *assumption* that the evidence, the facts, that she *hopes* to present in this case, that she *believes* will be presented, that those facts, when loosely strung together will make a damning chain. She wants to force you all to come to the conclusion which she has already drawn for you: that my client is guilty of first-degree murder. But I caution you, ladies and gentlemen, that things are not always what they might seem. And facts—no matter how vile and bloody they might be—when strung together don't always make a chain."

Lourdes rose now and stood before the jury, scanning their faces. Some jurors turned their eyes away, ashamed of themselves at having drawn the very conclusions that Lourdes now accused them of, of disobeying the oath that they had only last Friday sworn to uphold.

"All movie producers are the same, and their goals are the same. The ultimate goal is that they want you to see their movie. Their multimillion-dollar over-budget movie that they have spent months to create. And, in this endeavor, they will try to sell you on how great their movie is before you even walk in the theater. They want you to run around awed simply by their two-minute trailers, telling your friends and family, 'This is a great movie!' even though you have not even seen it. They want you to buy the posters and the T-shirts and the merchandise and cast your vote for best actor all before you have even taken your seat. And many will, even without having seen the movie. All because of the exciting two-minute preview that assured them the movie was going to be great. It was going to be fantastic. The next 'Best Picture' at the Oscars. And Ms. Townsend has certainly done her job well here today, ladies and gentlemen. She has filled her trailer with action and blood and grisly details and lots of special effects. It looks great. It sounds great. But, I caution you, don't buy your ticket just yet. Because just as a string of terrific-looking scenes run together in a magnificent trailer by a very talented producer"—Lourdes turned and deliberately faced C.J., subtly pausing for effect—"won't necessarily make a good movie, neither will a bunch of gory, vicious facts strung together make a very good case. No matter how many special effects that they throw at you to impress you. A bad movie is still a bad movie.

"My client is innocent. He is not a killer. He is not a serial killer. He is a talented, successful businessman who has never before gotten so much as a traffic ticket.

"An alibi? Mr. Bantling was not even at his home during the hours the medical examiner will tell you that Anna Prado was supposedly killed in the shed out in the back of his house. And he'll prove it, although he is under no obligation to prove anything.

"The murder weapon? Mr. Bantling is a renowned taxidermist, and his projects are on display at various local museums and establishments. The scalpel found in his shed is actually a tool he uses in his craft, not a murder weapon. The microscopic blood traces found on it are animal in nature, not human. And he'll prove it, although he is under no obligation to prove anything.

"The blood? The blood smears, as Ms. Townsend vividly described for all of us in her opening, that were detected 'all over the inside of his shed' by the chemical luminol are again, animal in nature, not human. Let me point out that *three*"—she raised three fingers up before the jury and walked slowly before them, watching their faces closely, never losing their attention—"count them, *three,* microscopic bloodstains matching the DNA of Anna Prado were found in that shed, a shed that the state alleges was actually sprayed with Anna Prado's blood when her aorta was severed, but where only *three microscopic drops* were found. Found, ladies and gentlemen, by a desperate FDLE special agent who has needed a name and a face for the serial killer Cupid he has hunted for over a year. An agent whose whole career rests precariously on finding that face, naming that name.

"The trunk? The Jaguar had been left at a repair shop for two days prior to being picked up by Mr. Bantling on September nineteenth. It was out of his care, custody, and control. He never even looked in the trunk before tossing his overnight bag in the backseat and heading to the airport on scheduled business that night. And he'll prove that, too, although he is, again, under no obligation to prove anything.

"Please note that not one single fingerprint, hair, fiber, scratch, stain, or substance has been found on the body of Anna Prado that links her death to Mr. Bantling. And although he is not on trial here today for the murders of any other women, and has not been charged with any other crime, let it be known that there is absolutely no physical evidence linking Mr. Bantling with even one of those other ten women. Not a fingerprint or hair, not a fiber, not a stain, not a scratch. Not a drop of DNA. Not one shred of physical evidence to those women. Not one."

"Objection," C.J. said, rising in her seat. "The facts of any other investigation have not been made part of this case. They are irrelevant."

"Sustained."

But the damage had already been done. Lourdes had made sure that the jury knew that there was nothing connecting Bantling to those other murders. Nothing at all.

Lourdes caught the eye of one woman who had before turned away from her prying stare. The woman was now nodding ever so slightly at Lourdes's words, while looking Bill Bantling over curiously. C.J. could practically hear her thought spring from her head: *He doesn't look like a serial killer.* Bantling smiled slightly at the woman and she smiled back, sheepishly looking away.

"The damning chain is not so damning now, is it, ladies and gentlemen? The movie is not so good. So don't be so amazed by special effects and bloody evidence and the evil words *serial killer* on the front page of the *Miami Herald.* Remember the oath you took as jurors, and . . . well, don't buy your ticket to this movie just yet."

On those words, Lourdes sat down in the silent, stunned courtroom. Her client covered her hand with his in a sign of his appreciation, while a perfectly staged crocodile tear fell from his eye.

And C.J. realized that her case was in big trouble.

73

"JESUS CHRIST, HOW could you not have known, C.J.?" Tigler paced her office, nervously running his hand over the top of his head. "We look like a bunch of fucking law students in moot court doing their first trial!"

"Jerry, I didn't know. He didn't engage in discovery. We thought we had it all locked down; obviously not."

"The man's car was in a garage for two days before the murder and the special task force, a task force of highly experienced detectives, mind you, could not have found that out unless someone told them to make sure to look?" Tigler's face was red. C.J. had never seen him this angry before.

"Just the fact that it was in a garage before he drove it does not make him innocent. He was still driving his car with a dead girl in the trunk."

"No. But it does make us look like bloodthirsty prosecutors who'll skip out on doing their homework just to nail a name on a serial killer and throw the terrified public a scapegoat. We look like amateurs and I don't appreciate looking like an amateur, especially in an election year."

"I'll work it out, Jerry. I'm meeting with Detective Alvarez and Agent Falconetti in ten minutes. I'll work it out."

"I hope so, C.J. Because even the feds won't touch this guy now. Tom de la Flors backed off the indictment when he heard the news. He feels the case warrants further investigation before a potentially innocent man is indicted on circumstantial facts." He stopped his pacing and wiped his hands on his pants. "Damn. We look like fools."

"I'll work it out, Jerry."

"I trusted you with this case, C.J. You had better work it out, that's all I can say." He straightened the toupee on his sweaty head, and reached for the doorknob, "And we better be doing all we can to make sure that we don't put a needle in the arm of an innocent man."

The door closed behind him with a loud bang. A few seconds later a light tap sounded, and the door opened again. Manny stuck his head in.

"Your boss looks like shit. I think he's gonna drop, C.J."

"That'll make two of us."

Manny walked into the room, followed a few seconds later by Dominick. Everyone looked at each other for a few seconds.

"What the hell happened, guys?" C.J. finally said, her hands spread on her desk, her voice exasperated. "How did we not know about this auto-repair place? Where exactly was he during the ten to fourteen hours before Anna Prado's body was found?"

"C.J., you know he never talked to us. He screamed for his lawyer before we even got off the causeway. No discovery, either," Dominick said in a low voice, obviously trying hard to control his temper. "We've talked to three hundred people. He wasn't with any of them on September eighteenth or nineteenth. And there was no reason to think the Jag would be at a garage—it's brand new."

"He's planned this all along. To get us to this point and then make us look like fools in front of the jury. I should have seen it coming, because it's been Lourdes's MO in the past—trial by ambush. I just didn't think she'd try it with this one because the stakes are so high. Because the evidence was so airtight . . ."

"Hey, she basically just accused me of manufacturing evidence to get an arrest. How do you think that makes me feel, C.J.?" Dominick angrily erupted, his voice booming.

"You know, you're not the only one working hard here to keep this guy behind bars."

Manny tried to smooth things over in as soft a voice as the Bear could muster. "Counselor, we're pulling everything, talking to every garage within a five-mile radius—"

"Make it ten. We need to find that garage. See if anyone saw anything."

"Fine. Ten miles. We're going back out and talking to the witnesses again. Every associate he's had in Miami that we know of . . ."

"You'd better work fast, because Judge Chaskel is determined to move this along. He's starting early every morning and ending late every night. We don't have much time."

"Well then, we're going to have to wait and see what he's got when he presents his case," Dominick said.

"By then it might be too late, Dominick. If the jury thinks we don't have what it takes, and worse yet, that we've been holding back, they'll let him walk. He can't walk. I won't let him!" As before, she could feel the small cracks in her fragile façade that had been glued back together with years of therapy begin to separate and splinter, spreading slowly and fanning out in all directions. She pulled her hands through her hair, hoping to hold her thoughts together. Dominick was watching her intently.

Watching her unravel. Watching her come apart before his very eyes.

"I need to look at all his records. Everything. I need to find out what it is he is going to spring on us. And I need to find it out before he puts his case on," she said aloud, but mainly to herself.

She looked up from her desk at both of them, watching her. The heavy silence was sobering.

"Don't you see? He planned this all along," she said finally, her voice a shaking, raspy whisper. "We've been ambushed. And I never even saw it coming . . ."

74

THE RING OF his cell phone played the musical score of Taps, and it immediately brought Dominick out of his deep sleep on the couch. The movie *Midnight Run* had been replaced on the television by an infomercial for a complete hair-removal system. He stared for a moment at the phone, blinking several times to make sure he was not still dreaming.

"Falconetti," he said, flipping open the Nextel.

"Who's DR?" the voice on the other end demanded.

"What? C.J., is that you?" He rubbed his eyes, looking around his apartment for a clock. "What time is it?"

"One A.M. Who is DR? What is DR?"

"What are you talking about? Where are you?"

"I'm at the office. I've just spent the last four hours going through Bantling's old date books and his business journals that were seized in the search warrants, and the initials DR keep popping up sporadically throughout 1999 and this year, without any other identifying info. In fact, there was a reference to DR the day before Anna Prado disappeared and then again the day before Bantling was arrested. Did you see that?"

"Yes, of course. We looked into it. Interviewed everyone we could find that had those initials. Nothing came up. We don't know who or what or where it stands for."

"Same thing goes with at least three of the victims. Two

days to a week before they disappear, there's a DR notation. What the hell is that?"

"It could be anything. It could be nothing. I don't know. What, is Manny not home?"

"What are you talking about?"

"I haven't heard from you in almost two weeks, and I know you call him when you need something, so I assume you are calling because he's not in." His sarcasm was met with silence on the other end.

"Yeah. I just thought DR might be something we missed," she said, purposely ignoring what he had just said. "Maybe someplace we haven't looked before. Maybe it's a place he goes to, where he's stashed—"

"We've already been down that road, and I think you have us grasping at straws. It's late."

More silence. The perfect opportunity for her to hang up, he thought. But she surprised him when she stayed on the line, and her voice softened. "I'm sorry about yesterday, in my office. I shouldn't have lost my temper with you. I guess I'm just a little anxious about where Lourdes is going with all this."

"Look, we all know the man's a nut. Throwing us off is a thrill for him. A high. That's why he didn't demand discovery. He wanted to make us look bad, like he outsmarted us. If he were innocent, he would have talked from day one and supplied us information that could prove his innocence. This is all a game to him, C.J. Remember that. Don't let him get under your skin, because that's what he wants."

"You did well today, on both direct and cross, in court. I wanted to tell you that, but you left so quickly. Lourdes didn't shake your tree."

"God knows she tried. She did, however, manage to paint me as a desperate cop on the edge of losing his career if he doesn't solve this case. Tell me, do I appear desperate to you?"

"No. Remember, *I'm* the one who called you."

He laughed. "Do you think the jury bought it?"

"No. Actually, I think you handled yourself well."

"How did Chavez do?" Potential witnesses for either side were not allowed in the courtroom during the trial so that their own testimony would not be influenced by listening to the testimony of others.

"Not much better than the motion to suppress. After that last slice of humble pie that Lourdes force-fed him, he toned down the arrogance by a few degrees. But even though his testimony was definitely more polished this time, it was also obviously more rehearsed, so in reality we gained nothing."

"What did the jury think?"

"That he's either evasive or stupid. Maybe both. They definitely picked up on the tension. Lourdes and he were like plaid and stripes at the school prom: They clashed from the get-go."

C.J. did not share with Dominick how Lourdes had again led Chavez to the dangerous waters of his previous testimony, with the same vague references to the rookie's ulterior motives for the initial stop of the Jaguar. And how C.J. had felt the perspiration form on her brow and lip, her heart in her throat waiting for the next question to come. The question to end all questions.

The tip. Did Lourdes really know about it, or had she been bluffing? Would she use it? Did she, too, have the 911 tape? Better yet, did she know who the caller was? Could C.J. expect the raspy voice to make an appearance as a defense witness later on, coming through the courtroom doors like an evil Matlock witness, here to ruin her case with his surprise testimony?

But once again, Lourdes had pushed the stubborn Chavez only so far, backing off suddenly, and leaving the jury with the taste that there was something more to the rookie's story. And C.J. had felt the heavy weight of fear slowly ease off her chest.

"How much more do you have left?"

"The ME, crime scene, Masterson for the porno tapes. Maybe two, three more days. Probably after the New Year, but you never know with this judge. It might be tomorrow."

"You weren't kidding that Chaskel moves fast. He's

done more in a week than most judges do in a month. Especially on a capital. What time are you starting?"

"Eight. We wrapped yesterday and today after nine. The jury is pissed. It's ruined their holidays. I fear they're blaming me, and I certainly wasn't the one who chose to try a murder during this most wonderful time of the year."

"How was your Christmas?" Their conversation had softened, lapsed back into the familiar. It was almost painful, how much he missed her.

"Okay," she lied. "Tibby got me a fur ball. A big one. Yours?"

"Good," he lied. "Manny got me nothing. He got himself a hickey, though. And in the true spirit of Christmas, I think he gave a couple, too."

"Really? Not to you, I hope."

"No. But I think your secretary will be wearing turtlenecks this week."

"Oh God. Men are so blind."

"Yes. Yes, we are."

She said nothing, but he thought he heard her sniffle.

"Is Tigler over his mad?" he asked, breaking the silence, feeling bad about that last cheap shot.

"Nope. Not until I win, which by the day is looking shakier."

He heard the quiver in her voice, the same anxious sound it held the other day in her office when she had called him and Manny in on the carpet. "How are you holding up?" he asked softly. "Are you okay? Do you want me to come ov—"

But she quickly broke him off, knowing what he was going to suggest. "Look, I'll let you get back to bed," she said quickly as the tears welled, and her voice started to choke. "Sorry I woke you. Good night."

She hung the phone up on him, and he knew she was crying. Crying alone in the darkness of her deserted office in downtown Shitsville. He stood up from the couch and walked his apartment, wide awake now.

She was walking too close to the edge. He could hear it

in her voice, see it in her eyes these last few months, these past few days. With just one stumble, or one slip . . .

He looked out his living room window in the direction of downtown, where he knew she was, alone and upset.

He just hoped that he would be there to catch her when she fell.

75

DR. THE SCRIBBLED initials appeared sporadically all over Bantling's date books. Different days of the week, different times. Day and night. The last one was entered just one day before Anna Prado was discovered in Bantling's trunk. *What did they mean? A place? A person? A thing? An idea? Nothing at all?*

C.J.'s brain hurt from thinking. She sipped on her cold coffee, refusing to give up and go home. If she stayed much longer, it really would not make much sense for her to go home anyway. Trial resumed at 8:00 A.M., and it was already 2:30. Her desk was literally covered with paper. Paper from the overstuffed box of business records, journals, date books, address books, bank statements, and tax receipts that had been seized from Bantling's house and cars and given to the task force by Tommy Tan. Everything and anything there was to know about William Bantling was spread before her like an open book. She had read through his journals and date books, looked at his daily business appointments, sifted through his taxes and receipts. She knew that some would think her obsessed, straying into territory that was too trivial, too familiar, where there, perhaps, was little or no evidentiary value. Especially since these were the same books, journals, records, and receipts that had already been combed over by experienced investigators with trained eyes. But still she had to look, had to see how it was he managed to live with himself every day, carrying on life as normal. And perhaps, just perhaps, somewhere along the way, those trained eyes had missed something . . .

She found his personal address book, the one seized with the day planner from his overnight bag in the backseat of the Jag, and flipped open the pages. The worn black Coach was overstuffed with address sheets, business cards, and tiny pieces of matchbook and cocktail napkins on which names and phone numbers had been hastily scribbled. She began reading the individual entries, carefully studying Bantling's almost illegible scrawl, looking for something, anything. She didn't know what. A handwriting expert had once told her that he could tell a sane person from an insane person just by watching him sign his name. She thought of his words now, wondering what opinion he would offer of Bantling and the scribbles in his little black book.

There were hundreds of names, some no more than a first name and phone number, and they were almost all women. He must have written down the name of just about every woman he had ever met; there were that many in the overstuffed book. Some of the names she recognized from task force reports of interviews. Others meant nothing. As she read through the names of dozens of women, a chilling thought suddenly seized her, and she quickly skipped ahead to the listings under L, making sure her own name had not made his creepy little black book. Her eyes scanned the names, but there was no Larson listing. Then she skipped back to the C entries, her eyes racing through the pages, expecting to see it scrawled before her across the page in his demented chicken scratch: *For a good time call Chloe! 202-18 Apartment 1B Rocky Hill Road, Bayside, New York.* One by one, her eyes read down the list of entries, her heart in her throat. But she was not there, and she slowly exhaled the anxious breath that had caught in her chest.

Any sigh of relief was short-lived, however, because her eyes caught on another name in Bantling's black book, scribbled in tiny, hurried script, that was almost, *almost* illegible. A name that took her quite by surprise and one that she would never have expected. One that she wished now she never saw.

> *Chambers, G.*
> *22 Almeria Street*
> *Coral Gables, FL*

76

GREG CHAMBERS. WHY would his name be in Bantling's book? How would they have known each other? And did they actually know each other, or did Bantling just pick up Greg's name someplace, possibly as a psychiatric referral, and put it in his black book for future reference?

C.J. stood and paced her office, her mind spinning. *If they had known each other, why would Greg not have told her?* He would have. There was no way around that, so he must not even have realized that Bantling knew him. He must not have known he was even in his book. The address book was obviously old; the entries could be from years back. The remote connection could have been a professional referral from long ago, or perhaps they were distant, forgotten acquaintances. Greg would probably be just as surprised as she to see his name in that book. That must be it.

But as she walked the room, her mind frantically scrambling to make sense out of the thoughts that spun inside her head, she felt the spiny, familiar fingers of paranoia creep up her neck, tightening their grip on her brain. And the *what-ifs* began to knock on her door, demanding entry.

What if they did know each other? What if they were friends? What if they were something more? She fought the paralyzing feeling of fear back down. The fear that even from his jail cell, he had planned this surprise. The fear that his words whispered years ago were coming true.

I'll always be watching you, Chloe. Always. You can't get away from me, 'cause I'll always find you.

The fear that he was everywhere, watching her, dictating even her most irrational thoughts.

She looked at her paper-covered desk, her cold cup of coffee, her drawn blinds in the dark office, illuminated only by a dim desk lamp and a gray computer screen. It was 3:00 in the morning, and she had to be back for trial at 8:00 A.M. She had not slept more than four hours a night since September.

You are jumping to conclusions. You are not thinking rational thoughts. This case is consuming you. Bantling is consuming you. He is eating you alive. And you are letting him.

Stress is a major factor in any illness, be it physical or mental. She knew it was a precipitating factor of her last breakdown. She had to control it before it ran out of control, before her life ran out of control. Her relationships, her career—everything was spiraling, the same as before. *It was all happening again, the same as before.* The parallel was frightening.

She crushed out her last cigarette and packed up her briefcase, stuffing the address book inside. She called downstairs and woke up the security guard and headed to the elevator.

She needed to get away. To remove herself for a while. She needed to think. She needed to rest, she told herself.

Before it all spiraled out of control.

Just like before.

77

ESTELLE WAS JUST packing up her large hobo straw purse to leave when C.J. tapped on the glass above her head. It was just past 7:00 P.M. on a Thursday night, and only three days from the New Year.

"Ooh, Ms. Townsend," she said, surprised, looking up from her bag, her red-clawed hand covering her chest, "You startled me. I didn't see you there."

"I'm sorry, Estelle. Is Dr. Chambers in?"

"Yes," she said, her voice distracted, as she thumbed through the appointment book, "but, well, he's with a patient right now." She looked up at C.J., her face frowning with obvious concern. "I'm sorry, but I don't have you down for an appointment this evening."

C.J. knew that Estelle was probably itching to ask her the question of the day: *Are you okay? You don't look so good.* Even Judge Chaskel had called her sidebar during the trial that day to make sure she was feeling alright. Concealer could no longer hide the dark circles under her eyes. She had lost five pounds off her slight frame in the past week alone, and anxious worry lines cut deeper across her pale brow. She had told everyone it was a lack of sleep, because she didn't think people would actually understand if she told them the truth—that it was entirely possible she was going crazy again. *Just a few more days till the nuthouse. Hurry up and get your tickets.* But Estelle dealt with crazy people every day, and knew better than to ask the question.

"I don't have an appointment, Estelle. I just need to see Dr. Chambers when he's done. It's very important; he'll understand."

"Oh. Okay, then. Well, um, I hate to disturb him when he's in session." She looked up at the clock in the waiting room. "And I have to go. I'm meeting my husband for dinner."

"That's okay, Estelle. I'll just wait until he's through. I need to speak with him tonight, though."

"Oh." She lowered her voice to a whisper, "Is it about your case? I see you every night on TV. It's always the top story at eleven."

"I just need to speak with the doctor."

Estelle mulled it over for a moment. "Well, you are friends. I guess he wouldn't mind. Why don't you have a seat then? This is his last patient for the day, and he should be done around seven-thirty. You can grab him on his way out."

"That's fine. Thank you, Estelle."

Estelle picked up her hobo purse and jacket and walked out into the waiting room. "Ordinarily, I'd stay, but we're meeting with Frank's boss and his wife, and well, you know how that is. We can't be late."

"Not a problem."

Estelle stopped at the door. Her voice lowered to that hush again. "Do you really think he did it, Ms. Townsend? I mean, really?"

"I wouldn't prosecute him if I didn't think he was guilty." *And I can do better than that, Estelle. I know he's guilty. I'm just not as sure as I was before that he's a murderer.*

"You never can tell about people, can you?" Estelle said and shook her head. "Good night, Ms. Townsend."

"No, you can't," C.J. murmured as Estelle left. She sat in the empty waiting room for a few minutes, collecting her thoughts. It was not working on this night. This was the first opportunity she'd had to speak with Greg Chambers since her discovery late last night. She wondered exactly what she would say, how she should say it. She didn't want to come off sounding paranoid and frantic, although she suspected that was how she looked.

The reception office door was slightly ajar. Estelle must have forgotten to pull it shut behind her when she left. C.J. got up and anxiously paced the waiting room, rolling an old issue of *Entertainment Weekly* magazine back and forth in her sweaty palms. At Estelle's reception window, she stopped pacing and saw that far down the hall, the doctor's office door was shut tight, as it always was while he was in session, while the secrets were being told. She glanced down at Estelle's desk and saw the open appointment book that Estelle had thumbed through five minutes earlier. The *what-ifs* screamed at her again in her head, demanding their answers.

She cautiously moved by the open door, and stood for a moment. She could not hear a thing. She pushed open the door slightly and saw that the door to his office was still closed. She looked above her head at the clock in the waiting room. It read 7:22.

Without really thinking, she pushed open the door and walked over the threshold of sanity to Estelle's desk. The appointment book was open to the week of Monday, December 25, through Friday, December 29. The last page for the year 2000. C.J.'s fingers hesitantly touched the page, and then she quickly flipped backward in time, past the penciled-in time slots of November and October, stopping at the week of Monday, September 18, through Friday, September 22.

Her eyes carefully scanned down Monday's appointment column. And there it was, the last entry of the day. September 18. The day before Anna Prado's body had been discovered.

She felt her breath suck in as she saw her worst, most irrational fear confirmed.

The penciled-in 7:00 P.M. appointment that night was B. Bantling.

78

SHE RACED BACKWARD to the seven dates that she had written down from Bantling's date book the night before. They all matched. The same dates, the same times, the same name: *B. Bantling.*

It was no coincidence. *DR.* Now it made perfect sense. *DR . . . Dr . . . Doctor.* Chambers was his doctor. *Chambers was Bantling's doctor.*

C.J. backed away from the desk, away from the date book, away from the truth that was in front of her eyes the whole time. The room spun, and she felt as if she would vomit. *What did this mean? How could this be?* He had treated both of them. He had treated her rapist. *How long had this gone on? Years?* Memories flipped through her head like a Rolodex in a hurricane. Had she met Bantling before? Perhaps sat next to him in this very waiting room, sharing a smile or a magazine or a comment about the weather while she waited her turn to see the good doctor? *What did Chambers know? What had Bantling shared with him? What did Bantling know? What had Chambers shared with him?* The thoughts she had dismissed the night before as irrational and paranoid rushed through her brain once again, threatening to shut it down. The air became heavy, and it was hard to breathe.

This couldn't be happening. Not again. *Please God, no more. One person can only take so much in her life. And this is it for me. I'm done.* She had to get out. She had to think. She backed into Estelle's chair and heard the thump as it careened into the wall, sending a picture frame crashing to the floor. She turned and ran through the open door, grabbing her purse off the seat in the waiting room. Behind her she heard a muffled voice yell, "What the hell was that? Estelle?" and then the sound of the office door opening down the hall, but it no longer mattered. She pulled open the heavy oak front door, and ran past the neat flower beds of yellow, white, and red, and down the path paved in Chicago brick. Away from the beautiful Spanish house on Almeria Street in posh, safe Coral Gables. Away from the kind, understanding doctor to whom for the last ten years of her life she had turned for help in dealing with the reality that was her life. For guidance and advice, and to fix the fears that paralyzed her mind. But now she ran as fast as she could away from it all. She climbed in the Jeep and sped off, swerving to miss the obscenity-screaming bicyclist who appeared suddenly in front of her car.

She disappeared down Almeria, heading for the Dolphin Expressway, just as Dr. Gregory Chambers stepped out into his now-empty waiting room to see what all the commotion was about.

79

"THE FIRST INCISION into the chest cavity was made beginning at the sternum, slicing vertically down across the breast plate, ending at the navel. The cut was clean, with no jags or tears to the skin."

Joe Neilson involuntarily twitched as he demonstrated on the plastic female mannequin that was set up across from the jury, and the pointer jumped slightly in his hand. "The second incision was made horizontally under the breasts, beginning just under the right breast and continuing laterally across and under the left breast. Again, there was only one cut and it was clean, with no jags or tears."

"Do you have an opinion as to what type of instrument made these incisions?" asked C.J. The courtroom was silent, hanging on every word.

"I do. It was a scalpel. The incisions were deep. They cut through to the bone, passing through three layers of skin, fatty tissue, and finally, muscle. There were no tears or indentations evidenced. The number-five scalpel that was seized from the defendant's residence was, in fact, tested against the skin tears made to Ms. Prado's chest. The depth and width of the cut matched. They were identical."

Two enlarged photographs mounted on posterboard sat side by side on easels next to the mannequin. One was of the scalpel blade seized from Bantling's home, magnified fifty times. The other was a close-up picture of the incision made in Anna Prado's chest cavity, also magnified fifty times.

"After the incisions, the sternum, the bone that supports the rib cage and protects the heart and lungs, was then cracked open and spread apart."

"Do you have an opinion as to what instrument was used to crack the chest?"

"No. Probably bolt cutters."

"Was Anna still alive at this point?"

"Yes. Death is determined when a heart stops beating. When that occurs, other functions cease in the body, including breathing, and things remain as they were at the exact moment someone expired. That is how we can tell what someone last ate and when, what sort of toxins were in her bloodstream and liver, et cetera. When Ms. Prado's sternum was cracked, the lungs were exposed to air and outside pressure, which would, in turn, cause them to collapse. As the lungs deflated of air, oxygen would stop circulating to the heart and brain, and death from suffocation would ensue in approximately two to five minutes. However, air was still found in Ms. Prado's left lung during the autopsy, so we know that her death did not result from suffocation. And that, yes, she was still alive, when—"

A wail let out suddenly in the room, followed by a gasp. It was Anna's mother. She was sobbing uncontrollably, being held up by family members. "Monster! Monster!" she yelled.

"Order!" demanded a red-faced Judge Chaskel. "Hank, please escort Mrs. Prado into the hall for this part of the testimony. I'm sorry, Mrs. Prado, but such outbursts cannot be permitted in the courtroom."

"He took my baby!" she screamed as family members led her to the doors while the jurors' eyes followed. "That bastard took my little girl and cut her up! And now he sits there smiling!" The doors closed on her screams.

"The jury is hereby instructed to disregard those remarks," the judge warned sternly as Lourdes stood to object. The twelve members of the jury all looked in the direction of an obviously upset William Bantling, who shook his bowed head from side to side, his face buried in his hands.

Uncomfortable silence hung in the air for a few moments, while the sounds of Mrs. Prado's wails faded as she was escorted down the hallway to the escalators.

"Okay, Ms. Townsend, you may continue," Judge Chaskel said.

"What caused her heart to stop, Doctor?"

"The severing of her aorta, the artery that supplies blood to the heart. Her aorta was cut and the heart muscle removed immediately after the sternum was cracked, and before the lungs could fully deflate. That caused her immediate death." The pointer now moved to another posterboard of a gray, nude Anna Prado, lying flat on the steel gurney at the medical examiner's office, a black hole where her heart used to be.

"Was she conscious at the time?"

"That is impossible to determine, although, as I already stated, the mivacurium chloride found in her system would not cause her to lose consciousness. It would simply cause paralysis. Its relaxant effects on the skeletal muscles, however, would probably slow or prevent the body from going into shock, its natural defense when attacked. So I'd say that yes, there is a distinct possibility that she was conscious when her heart was cut out." A collective murmur rolled through the courtroom, like the wave at a baseball game.

"Thank you, Dr. Neilson. I have no further questions."

"Very well. Ms. Rubio? Cross?"

"Just a couple of questions. Doctor, you testified that the incisions on Ms. Prado's body were consistent with those of a number-five scalpel, is that correct?"

"Yes."

"And that could have been any number-five scalpel. Is that correct? Not the particular scalpel allegedly found at Mr. Bantling's residence?"

"Yes. Any number-five scalpel."

"And number-five scalpels are not peculiar, are they? In fact, they are rather common, particularly in the medical and taxidermy professions, correct?"

"I couldn't say about the taxidermy profession, but, yes, they are quite common in the medical profession. They can be purchased at any medical-supply store."

"Thank you, Doctor." Lourdes crossed the courtroom to her seat, then turned. "Oh," she said, as if the thought had just occurred to her, "and who was it that brought you this scalpel, this alleged murder weapon, for testing and comparison? Which detective was it?"

"FDLE Agent Dom Falconetti."

"Oh," she said, thoughtfully, sitting down. "I have nothing further."

"State, do you have anything else?" asked Judge Chaskel.

It was 6:10 P.M. on Friday, December 29. The last working day of the calendar year 2000. C.J. had headed into the courthouse this morning, with reality crumbling and cracking and threatening to collapse around her, another sleepless night swallowing her eyes in deep circles and cutting lines of damage further into her brow. She did so because there was nothing else she could do at this point, and forfeiting to the other team was just not an option.

Just like Lourdes's cross, everything was innuendo and everyone was now suspect. Answers led to more questions. Absolutes were now equivocal. And nothing was real anymore; nothing was certain. She had no control over anyone, over anything in either her personal or her professional life. Witnesses who were supposed to be hers gave answers for the other side. Doctors who were supposed to help her also aided the enemy. Confidantes may now be spies. And the cracks in the façade ran deep, fanning out in a million directions. *Just like before.*

"No, Judge. I have nothing further," she said, rising. Joe Neilson had been her last witness, finishing her case with a painful and telling description of the final tortured moments of Anna Prado's life. "The state rests."

"Very well. That's a perfect place to end this for the holiday weekend," began Judge Chaskel. Then he turned to give his standard list of admonishments to the jury before discharging them.

C.J. turned and looked down at Bantling in his seat next to Lourdes. He still had his face buried somberly in his hands for the jury, his head shaking softly back and forth. But only now she saw why.

It was because he was laughing.

80

"HAVE YOU TRIED calling her, Dom?" Manny asked, the New Year's party hat dipped in gold glitter tipping precariously off the side of his head. He was already three sheets to the wind, as was almost everyone else in the room.

"Yeah. I keep getting her voice mail. I'm a little worried, Manny."

"I know you are, *amigo*. Have another beer. Mari!" he shouted across Eddie Bowman's crowded living room, packed with cops and analysts and agents and detectives, all adorned with glitter party hats and drinking shots from plastic champagne glasses. "Bring Dommy Boy another beer!"

Marisol looked up from her conversation with six other women. She was dressed in purple sequins from head to toe, with a large swath of material missing conspicuously from her midriff. She shot Manny an annoyed look and a silent tsk.

"Okay, Okay. *Please* bring Dom another beer." Manny turned to Dominick. "Jesus Christ, one roll in the sack and now I've gotta use fucking manners. I'm thinking back to my single days again, Dom. Maybe you should stay put, too."

"No more drinks for me anyway, Manny. I'm headed home soon."

"Hey, it's almost midnight. You can't leave before the

ball drops. Maybe she's not in. Maybe she went away for the weekend."

"Maybe. But her car's still there at her apartment."

"Now don't turn stalker on me, buddy. Driving by her apartment and shit."

"I'm worried, Bear. She looks like crap. She's lost weight. She's not eating, she's obviously not sleeping. She won't call any of us back. Even you. This guy Bantling is fucking with her head. And he's winning. He's got something on her. You've known her for years. Have you ever seen her like this before?"

"No, I haven't. And it worries me, too. Maybe this case just has her burning too many candles at both ends. Maybe she's taking it easy this weekend." He paused and slugged down a guzzle of beer before finishing his thought. "Or, maybe she has someone else, Dom."

"You know, if that was it, I'd back off. But I don't think it's someone else. I think she's taken on something by herself, something that's too big for her to handle alone, and she won't let anyone share it. She won't let anyone in, and it's pulling her apart, breaking her down. I see it in her eyes. When she lets me look, that is."

"Well, the state just rested. So what more is left? A few more days?"

"Just the defense."

"That's a problem. No one knows what Psycho is going to say, or for that matter if he's even taking the stand. No luck on that garage, huh?"

"Nope. We checked everything. Eddie even followed up a lead this morning. Nothing. We just have to wait and see what Bantling does. Take it from there."

"His lawyer is so full of shit." Manny raised his voice to a high-pitched whine: " 'We'll prove it's animal blood. We'll prove he didn't know what was in his own fucking trunk. Even though we are under no obligation to prove anything.' Bullshit. Luminol won't let us type the blood that was splashed all over that shed. It only lets us see it. She knows that, but she's gotta twist it. Same goes for Bantling's fucked-up tale that it's bird blood. She can't prove that. What fucking bird do you know that spurts blood on a ceiling like Ol' Faithful? But that don't matter to Rubio. She's leading that jury by their dicks to her bull-shit."

"Or by something else."

Manny shook his head in disgust. "Did you hear that shit? Chaskel's clerk told me that juror in the front row is still making goo-goo eyes at Bantling. Even after Neilson gave his slice-and-dice testimony. What kind of woman is that desperate?"

As if on cue, Marisol appeared suddenly from the kitchen with two beers. "Here, Bear," she cooed, handing him the beers, "because you said 'please.'"

"Alright, Manny, I'm out of here. I have a few things I want to get done tomorrow. A couple of people I need to reinterview. Maybe get some answers before Bantling puts on his show this week."

"On New Year's?"

"No rest for the weary. Keeps my mind free."

"Call her again, tomorrow, Buddy. Hang in there. This is almost all over."

"Call who?" Marisol asked Manny in a hushed whisper.

Dominick made his good-byes as he headed through the crowd to the door.

"Five, four, three, two, one . . . Happy New Year!" Dick Clark yelled behind him from the TV, and the room erupted in cheers and whistles and honks and noise. "And what a great year 2001 looks like it's gonna be!" "Auld Lang Syne" blared on the speakers.

"I don't think so, Dick," murmured Dominick to no one but himself as he closed the door and headed down the path out of the house. "I just don't think so."

81

LOURDES RUBIO BEGAN her case Tuesday morning at nine. First up was the owner of Louie's House of Tinting in North Miami Beach, then the head of the American Taxidermy Association, then the head of Pathology at Albert Einstein College of Medicine. In one day C.J. watched as her case was chiseled to a mountain of reasonable doubt.

Bantling's Jaguar was getting tinted all day Monday the eighteenth and Tuesday the nineteenth. It was picked up at approximately 7:15 P.M. that Tuesday. Louie testified that it had sat overnight in an unsecured parking lot, and that more than ten different employees had had access to the Jag during the day. He also testified that no one had looked in the trunk since Bantling had dropped it off on the eighteenth. There would have been no need to.

William Bantling was a renowned taxidermist, recognized many times over for his talents by the Southeast Chapter of the American Taxidermy Association. A number-five scalpel is often used as a tool in the craft. Normally, the animal is dead before the procedure is done; however, in certain instances, a live animal may be used to achieve a more "realistic look," particularly in the animal's eyes. That, of course, would explain the luminol-illuminated blood smears.

The blood smears on the number-five scalpel found in Bantling's shed were too small to achieve an accurate sample for DNA testing. Tests did indicate the presence of animal blood, though, most probably from a bird. The red blood cells discovered on the blade had nuclei, something that human red blood cells do not have. The swirls left on the blade that initially matched Anna's blood type also appeared to be "manufactured," as were the three drops of her blood found on the floor in the shed. So said the Chief of Pathology from Albert Einstein.

C.J. knew that you could find an expert somewhere who would say almost anything, refute even the most airtight evidence with conviction, if paid enough. Psychologists who would blame pro wrestling for a teenager's act of cold-blooded murder; doctors who would blame death on a heart attack rather than on a drunk driver. For the right price, there were witnesses for any defense, any legal theory. And sometimes it worked. But to actually watch her case crumble, come apart at the seams . . . to see Bantling's smile grow more and more confident as the jury nodded involuntarily at the testimony of his parade of witnesses, the coquettish glances in Bantling's direction of Juror Number Five occur more frequently, the fear that once appeared in her eyes replaced now by an inquisitive lust . . . it was all too much. C.J. knew that her cross-examinations were not up to par, her tone of voice sounding more and more desperate with each witness. It was obvious that she had not prepared questions on these witnesses, that she had been taken by surprise, *ambushed,* and she felt the jury's trust in her wane.

She had not slept all weekend. Nightmares of her rape were now replaced with nightmares of Bantling's acquittal. His twisted bloodred smile in the clown mask, turning to her in the courtroom and laughing. Laughing as Hank the bailiff unlocked the handcuffs and leg shackles and let him go free. And then him walking toward her, at her, while everyone just watched. Dominick, Manny, Lourdes, her parents, Michael, Judge Chaskel, Greg Chambers, Jerry Tigler, Tom de la Flors. All just watching while he threw her on the prosecution's table and stuffed her panties in her mouth, a shiny new jagged knife in his hand slicing the buttons off her blouse.

Her appearance was almost scary, she knew. The dark circles were impossible to hide now on her pale, sallow face, the chewed fingertips too gnawed for even fake nails. Her suits hung on her as if she were a mannequin at a bad dress shop.

Just get through today, and tomorrow will surely get better, she continually told herself, although she knew otherwise. She knew from past experience that the spiral only headed one way. If Bantling walked, she was done. It was over. Now that seemed like only a matter of time.

At a quarter to six, Judge Chaskel dismissed the jury for the day. "Ms. Rubio, how many more witnesses do you intend to call so I can get an idea of scheduling?"

"Just two or three more, Judge."

"Does your client intend to testify?"

"I'm not prepared to answer that just yet, Judge. I don't know."

"Well, if he does, do you think you will be done by tomorrow evening?"

"Yes, Judge. Of course, that also depends on the prosecutor's cross." She looked in C.J.'s direction.

"Let's take it as it comes, Judge. I don't know how long my cross will be. I will probably need time to prepare if the defendant testifies," C.J. said wearily. *I will probably be disbarred if he testifies, Judge. Then come the men in the crisp white suits.*

"I understand that. We are moving along nicely, though. I'd like to do closings on Thursday then, unless, of course, you need some additional time, Ms. Townsend, and a charging conference on the instructions to the jury on Friday morning. Then we'll give it to the jury by Friday afternoon. A quick verdict and we're done by the weekend."

And then we're done by the weekend. And it will all be over. Just like that. By the weekend. In time for the Dolphins' playoff bid, and the Coconut Grove Art Festival.

By the weekend, fate would be forever decided.

82

SHE SAT IN her office, the blinds of course drawn, the sound of the Channel 7 news anchor barely audible on her small portable television, a mountain of paperwork lying uselessly on her desk, next to a cold bowl of soup and her fifth cup of coffee. The Cupid trial, of course, was the lead story on the six-thirty news, followed by a spin on a fraudulent investment company that had bilked South Florida seniors out of millions, and a blurb about a missing college student from Fort Lauderdale with epilepsy. She hated going home. She hated staying here. There was no escape anywhere. And that was the problem. At least until the weekend. *And then we're done by the weekend.*

A faint rap sounded at her door, and before she could answer, it slowly opened. She expected to see an irate Jerry Tigler before her, maybe even a concerned Dominick Falconetti and Manny Alvarez, whose calls she had avoided all week. She didn't expect a smiling Gregory Chambers.

"May I come in?" he asked, entering anyway, looking about her office.

Her back stiffened and she shook her head, but strangely enough, could not find her voice in time and he sat down before her.

"How have you been?" he asked, his brow furrowing with a look of concern. "I just came from the sex offender training symposium downstairs, and I thought I'd stop up.

You haven't made our last two sessions, and I am a bit worried about that. With all the stress that you are under."

"I'm fine. Just fine," she said, her head still shaking. "I think you should go," was all she could say.

"You don't look fine, C.J. You look sickly. I have watched you on TV and I am downright worried about you."

"Worried about me? You are worried about me?" She couldn't hold the anger in anymore, the hurt, the confusion. "I came to you for help, Greg—Dr. Chambers—I trusted you as a doctor, as a friend, and you were fucking with me the whole goddamn time!"

A look of hurt and surprise crossed Greg Chambers's face. "What are you talking about, C.J.?"

"I was there. I was at your office!" she screamed.

"Yes, Estelle said you came by last week," he began defensively, the look of confusion still on his face, "but you were gone when I came out. That's exactly the behavior you're exhibiting that I am concerned about—"

She cut him off, her voice now choked with tears. Tears that she could not hold back. "And I saw. I saw it, right there, in your office. In your appointment book."

"You looked through my appointment book? C.J., how could you—"

"You were treating him, too! Bantling, that son of a bitch. All this time and you said nothing. You knew all along that he had raped me and you played me like a fool."

Greg Chambers's shocked face now grew dark at the sound of her allegation. "I knew nothing of the sort. Listen to me, C.J. I did treat him, Billy Bantling, that is true—"

"And you said nothing! How could you do that? How could you not tell me?"

"I do not owe you an apology or an explanation, but I will afford you a limited one because of our long-term relationship. Our friendship." The anger rose in his voice as he spoke, and although he struggled to contain it, his tone was cutting and she suddenly felt small and unsure. Weak. "As a prosecutor, you know full well that I cannot divulge the fact that I am treating someone. The very fact that someone is a patient of mine is confidential and privileged. And I would never disclose that information. Never. I took an oath. Not for anyone or anything, without the consent of the patient. Unless there was a known conflict, which there was not.

"I never knew that there was a connection until you came to me and told me that the subject arrested in the Cupid investigation was the man who had raped you. And at that time my relationship with Bill Bantling was severed, obviously, because of his arrest. Of course, I will not share anything with you that occurred in my sessions with Bill, so please don't even ask. Just know that I would never compromise any of my patients. Never. And while this might sound cold, C.J., to attack my professional integrity and imply such a thing without first consulting me is offensive and insulting. I was in a difficult position and I did what I ethically was required to do.

"Now I came here to see how you were doing, to see if I could help. But I no longer think that that is a good idea. As your doctor, I do suggest that you continue therapy with someone else, however, because you are exhibiting signs of a breakdown." He rose to leave.

A sudden, inexplicable feeling of shame overwhelmed her. Her thoughts ran together clumsily, colliding now in confusion. "I don't know what to do anymore," she whispered. "I don't know who to believe, what to believe. It's all coming apart and I can't control anything. Nothing is real. I don't know what is real anymore, Dr. Chambers." The tears flowed from her eyes, even though she thought there were none left.

It was too late. Greg Chambers was angry, the words had been said and could not be taken back. "I warned you not to take this case on because you were too close, C.J. Perhaps that lack of distance has warped your perspective on things, on relationships. Perhaps you've made the wrong alliances, ones you now no longer trust. Decisions made under stress and confusion are often poor ones."

"Dominick? Do you mean him?"

"I'm simply advising you as I did months back. Distance adds perspective, which is what you seem to need. Continue therapy and you will see that. Good evening."

He shut the door behind him with a dull thud, leaving her alone again in her office.

She buried her face in her hands, sobbing, the façade fracturing under the stress, the splintering cracks threatening everything she had sought to rebuild over the past decade.

And she never even saw the picture of twenty-one-year-old Florida Atlantic University college student Julie LaTrianca that flashed momentarily across the TV screen behind her, or heard the comments of the perky and doe-eyed news anchor who described the dark-haired beauty's disappearance from a Fort Lauderdale bar on New Year's Eve as "mysterious."

83

TWENTY MINUTES AFTER Greg Chambers walked out of her office, the phone rang on her private line at her desk. She let it ring at first, but it kept up, and finally on the tenth ring she picked up, wiping the tears on her face with the back of her hand.

"Townsend. State Attorney's."

"C.J., it's me. Dominick." She heard police sirens in the background, lots of them, mixed with loud shouts from many different voices.

"Dominick, it's not a very good time for me. Can I call you—"

"No, you can't call me back. And it is a very good time for you, trust me. We found them, and you need to get down here."

"What? What are you talking about?"

"I'm at a mobile home in Key Largo, just off of U.S. 1. It belonged to Bantling's dead aunt, Viola Traun. We found the hearts. All of them. Stored in a freezer in her kitchen. We also found pictures, C.J. Tons of pictures of each victim, taken on some black background while they were being tortured on this metal gurney. Some even while they were being killed. Snuff pictures. Looks like maybe his shed. He had everything here."

"How did you find—?" Her heart was pounding in her

chest, a mixture of relief, excitement, fear, panic. Too many emotions overloading the circuits.

"I found a bench warrant issued by a judge out of Monroe County for Bantling. Just issued a few weeks ago; that's why we never saw it. It's a civil contempt warrant. Bantling was the guardian of his aunt's property when she was alive, and he failed to file some sort of bullshit accounting within sixty days of her death, so the judge issued a warrant, not realizing, I suppose, that Bill Bantling was the very same William Bantling on trial for murder in Miami. I found out about the house and came down with Manny, and the owner of the trailer park let us in. What a place. The pictures were in the freezer with the hearts. Don't worry, it's all kosher, because the trailer was going into foreclosure for nonpayment of back rent on the land. The landowner had right-of-possession papers and all. I made sure. But we need a warrant before we go any further. I don't want to fuck this up."

"Oh my God." She struggled to catch her breath. "Okay. I'm on my way."

"We got him, C.J.," Dominick said, his voice a whisper of excitement. "He's all ours now."

84

JUROR NUMBER FIVE stopped smiling and Bill Bantling stopped laughing when C.J. announced on Wednesday morning that she was reopening her case. And by noon, after Special Agent Dominick Falconetti had retaken the stand for two hours, none of the jury members would even glance in Bantling's direction, and an emotional chill could be felt taking over the courtroom. By the end of testimony that afternoon, two male jurors had broken down in tears, and three female jurors had vomited after viewing the actual heart of Anna Prado, now preserved in a see-through evidence bag, followed by the horrific pictures found in Viola Traun's freezer. That included a pale-faced Juror Number Five, who perhaps saw herself a few months down the road caught on film in one of Bantling's trophy photos. Anna Prado's mother was again escorted sobbing and screaming hysterically out of the courtroom, but this time around Judge Chaskel somberly decided to break for lunch. The tide had definitely turned.

During the lunch break, Dominick charged William Rupert Bantling with ten additional counts of first-degree murder, and dropped ten more pink arrest forms on the Dade County Jail as a hold, in the what now seemed unlikely event that this jury let him walk. Lourdes waived her client's right to a First Appearance Hearing, and by late afternoon announced to Judge Chaskel that her client would not be testifying on his own behalf. Bantling's cocky smirk was now replaced with a nervous, defiant twitch, and his face had grown pasty and pale-looking. Violent, hushed squabbles could be heard erupting between Lourdes and him at the defense table.

Closing arguments concluded on Friday afternoon, although Lourdes's lacked the conviction she had mustered for Bantling in her opening. After the charging conference, the two alternate jurors were dismissed from service and their opinions devoured in the hall by dueling MSNBC, CNN, and Fox News correspondents, and the remaining twelve jurors instructed on the law. Finally, at 4:27 P.M., the jury was sent out to deliberate the fate of the defendant.

Less than an hour later, at 5:19 P.M., a knock was heard on the jury door and Hank delivered a note to the judge in his chambers.

They had a verdict.

85

"IS THIS YOUR verdict, so say you all?" asked Judge Chaskel over his reading glasses to the jury foreman as everyone in the courtroom quickly scrambled to their seats. No one had expected a verdict this quick in a capital case. Particularly C.J., who had barely made it to the first-floor coin-operated coffee machine for a cup of joe on her way back to wait for the verdict in her office. That's when Eddie Bowman had jumped on the escalator, yelling to her that the jury was back.

The judge's face showed no emotion as his furrowed eyes perused the verdict form. The courtroom was standing-room-only—jammed with prosecutors, defense lawyers, press members, spectators, and family. An electric buzz of excitement ran through the room.

"Yes, Your Honor, it is," anxiously replied the foreman, a garbageman in his forties from Miami Beach. He was trying hard to ignore the cameras and microphones that were hanging on his every breath, recording his every nervous tic. Small beads of sweat appeared on his upper lip, and he brushed them away with the back of his hand.

"Very well, then, you may be seated, sir. The defendant will please rise." Judge Chaskel folded up the verdict form and handed it back over the bench to Janine, the clerk. The foreman, obviously relieved to be out of the spotlight, sat back down with the other eleven members of the jury, all of whom then stared at the bench uneasily, purposely avoiding even a glance in the direction of Bill Bantling. "Madame Clerk, please read the verdict." Then Judge Chaskel sat forward in his high-backed leather chair, his hand firmly resting on the wooden gavel on the bench.

"We the jury, in the county of Miami-Dade, Florida, on this the fifth day of January, two thousand and one, find the defendant, William Rupert Bantling, guilty of murder in the first degree."

Guilty. Guilty of murder in the first degree. A choked sob sounded in the courtroom, which C.J. suspected came from Mrs. Prado.

"This courtroom will remain in order and everyone will remain seated," said the judge sternly, his deep voice still commanding attention over the now-overanxious, excited, fidgeting crowd. "Ms. Rubio, would you like the jury polled?"

"I would, Your Honor," Lourdes said blankly after hesitating a moment, her hands resting on the edge of the defense table for support. Bantling stared at the judge, as though he had not yet heard the news.

"Ladies and gentlemen of the jury, I will now individually poll you to see if the verdict rendered was, in fact, your own. Juror Number One, what was your verdict?"

"Guilty," said the retired secretary from Kendall, crying.

"Juror Number Two?"

"Guilty."

And so it went down the line. Some of the jurors' eyes were red with tears, others looked relieved, and still others shared looks of disgust and anger when their turn to speak came.

After Juror Number Twelve reiterated the defendant's guilt, the courtroom erupted in complete chaos. Mrs. Prado began to wail, family members of Cupid's other victims who had attended the trial shouted and cheered, reporters rushed out to the hall to call their news agencies, and C.J. hung her head in a silent prayer of thanks to a God she had thought no longer existed.

It was over. It was finally over.

86

THAT WAS WHEN William Rupert Bantling began to scream.

It was the same bloodcurdling, angry screech that she had heard before when she was locked in with him and Lourdes in DCJ. The excited courtroom chatter quickly drifted into stunned silence as everyone's eyes and cameras turned to Bantling.

He had his hands on his head, pulling at his hair, and was shaking his head furiously from side to side. His face was beet red, his eyes wide and furious, and from his mouth came that awful screeching sound. He turned in C.J.'s direction and pointed at her.

"You fucking cunt!" he hissed. "I should have fucking killed you then, you little bitch! I should have fucking killed you! You're not gonna get away with this!"

"Order, I want order in this courtroom! And I want it now!" Judge Chaskel bellowed, his face red, matching Bantling's. "Mr. Bantling, are you listening to this court? I want you to be quiet!"

Lourdes put her hand on Bantling's arm to quiet him, but he violently threw it off, almost sending her into the chair railing. "Don't you fucking touch me, either, you two-timing bitch! You're in on this with her—I know it!"

"Mr. Bantling, I will no longer tolerate this outburst in my courtroom. I will have you gagged, if that's what it takes to shut you up!" He looked at Hank. "Remove the jury now, Hank! Now!" Hank hustled to push the jury members, who all stood with their mouths open watching Bantling's breakdown, through the door leading to the soundproofed jury room.

Bantling turned and faced the bench. "Your Honor, I want another lawyer. I want another one right now."

"Mr. Bantling, you have just been convicted of capital murder. You can have any lawyer you want to represent you during the appeals process, as long as you can afford it. And if you can't, the court will appoint one for you. But you can't have another one right now."

"Judge, you don't understand! I didn't do this, and they both know it!"

"You need to calm down, sir, and control yourself."

"I fucked that prosecutor years ago. I fucked her bad in her apartment in New York, and now she's framing me for these murders! I want a new trial! I want a new lawyer!"

Judge Chaskel furrowed his brow again. "Mr. Bantling, this is not the time or the place for these sorts of allegations, which sound rather ludicrous to me. You can take up whatever issue you want with your appeals attorney at a later date."

"Just ask her! She'll tell you! She'll tell you she was raped! And she knows it was me who did her! And my attorney, she knows it was me but she feels bad for Ms. Townsend. She feels bad for poor Chloe. So she's not fighting for me like she should. She should have had this case dismissed!"

"Ms. Townsend? Ms. Rubio? Do you know what this is about?" Judge Chaskel looked perplexed.

This was it. The moment she had always dreaded. The moment she knew would come, but today had thought somehow she might escape. *How would it feel when it all came crashing down?*

C.J. swallowed hard and stood from her seat to face the judge. "Your Honor," she said slowly, "I was, in fact, the victim of a violent rape some years back when I was a law student in New York."

One huge, enormous gasp could be heard simultaneously throughout the courtroom. A voice said, "Oh my God!" Another, "Holy shit!" Another, "Did you hear that?" *Tonight's CNN Headline News, coming to you live from Miami: Shocking In-Court Revelation by Prosecutor in Cupid Murder Trial!*

She cleared her throat and continued in as strong a voice as she could muster. "Apparently, Your Honor, the defendant has become privy to this information through old police reports and public records searches and is aware that my rapist was never caught. In an effort to fool this court and to cloak these proceedings in accusations of impropriety and railroading, Mr. Bantling has made a midnight confession that he was the man who raped me. However, Judge, I can assure this court that that is not the case. Mr. Bantling is not the man who attacked and raped me, and I have advised his attorney as such in a prior meeting. I believe she also finds no merit in his accusations before this court today."

Judge Chaskel stared dumbfounded out from the bench. He did not like being put in this position. Not after he had just run what he thought to be a perfect, appeal-proof trial. "And this is the first time I am hearing of this? Now?" He looked at Lourdes. "Ms. Rubio, do you wish to be heard on this matter?"

Lourdes Rubio looked straight out before her at the judge, never once even glancing in C.J.'s direction. "Judge, I have spoken with my client and I have read the police reports concerning Ms. Townsend's assault. I have also spoken with Ms. Townsend herself." She paused slightly, then continued, "I believe my client's accusations against Ms. Townsend are without merit and I do not support them."

Judge Chaskel sat in silence, contemplating his reaction and his next words. The courtroom stayed silent as well. Finally he spoke. Although sounding sincere, his words were carefully chosen for the court reporter. "Ms. Townsend, I am sorry that you were compelled to disclose a very private matter before this court today. I should only hope that the media that is present here and now armed with this information will treat it with the privacy and tact that it so deserves."

"This is fucking bullshit!" Bantling violently pushed the defense table with both hands, sending it toppling over and Lourdes's files flying everywhere. "All of this! All of you are gonna kill me because you feel sorry for that lying bitch!" Three corrections officers grabbed him from behind, holding his arms and legs while he struggled against them. As they handcuffed and shackled him, he snarled in C.J.'s direction, his eyes filled with pure hatred, his mouth foaming.

Judge Chaskel raised his voice to almost a shout. "You can have your appeals attorney take up any issue you want. Right now, this matter is concluded. Gag him, Hank."

"You lying whore, Chloe! This isn't over! This isn't over!" Bantling screamed.

Then he fell silent as the bailiff taped his mouth shut.

87

SHE COULDN'T GO home. The media had somehow found her carefully guarded address and were camped out in the parking lot of Port Royale awaiting her return. They'd obviously paid the security guard to look the other way while they pulled past him in their bright blue Channel 7 News Team trucks. So she sat in her office at 10:30 that night calling hotels to try to find a room for a few nights until the media got bored and moved their trucks away from her parking spot and their boom mike away from her front door. She didn't even notice him standing in the shadow of her door frame until he softly called her name.

"C.J.?"

She looked up, hoping it was the State Attorney again, but instead found Dominick.

"Hi there," was all she could reply. He had been in court when the verdict was read.

"What are you doing?"

"Well, actually, I am looking for a place to stay for a few days. Mrs. Cromsby, the elderly lady in apartment ten-sixteen below me who takes care of Lucy and Tibby while I'm working, has suggested I 'lie low' for a while. It's a circus, apparently." She would not look at him.

He came in from the doorway and walked around the side of her desk, sitting finally on the edge. She felt his eyes upon her, studying her as if she were a specimen, and she wished he would just leave.

"You told me you were in a car accident. Those scars are from no car accident, are they?"

She felt her lip tremble and she bit it, hard. "No, no they're not."

"Why didn't you tell me?"

"Because I didn't want you to know. I didn't want anyone to know. Now, isn't it ironic, that my rape is tonight's top story around the world? Translated into twenty-four languages as we speak." She pulled her fingers through her hair and rested her head in her hands. "I didn't want you to know, that's all."

"Did you think things would be different between us if I knew? Is that it?"

"I don't need your pity, Dominick. I really don't."

"It's not pity, C.J. I thought it was a lot more than that. Do you think I'm that shallow?"

"Look, it's not about you. Okay? It's in the past. *My* past. And I still try to deal with it every single day in the best way that I can. Today was just not one of those better days."

"Don't just shut me out."

"I can't have children, Dominick. There, I've said it. Maybe it matters to you, maybe it doesn't, but I can't. And now you know. Now you know."

A long silence hung in the room. Her cheap wall clock ticked off the minutes, and no one spoke. Finally, Dominick broke the silence in a low voice, "Was it him? Was it Bantling?"

Within hours, the media had amassed and then released for public consumption, vivid details of C.J.'s rape. And now he remembered Manny's voice on the Nextel, telling him about the clown mask he had just found in Bantling's closet. And then C.J., startled by him in the task force conference room with the unattended evidence. It was all there. *You just had to know where to look.*

She pondered the question for a few long seconds. She felt the tears well up and then trickle in a hot stream down her cheeks, but there was no stopping them. She looked up at him, straight in his probing, questioning brown eyes and when she finally spoke, her voice, barely a whisper, was resigned. "No. No. It wasn't him."

He studied her. Her beautiful tan face, framed by chestnut blond hair, lighter at the roots than at the ends, like a child's. Her deep, emerald eyes, underlined with troubling, dark circles. He imagined for a moment what Bantling had done to her to give her those scars. He pictured that face, the face he had now grown to love, crying and twisted and tortured under the weight of a barbaric monster. He knew she was lying to him. Somehow it didn't matter.

"Close the book."

"What?"

"Close the telephone book. Put down the phone."

"Why?"

"Because you're coming home with me, that's why. I'm taking you home."

He took her hand and pulled her up and out of the chair. Then he wrapped her in his arms and kissed the top of her head. He held her tight against his chest, listening to her sobs, and stroking her hair. Not wanting ever to let go.

88

THE CUPID STORY dropped to the second page of the paper after a couple of days, and after a week was no longer even a mention on the evening news, the press having moved on to feast on yet another tragic murder or fire or flood. Painful details of her rape and speculation about motive and retribution were front-page news initially, but then the tide of public opinion washed over the editorials and suddenly rape victims' rights to privacy became an issue and the press became villains.

C.J. took some time off from work to reflect and regroup and allow the press to lose interest in her. Bantling's indictment for another ten counts of first-degree murder was handed down quietly and without much fanfare, and surprisingly, passed in the press without more than a remark or two about the rape allegation. It didn't much matter anyway. Those murders were being handled by Rose Harris. For C.J., there was only one final hearing to get through, one more meeting with the monster, one more encounter with the hungry press, and then her job was done.

She spent a few days in Key West with Dominick, while the furor died down in Miami. It was quiet and relaxing, and they spent hours together just talking over bottles of wine and glorious sunsets. It was amazing this feeling of relief she had now. Relief that she could finally share with someone this lonely, isolated part of herself—a part that had been shuttered and locked away from all for twelve years. Even though Dominick and she did not really talk about it—the actual rape—just knowing that he *knew* and that it didn't matter and that he loved her was a deeply profound experience. It elevated her, and, in turn, made her fall even more deeply in love with him.

The penalty phase began six weeks later. On Judge Chaskel's orders, Bantling was gagged, handcuffed, and shackled. The judge had, of course, first held a hearing to determine if Bantling could conduct himself without restraints and Bantling had told him in the first four minutes to go fuck himself and the prosecutor, too. So Chaskel had ordered the gag and shackles. The last thing he wanted was the jury damaged now, witnessing another violent prejudicial fit, after the whole trial was finally over and done with. He had afforded the defendant the opportunity to respond, and his own attorney had denied his bizarre accusation. Let the Third District Court of Appeal listen to his ravings and make sense of them. Because after the jury handed down sentence, it would be their problem, not his.

In a capital case, the penalty phase was a mini-trial, with both sides allowed to present testimony. But the guilt or innocence of the defendant was no longer the issue to be decided. It was simply whether he should live or die for his crimes. C.J. presented the state's case for the death penalty in three days. The jury heard about the other evidence recovered in the search of Viola Traun's trailer. They saw the crime-scene photos of the other ten hearts that, along with Anna Prado's, were found in the freezer alongside the gruesome trophy pictures. They heard about the other ten abductions, the other ten victims, found with the same black cross carved in their empty chests. Evidence that could not have been used to support his conviction, but could now be used to condemn him. And all the while, Bantling sat defiantly next to Lourdes Rubio with his mouth taped shut.

On the fourth day, after the state had rested and before the defense was allowed to present its case, Judge Chaskel removed the jury from the courtroom.

"Ms. Rubio, do you intend to call witnesses at this time on your client's behalf?"

"Just one, Your Honor. Mr. Bantling wishes to call just one witness. He wishes to testify himself on his own behalf."

Judge Chaskel blew out a slow breath. "Very well, then. He has a right to do so. Let's see first if he can follow the rules. Hank, remove the gag."

C.J.'s heart began to pound in her chest. *Calm down. It was just crazy words. There was no proof. She had made sure of that.* She looked to her left and saw Dominick watching her from the back of the courtroom. He nodded in her direction. Nodded that everything was going to be okay.

The judge stared at Bantling over the top of his glasses, his eyes narrow slits that read caution. "Mr. Bantling, your attorney has advised me that you wish to testify on your own behalf, which is your right. However, it is not your right if such testimony is disruptive to this court, and will not be permitted if you cannot control yourself," he said sternly. "That being said, can you assure this court that there will be no further inappropriate outbursts, such as the one you demonstrated at your conviction? If you can make that promise to this court, I will allow you, of course, to testify. However, I will not tolerate that conduct again in my courtroom. And if you cannot promise this court that there will be no such outbursts, then you will not be allowed to testify and you further leave me no choice but to keep you gagged. What's it going to be, Mr. Bantling?"

"Inappropriate outbursts?" Bantling shouted. "Fuck you and this kangaroo court. I am being framed. That fucking bitch is framing me!"

The gag went back on.

It took the jury less than twenty-five minutes to return a unanimous sentence recommendation. Death.

There was no need to drag this out one day further. Judge Chaskel immediately sentenced Bantling to death by lethal injection. Then he ordered Bantling to be removed and the courtroom cleared, and he quickly left the bench. Bantling was dragged out, screaming under the gag, by

three corrections officers. The press ran out into the hallway to call their editors and catch the jury members for
interviews on their way out. Dominick, Manny, Chris Masterson, and Eddie Bowman were pulled outside by different television stations for their live opinions. All that
remained in the courtroom were the clerk, C.J., and Lourdes, each packing up what remained of their massive files
in *The State of Florida* v. *William Rupert Bantling*.

Lourdes approached C.J. at the prosecution table, on her
way out of the courtroom, her two boxes balanced precariously on a metal pulley cart. This was the first time Lourdes had even looked at her since that day in DCJ.

C.J. held her hand out. A peace offering. "Good working with you, Lourdes."

Lourdes ignored both C.J.'s outstretched hand and her
comment.

"Will you be handling the murder trials for those other
ten women, C.J.?"

"No. No, I don't think so."

"That's probably a good idea."

C.J. ignored the slight, turned her back to Lourdes, and
finished packing up her briefcase.

"There are a lot of aspects of this case that trouble me,
C.J. Some of which may be of my own doing and for those,
I will take full responsibility. Do the ends justify the
means? I don't know. I just don't know." She looked
around the empty gallery, as if taking in this scene one last
time. "But there is just one thing that I can't get out of my
mind that keeps bothering me. And, I thought, may be
bothering you as well."

C.J. stared at her files, wishing Lourdes and her struggling conscience would just leave.

"At the midnight hour, right before closing arguments,
Agent Falconetti suddenly finds the house of Bill
Bantling's dead great-aunt. Bantling—a man whose past he
has scoured over like Brillo on a dirty dishpan. How fortu-
itous, C.J., that he should find that relative with only hours
left in this trial, when he had months to do so and couldn't.
Quite the hero. And quite ingenious of him to run
Bantling's criminal history again so late in the trial. Bril-

liant police work or bizarre coincidence? Perhaps he got the idea from another anonymous little birdie. That, I guess, we'll never know."

C.J. looked up from her files, her eyes meeting Lourdes's stare. *Now you know that I knew. All along I knew.*

At that, she turned and walked down the aisle away from the gallery, the empty bench, and deserted box, past the abandoned rows toward the door. When she reached it, she called out behind her one final comment.

"They say justice is blind, C.J., but I think that in some instances it is simply because she chooses not to look. You'd do well to remember that."

89

"I OWE YOU an apology," C.J. began. "Actually, I probably owe a few people apologies, but you are the one I wanted to talk to first."

She stood in the blue-and-yellow waiting room, in the "needs help" section, while Greg Chambers stood on the other side of the reception office. The square, bulletproof window separated them, so she spoke awkwardly into the intercom. "Besides," she added with a difficult smile, "I think I have a standing appointment on Wednesday nights."

He looked surprised to see her. Surprised, but not shocked. He nodded, and the door buzzed. He was waiting for her on the other side when she opened it.

"Dr. Chambers," she started, "I jumped to conclusions. I realize now that I shouldn't have. That you have been not just a doctor but a friend to me for ten years and—"

"Please, C.J. There is no need for apologies, although yours is appreciated. Come in. Come in. You just caught me."

He walked her back into his office and flipped on the lights. "Have a seat, please. I'm sorry myself. I haven't seen you since we last spoke in your office. I wasn't expecting you this evening. I'm afraid we gave your standing to a depressed housewife from Star Island. She just left for dinner at the Forge in her Mercedes," he said lightly, smiling.

"Glad to see you're still helping the community at

large," she replied, smiling back. "One hour at a time." The tension wasn't as bad as she'd thought it would be.

"I heard about the sentence today. So you are finally done, are you not? Or are you going forward on the rest?"

"No, I'm done. Rose Harris will be taking the other ten murders. I don't want to be beauty queen anymore, thank you."

"Well, I should congratulate you on getting through this. In fact, I have a bottle of champagne that I keep in the fridge for special occasions. Patients who break through and end their therapy, getting season tickets to the Dolphins, that sort of thing. I've had one in there for you, hoping someday to break it out. I think now may be the time. You did it. You have closure." He looked at her with those eyes she had always thought of as kind, and his voice became very serious. "Let me break it out now as your friend, not your doctor, please."

She nodded and smiled. She knew where he was going. After what had been said the last time they met, there was no way he could continue as her doctor. It would not be good for either of them. "Only if I can have a cigarette with it. I can only handle giving up one addiction at a time, and my psychiatrist is the biggie sacrifice of the night."

He laughed. "I have some cheese and crackers here, too. Let me feed you before I get you drunk."

"Don't go to any trouble."

"No trouble at all." He rose and walked to the wet bar and fridge behind her. "How did you fare under all that press, C.J.?"

"I ran and hid out, to tell you the truth. At Dominick's. Then, when I was no longer the flavor of the day in the news, I moved back home. It passed quickly enough. I think the polls are with me. Bantling is an evil nut and I'm his scapegoat." It felt strange to actually use Bantling's name in front of him, and she made a mental note to be more careful. He was speaking to her as her friend now, not her doctor, but he still could not change what his relationship with the man had been. No matter how much either of them would like to. "Tigler gave me a raise and

three weeks off. It felt good to be away from the office."
She heard a loud pop when the champagne opened.

"Agent Falconetti and you. Is that still happening?"

"Yes. It wasn't for a while, but it is now. I think he's good for me."

"Don't be too impressed," he commented, as he placed a tray arranged with the champagne, two glasses, and a plate of canapés on the coffee table that separated the two wing-backed chairs. "They're leftovers from Estelle's birthday party last weekend." Then he sat down in front of her. "He broke the case, didn't he? Turned the tide, so to speak."

"Yes, he's a great investigator. He found the trophies. And those pictures. They were just awful. The worst I've seen."

"I'm sure they were."

"I shudder when I think what the outcome might have been if he hadn't found them."

"Or known where to look. I'm glad I spoke with him after that conference. Or else he never would have had a clue."

"A clue? About what?" An inexplicable, uneasy feeling came over her.

"Where to look. I told him to run another criminal history. Because you never know what you might find. Champagne?"

Her mind began to race with questions. Questions she was not sure she wanted answers to. And she remembered Lourdes's final words to her in the courtroom. "I'm sorry about what I said that night," she said slowly, changing the subject to buy time and rein in the thoughts that were rushing her brain. "I was in shock. The case was falling apart. I guess I said things I shouldn't have."

"You were under a lot of stress."

"Yes, I was."

He gestured toward the champagne, for her to pour. She could not shake this cold feeling. Her instincts sensed that something was not right.

"I hope you understand my difficult position back then,

C.J., what with Bill being my patient and all," he said. "And the even more difficult position that you put me in now."

She shook her head slowly as she pulled the bottle of chilled Moët Rose out of the beautiful antique bucket made of thick lead crystal. A dark red object lay in ice at the bottom.

"A difficult position, what with me wanting to fuck you and all," he said.

A scream pierced the calm of the office, reverberating off the walls, again and again and again. He sat across from her, watching, in the wing-backed chair, his legs casually crossed, an amused smile on his face.

It was several moments before the horror became clear to her, before her brain comprehended the incomprehensible, and threatened to shut down from the shock of it all. Before she finally realized that the dark red object that she was staring at was actually a human heart, and the scream that she kept hearing was, in fact, her own.

90

SHE STILL HAD the champagne bottle clutched in her hand when she jumped out of the chair, pushing it backward, where it toppled over with a crash. *The door! Get outside!* She ran as fast as she could for the closed door. She felt his hand then on the back of her suit jacket, grasping, pulling her back, and she turned and swung the bottle full force at his face.

He was quick. His right arm blocked the strike and she heard a grunt when the bottle slammed into the bone on his forearm. The bottle shattered and champagne exploded everywhere, drenching her hair and face. She turned again to the door, but felt his fingers still on her back, pulling her back to him. She writhed under his grasp, slipping her arms out of the sleeves and leaving the empty jacket limp in his hands behind her. Her hand reached the doorknob and she pulled it open and she dashed down the hallway into Estelle's empty and dark reception office. She had almost made it to the waiting room door when she felt him on top of her, his breath heavy in her ear, his hands pulling her back by the shoulders. Her fingers slipped off the knob and she fell backward, landing hard on the Mexican tile.

A sharp, excruciating pain exploded in her leg, and the back of her head smashed violently on the tile. The room faded for a second, and then she felt her twisted leg throbbing underneath her body. At first she thought that she had broken or even shattered a bone in the fall.

Chambers was squatting next to her, trying to catch his breath, watching her roll on the floor. She could see he was smiling. *Why was he smiling?*

She looked down at her leg, thinking perhaps that he had stabbed her, half expecting to see her own blood running down onto the floor and through the maze of ash-colored grout. Then she saw the needle in her thigh, its syringe empty. The room began to swim, and her thoughts blurred together incoherently. She tried to grab at it, but her arms fell uselessly to her sides. She lay back on the cold floor, her body suddenly heavy and tired. He sat down against the wall next to her, watching her intently, his smiling face blurring in and out of focus. The fluorescent lights above her were blinding, flashing slowly when she blinked. She tried to say something, but could not form the words. Her tongue was too thick. The last thing she heard was the sound of Bach playing overhead in Estelle's office. Classical music. Music to calm the crazies.

And then the room went black.

91

SHE OPENED HER eyes slowly, expecting to see the blinding fluorescent office lights above her, but instead saw herself. Her own image stared back at her, laid out on a metal gurney in her olive green suit, arms strapped to her sides, legs buckled down. She blinked and realized that it was a mirror. She was lying on her back and staring up at a mirror on the ceiling. Surrounding the mirror were the bright fluorescent lights she had expected, illuminating a room that was painted entirely black. Although she could not see behind her, from what she could make out, the room looked small, maybe twelve by fourteen, and she could not see a window. A tripod and camera were set up across from the gurney. Mozart's "Alleluia" played softly around her.

Her body still felt heavy, her limbs disassociated from her torso. When she thought to move her finger, she wasn't sure if it moved or not. She had no sensory perception. Her eyelids opened and closed slowly, and each time they did, her eyes struggled again to focus. She smelled old champagne in her hair. She tried to speak, but her tongue felt useless and the words that she spoke sounded garbled and choked, as if she had no tongue at all.

She rolled her head to the right and saw him standing in the corner, his back to her. He was humming. She heard the sound of running water and the tinkle of light metal objects tapping together. The sounds in the room pounded in her ears, then softened. Pounded and then softened, like the throb of a headache.

He turned to her and tilted his head, frowning. "You must have a high tolerance. I didn't expect to hear from you for a few hours."

Again she tried to speak, but only an incoherent mumble came out. Behind him she saw a metal pushcart. On top of a white cloth, the sharp, silver instruments shone in the glare of the fluorescent light. And then she saw the bolt cutters.

"Maybe the shelf life is off. No matter. You're here. That's what counts. How are you feeling, C.J.?" He shone a penlight in her eyes. She felt her eyelids struggle to close. "Not too good, I would imagine. Don't bother trying to speak; I can't understand you, anyway." He unbuckled the arm strap and put his fingers on her wrist, feeling for a pulse. "Ooh, you should be asleep. You should practically be in a coma, but your pulse is racing. Quite the fighter, aren't you?"

He dropped her arm and watched it fall on the gurney with a thud. She saw then that his own arm was wrapped in a bandage, and she remembered the champagne bottle.

"Don't fight. Don't stress. It increases the heart rate, the blood flow, and, quite frankly, it makes more of a mess. Not that I wouldn't love being bathed in your blood, but there is cleanup to be considered."

She struggled to move her head.

"So now you understand, do you? Now you get it?" He smiled, watching her, letting her absorb the horror he was feeding her. Even through the drugs, he could see her struggling to comprehend. "Now don't go thinking that I'm going to reveal the secret family recipe, give a last-second detailed confession so that it all becomes clear, because I won't. Some things you will have to go to the grave wondering about." He sighed and touched her hair. "Suffice it to say that I am a gentleman, and gentlemen do prefer blondes. I know that I always have, C.J. Since the moment I met you ten years ago, I have had you on my mind. Beautiful C. J. Townsend, attorney *extraordinaire*, struggling not to be so beautiful, so noticed, trying hard just to get through each day. And carrying a dark, sad secret that she chooses to unburden on only one person. Her psychiatrist. Living her sad and lonely life out, haunted by memories and dreams that make it impossible for her to sleep, impossible for her to find someone so that she won't be so sad and so lonely. A diagnosis of posttraumatic stress is in order. And, at triggering times like Christmas and Valentine's Day, clinical depression. Does that sound familiar, C.J.? Does that about sum things up? Let's see, seventy-five dollars an hour, the police discount, times how many months of therapy? For how many years? And I can access you in a few sentences."

He continued stroking her hair, brushing it off her sweaty face. He leaned over, his face close to hers, the blue eyes she once thought of as kind examining her with pity. A hint of contempt, perhaps?

"I'm going to make you feel really good about yourself now, C.J.," he whispered in her ear. "You were never really that sick. No more than your average bear. Or the average Star Island housewife who's bored with the luxury of her life. You just took the time to notice that your life was a mess and, unfortunately, chose me to help you fix it."

He stood back up and she saw him pull a syringe and a small bottle out of his jacket pocket. "Now, I promised you that I would not bore you with a midnight confession of all my dastardly deeds. But I must say that you and Bill were a perfect case study. A great working thesis. The rape victim and her rapist. What would happen if the tables were turned? What if the persecuted became the prosecutor? Given the opportunity, what road would she take? The ethical one or the just one? How far would she go for retribution? And what would that mean? How much would Billy Boy have to pay for his crimes of passion? Would his life pay the debt?

"I must say, C.J., it has been some ride, watching you. Watching a clueless Billy Boy, whose only problem seems to be that he can't keep his dick in his pants, and of course, he can't control his anger." Chambers motioned toward her stomach while he filled the syringe with a clear liquid in a glass bottle. "I saw the work he did on you while you were napping. You're right. It was barbaric," he said, his lip curling in distaste. "Watching him and his ego thinking he'd get off this whole time. Underestimating you all along.

"I was tempted to let him walk. To keep my trophies. All of them. And see what you would do when they opened up his jail cell and gave him five dollars for the bus ride home. Would you have been there, waiting in the shadows, with your daddy's Saturday night special, ready to pump him full of lead?

"But, I decided that this would be a happier ending. Now you will go meet your maker, knowing that you caused other people to kill an innocent man for you. Try to explain that to God. Or, then again, will they do it? Hmmm . . . Maybe, just maybe, Billy will win his appeal. And he'll walk. Wouldn't that be ironic? You're dead and he's alive, fucking some more women with his big, ugly knife."

She said something, but the words were desperate, incomprehensible slurs.

"Oh, C.J. Don't be so scared. I'm only going to leave you for a little while. I'll be back. I wanted to leave you with a few thoughts for our next session. And now, I have to bring home the bacon. I have a nine A.M. patient waiting anxiously for me—he has obsessive-compulsive disorder—and Estelle is tied up in traffic. So I've got to get to the office." He slid the needle into her arm.

"This should keep you happy. I'm sure you've heard of it. Haloperidol? Have a nice nap, and I'll see you in a few. We'll take some pictures, have a few laughs."

She heard the jingle of keys, and then the door opened with a creak.

The black room went fuzzy again, out of focus. She felt her eyelids close, her clenched fist relax and go numb. She felt her weightless body falling. Falling, but not landing, not stopping.

"See you later," was the last thing she heard.

92

DOMINICK FELT HIS breath catch when the line was finally picked up, and he heard the familiar sound of her voice on the other end. After a moment, though, he quickly realized it was the answering machine again and acid churned in his stomach.

Where is she? Where the hell is she? She had stood him up for dinner last night, and hadn't shown up for work this morning. She wasn't at her apartment, and no one had heard from her since the sentencing hearing.

Has she gotten spooked again by their relationship? Has she run off, needing time for herself, without telling him?

He could not shake the bad feeling that consumed his thoughts. A foreboding, dark feeling, deep in his gut that something was terribly amiss. He had not slept all night, worrying where she might be. An accident, perhaps? But there was nothing in the hospitals, no reports with any of the departments.

It was now more than twenty-four hours since she had disappeared. He could wait no more. He picked up the Nextel and called FDLE dispatch to put a BOLO out on her car and to report a Signal 8. A missing person, suspicious circumstances.

93

SHE OPENED HER eyes again, but this time everything was completely black. *Was she dead? Was this it?*

She felt her head turn to the side, and then to the other side. There was no light whatsoever. Maybe she was dead. But then her cheek met the cool metal of the gurney and she remembered that the room was black, windowless. There was no light because he had turned off the light switch.

How many hours had passed? How many days? Was he still here? Was he in the room right now, watching her? She tried to move her fingers, but they were too heavy. She tried to wiggle her toes, but could not tell if she had. Her mouth was dry, her tongue thick from the drugs. How much had he given her?

Greg Chambers. Cupid. Brilliant psychiatrist. Trusted friend. Lethal serial killer. Why? How? It made no sense. Her therapy, all these years, it had been a game to him. An amusing, entertaining game. Watching her struggle with the devastating effects of a rape. Then he had met twisted Bill Bantling, and he had played the two of them like pawns in a game of chess. To the death.

The room was ice-cold, like a hospital operating room. She felt herself shiver, her teeth knocking together. She knew who he was, what he had done, and she remembered his words to her.

Don't fight . . . quite frankly it makes more of a mess.

Whose heart was in that bucket? The hearts of all eleven Cupid victims had been recovered and matched with DNA. What she had seen meant that there were more victims. After her own death there would be yet another, but no one would put them together. No one was looking. The scare of a serial killer would not become reality for a long while. If ever.

He was going to kill her. And she knew how he was going to do it. She could describe it in the bluntest of medical terms, having witnessed his handiwork eleven times over, listened to the medical examiner, read the autopsy reports, seen it happening in his macabre trophy pictures.

And she knew that he was going to make her watch. She remembered the adhesive found on Anna Prado's eyelids. He was going to tape her eyes open and make her watch in the full-length mirror on the ceiling in this black room, her death chamber. Where no one would hear her scream.

A whimper sounded in her throat. She tried to call out, but still could not. The tears ran helplessly down her cheeks, running onto her neck into a puddle on the gurney.

She remembered then the metal pushcart in the corner, the shiny, sharp instruments. Dr. Joe Neilson's face flashed in her mind, and she heard his words on the stand while the pointer in his hands jumped across the female mannequin's chest.

"It was a scalpel. The incisions were deep. They cut through to the bone, passing through three layers of skin, fatty tissue, and, finally, muscle."

She knew how it would end. She even knew how it would feel.

When would death come for her? Or was he already here, watching her silently in the dark? Watching her cry and hearing her whimper? Seeing her struggle, hoping her heart would not race under all the stress?

She could only wait in the blackness. Wait and see.

94

·

"I'M SORRY TO disturb you, Dr. Chambers, but there is some-one here to see you," Estelle said, her voice suddenly crackling to life on his desk. Gregory Chambers stared at the intercom for a moment. "It's Special Agent Falconetti with FDLE."

"Very well. Please have him wait for a few minutes in the reception area, while I finish up here," he replied back to Estelle. Then he finished reading the notes he'd jotted down from his last patient into the dictaphone.

Estelle looked back up from her desk at an obviously worried Dominick Falconetti. She had seen him before, on TV during the trial, but there he always looked so con-trolled, so confident. Today he looked incredibly anxious. It must be the news, she thought. "Agent Falconetti, the doctor can see you in a few minutes, if you would just have a seat." Estelle nodded toward the leather chairs in the waiting room.

"Thank you," Dominick said.

She studied him curiously while he moved away from the reception window toward the chairs. She noticed that he did not sit. His eyes perused the waiting room, and he looked at his watch two times.

The door opened then, and Dr. Chambers appeared in the reception area. He walked past Estelle and opened the door to the waiting room. "Agent Falconetti. Please, come in," he said, motioning toward his office.

Dominick followed him past the reception desk and down the Mexican-tiled hall into the soft yellow-and-blue office. "What can I do for you, Dom?" Dr. Chambers said as he closed the door behind them.

"I'm sure you've heard about—" Dominick began.

"About C. J. Townsend? Yes, yes, of course. It's been on the news for two days. Are there any developments?"

"No. Nothing. That's why I'm here." He hesitated slightly before continuing. "I don't know if you knew this, but we were involved. She told me that she had been seeing you, professionally. With that in mind, I wanted to ask you some questions."

"Dom, please, I'll help out, of course, in any way that I can, but please don't ask me what was discussed between C.J. and myself. I can't divulge that, and I won't."

"I understand that. I need to know, when was the last time that you saw her?"

Greg Chambers studied him for a moment. He had already thought this possibility through, this encounter. But if the great Special Agent had known or even suspected the answer to his very own question, he would have rung the good doctor's doorbell two days ago. And it was just as obvious that he did not know of the others included on his list of special clientele. Apparently, C.J. had kept some things to herself. "Oh, not since the trial. It's been weeks, actually."

"Have you spoken with her at all?"

"No, not since that time. We were no longer seeing each other professionally. I wish I could be of more help." He shrugged his shoulders.

"I understand. Is there anything that you can think of? Where she might go? Anyone she might go with? Anyone she was afraid of, perhaps?"

It was clear that they had no idea. None. They could not even figure out if they had a missing person or a person who wanted to be missing. And it was sad, watching the great detective struggle with the thought that his lover might have left him. Picked up and gone with someone else, leaving him to entertain the thought that he never really knew her after all.

"No, Dom, again, I'm afraid I can't help you. Except to say . . ." His voice trailed off and he pondered a moment before slowly sharing his next thought. "C.J. has a mind of her own. If you are asking for possibilities, it would not be out of the realm of them to say she would take some breathing room if she felt she needed space." He looked straight at Dominick, his telling eyes providing the detective with the answer he was looking for, but might not want to know.

Dominick nodded, slowly. Then he handed the doctor a business card and said, "Okay. Thanks. Please call me, direct, if she gets in touch with you. I wrote down my home number on the back as well, although I'm available twenty-four/seven on the Nextel, but just in case for some reason you miss me . . ."

"I will. And again, Dom, I'm sorry that I couldn't be of more help."

Dominick turned and walked down the hallway, his head down, the dejected shoulders slightly sagging. Classic, subtle, and very telling body language. Dr. Chambers watched him go, watched him nod ever so slightly to himself as he opened the door to Estelle's reception room, watched him absorb all that the good doctor had said and had not said. And all that it implied.

Then he watched as Special Agent Dominick Falconetti opened the heavy oak front door, got into his car, and just drove away.

95

THE DOOR OPENED and the room exploded in light. The jingle of keys sounded behind her.

He walked over to the corner sink and began to wash his hands, his back to her. Next to the sink was the metal cart laid out with tools. Scalpels in assorted sizes, scissors, bolt cutters, needles, tape, an IV line kit, straight razors, and an IV bag. He spent at least five minutes scrubbing his hands, like a surgeon, over the sink, and then carefully drying them with paper towels. He opened one of the cabinet drawers below the sink and pulled out a box of sterile rubber gloves and delicately pulled on a pair.

"Sorry that I'm so late," Chambers called out. "I got stuck in session. You think you have problems. You should hear what's out there. Schizophrenic seventeen-year-olds that threaten their own mothers with knives. Can you imagine? Your own mother?"

He walked over to the tripod and looked through the camera, focusing the lens on her face, which was turned up, facing the ceiling, her eyes open. Then he snapped off a picture. "I bet you are photogenic. You have wonderful features." He snapped off another and then refocused to capture the whole gurney.

He walked back over to the metal rolling cart and paused for a moment, thinking. Then he reached under the sink again and took out a pair of green scrubs. In the corner of the room was a metal chair. He removed his jacket and neatly draped it over the back, then removed his tie, dress shirt, and slacks, folding them neatly on the chair. He dressed in the scrubs, and all the while he hummed. "Your friend stopped by the office this morning," he said while slipping mint-colored cotton booties over his shoes. "Dominick. He wanted to know if I could help him. If I could tell him where you might have gone, and maybe who with. He was very sad when I told him my opinion. Very sad, indeed."

He pulled the metal cart over to the gurney on her right side. From the cart he took a surgical cap and placed it on his head. "You know, I did my residency in surgery, initially." He looked down at her right arm and frowned. It was not strapped. He had forgotten to strap it after he had injected her. He raised her arm and let go, watching it crash to the gurney with a thud.

She mumbled something that he couldn't understand. More garbled nonsense. Tears flowed down the side of her head and onto her hair.

It was sad. This beautiful specimen, this fabulous work in progress. He had thought that when it ended he would have a sense of joy, a sense of validation, to see his hypothesis come true. But when Bill had finally been sentenced to death, when the game had ended and the final play set in motion, he was, well, he was *sad*. He had engineered this experiment from the very beginning, when Bill had walked into his office three years ago with a shitload of problems, down on his luck, and with no one to talk to. But he had listened when Bill ranted and raved. Listened when he had told the nice doctor of all the nasty things he had done to all the nice women he had met over the years. And he had learned. Learned that while coincidences were hard to come by, they did still happen in this world. And that was when Dr. Gregory Chambers, M.D., F.A.P.A., knew that he had found the most amazing specimens with which to conduct the most amazing experiment in all of modern psychiatric scientific history. And although he had dabbled in death long before his sessions with the clinically depressed C.J. or the narcissistic sociopath Bill had ever even begun, those efforts had been immature. The others had not even been missed. Their deaths had been insignificant, inconsequential. But this, well, this experiment had been an *orchestration*. He remembered the thrill of the moment when he had actually decided to do it—and the look on poor, sweet Nicolette's face when he had sliced her open. She had not realized how important her role was in all this. She had been the first. The first of many in this blind study.

And now that it was over he was sad. Sad because he knew he could not share this great work, this enormous feat with the world. His peers could never know; the observations and results could not be shared and studied by his contemporaries. To them he would still be Dr. Joe Anybody.

"Now, now. No tears," he said in a sympathetic voice. "I'd like to tell you that this won't hurt a bit, but I'm afraid that's just not true. As you know, we need to set you up first with an IV." He reached behind him and grabbed a syringe and a rubber band, with which to tie off the vein.

Suddenly, he turned and his hand violently grabbed her right wrist, crushing it in his grip and smashing it hard against the gurney. He moved his head over hers, till his face was inches from her own. He searched her vacant eyes, which stared helplessly at the ceiling.

"But before we begin"—he smiled at her from above— "why don't you be a good girl and give me back my scalpel?"

96

HOW CLEVER. HOW very clever. Of course, he had noticed the missing scalpel the moment he had walked in the room. Did she think him that stupid, that he wouldn't notice? A classic mistake, one that others far more clever than she had made. In her haste, she had underestimated him, taken him for a fool.

Victory in the game of chess comes by ensnaring your opponent in a trap from which he cannot escape, through a series of complicated, but seemingly insignificant, moves. The thrill is won by whispering the word *checkmate* to the dumbfounded fool across from you, who, until that very moment, had been plotting his next move against your queen.

This game was no different, the thrill made even sweeter by a worthy opponent. He moved about the room, setting up his board, laying the trap, giddy with thoughts of seeing the dumbfounded look cross her beautiful face.

He saw the wrist strap unattached, her clenched hand trembling with nervous anticipation before she attempted to save her own life with one last desperate attempt on his. He watched her eyes, wide with fear, and allowed her mentally to move her pawn into position. Then his hand, quick as lightning upon hers, his words to her a final checkmate, her preemptive strike foiled.

Her fist was clenched into a tight ball, and he saw the

bright red blood as it oozed out between her fingers, trickling down her wrist and dripping onto the gurney. Using both of his hands, he pried open her palm. She moaned in protest. There he could see the number-five scalpel, and then the raw, deep cut that it had made in her flesh when she had clenched it so tightly. He plucked it from her grasp, as a parent would do with a toy hoarded by his naughty toddler.

She shook her head slowly from side to side, an obvious acknowledgment of defeat, and tears spilled from her eyes. Her last best effort had failed. It amused him that she had so much strength. A worthy opponent, perhaps—better than all the rest. But, unfortunately, not good enough.

He heard the scream first then in his ear, her words clear, not garbled, and that was when he realized that most of the Haldol had worn off. Much more than he would have thought. Pain, hot and wicked, sliced through his neck, and he felt the warmth of his own blood as it drained onto his scrubs, the green slowly transformed to a dark red.

Surprise replaced amusement, and he watched her shout the words at him, her tearful face now dark and angry. His hands flew to his neck, uselessly covering the small hole that spurted blood violently through his fingertips. He could feel himself drowning in his own blood, heard his own garbled chokes as he tried to speak to her. He watched as the life poured out of him, spilling onto his shoes, slowly seeping away from him across the floor.

He struggled to grab her, to crush and twist her neck, but she was just out of reach as he stumbled backward, and he felt the wall behind him. She sat up on the gurney and he saw the hatred in her eyes. In her left hand she held another blade, dripping red droplets of blood onto the gurney. His blood.

And at that moment he feared, because he knew that he had made the most classic mistake of all.

He had underestimated her.

97

SHE KNEW SHE had only one chance. Just one chance to get him close enough to her so that she could stick the blade in his eye or ear or neck. She knew her strength was limited, her arms still weak.

He crossed the room in his green scrubs, all the while humming. Then he was next to her, frowning just above her. She knew something was wrong. She tightened the tension in her thumb, clenching the blade tighter against her palm. Had she not pushed the gurney into the same spot? Had she moved the instrument cart too much? In the complete blackness, it had been impossible to discern how things in the room had looked, exactly where they had been placed before.

He was close, but not close enough. But it was clear he knew that something was amiss. *The strap.* He saw that she was not strapped in. She felt the sweat form on her face, even in the freezing-cold room. He grabbed her hand suddenly and dropped it with a thud on the gurney. She let it fall, trying hard to let her hand fall naturally, but without letting go of the blade. *Don't let go. Whatever you do, don't let go.* He seemed satisfied and turned away from her to the cart behind him.

Inside, she breathed a sigh of relief. *Closer, just come a little bit closer now with that IV. Just a few more inches.*

Suddenly, his hand violently on hers, crashing it to the cart, prying her fingers apart. *No. No. Don't let go!* She clenched her fist tight, and felt the blade slice through the layers of skin and tendon and muscle. But still she wouldn't let go. Not until her last finger was pried open and she was robbed yet again. He was smiling above her, a smug smile at having figured her out. Foiled her plan. Tears rolled down her face. *God, no. It can't end like this.*

Closer, just come a little bit closer, you bastard. I still have one last trick up my sleeve. One last hurrah before you put me to sleep forever. With any luck, I'll get it right the first time. Because after that, I'm definitely out of chances.

His smug face, inches from her own now. The rubber tube and the syringe in his hand.

"Go to hell!" she screamed.

She spit the words out in his ear. The number-three scalpel was tucked in under her left hand, with the strap loosely fitted over her wrist. Using all the strength she could muster, she raised the blade and brought it down hard into his neck. Blood squirted like a fountain. His eyes, which had been locked on hers in a triumphant look of smugness at having figured her out, grew wide with shock.

He staggered back, away from her, his hands on his neck. He crashed into the metal cart, sending it careening into the wall. The surgical instruments flew on the cold black tile with a tinkle, scattering across the floor. One hand left his neck and he reached out for her, his eyes wide with shock, but then he fell against the wall.

Blood was everywhere. She must have nicked the carotid artery, and he was bleeding out all over his green scrubs. His eyes still stared at her, but his face was dark with anger. His words were choked, as though he could not breathe.

She rolled off the gurney, hitting the floor hard. A searing pain flared in her side and she felt bone snap. She still could not fully use her legs, the powerful haloperidol making them useless, like deflated rubber tubes. With her hands she pulled herself to the black painted door that he had come through, reaching up and feeling the doorknob above her head, her eyes never leaving his. The pain in her side was intense, and it was difficult to catch her breath.

Blood from his neck wound began to seep across the floor toward her, making the black floor appear glossy, shiny. She tried to scream for help, but the sound was low and raspy and ineffective. He made a gurgling noise just then, and she saw one hand moving next to him, grasping for something.

She had to get out, had to get help. She turned the knob, but it would not open. Then she remembered the jingle of the keys.

He had locked them both in.

98

THE KEYS. THE goddamn keys! They were in his jacket pocket on the chair. Next to where he sat slumped against the wall, his fingers still moving like a crab, against the floor. His eyes were open, but they were not blinking and, but for his moving fingers, he looked dead. He was probably in clinical shock, his organs beginning to shut themselves down. She pulled herself through the blood, which now covered the tile, to the chair. The jacket sat draped on top of it. The pain in her chest was excruciating. With every move, it became even harder to find her breath.

She pulled the jacket down onto the floor and frantically dug through the pockets, her eyes not leaving him. His blood, still warm on the floor, was everywhere. *Breast pocket, nothing. Inside pockets, nothing. Left-hand pocket, bingo.* The jingle of a key ring. She pulled them out and began to drag herself back to the door. Her legs were tingling, but she still had no strength in them.

The hand fell on her ankle quickly, pulling her back to him. She screamed, trying to kick it off with her useless legs. She turned and saw that the other hand had moved off his throat, and in it he held the syringe.

"No! No!" she screamed. "God, no!" Her hands moved across the slippery tile trying to pull herself back, but found nothing to grab onto. She slid in his blood back to where he sat. She saw the syringe, its body filled with a

clear liquid, its sharp needle spurting drops of poison in
the air. His finger was on the plunger, ready to thrust it in
her flesh, and he pointed it at her thigh as he pulled her
toward him. That much Mivacron injected directly into the
bloodstream without the dilution of an IV would kill her.
Her hands thrashed about desperately seeking leverage,
anything to hold her back from where she was going, but
she found nothing and the needle came closer, until it was
inches from the skin. Even as she was sure that he sensed
his own death was near, a look of triumph passed on his
face at the thought, probably, that they would die together.

Then her hands found something cold, something metal
on the floor. Scissors. She grabbed at them and with all her
might pulled herself forward, at him, on him. Her hand
flew out first, the scissors finding his chest. His grip less-
ened suddenly, and his hand slipped to the floor off her
ankle. The syringe dropped to the floor, rolling in the blood
to the wall. His eyes remained open. The look of triumph
never passed.

She pulled herself back to the door and felt for the handle above her. Grabbing it, she pulled herself up and found
the lock. Her right hand, wet with blood from the gaping
wound in her palm, slipped off the knob and she landed
hard on her chin on the floor. Intense pain ran through her
head like a shock wave, and the room began to blacken.

No. No. Get up! Don't pass out here! Not here, not now!

She shook her head to lift the fog, and pulled herself
back up on the knob, the fingers on her hand finding the
lock above it. The key ring jingled, her shaking hands fum-
bling to find the right one. The pain in her right palm was
intense, and she could not grasp with her fingers. The third
key finally found the lock and slid in and she heard the
click. She turned the knob and pulled it open a crack, slipping to the floor. Her fingers found the small opening and
she pulled the door, finally falling into a carpeted dark hallway. The tick of a grandfather clock could be heard somewhere.

*Where was she? Where the hell was she? What other
surprises did he have in store for her?*

She cast one more look behind her. He sat still and

motionless against the wall, his vacant, lifeless eyes open wide. She pulled herself down the hallway looking for a phone. The hallway was dark, almost as black as the room she had just left behind her. There were no windows, no light.

Find a phone. The police can trace the call. They'll know where I am. I'm probably at his house, wherever the hell that is.

It was now almost impossible to breathe. The air was heavy, the pain numbing. *Not here. Don't pass out here, Chloe!*

Some ten feet later she found wooden stairs and, holding on to the railing, slid down them, landing in the dark on cool tile. There was more light downstairs than up, and there were windows. Outside she could see it was dark, nighttime. Streetlights sent soft light through the wooden blinds. Down the pale-yellow-and-blue hallway, on a wooden antique desk stacked with pictures of Estelle and her family, was the phone.

She knew exactly where she was, where she had been all this time. And in the nice Spanish-style house on Almeria, in the comfort of her psychiatrist's office, she lay in the dark crying on the cool Mexican tile floor, just waiting for the police to come.

99

"COUNSELOR, YOU ARE one fucking lucky lady. That place looks like a scene from a bad horror movie. Blood everywhere," Manny said when he walked into the room, his clothes disheveled, his face a carpet of black. In one hand he held a basket of exotic tropical flowers. In the other, he held a plateful of *pastelitos*. "The flowers are from the guys. Even Bowman, that cheap fuck, pitched in. And the *pastelitos* are from me. The doc outside said no *café con leche* for you for a while, so it'll have to be milk."

"Lucky?" C.J. grimaced from her bed. "You go buy the Lotto ticket, Bear. I don't think I'm up to it." Breathing was painful. Talking was worse. "Thank you. They're beautiful."

"Well, you do look like shit, but at least you're alive. More than we can say for Dr. Friendly. I just came from his office. Nice hole you left in his chest, Counselor. Even nicer one in his neck. Remind me not to get you mad. What does the doctor say? Will you be coming back to us, or do I need to find another ASA who will let me profile on the phone?"

"Three cracked ribs. A severed tendon in her right hand. Concussion. A collapsed lung. But she'll be fine," said Dominick who was sitting at the side of the hospital bed in an armchair, where he had been all night, ever since she was brought in.

"I'll just put them flowers here. Right next to the forty zillion roses someone sent you. I wonder who that could be?" He laughed and shot Dominick a knowing look. "You look like shit, too, Dommy Boy. But you don't have no excuse." Then he turned to C.J. again, and his face grew soft. She could see the worry hidden deep in his otherwise-tough-looking face. "I'm glad you'll be okay. I'd miss you, Counselor. You had us worried there."

"What did you find—" She swallowed, trying to finish her sentence.

"Don't talk. It's painful hearing you," said Manny, his gruff demeanor making a welcome comeback. "There's not much to find, tell you the truth. Dr. Friendly's death chamber had the makings of an ER operating room in tools and bodily fluids, but so far, that's it. We can't find the heart you think you saw. The crystal ice bucket is clean. No dead body in the office or at his house, which we're ripping apart right now. Everything is spotless. No prints, no blood, except, of course, the evil doctor's, which is every-where and on everything. He was drained when we found him. If there was anyone else's blood in that room, we're sure as hell not going to find it now. Fort Lauderdale P.D. is going over the club on Las Olas where that college student disappeared, but at this time of year, it's mainly tourists and so far, no one's recognized him."

"I don't think we're gonna find anything, C.J.," Dominick said softly.

"What? You think I imagined what I saw?"

It all made sense now. Too much sense. Chambers had the police connection. The police credentials as a consult-ant. The inside scoop. *You just had to know where to look.* Of course, every action has a reaction. And if one theory was pushed too far, exposed too much, then the reaction could prove just as deadly. He was careful not to push this one. Some things were better left alone.

"No. I think maybe he wanted you to think that's what you saw. I think he was obsessed with you. Maybe he was going to try a copycat. That's the theory we're progress-ing on."

Manny nodded. "We got the right nut behind bars. This

one was just a work in progress. Hey, I gotta head out and keep Bowman awake at Chambers's house. He was at a bachelor party when we got the call. I yanked him out of there right before it was his turn for a lap dance. Now he's crying exhaustion. So I'll call you later to tell you what we've found." He turned at the door and said again, "Glad you're with us, Counselor. Real glad."

The door closed, and they were alone. Dominick's hand found hers on the bed. "You'll be fine. Just fine." She could hear the relief in his voice. The fear, too.

"Did he?" Her voice cut off with a choked sob. She couldn't look at him at that moment. She just stared up at the ceiling.

"There's no evidence of that." He knew what she was thinking. The rape kit had come back clean.

She nodded, feeling the tears stream down her cheeks. She gripped his hand even tighter.

He had been in that house, and she had been right there, right above him, in the web of a monster, but he had missed her. He had walked out, and the unthinkable had almost happened. Again.

"It's going to be okay this time, C.J. It will. I promise." He raised her hand in his and kissed it hard. His other hand stroked her cheek softly. His voice was choked, his words shaking with conviction. "And I never break a promise."

EPILOGUE

NOVEMBER 2001

THE DOOR TO Courtroom 5-3 opened onto the crowded hall-way, packed with weary and confused family members of both victims and defendants alike, waiting for their cases to be called up on calendar. Judge Katz, in a particularly foul mood at being forced to actually work the day before a holiday, commanded court inside, buzzing through the morning's First Appearance Hearings, dispensing justice and setting and denying bonds at a blinding pace.

C.J. stepped out of the courtroom, letting the door close on yet another Judge Katz tirade in progress. "No bond! Not now, not ever!" the judge yelled. "If you love him that much, go visit him in jail. And get your eyes checked by an optometrist before you walk into any more baseball bats!" was the last thing C.J. heard before the door closed completely. Just another day in paradise.

Paul Meyers, the Division Chief of the SAO Legal Unit, was waiting for her in the hallway, leaned back against a wall, legal books in hand. His expression was serious, reserved.

"C.J.," he said, pushing himself off the wall and making his way toward her in the crowd, "I knew you had a bond hearing this morning. I need to talk to you. Before this gets out and the phone starts ringing."

A knot tightened in her stomach. So much for a quick escape to a four-day weekend. A personal visit in the courthouse from the Chief of Legal was not usually a good thing. "Sure, Paul. What's up?"

"It's the Bantling appeal. It just came back this morning. We got it faxed from the Attorney General's Office, who just had it faxed from the clerk at the Third DCA. I wanted to be the first one to go over it with you. I'm sure the press will be calling."

Oh, shit. Here it comes. Pick a new exciting destination for your life because he's a free man.

The nightmare that she had put in the past for almost a year was about to start up again. The knot in her stomach tightened, and her mouth went dry. She nodded her head slowly. "And?" was all she could say.

"And? And, we won. On all the issues." He finally broke out in a smile. "The court unanimously upheld his conviction. I have the opinion right here." He flashed a stack of papers in her direction. "I'll have to get you a copy. But basically, they said that there was no conflict with your prosecuting him. They said his argument that he had been the one who, well, had assaulted you was 'opportunistic and inflammatory and was not corroborated by independent evidence.' They said that if they found merit in his argument, it would, and I quote, 'open the floodgates to other defendants to dig up dirt on the prosecutor or judge handling their cases in the hope of diverting justice off its course. To simply allow a mere allegation to support a conflict or recusal argument, conveniently made in this case after the statute of limitations had expired, would thus permit a defendant to not only forum-shop, but also now to prosecutor-shop, without any substantiation required of his prejudicial claims.'" He pointed out the highlighted portion of the opinion and let her read it.

"They also didn't buy into his conspiracy theory or his ineffective assistance of counsel. They said Rubio was more than adequate, and his decision to testify or not testify was clearly reflected on the record as his own.

"And finally, on the most important issue, they didn't go for his newly discovered evidence argument either. I highlighted that for you, too. They said Judge Chaskel heard that argument on Bantling's Motion for New Trial last spring, and that they, too, found no merit in it. Chambers's assault on you, in and of itself, with nothing more, does not constitute newly discovered evidence. They also noted that the jury in his trial last summer also didn't buy that argument and convicted him of murder ten times over. Period. End of sentence. That's all she wrote. You can breathe again, C.J."

"What's next?" Her heart was beating a mile a minute.

"The Florida Supremes, but I wouldn't worry. I think the Third DCA wrote a really strong opinion. After that, well, he can then start making his way through the federal system until he hits the U.S. Supreme Court."

She nodded thoughtfully, absorbing everything he said and all that it implied. She was surprised that she felt no guilt, no remorse. Just a sense of calm.

"It'll still be about eight or ten years before they execute him, with the way justice works in Florida. Maybe longer. We probably won't even be around to see it happen."

"I will," she said, her voice flat.

"Well good luck to you. I'll be enjoying my measly state retirement out on my boat off the Keys. Six years and counting. Just me and the fish. I'm not even inviting my wife. I've got to run, C.J. I'll drop a copy off on your desk later on today. Are you going out of town for Thanksgiving?"

"Yes, actually. My flight leaves late this afternoon. I'm going to visit my parents in California for a few days." That was a relationship she hoped could be repaired. That she thought she wanted back.

"Well, this news should make your vacation even better. Have a nice trip." He took off down the hall, making his way through the restless crowd toward the elevator, happy thoughts of retirement and turkey probably dancing in his head at that very moment.

Oh, I'll be there, Paul. If and when it ever comes to pass. Just as I promised. I'll be there to watch it happen. To make sure justice gets done.

She watched him get on the elevator and waved as the doors closed. Then she glanced at her watch. It was almost noon, and she still had to go home and pack. She took the elevators down to the first floor, and walked past the Pickle Barrel. Because of the holiday it was not as full as usual, as most of the defense attorneys and prosecutors and judges had jump-started their weekend right after morning calendar.

C.J. pushed open the glass doors and walked down the cement steps. The back doors of the courthouse led out to Thirteenth Street and DCJ. For security reasons, it was blocked to all traffic except police vehicles. She recognized the state car right away.

Dominick sat in his Grand Prix, right in front of the steps, just waiting for her. He lowered the passenger-side window as she approached. "Hey, pretty lady," he called out, "want a ride?"

"My mom taught me not to talk to strange men in cars," she replied, smiling. "What are you doing here? I thought you were going to meet me at my house."

"I was. But I wanted to rescue you early from this place. Get a head start on those canned airline Bloody Marys, maybe."

She opened the door and climbed in next to him. He reached across the seat, his hand on the back of her neck, gently pulling her toward him, his warm lips meeting hers.

"Well," she said, when their kiss had finally ended, "What a welcome. I'm glad you did. I could go for something cold and tropical right about now. A 'we're on vacation' drink. Are you packed?"

"Yup. It's all in the back. Are you?"

"Of course not," she replied, "but maybe you can help me. It shouldn't take too long."

"Let's get going then. Drop off those nasty files. I'll follow you back home. And then it's just you and me, baby."

"And my parents. Don't forget, you get to meet them."

"I can't wait," he said, meaning it.

She smiled, kissed him softly again, and hopped out of the car to drop off those nasty files and jump-start her own vacation. Their flight to San Francisco left at 5:30, and she didn't want to miss it.

ACKNOWLEDGMENTS

A necessary thank you is due the following individuals for their assistance on this project, all of whom provided their invaluable knowledge without reservation or hesitation, and for that I am especially grateful: Dr. Reinhard Motte and Dr. Lee Hearn of the Miami-Dade County Medical Examiner's Office; Special Agents with the Florida Department of Law Enforcement, particularly Special Agent Eddie Royal; Domestic Violence Division Chief Esther Jacobo of the State Attorney's Office, Miami-Dade County; Assistant Statewide Prosecutors Julie Hogan and Marie Perikles of the Office of Statewide Prosecution; pharmacist Liz Chasko; and, finally, Mr. Dean Mynks.

A special thank you is also due Marie Ryan, Esq., Leslie Thomas, Penny Weber, Thea Sieban, and John Pellman, Sr., for their precious time, as well as their insight, and to my friends and family for their support, and my mother for her gift.

ABOUT THE AUTHOR

Jilliane Hoffman served as an Assistant State Attorney in Miami, Florida, from 1992 to 1996. She was a felony prosecutor with special assignments to the Extradition/Legal Unit and the Domestic Violence Unit. Until 2001, when she left her job to concentrate on her writing, Ms. Hoffman was the Regional Legal Advisor for the Florida Department of Law Enforcement in Miami, responsible for advising Special Agents on criminal and civil matters in complex criminal investigations including narcotics, homicide, and organized crime.

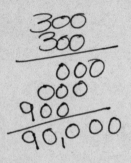

```
    300
    300
  ─────
    000
    000
  900
 ─────────
 90,000
```